SONGS INSPIRE

An

American Hometown

❦

Terre Haute, Indiana, 1927

TOM ROZNOWSKI

This Place in Time

FREE MUSIC DOWNLOADS FROM TOM ROZNOWSKI'S CD
This Place in Time

Eugene Debs 2:55 · Sole Leather 2:43 · A Vigil of Friends 4:14

.

"This is one of those CDs that just puts a smile on your face from the first
note and manages to maintain that feeling all the way through. The
songs are absolutely perfect invocations of the place in both lyrics and
melody. Tom Roznowski has a powerful, down-home voice which is perfect for the feel of the enterprise. The whole album is a joy from start to
finish and I can't recommend it highly enough."

—*Maverick* (UK) (five-star review)

Music downloads can be accessed at www.tomroznowski.net/1927

M000233803

An
American
Hometown

SARAH —
FROM ONE
TRANSPLANT TO
ANOTHER .... ISN'T
INDIANA GREAT?

Terre Haute, Indiana
1927

QUARRY BOOKS

AN IMPRINT OF
Indiana University Press
Bloomington • Indianapolis

An
American
Hometown

Tom Roznowski

Foreword by Scott Russell Sanders

This book is a publication of

Quarry Books
an imprint of
Indiana University Press
601 North Morton Street
Bloomington, IN 47404-3797 USA

www.iupress.indiana.edu

Telephone orders   800-842-6796
Fax orders   812-855-7931
Orders by e-mail   iuporder@indiana.edu

© 2009 by Tom Roznowski
All rights reserved

No part of this book may be reproduced or utilized in any form or
by any means, electronic or mechanical, including photocopying
and recording, or by any information storage and retrieval system,
without permission in writing from the publisher. The Association of
American University Presses' Resolution on Permissions constitutes
the only exception to this prohibition.

∞ The paper used in this publication meets the minimum
requirements of the American National Standard for Information
Sciences—Permanence of Paper for Printed Library Materials,
ANSI Z39.48-1992.

Manufactured in the United States of America

Library of Congress Cataloging-in-Publication Data

Roznowski, Tom, [date]
  An American hometown : Terre Haute, Indiana, 1927 / Tom Roznowski ;
foreword by Scott Russell Sanders.
     p. cm.
  Includes bibliographical references and index.
  ISBN 978-0-253-22129-2 (alk. paper)
  1. Terre Haute (Ind.)—History—20th century. 2. Terre Haute (Ind.)—
Social life and customs—20th century. 3. Terre Haute (Ind.)—Biography.
4. Sustainable living—Indiana—Terre Haute—History—20th century.
5. Terre Haute (Ind.)—Economic conditions—20th century. I. Title.
  F534.T3R69 2009
  977.2'45—dc22

                            2009021708

1 2 3 4 5 14 13 12 11 10 9

TRISHA

Most of the commonest assumptions, it seems to me, are arbitrary ones: that the new is better than the old, the untried superior to the tried, the complex more advantageous than the simple, the fast quicker than the slow, the big greater than the small, and the world as remodeled by man the architect functionally sounder and more agreeable than the world as it was before he changed everything to suit his vogues and conniptions.

E. B. WHITE

Contents

Foreword

Scott Russell Sanders

The earth is a patchwork of places, each with its own natural and human history. In recent decades, however, the qualities that distinguish one place from another have been eroding under the impact of global corporations, electronic communications, and the uniform design of everything from high-rises to highways. In our quest for efficiency, we have been moving toward ever greater homogeneity in how we eat, dress, speak, work, play, travel, communicate, and learn. Nowhere is this homogenization more evident than in the United States, where, from coast to coast, box stores sell the same products, fast food chains peddle the same grub, networks broadcast the same shows. Television flattens regional accents, so that teenagers from Texas sound increasingly like teenagers from Minnesota or Maine. Pushed by advertising, the current fashions in eyeglass frames or phones crop up everywhere at once, like mushrooms after rain. Unless we look beneath the surface, we may be lulled into believing that we dwell, not in particular places, but in a realm of money, merchandise, information, and toys.

Tom Roznowski knows better. In this captivating book, he delves beneath the surface of Terre Haute, Indiana, to reveal one city's rich particularity, and in doing so he illustrates how any of us might gain a deeper sense of our own home places. In 1927, the year Roznowski has chosen to enter the history of Terre Haute, the city billed itself as "The Crossroads of America," because of its location at the intersection of major east–west and north–south highways and railways. (The state of Indiana later appropriated the slogan for itself.) Working from A to Z through a city directory published that year, he profiles individuals, examines their occupations, surveys businesses and civic institutions, explores neighborhoods, and traces the web of relationships that connected citizens to one another and to their hometown.

Roznowski's cast of characters includes a metaphysician as well as mechanics, a physiognomist as well as physicians, a spiritualist medium as well as ministers. We meet boxers, confectioners, dancers, farmers, miners, welders, waiters, plasterers, bicycle racers, cigar sellers, cake icers, chicken pluckers, stage hands, sign-painters, sausage-makers, innkeepers, locomotive engineers, and practitioners of a host of other trades. A number of those trades reflect the old-fashioned virtue of thrift—a rag collector, a junk dealer, a repairer of barrels, a maker of replacement handles for tools, a seamstress who mended clothes, and a sharpener of saws. Factories and workshops in the city manufactured bottles, brooms, barrels, boxes, bread, and butter; caskets and corsets and coffeepots—along with items starting with every other letter of the alphabet.

As a talented singer-songwriter, Roznowski shows a special affection for the many musicians who earned their living by playing at weddings, church socials, house parties, and theaters. And as a connoisseur of regional cuisine, he pays tribute to the cooks who transformed the produce of local farms into hearty meals at cafés, boardinghouses, and hotels. The Parks Purity Pie Company, he assures us, was "the original heaven of pies." The Bon Ton Pastry Shop continued baking delicacies until the early 1970s, he reports, and there are still quite a few people "whose mouths water at the mere mention of the name." Throughout the book, he savors the music of names—Rosebud McGrew, Cinderella Smith, Otis Duck, E. Blanche Rippetoe—and he relishes the wry conjunctions of names and professions, such as the two sisters, both teachers, with the surname Failing, or the supervisor of penmanship called Miss Paine, or the watchmaker nicknamed Tick-Tock Tucker, or the janitor named Broome.

Woven through these profiles are dozens of stories, each as compact and finely cut as a gem. We read about two mayors, one whose father was an immigrant shoe shiner, and another who started life in the city orphanage. We read about a doctor married to an undertaker, a coupling in which even a failed treatment could be good for business. We learn that Terre Haute produced more World Series ballplayers in that era than any other city. We learn that the owners of clock shops still set their wares to 7:22, the hour of Abraham Lincoln's death. We discover the origins of civic institutions designed to care for the needy, ranging from the County Poor Farm and Rose Home Orphanage to the Boys Club for Homeless Children and the Home for Aged Women. In the shadows, behind the forthright Rotarians and Elks and Moose, we glimpse a band of secret societies, such as the Tribe of Ben Hur, the Knights of the Maccabees, the Independent Order of Oddfellows, the Improved Order of Redmen, and, most evocatively named, the Mystic Order of Veiled Prophets of the Enchanted Realm.

While there is a great deal about Terre Haute in the 1920s that Roznowski clearly treasures, he also acknowledges the dark side of the community. There were speakeasies where bartenders served bootleg booze. There was a red light district where ladies of the night accommodated traveling salesmen and hometown customers alike. Blacks were crowded into a section of the city known as Baghdad; schools, swimming pools, drinking fountains, and other public facilities were segregated; and the Ku Klux Klan periodically marched through the streets in their silly, ominous garb. Women were prevented from entering many lines of work, and they were often subordinated to men. There were deadbeats and drunks and crooks. (However, John Dillinger and other bank robbers, active elsewhere in Indiana at the time, avoided Terre Haute for fear that a train on one of the railroad tracks crisscrossing the town would foil their getaway.) Despite significant local philanthropy, the provisions for the needy were Spartan at best. By comparison with middle-class life in our own day, life for many residents in the 1920s was austere, characterized by wearying labor, cramped quarters, and narrow horizons. While citizens knew their own place with an intimacy that few of us could match, they had to work harder than we do to learn about the rest of the world.

What emerges from these historical excavations is the portrait of "a once sustainable society," a city that was largely self-sufficient. The Terre Haute of 1927 had not yet been overrun by cars or blighted by franchises. The vaudeville houses had not succumbed to movies. The city still drew most of its food and building materials from the nearby countryside, manufactured many of the goods needed for a comfortable life, provided most of its own entertainment through performances by local musicians and actors, and allowed residents to go about their daily rounds on foot within compact neighborhoods or to ride further afield on electric trolleys. Citizens responded to social problems by rolling up their sleeves and setting to work, without waiting for help from outside. The rolls of service organizations were filled by laborers as well as tycoons. The schools, both public and parochial, were well-funded and well-regarded. Civic leaders made sure there was an abundance of parks and public gathering spaces. At the edges of the city, streets gave way to fields and woods without any intervening sprawl. These qualities of self-sufficiency began to fade with the onset of the Great Depression a few years later, and over the subsequent decades they have all but disappeared.

Today, advocates of sustainable communities embrace many of the features exemplified by 1920s Terre Haute: a vigorous local economy, nearby sourcing of food and energy, compact development, an integration of shops and workplaces in residential neighborhoods, enhanced civic engagement, improved public transportation, and a renewed concern for the common good. While granting that there is much in our past we should relinquish without regret, Tom Roznowski helps us to envision those qualities we might recover and those we might cultivate in our efforts to create wholesome, humane, and distinctive home places.

Acknowledgments

This book would not have been possible without contributions from a mighty cast of characters. I am forever indebted to the inspiration, encouragement, and research made available to me by three exceptional historians: Dorothy Jerse, Judith Calvert, and Mike McCormick. It was Dorothy and Judith's book, *On the Banks of the Wabash,* published by Indiana University Press some 25 years ago that first opened up Terre Haute, Indiana, to me. Mike, longtime Vigo County historian, continues to know more about the city's past than anyone alive.

I've also benefited over the years from the tremendous resources available at the Vigo County Historical Society and the Vigo County Public Library. This begins with the people who have helped me navigate the volumes of historic material: Marilee Hagan and Barbara Carney at the Historical Society and David Lewis, Susan Dehler, Jim Gilson, Joanne Spann, J. J. Coppinger, and Nancy Sherrill at the VCPL. Special thanks go to Harriet McNeil and Barbara Carney for their eleventh-hour fact checking.

Over the years, I've gotten to know some very kind and fascinating people who call Terre Haute, Indiana, home: among them, Carolyn Toops, Jeffrey Marks, Harriet McNeil, Jan Cockrill, Jessie McCune, Effie Hunt, Kevin Burke, and Nan McEntire. It was my pleasure and privilege to speak with a number of individuals with actual memories of Terre Haute in 1927. Included were Clifford Tapy, Ethel Maxwell, Dick Tuttle, Martha Newport, Earl Kickler, John Moseman, and two spirited women whose memories I hold dear: Frances Hughes and Gertrude Shower.

I received essential support for my early research on Terre Haute from the Hollie and Anna Oakley Foundation and the Sony Corporation. My profound gratitude to Bud Perry and Jeff Perry at Oakley and Warren Macaroni at Sony for their willingness to extend a helping hand.

This journey began as a public radio series on WFIU-FM in Bloomington, Indiana, back in 1995. My eternal thanks go to Christina Kuzmych, the station manager, who gave me an opportunity to work in a medium I was familiar with and who remained steadfast in her support while I struggled to find the form I needed. Mike Paskash has been my studio engineer for over a dozen years and has been indispensable in achieving quality and consistency in the broadcasts.

Judy Witt was very helpful in building a regional presence for the program. The dedicated and talented staff at WFIU continue to be an inspiration to me.

In 2004, the story of Terre Haute in the 1920s emerged on public television. My valued creative collaborator for that project was director Susanne Schwibs, with essential support in the process coming from producer Steve Krahnke and WTIU station manager Phil Meyer. Milt Hamburger provided excellent graphic designs for both series.

Throughout the process of researching and writing this book, I've had extraordinary guidance from the folks at Indiana University Press. My initial editor, Dee Mortensen, patiently listened to my ideas, believing throughout, as she said, that there was a good book in there somewhere. Linda Oblack brought a sure knowledge of regional themes and an emerging love for Terre Haute to the table and Peter Froehlich offered steady perspective as the book took flight. Editor Miki Bird, with the aid of Chandra Mevis, provided a soft landing.

I have been privileged to work with two outstanding personal editors throughout the years: for the Hometown series, my wife, Trisha Bracken, and for this book, Lucinda Berry of Terre Haute, Indiana. They each displayed incredible patience and care with my efforts as well as a finely honed sense of what good writing should be.

This brings me to my own experience of home. My parents, Donald and Grace Roznowski; my sisters, Ellen and Fran, and my brother, Joe, formed my first home in Albany, New York, where my habit of loving places and the people in them began. As to my home now, Bloomington, Indiana, my dear friends there are an incentive for daily living that I deeply treasure.

And my darling Trisha—my light, my heart, my soul. Sometimes the clearest expression of love is a faith in what you cannot completely understand. Through this long period of searching and discovering together, my dear wife and partner, Trisha Bracken, has been truly mighty in her love. While creative expression has given my life a form, Trisha, you have given it being. Thank you for the gift of yourself.

An
American
Hometown

Introduction

Terre Haute, Indiana, was once one of America's shining jewels. Set along the banks of a legendary river, it was a thriving Midwestern city, surrounded by fertile farmlands, rich coalfields, and mature hardwood forests. In the early decades of the twentieth century, Terre Haute became known as "The Crossroads of America," due to the fact that two national highways, U.S. Route 40 and U.S. Route 41, intersected right in the heart of its downtown. Gradually, as the city assumed an even greater prominence in the American consciousness, this title came to symbolize much more.

By the mid-1920s, Terre Haute was at the intersection of another type of crossroads—that of a profound shift in American life. The United States was completing the transition from being a rural nation to an urbanized one, wholeheartedly embracing science and technology as the primary means of improving daily life. Most households had begun to acquire advanced appliances like electric iceboxes and vacuum cleaners while laying aside their straw brooms and pie safes. This included working-class families, even as they incurred significant debt to do so. Increasingly, muscle and mind were being displaced by machine, while synthetic materials, like plastics and complex metal alloys, were gradually being substituted in place of wood, stone, and iron ore.

Still another crossroads would be reached with the exponential rise in worker productivity. The increased mechanization of farms and factories would result in record crop harvests and huge inventories of manufactured goods. With much of Europe still recovering from the devastation of World War I, attention focused on expanding the domestic consumer market to absorb the surplus.

Throughout the 1920s, a vigorous debate was being engaged by pundits and politicians. On one side were those who called for these gains in productivity to be translated into more leisure time and greater support of public services. Others extolled the benefits of expanded personal wealth and discretionary spending.

Now, at the beginning of the twenty-first century, we can see how this debate was resolved. Today, two-thirds of America's Gross Domestic Product is directly tied to consumer spending. Currently, the United States, which constitutes 5 percent of the world's population, consumes over one quarter of the world's energy resources. Meanwhile, the emergence of an American society dedicated to increased personal mobility, material acquisition, and resource use has, not surprisingly, accompanied the steady decline of Terre Haute, Indiana.

In 1927, Terre Haute was a prominent part of the American cultural landscape, visited by national figures from politics and the arts, mentioned in the prose of writers such as O. Henry and Ring Lardner. In the city's residential neighborhoods were a wide variety of locally owned stores, businesses, and factories that nearby households worked in and patronized daily. This city of ten square miles and 65,000 people contained more than 400 grocery stores, two Jewish synagogues, and a host of active union locals for occupations ranging from commercial bakers to theater stage hands. Elementary schools were constructed without cafeterias since children and teachers could easily walk home for lunch.

Three daily newspapers were published in Terre Haute in 1927. The two largest, the *Tribune* and the *Star,* supported the Democratic and the Republican parties respectively. The previous December, the Terre Haute Symphony had been founded. This 48-piece orchestra, which performed works by Grieg and Hayden at its premiere, drew the majority of its members from the skilled amateur musicians in the general public.

Terre Haute's subsequent decline occurred in no small part because much of what the city had represented during its peak in the 1920s became more difficult to sustain in a modernized society. The exponential growth of automobiles meant that people habitually began driving to shop, work, and worship. Core neighborhoods became less self-contained. The proliferation of broadcast and recorded media meant that residents relied less often on their neighbors and themselves for entertainment. Vaudeville in Terre Haute and minor league baseball disappeared as people attended double features or stayed home to listen to radio. In the midst of this cultural shift, fewer children learned to play musical instruments or visit the library.

Over time, the very concept of the hometown became almost quaint to Americans. Elements that had traditionally created a community's identity—long-standing family businesses, locally produced manufactured goods—were considered inefficient for a global economy. Neighborhood schools were consolidated. Civic groups struggled to maintain a functioning membership.

Today, as distinctive local characteristics continue to disappear and communities become more generic, residents find less that connects them directly to the experience of living in a particular town. In a sense, this softens the inevitable adjustment involved in moving elsewhere, which a significant number of Americans now do multiple times during their lives.

Residential and job mobility have become so common that few Americans spend even a portion of their adult years in their original birthplace. Accordingly, the services that Americans have grown accustomed to now follow them everywhere they go. Today, every midsize American city provides access to Starbucks, premium cable channels, and *USA Today.* The retail landscape of America's outskirts offers an almost identical sequence of big box stores, fast food franchises, and chain supermarkets. Conversely, very few cities still contain a locally owned drugstore, newspaper, or movie theater.

In many ways, the Terre Haute of 1927 functioned as a sustainable environment. Many of the small industries that flourished in the city accessed raw materials from the greater Wabash Valley. Locally harvested corn was used to make solvent. A certain grade of sand abundant to the area was suitable for glassmaking. Meanwhile, thousands of street trees and acres of public parks helped to cleanse the polluted air of this industrial city. Cloth awnings and skylights regulated the natural light of the sun. Transoms and high ceilings improved the flow of air indoors.

The Wabash River was an integral part of the city's identity. On summer weekends, it was navigated by excursion boats that carried passengers to picnic grounds and wooded retreats. Terre Haute's electric mass transit system carried more than 10 million passengers annually. A larger regional streetcar system, the interurban, connected the city to outlying rural areas in Indiana and Illinois.

The people who lived in Terre Haute in 1927 commonly employed a personal resourcefulness and frugality in their everyday lives, resulting in more modest consumption. Shoe heels were repaired when they wore down from constant use. Peels from cucumbers grown in backyard gardens were used to repel ants. Slivers of soap were saved, much as one might collect loose change in a jar.

This sustainability at both the personal and community level reflected a direct and intimate relationship with the natural world. In 1927, over 40 percent of the food consumed in Terre Haute came from area farms. The organic nature of this food was sourced in basic agricultural methods and the dominance of small farms rather than a philosophical approach to health and diet. Still, the end result was that local consumers gained access to a wide variety of fruits and vegetables that are no longer found in the produce sections of today's megamarkets.

While this constant engagement with nature often originated out of necessity rather than design, it clearly influenced the quality of everyday life. Residents of Terre Haute planted fruit trees, maintained small chicken houses, and consumed the food they produced. Shade trees were positioned to help cool a house in the summer months. Martin houses were built for these bug-eating birds to regulate the seasonal scourge of insects. Windows were opened in the evening to refresh a home after a hot summer day.

Examining this particular, seemingly unexceptional time and place through the people who once lived there can reveal resources and perspectives that have since been lost or overlooked. Years of economic prosperity have led some in America to believe that earlier strategies for building community and engaging nature have been discarded simply because they have been surpassed and improved upon. But just as we are all likely to make hasty decisions as individuals, we are also capable of making them as a society. We are now witnessing the larger impact of scrapping mass transit systems, demolishing urban neighborhoods, paving green spaces, and shifting from the reusable to the disposable. We have found that turning our backs on the past does not always guarantee a brighter future.

Terre Haute, Indiana, would undergo a decline after the 1920s for a host of reasons. Industries that had characterized the city's growth, like railroads and bituminous coal mining, became less essential to American life. Much of the city's local manufacturing relocated to other parts of the country where unions weren't as organized, or to other parts of the world where wages weren't as high. The population of Terre Haute spiraled downward, which in turn lowered the quality of community services and the support of once-committed residents.

Hidden beneath these broader historic trends are the lives of real people—people who had jobs, kept homes, and made love as they turned the pages of their wall calendars. Many testimonials survive from Terre Haute residents of the 1920s describing how delighted they were to be living in this town they called home. Walking through the older sections of the city today, a visitor can still get a sense of the city in full flower and perhaps begin to understand exactly what these proud residents were talking about. It is what Terre Haute resident Theodore Dreiser referred to as "the lovely morning dream of America."

Nineteen twenty-seven was less than a century ago. But sometimes with the frantic pace of change, even the recent past can seem like an ancient civilization. That may be the challenge Americans will always struggle with: we often move forward too quickly to set down roots and absorb the richness of what lies right beneath us. Since the settlement of the frontier, our dreams always seem to be found on some distant horizon.

The lives of the people in these pages spanned a crucial transition between down home and downtown, tradition and progress, self-reliance and technology, sustainability and resource depletion. While their responses to everyday life were often rote and unconscious, or rooted in misconception and superstition, the community they built resonated with nature, with the senses, and with personal skills and qualities in ways that still fascinate us today. While it's too simple to say they did more with less, they may have gone a long way toward reaching beyond that distant horizon—all by standing still and working with what was right nearby. That perspective may ultimately be the essential gift they have to offer us.

Notes on the Entries

There are two descriptive categories used in this book that require some explanation: residents of the County Poor Farm and some names I wish to bring to your attention. Below I clarify these and also explain the layout of the book and some abbreviations used.

The Vigo County Poor Farm

The County Poor Farm in Terre Haute operated in 1927 on the east side of the city at 29th and Maple Avenue. In the absence of safeguards like unemployment insurance, Social Security, and IRA accounts, the County Poor Farm was a local effort to provide food and shelter to adult individuals without financial means or an extended family's support. This often included the elderly, the chronically unemployed, or those with debilitating emotional or physical challenges.

There was a curious mixture of pride and shame operating at the County Poor Farm. Residents of the Poor Farm were listed in the 1927 Polk Directory only by name. Prior to the Great Depression, being a poor, able-bodied adult in America was not only considered unnecessary, but also made one unworthy of any real dignity.

At the same time, though, postcards were printed and presumably sold featuring a color illustration of the Vigo County Poor Farm. Enough blank space was provided on the reverse side for a variation on the classic postcard message: "Having a miserable time. Wishing I weren't here."

Residents' Names

Many chapters include references to individuals whose names I find unique or just lovely to say. These are designated with an (N) with a full listing available on the website (www.hometown.indiana.edu/1927). You'll notice names from ancient mythology (Hercules, Narcissus), more recent history (Oliver Cromwell, Benjamin Franklin), and even late twentieth-century pop culture (Felix Unger).

I don't expect any of these names to provide inspiration for prospective parents. In some cases, it was difficult to even establish the gender of the name. I would encourage you to say the names aloud as you read them, though. The longer ones especially are pure poetry. As hard as it is to imagine anyone today navigating life with one of these names, at the same time you can't help but wonder why these mellifluous monikers have pretty much disappeared.

Resident and Business Listings

This book follows the format of the 1927 Polk Directory for Terre Haute: residents and businesses are listed by name, followed by the spouse's first name in parentheses, the occupation, the location of that occupation, and finally, the address of the residence.

The prefix "r" before an address indicates a rented dwelling while the prefix "h" denotes home ownership. The letters "h do" or "r do" after an address means the residence and listed occupation were located in the same structure or property.

Workers at Abel Manufacturing
Martin Collection, Indiana
Historical Society

ABEL MANUFACTURING COMPANY, 101½–107½ Wabash Avenue, Phone: Wabash 1999, Mfrs. of Over-Stuffed Living Room Furniture, **Wm. H. Abel**—*president*, **Meyer Mannberger**—*secretary-treasurer*

Mrs. Amelia Abel—*cutter*, Abel Mfg. Co.—r 1738 N. 12th

Walter E. Abel (Lestia F.)—*upholsterer*, Abel Mfg. Co.—h 1124 S. 8th

Warren L. Abel (Florence)—*upholsterer*, Abel Mfg. Co.—h 615 S. 20th

William H. Abel (Amelia)—*president*, Abel Mfg. Co.—h 1738 N. 12th

As good a place to start as any. The Abel Manufacturing Company was the kind of small local production facility based on a skilled handicraft that flourished in Terre Haute and throughout America, up until the Great Depression. Despite the ambitious corporate titles here, Abel's Manufacturing was really just a step or two removed from the home-based cottage industries of the early nineteenth century.

Abel's was a family-inspired effort, with William providing the business savvy, Warren and Walter the hands-on creative direction, and Amelia the trusted precision with all that expensive fabric. In addition to Meyer Mannberger, there were about 20 other employees involved (list of Abel employees at www.hometown.indiana.edu/1927). Rose Atkins, a widow and single mother who lived at 518 North 8th, was listed as a cushion filler at Abel's, ultimately responsible for the overstuffing of every piece of furniture the company produced. Mr. and Mrs. Frank Allison rode the interurban line everyday from Clinton, Indiana, to work at Abel's; Frank was a woodworker, Mary a seamstress, using heavy thread and thick curved needles to stitch the upholstery.

The Abel Manufacturing Company operated without the help of conveyor belts or fork lifts. In fact, a freight elevator was probably the only mechanical assistance used in the course of a work day. By and large, the daily work at Abel's in 1927 was done by hand. Amelia, measuring twice then cutting once with a tailor's shears. Walter and Warren, holding upholstery tacks between their lips as they hammered. Beyond those steady sounds, the noise probably wasn't that intrusive. At Abel's, after all, they were building soft places to sit.

This was all small-scale mindful production; just a few pieces of furniture being created over the course of a day or week. The work space was a vast upper-story loft that relied on skylights and tall windows to illuminate the beamed brick interior. At least one of those windows would have offered a good view of the river.

The wearing effects of time tell us how unlikely it is that any of the Abel company's work survives today. In any event, this particular business, with its beginnings upstairs at 101½ Wabash, would survive the partnership of the brothers Abel. By the late 1930s, Warren was making his own furniture on Ohio Boulevard, Walter had taken to selling furniture others had built, and as for William, he continued with the modest operation the family had originally founded. Long after his brothers had left Abel Manufacturing, William's partnership with Meyer Mannberger was somehow still intact.

ACME EXPLOSIVES COMPANY, 806–807 Terre Haute Trust Bldg., Wholesale Explosives, **John F. Murphy**—*secretary*

What remains fascinating about Terre Haute, Indiana, in 1927 is how it continually represents what we've come to regard as the classic American hometown: groups of kids walking home from school, a trolley car easing down a shady street, a corner grocery with the proprietor living on the floor above.

These idyllic images and many others like them became part of American popular culture in the first half of the twentieth century. That said, there doesn't seem to be an easily identifiable source for the all-purpose Acme Company that appeared in the old Roadrunner cartoons created by Chuck Jones for Warner Brothers. The name "Acme" was simply how something generic was labeled around that time. So it makes sense that included in Terre Haute's iconic status is the fact that it was once home to the Acme Explosives Company, which stood ready to ship volatile products in large wooden crates to remote desert locations per the order of one Wile E. Coyote.

David C. Adams (Lula)—*musician*—h 1210 N. 8th

Playing a musical instrument in early twentieth-century America was a valuable social skill, regarded as an outright necessity within many communities and families. While mechanical reproduction of music was certainly well-established through phonographs and player pianos by the 1920s, most of the music being heard was still being performed live. Four theaters in Terre Haute maintained house orchestras in 1927, though with the advent of talkies and the continuing decline of vaudeville, the handwriting was already scrawled on the dressing-room wall.

All across Terre Haute, an upright piano was often featured in the living room, with an ample supply of sheet music stored in the piano bench, and at least one family member who could play passably. By 1927, these impromptu recitals, not to mention the actual pianos themselves, were increasingly being pre-empted by newly purchased radio sets. Even so, the immediacy and beauty of live music was revered. If Sis could play, the family still found time to listen.

Like other everyday skills that flourished in the 1920s: dressmaking, carpentry, or baking—musicianship in Terre Haute was informally structured into a type of pyramid. At the base of this pyramid were literally thousands of gifted amateurs who performed gratis for gatherings of family and friends. Just above it was a large middle tier of individuals whose cultivated talents might have attracted occasional payment. This group would have included music teachers with perhaps one or two after-school students or choir directors for small church congregations in their neighborhood.

At the top of this pyramid were the individuals who actually listed their primary occupation as musician or music teacher (list of musicians at www.hometown.indiana.edu/1927). There are a surprising number of these in Polk's Terre Haute Directory for 1927. Some held a steady position with one of the theater orchestras (*see* William R. Joyce). Certain others apparently taught music consistently enough to consider their homes as places of business (*see* E. Blanche Rippetoe).

Due to their tender age, scant income, or female gender, the clear majority of these music professionals continued to live in extended family households. In 1927, many of them were dues-paying members of Musicians Local 25, which met the second Sunday of every month at the Central Labor Union. Local 25 had been founded in Terre Haute in 1897 with a charter membership of 380 musicians. For the musicians working then, paid performances at dance socials, company picnics, park concerts, parades, and vaudeville shows had been plentiful. The hearing of music in those days was almost exclusively a live experience. Recorded music on gramophones was considered a rare novelty. Nationwide radio broadcasts and music in motion pictures could scarcely be imagined. By 1927, though, that future was clearly in sight.

David C. Adams is unique in that he is listed as the head of a household, one that in 1927 included his wife Lula and their daughter Lynn. The Polk Directory from that year also tells us that Edwin and Gertrude Adams were living right across the street at 1215 North 8th Street. We don't know David's instrument of choice, but the proximity points to frequent family gatherings and likely one of David's favorite venues.

(N) Miami Adams (spouse of James—*miner*)—h 848 Lafayette

(N) Luella Ades (spouse of Isaac—*president*, Terre Haute Tent and Awning Company)—h 2026 South Center

Luke Adkins (Mary)—*laborer*, Street Cleaning Department—h 1566 S. 13½

Street cleaning was one of the most essential daily services provided by municipalities in the late nineteenth and early twentieth centuries, due in no small part to the unregulated presence of the natural world. Streets in residential neighborhoods were usually lined with large elm trees, which inevitably left clumps of wet leaves on paved surfaces. In Terre Haute, festive parades involving animals were common to celebrate national holidays or announce the return of the circus to town. The street sweeper often signaled the end of the parade, pushing his broom behind the last animals.

Much of the daily effort at street cleaning, however, was a response to the presence of horse-drawn vehicles. In 1907, the city of Milwaukee was dealing with an average of 133 tons of horse manure a day, or roughly three-quarters of a pound for every resident. At the same time, health officials in Rochester, New York, estimated that the 15,000 horses in that city were producing enough manure annually to form a pile 175 feet high that could easily cover an acre of ground. In the process of gathering all this information, statisticians somehow calculated that this enormous dung heap would be capable of breeding 16 billion flies. Flies were also drawn to the carcasses of dead horses. As late as 1912, more than 11,000 of them were removed annually throughout the city of Chicago.

Besieged by these ominous statistics, it's not surprising that many observers at the time considered the steady increase of motor vehicles to be an asset to public health. Whether Luke Adkins counted himself among these observers remains to be seen. His job in 1927 still occasionally involved cleaning up after horses. Milk delivery wagons, farm wagons loaded with produce, peddlers urging their tired horses on, all of these were common sights in Terre Haute, even in the heart of downtown.

Luke would have dealt with this familiar challenge as he would a spent plug of tobacco; by nudging it with a push broom toward a sewer grate and on its way to the Wabash River.

Victor Aldridge (Cleta)—*baseball player*—h 2412 S. 8th

In 1925, it was noted that Terre Haute, Indiana, had placed more of its hometown players in World Series games than any other city in the nation. Up to that point, various residents of the city had appeared in 13 different World Series games. Terre Haute had earned this distinction somewhat unfairly. In the early part of the twentieth century, a huge bumper crop of young players rose from the flat expanses of the American Midwest, nurtured by minor league teams that seemed to exist in almost every small town. Of course, to actually have played in the World Series or the major leagues up to this time, you had to be white.

Enter Vic Aldridge. He was born in the tiny rural community of Indian Springs, in nearby Martin County (*see* James W. Thompson). Much like Joe E. Brown's character in the 1933 movie *Elmer the Great,* Vic was drawn to the bright lights of Terre Haute, Indiana, to play baseball.

Vic stood only 5'9". He understood quickly that his best chance to get to the majors was by standing a little taller on the pitcher's mound. He developed a nasty curve ball that eventually got him there in 1917. Rogers Hornsby, an excellent hitter who was known to be quite nasty himself, deemed the pitch one of the finest curves he'd ever seen. It proved to be the basis for a successful career as a professional athlete. By 1927, Vic Aldridge had been pitching in the major leagues for eight years and had even won two games in the World Series for Pittsburgh in 1925.

In the early decades of major league baseball, hometown nicknames for players were very common. These nicknames often defined a career more clearly than individual statistics or game exploits. Vic's nickname was The Hoosier Schoolmaster, and three other pitchers with Indiana roots had some real beauties: Amos Rusie was The Hoosier Thunderbolt, Sam Leever was The Goshen Schoolmaster, and George Mullin was Wabash George. Pitcher Mordecai "Three Finger" Brown, who eventually owned a gas station at the corner of 7th and Cherry Streets in Terre Haute was also known as "Miner." (See photo of Mordechai Brown's gas station at www.hometown.indiana.edu/1927.)

With his bonus money from the 1925 World Series, Vic Aldridge purchased a modest clapboard home on South 8th Street where he and Cleta lived throughout 1927. In October of that year, Vic Aldridge would pitch in his final World Series. In the eighth inning of Game 2, a clutch double by Lou Gehrig of the New York Yankees sent Vic and his Pirates team to defeat. After the subsequent four-game sweep, Vic must have been happy to return home. The following season would prove to be Victor Eddington Aldridge's last as a major leaguer, during which he would pitch for a new team, hit his second home run against major league pitching, and lose almost twice as many games as he won.

Through it all, his adopted hometown seemed to suit him just fine. Vic Aldridge would live the rest of his days as a Terre Haute resident, closing in on 80 when he died in the spring of 1973.

Minnie G. Allen—*seamstress*—r 1656 N. Center

Operating with needle, thimble, and thread, and maybe—occasionally—a treadle sewing machine, Minnie was practicing her craft in a city filled with worthy amateurs. In this case, her skills would have been measured against nearly every post-adolescent female in Terre Haute. For a moment, imagine how good she must have been to make it her living.

Carl Anderson—County Poor Farm

Flora Anderson—*seamstress*, Stahl-Urban Company—r 2116 Dillman

Unlike Minnie Allen, Flora was on the clock and on a machine, one of about 160 machines that operated at the Stahl-Urban Plant at 918 Ohio Boulevard (*see* Darrell D. Donham). The Stahl-Urban Company made overalls and work clothes, so handling heavyweight denim all day probably rubbed Flora's fingers raw. But there were a couple of bright spots for Flora in addition to her weekly pay voucher: The sewing machines at Stahl-Urban were powered by electricity in 1927, which at least saved Flora's ankles, and her job as seamstress probably put her in a position to obtain factory seconds for her husband, Elija, listed that year in the Polk Directory as a laborer.

William J. Anthony (Margaret)—*equipment manager*, Indian Refining Company—h 920 N. 4th

In 1924, Toscha Seidel of Terre Haute, Indiana, was one of the few and fortunate violinists in the world to possess a "Da Vinci" Stradivarius. This rare violin, one of approximately 1,100 instruments created by the master, had acquired an uncertain history over the years. Mr. Seidel had initially purchased it from a dealer in Berlin, who could only verify its ownership back to 1886. Apparently, the rare violin had vanished and reappeared numerous times since it was finished by Stradivari's sons just after his death in 1737.

In 1927, William Anthony also had a rare eighteenth-century artifact that he would occasionally display to curious visitors. This was an original Franklin penny, struck in 1787. It was the first copper coin authorized by the new Congress.

Just as Toscha Seidel's Stradivarius produced extraordinary sound, Mr. Anthony's single penny offered invaluable wisdom. Inscribed on one side just beneath a sundial indicating the sun's meridian, was the ageless advice: "Mind Your Business." On the coin's other side, printed in the center, was an important reminder to those fortunate enough to actually hold something that old: "We Are One."

(N) Salome Apman—*janitress*, Greenwood School—h 2831 S. Center

(N) Apolina Appler—(spouse of Adam—*laborer*)—h 437 S. 14th

John Archer (Laura B.)—*blacksmith*—h 531 N. Center

In just five years, between 1920 and 1925, the number of horses in the state of Indiana declined by more than 20 percent. It wasn't just the automobile that was responsible for this, but the sudden explosive growth of all motor vehicles, including tractors for plowing and trucks for hauling. In this place in time, using the term "horsepower" to explain an engine's capacity made perfect sense to people raised on the farm.

In 1927, the Classified Business Section in the Polk Directory listed 13 blacksmiths in Terre Haute. John Archer's name does not appear in this section, but this anonymity was common among the blacksmiths working in town. Smithing had never been a business you went out of your way to advertise. Most of the remaining smiths working in Terre Haute operated out of old carriage houses or sheds along alleyways. If someone in the neighborhood needed to have a broken hoist chain repaired, they knew right where the smith could be found and also knew he probably wouldn't be all that busy. Much of a smith's daily work involved extending the life of a tool or machine part.

Since many blacksmiths didn't even bother to post a sign, they would have certainly been unlikely to pay for a listing in some business directory that would be shelved in a downtown office. But even in the face of dwindling opportunities, this group of skilled professionals still maintained an active community. Blacksmiths Local 484 continued to meet on the second and fourth Saturdays of every month, though by 1927 the roll call was probably getting quicker with every meeting. Much like the horses they shod, them that was dying wouldn't soon be getting replaced. Yet even at this late date, the membership contained a rich diversity of names. There were still three men in Terre Haute named Davis who listed their occupation as blacksmith. In addition to Edward, two of them had names as blunt as their trade: Count and Vote.

These survivors of the blacksmith's trade, these men who used fire and physical strength to bend natural elements to their will, must have understood that they were quickly being left behind in the world, by a distance that even the most ambitious among them couldn't travel. Of the 13 blacksmiths who paid extra to have their names in the Polk Business Section for Terre Haute in 1927, not one found it necessary to be listed in the city's latest phone book. Perhaps they couldn't imagine their customers would ever locate them that way. Or maybe it was because the sound of a ringing hammer always drowns out a ringing telephone.

Stanley B. Archibald—*musician*—r 614 S. 5th

A more common example of a musician's life can be found here. This is a twist on an old joke: Question: What do you call a musician who breaks up with his girlfriend? Answer: Homeless. In 1927, Stanley was 24 years of age and living with his parents, William and Anna, and his 28-year-old sister, Jean. Both Jean and William were teachers in Terre Haute's public school system, so whenever Stanley slept late Mama likely had breakfast already waiting for him.

(N)—Lycurgus N. Arick (Belle)—*laborer*—h 35 Rose Ave.

Carrie Arney—*maid*—r 1000 S. Center

In the 1927 Polk Directory, maids, domestics, and housekeepers were each listed separately. What they shared were their everyday duties (cooking, cleaning, laundry, shopping) and their gender. Maids tended to live onsite, usually in households wealthy enough to include serving dinner and answering the telephone among the assigned tasks. This arrangement generally involved a lace apron and one afternoon off during the week.

Carrie Arney lived and worked in the home of Omar and Gwendolyn Mewhinney. Omar was the founder and president of the Mewhinney Candy Company, a manufacture of boxed chocolates, located on North 9th Street (*see* Reba Deardorf). It's fairly likely, don't you think, that there were dishes of candy set out in the living room and foyer? A gentle warning from Mrs. Mewhinney was probably made on Carrie's first day.

Forrest B. Arnold (Everal K.)—*bus driver*—h 2343 Cleveland Ave.

Joseph E. Asay (Addie)—*street car operator*—h 2622 Schaal Ave.

At the beginning of the twentieth century, Terre Haute, Indiana, was already a city of 35,000 people. Many of the public amenities the city offered to residents were comparable to those found in larger municipalities like New York and Chicago. For example, Terre Haute had an impressive urban park system. By the mid-1920s, this city of ten square miles had committed more than 600 acres to urban green space and had assigned 120 public employees to maintenance.

Like most mid-sized cities at the time, Terre Haute featured an extensive mass transit system which included 25 miles of streetcar track. In 1927, electric trolleys were carrying an average of 30,000 passengers in the city daily, more than 10 million annually. The fare was 5 cents, with no additional charge for transfers. Since these trolleys traveled not quite as fast as an average man could run, the convenience provided to passengers was not so much time saved as energy conserved. In this walking city, it simply meant you could take a load off your feet.

The seven streetcar routes within city limits were supplemented in 1927 by six motorized bus routes. In addition, there were four separate taxi companies as well as a large number of driver-owned jitney cabs. Inevitably, along the busier streets, there was competition for ridership. For all practical purposes, it meant that no city resident was more than a short walk from a public transit stop.

In May of 1925, motorized buses operating in Terre Haute appealed for relief from an existing ordinance which prevented them from loading and unloading passengers wherever there were trolley lines. This request would foreshadow a high-stakes competition between buses and trolleys that would play out across

Terre Haute Trolley Car with Crew

America in the coming decades. Now, over half a century later, we're aware that the playing cards were dealt from a marked deck.

All throughout the 1920s, electric streetcar systems in America had continued to attract customers and substantial capital investment. The per capita ridership during this time actually exceeded the trolley systems of Europe. In 1920, Terre Haute became the first American city with a complete fleet of lightweight Birney electric trolley cars. By the close of the decade, an estimated 14 billion riders across America were taking the trolley.

But during this same time, automobiles were consuming 90 percent of the nation's petroleum, 8 percent of its rubber, and 25 percent of its repair and service facilities. The large corporations that competed for the allocation of these resources quickly determined that electric trolleys, in fact public transportation generally, formed an obvious impediment to future profits.

In 1932, four of these corporations quietly decided to form a syndicate. General Motors, Firestone, Standard Oil, and Mack Truck had realized that with the Depression creating a scarcity of credit for infrastructure development, an opportunity existed to regulate, perhaps even eliminate, competition from mass transit.

Over the next 17 years this new partnership, called National City Lines, would persuade 45 cities to scrap their street rails for motorized buses, which not surprisingly would be built and maintained by members of the syndicate. Subsequently, the hours of operation for public transit systems were cut and ridership fell drastically. By 1940, half of all streetcar passengers had been induced to abandon the trolley for cars and buses. The experience of riding public transit became less enjoyable as it became less convenient.

The change for Terre Haute would occur on June 4, 1939, when the last electric trolley line in the city stopped service. A fleet of 36 motor bus coaches were introduced to the public the very next day.

(N)—America Asher (widow, W.H.)—h 2300 S. 10½

Anna Asher—*cottage manager*—Rose Orphan Home h do

It would be impossible to consider the Rose Orphan Home as a welcoming place to live. It contained far too much misery for that. Nevertheless, from a respectful distance, say, the corner of 25th and Wabash, the 20-acre property on Terre Haute's east side did exude a kind of dreamy splendor to passersby.

The three-story main building, constructed in 1883, had been modeled after the Sandringham Palace in Lynn, England. On the main floor, the banisters had been fashioned from hard Georgia pine with windows of leaded stained glass brightly illuminating the turn in the staircase. An enormous, framed mirror, imported from France, hung in the foyer. The domed cupola atop the building housed a large bell which announced the start of the day to as many as 150 children. (See photo of a view from the bell tower at www.hometown .indiana.edu/1927.)

Ever since its founding, the Rose Home had divided the children into three cottages, one for the girls, two for the boys. This separation was the first of the many hard adjustments for any child brought there to live. At the Rose Orphan Home, brothers were separated from sisters, no matter their age. Upon their arrival, each child was given a bed with clean sheets, issued two changes of clothing in approximately their size, and assigned a 2'-square cubicle to store their clothing, a nightshirt, and a washcloth. Three meals a day were provided, as well as hot water to wash in, and a free movie once a month at the Liberty Theater downtown. Though virtually every waking and sleeping moment was spent in a crowd, each child quickly discovered what it meant to be completely alone in the world.

Anna Asher's position as cottage matron allowed for little flexibility. Anna was already dressed when the first bell from the main building rang at 5:30 AM. She would then climb the cottage stairs to the second floor and face a dark, open room with two rows of sleeping children in cots set against opposite walls. On the coldest mornings, Anna might pause for just a moment before beginning her daily ritual. Then all at once, the overhead lights would be switched on from the power plant. Anna would stride across the hardwood floor and forcefully clap her hands without saying a word.

In the next 45 minutes, 30 to 40 children, including toddlers, would be washed and dressed to face the new day. Anna would rely on the older children to assist the younger ones in most every task, from tying shoelaces and hair ribbons to wiping noses and drying tears.

At 6:15, all of the children in Anna's cottage would line up, tallest to shortest, and descend the stairs. They would then take their place at one of two long wooden benches facing each other on the first floor. The children's position on

The Rose Orphan Home

the bench corresponded almost exactly to the placement of their bed on the floor above. Set between the benches were long oak library tables, where Anna would supervise all the homework done in the evening.

Promptly at 6:30 AM, a second bell would ring out from the main building to announce breakfast. The children would then walk in single file from their cottage through the fading darkness to a dining hall located in the rear of the main building.

Breakfast consisted of either oatmeal spooned out of large metal pots or canned plums saturated in heavy syrup, the two selections apparently chosen to eliminate the likelihood of favorites. Although seconds of milk or bread were allowed, conversation between the children was not.

After breakfast, the children returned in a straight line to their cottage to make their beds. Here again, the older children would assist the younger ones. Then, until school began at 8:00 o'clock, every child in Anna's cottage would begin the work tasks that they had been assigned somewhere at the Home. These tasks varied little from day to day. They might involve housekeeping under the supervision of Mrs. McKimmey, laundry under the direction of Mrs. Leslie, or for the boys, work in the barn or the fields with Mr. Griffith. The assignments and instructions were always very precise, for instance, to clean 15 windows daily at the main building. Whatever part of the job remained once school began would be continued after school up until the bell announcing dinner at 5:00 PM.

Anna Asher was the first and last adult the children in her cottage saw every day. The toddlers were put to bed first at 7:00 o'clock. Children up to age 14 could stay up until 8:00 o'clock. The older adolescents would have still another hour to mend socks or continue with their homework; most any task to keep the time from moving too slowly.

At the Rose Orphan Home, too much time spent in reflection could cause one's inner resolve to crumble, whether you were a cottage matron combing her hair or a child lying sleepless in bed. Anna Asher's working day at the Home included stark reminders of how ruthless life's fortunes could be. From time to time, Anna's cottage would be assigned a new child who would need changes of clothing, socks, and a pair of shoes from the random assortment that had been donated to the Home. Often, the donated clothing had originally belonged to a child who had died suddenly. Anna would lead the newest orphan to the storage room on the first floor, open the door, switch on the overhead light, and together, the two of them would stare at a limp pile of clothes once intended for other children. Anna might have mentioned the source of the donations just to remind the new resident how lucky they were, or she might have kept that information to herself. Either way, that moment must have hung heavy in the air.

At the end of every day, there was the last of her duties, just a little after 9:00 PM when all of the children were finally in bed and the overhead lights on the second floor had been turned off from the power plant. This would offer

Orphans at the Rose Home
Martin Collection, Indiana
Historical Society

an extra moment for Anna to listen to the steady soft breathing of the younger children, holding out the hope that this day might end without her noticing the sound of one of them crying.

(N) Odetta Axe—r 1525 Eagle

Robert Axlander—*fruit grower*—south side of Hulman at E. 28th St.

The presence of a fruit grower well inside city limits might surprise you, but probably not as much as learning how common it actually was. In 1927, there were literally dozens of Terre Haute city residents who listed their occupation as farmer, gardener, or fruit grower (list of farmers and gardeners at www.hometown.indiana.edu/1927). These city residents supplemented the vast amount of fresh local produce already being grown in Vigo and surrounding counties. Their homes usually sat on the parcels they cultivated; enough land, in Robert Axlander's case, for a modest orchard and a small wooden stand on the roadside.

You're likely imagining an apple orchard here. But the varieties of fruit cultivated on these small parcels would surprise you as well. As late as the mid-1920s, Indiana was still producing 380,000 bushels of peaches annually. Plums, 209,000 bushels of them, were also being harvested. Cherries thrived in Indiana up until the early years of the twentieth century. In the year 1909, the state still produced 364,000 bushels of cherries for pies, jams, and ciders. Although a state report in 1924 had called the cherry crop good for that year, there weren't enough bushels harvested to be calculated statewide.

Unlike the apple trees, peach trees and plum trees required constant pruning and, occasionally, a late frost might kill the entire crop. But in 1927, there remained a strong commercial market for locally grown fruit. In addition to family canners and cobbler makers, independent grocers regularly attended the daily farmers market, located at 2nd and Mulberry. In Terre Haute, one could cultivate a local reputation based on a particular variety of fruit: Stump the World Peaches, for instance, or the Imperial Gage Plum, or the Early Richmond Cherry. And if your crop happened to fall victim to the whims of the weather; well, it wasn't like your competition was making out any better.

BACHELOR CLUB—**Paul Pfeifer,** *secretary*—606 Poplar

The origins of the club date back to 1914, when Everett Cole decided to organize a group of 15 male friends into a social club that would sponsor dances, outings, and other planned events with the eligible young women in town. By 1917, the group had formalized its operations with Robert's Rules of Order, monthly meetings, and a few elected officers. The military draft in World War I placed a temporary damper on the club's activities, but by 1919, the now-named Young Bachelor's Club was renting dance halls, hiring jazz bands, even printing invitations. Each event involved approximately 20 couples, club members or by invitation. The dances were pretty classy affairs. Suit and tie required, except for the costumed Halloween Dance, with a stiff cover charge of $1.00 per couple. Being that the dances were always held in a rented hall, they regularly ran until after midnight.

The purpose of the Young Bachelor's Club was really no different from Weight Watchers: its sole mission was to create former members. This first version of a club for bachelors put itself out of business in 1920 when the president, secretary, and treasurer finally found their brides and the vice-president headed out to California in search of better prospects.

In 1927, the new secretary of the revived Bachelor Club, Paul Pfeifer, was living with his mother, Amelia, at 525 South Center Street. The primary qualification for club membership apparently hadn't changed. But since there were literally hundreds of fraternal organizations, barber shops, and pool halls throughout Terre Haute serving the networking needs of men only, one might wonder what particular advantages this exclusive club offered to potential members. After all, the initiates of the first Young Bachelor's Club all had a prior connection; they were Everett Cole's friends. The new club did at least have an actual headquarters: a small clapboard building at 606 Poplar, on a corner lot three blocks from downtown. The building appears too small to have accommodated dances. In any case, with Prohibition in place it's hard to imagine how that type of event could have attracted sophisticated bachelors and their dates. It's possible that like many fraternal organizations and speakeasies operating then, the structure simply provided a refuge to drink alcohol.

It would all be swept away within a couple of years. Paul Pfeifer married Miss Margaret Shea in the spring of 1929 and they moved into an apartment located a block away from mother Amelia. The club's headquarters was soon demolished to make way for a gas station, perhaps anticipating a time later that century when the social designation of "bachelor" would pretty much cease to have any real meaning.

(N) Mary Bad (widow Richard)—r 1726 S. 4th

(N) Zipporah Baganz (widow Charles)—h 1414 Chase

As is often the case with the most unique female names, they each married into them. Not even marrying a Smith would have changed things for Zipporah.

Hamill W. Baker—*investments*—408 T. H. Star Bldg.—h 1136 S. 6th

He was a financial advisor in a strong bull market in 1927, which sat about two years from Black Tuesday, October 29, 1929, the massive collapse which laid waste to most of the sage predictions about stock futures. And boy, what Hamill W. Baker wouldn't have given to get that one right. Then, like the singer of Vernon Duke and Ira Gershwin's "I Can't Get Started," he could have sold short. As it turned out, Hamill gave up his office in the Star Building soon after the Crash. By 1934, lawyers had practically taken over the entire fourth floor.

Joseph M. Ball—*drugs*—423 N. 13th–423½ N. 13th h do

It was common in 1927 to find grocery stores in Terre Haute with the proprietor living upstairs or a drugstore that was locally owned. But this was a rare hybrid. And picture this: The 400 block of North 13th Street was almost entirely made up of residential homes with a drugstore, a broommaker, a restaurant, a shoemaker, and an upholsterer operating in their midst.

Compared to the retail pharmacies of today—multinational chains with millions of square feet devoted to identical floor plans—Joseph M. Ball's operation was more than just a rare hybrid. It was a separate species altogether.

(N) Ottis Ballou (Edna)—*motorman*—h 1700 N. 4th

Hopefully the surname was pronounced with clear emphasis on the second syllable: like the movie *Cat BalLOU.*

Baker A. Bannon (Ethel)—Upholstering, Furniture Repairing, Packing and Crating for Shipment; Our Motto: Good Work, Second Hand Goods Bought and Sold, Work Called For and Delivered, 409–413 Lafayette, 413 Lafayette h do

Baker A. Bannon (Ethel)—*restaurant*—413 Lafayette h do

We've obviously got ourselves a real character here. There are many signs to suggest this: the phonetic beauty of the name, the wide variety of business activities located at one address—an address that also happened to contain the Bannon family home. There was, at best, a marginal living to be made from covering and repairing, packing and crating, calling for and delivering. At least the restaurant promised to provide the family with money and meals at the same time. Adjustments were probably made hour to hour. One guesses that Ethel was flipping the eggs if there happened to be a crate to build that day.

In 1927, Baker A. Bannon's presence in his hometown was strengthened by the neighborhood where he lived and worked. The Twelve Points section of Terre Haute was one of the city's most distinctive communities. It first emerged in the late nineteenth century with the dedication of Collett Park and the growth of large industrial employers like the Columbian Enameling and Stamping Company. This produced a lot of air pollution and so a lot of trees were planted to ease its effects.

In 1897, local businessman Walter Phillips decided to create a business district along Lafayette Avenue. By the 1920s, this commercial section had grown to include a local bank, a hotel, a movie theater, three doctor's offices, four bakeries, seven drugstores, 20 groceries, and dozens of other businesses ranging from the Twelve Points Bicycle Shop (*see* J. Wood Posey) to Lawrence W. Patton, vulcanizer. All of this activity sat along one street, contained within ten short city blocks.

Since the vast majority of these shops and offices were owned by individuals who also lived in Twelve Points, there was a strong incentive to be one's own best advertisement. Accordingly, the Twelve Points section developed a reputation for outsized characters who just so happened to run their own businesses. Since the commercial was personal in Twelve Points, this made perfect sense. Transactions were customarily conducted face-to-face using first names or barring that, a well-known nickname. Take a name like Baker Bannon and put a distinctive personality behind it, and you'd really have something.

In the early 1920s, a small group of merchants from Twelve Points pooled their resources and purchased an ad in the *Terre Haute Tribune,* the city's evening newspaper. The businesses included Mike the Tailor, Morris the Tailor, and Boyer the Printer, apparently the only names by which these merchants needed to be known in Twelve Points. The Teco Tavern, misnamed somewhat since Prohibition, would tout their homemade chili as the best in town. The Teco also seemed particularly proud of another delicacy, homemade not only in its recipe but in its name: Limburger sandwiches à la Billy Smith. Unique tastes and characters just seemed to find each other in Twelve Points. Next to the Swan Theater, there was a small booth occupied before every show by Sam the Popcorn Man. His particular specialty was a nickel bag of popcorn sprinkled with celery salt.

Although the Teco Tavern had changed hands by 1927, Billy Smith could still be found around Twelve Points, working as a plasterer and living with his wife, Ida, at 662 Lafayette Avenue. His fame was secure in the neighborhood, having once had his name attached to a Limburger sandwich. But for those positions that involved a little more outside competition, it was thought that perhaps a catchy slogan might separate an individual from the field. For Mike the Tailor, a quotation of his own devising: "Mike Has Fits." With his full name standing in front of all that lay behind it, Baker A. Bannon had also achieved his measure of fame within a small neighborhood, even as he built the occasional wooden crate for shipment overseas.

(N) Delphia Barbee (spouse of Ernest L.—*laborer*)—h 1101 Voorhees

Again, let's hope the emphasis was on the second syllable: *not* like the Aussie delicacy Shrimp on the BARbee.

Raymond J. Barnaby (Effie)—*musician*—h 1022 S. 9th

He wasn't living with his parents, and Effie isn't listed as working outside the home. It's fascinating to realize that they just must have gotten by somehow.

Anna Barton—County Poor Farm

Ferdinand Bayard—County Poor Farm

Alex Bayauskas—*shot firer*—r 2101 Buckeye

And your guess would be as good as mine. There were two gunsmiths operating in Terre Haute in 1927: Edward Brown and Edmund Tetzel. Oddly enough, they did business on the same block of Ohio Boulevard, right across the street from one another. Maybe there was some superstition gunsmiths had about turning their back on the competition.

There's no evidence that Alex worked for either man. In any event, you'd think a gunsmith would check his repair work personally without the need for live ammunition. We can probably eliminate hired assassin and circus cannon operator here, as well. Which leaves what? A complete mystery. By 1928, Alex Bayauskas had left Terre Haute and there's no subsequent record of him in any federal census.

Birch E. Bayh (Leah W.)—*supervisor*, Physical Education, Public Schools—h 242 Barton

Father and mother to a United States Senator. Grandparents to yet another Senator, who also served as governor of Indiana.

Rev. Orval W. Baylor (Helen E.)—*manager*, Klan Home—h 1941 N. 10th

In 1925, the statewide membership in the Ku Klux Klan for the state of Indiana was estimated at 194,000. One might dismiss this number as excessive, if it weren't for the fact that the Klan's internal rolls at the time claim to have registered half a million members. Terre Haute, Indiana, supported two local chapters of the Klan. Terre Haute Klan #7 had a membership of 7,250. In North Terre Haute, Otter Klan #91 had organized with 990 members. Both chapters met at the Klan Home, which sat in Klan Park—located on a corner parcel at 1501 North 13th Street.

It's been said that the immense popularity of the Ku Klux Klan in Indiana during the 1920s was due in part to the organization adapting its message for both the changing times and a changing audience. To an extent, its platform was redirected against a variety of perceived threats; which supposedly originated from selected immigrant groups, Jews, Roman Catholics, and even chain stores. This, of course, was in addition to the Klan's longstanding tradition of violence and intimidation against the local Black population. Beyond the hateful rhetoric, introducing the Klan to Indiana was certainly a lucrative proposition. Every member paid $10.00 to join and $6.50 for the white hood and robe.

But membership in the Klan was not simply a matter of exercising private prejudices or the lure of a secret organization. There is ample evidence that it influenced the conduct of public policy. In January 1925, it was estimated by the *Saturday Spectator* that two-thirds of those running for public office in Terre Haute were Klan members. In July of the following year, the Klan announced their intentions to build a new auditorium in the city. The fundraising goal was set at $30,000. At the time, there was little doubt that their broad base of support would enable the group to quickly raise the full amount.

In the absence of membership roles for the Terre Haute and Otter Klans, the names of the 8,000-plus individuals who took the vow remain unavailable to us today. That is, with a few notable exceptions. Orval W. Baylor would be one of them.

Beyond the white robes of the Klan, Orval Baylor was a man of the cloth by serving as assistant pastor at the First United Brethren Church on Barbour Avenue. This connection was not as rare as you might think. A few years earlier, a Ku Klux Klan rally in Kokomo, Indiana, drew a crowd of 100,000 people. The high school band played. The local clergy offered prayers.

But by 1927, even as personal prejudices remained strong, the Klan movement in Indiana was in steep decline. D. C. Stephenson, the Grand Dragon of the Indiana Klan, had been found guilty of second-degree murder in the death of Madge Oberholtzer and subsequently sentenced to 30 years in prison. Statewide membership in the Klan would drop to 7,770 by 1928. The local chapters in Terre Haute, which just a few years earlier had announced plans for a 5,000-seat auditorium, wound up selling the property on North 13th Street to the Modern Machine and Pattern Company.

This was apparently Orval Baylor's cue to leave Terre Haute and head south. The 1930 census reported that he and Helen were living in Louisville, Kentucky. Their 6-year-old son, Robert, was probably old enough to have remembered Terre Haute. How much he might have remembered of his father's motive for being there is unknown. The same census reports that in 1930 Helen had just given birth to a daughter, Edna. One hopes that a new decade and a new child marked a fresh start to the family legacy.

Kathleen Beck—County Poor Farm

Edward C. Bell (Mildred C.)—*weighman*—Terre Haute Pure Milk and Ice Cream Company—h 608 N. 5th

In 1927, Terre Haute Pure Milk and Ice Cream Company, located at 531 North 5th Street, was the largest dairy in the city. It produced pasteurized milk and cream, cottage cheese, butter, and ice cream. The daily output required to be the largest commercial dairy in Terre Haute was quite modest by modern standards: 3,000 gallons of milk, 1,000 gallons of ice cream, 1,500 pounds of butter. These figures, and Edward Bell's job as weighman, illuminate how Terre Haute's local economy operated in 1927 and, more importantly, how the city businesses built relationships with the many small farms that surrounded it. (*See* Loudon Packing Company.)

The Terre Haute Pure Milk and Ice Cream Company was actually one of seven dairies operating in the city at the time. To give a sense of scale, the proprietors of two of these dairies, Walter Denehie and Harry Hamilton, actually lived adjacent to their small processing facilities. With one exception, all of Terre Haute's dairies were locally owned. The president of the Wadley Company, a wholesale dealer in poultry, eggs, and butter resided in Indianapolis, 70 miles away.

In 1927, the process of milk production was local. The Terre Haute Pure Milk and Ice Cream Company dealt exclusively with members of the Vigo County Milk Producers Association for its daily supply of milk and cream. This is where Edward Bell came in, literally, from his home located just half a block from the dairy.

A Local Farmer
with Milk Cans

From 9 to 10 AM daily, the Terre Haute Pure Milk and Ice Cream Company received milk shipments in 3-foot-tall metal cans from area farms. It was Edward's job to inspect and weigh them. He likely knew each of the local producers by name, as well as the name of the horse whenever a farm wagon was involved.

Edward's role in this process invites us to reconsider the economies of scale. In 1927, the individual calculations that Edward made and the numbers he wrote down totaled in the hundreds at most. The raw milk he weighed would have originated from local farms less than 20 miles away. And later in the day, when the milk, cheese, and ice cream were finally processed, those products would only travel a few city blocks to their destinations. In 1927, home delivery for Terre Haute Pure Milk and Ice Cream Company would be accomplished every morning with 29 wagons drawn by horses, who had memorized every stop with their footsteps.

Harry E. Bennett (Ola A.)—*proprietor*, Rex Theater—h 834 N. 6th

The Rex was like the Swan or the Alhambra in Terre Haute, a tiny neighborhood theater that didn't even bother to advertise in the daily newspapers. With more than 650 motion pictures being produced in the United States annually by 1927, the available supply of films far exceeded the number of exhibitors. Harry Bennett probably figured that since his business was surrounded by plenty of houses, that in itself would guarantee plenty of customers. The Rex Theater was located at 838 North 6th, literally right next door to where Harry and Ola lived.

The Rex would still have been showing silent films in 1927. The nation's first talkie, *The Jazz Singer* didn't premiere in Terre Haute until February of 1928. By then, there were more than 15,000 movie theaters operating nationally. In many towns, the number of weekly ticket sales easily outpaced church attendance.

All that said, it's really not surprising to learn that the Rex Theater had completely vanished by 1931. Reinvestment in new sound projectors was suddenly required for movie theaters and the exhibiting fees for new feature-length pictures had increased. Up until this point, the only concession Harry had to make for sound was a piano and a person to play it (*see* Fern Garden). More challenging for Harry was the fact that many of the larger downtown theaters in Terre Haute had begun to show double features for the cost of a single admission. With such a business model, in-house concessions probably provided the greatest profit. For the Rex to compete it would have required further investment at a time when the Depression made credit unavailable to small business owners. So often, the money you can't spend leads to the money you'll never make.

(N) Stephania Berlot (spouse of Frank—*molder*, Terre Haute Malleable and Manufacturing Company)—h 2022 N. 20th

In Indiana, there's a tradition of "hoosierizing" the French language. To the locals, Versailles is "Versayles," Lyon is just like the animal, and the pronunciation of Lafayette, Indiana, only honors the hero, not his actual name.

One hopes for a soft treatment of the surname here, like merlot. But who knows? Stephania herself might have called her hometown "Terry Hut."

Joseph Bermagar—County Poor Farm

Samuel N. Berry (Grace A.)—*janitor*, Rose Polytechnic Institute—h 1634 Spruce

In 1927, Samuel N. Berry had already held his position for 27 years and remarkably, he would hold it for 23 more. Robert L. McCormick, helping to keep Samuel busy every day as a professor of civil engineering, would come reasonably close with 46 years.

Leon F. Bingaman (Mayme)—*metaphysician*—h 324 N. 4th

His death certificate tells us that Leon Bingaman was 73 years old in 1927. Apparently, he chose to take eight years off his age when the census taker visited his home three years later. Hard to say what first brought him to Terre Haute, or to metaphysics, for that matter. But in 1927, Leon was presenting himself as a philosopher-for-hire and hung a shingle outside to prove it. Since many of his potential clients must have asked, Leon likely had a thumbnail description of his practice at the ready.

Metaphysics would be broadly defined as a personal inquiry into the eternal, universal nature of things; that which cannot be quantified or explained purely by science. The questions raised by metaphysics generally arise from an awareness that all is not as it appears to be. One could be drawn to this inquiry by wondering if something significant might lie behind what we experience with our senses and think about with our minds.

A slightly more pedestrian explanation for Leon's personal inquiry might be the teachings of one James Schafer. In the 1920s, Schafer founded the Royal Fraternity of Master Metaphysicians. The movement was later described by *Time* magazine as a "theological goulash of Rosicrucianism, Christian Science, Christianity, Supermind Science, faith healing, and how to win friends and influence people." When Schafer appealed for tax exempt status as a religious movement, the New York State Supreme Court rejected his claim, saying the only way the Royal Fraternity compared to a religion was in "the solicitation and receipt of funds."

Formal certification as a metaphysician could be obtained from the Royal Fraternity with the payment of $100. Schafer's most fervent followers tended to be middle-aged women, but a core group of men distinguished themselves within the movement as the Storks. This select fellowship wore diaper pins on their coat lapels, which designated them as messengers of a new beginning—the type of message presumably being carried by the stork rather than the diaper.

It's also possible that a book first published in 1925 inspired Leon Bingaman's relationship with the great forces beyond. *The Game of Life and How to Play It* was authored by self-described metaphysician Florence Scovel Shinn. She was a former children's book illustrator who popularized the belief that a person's positive intentions directly led to positive results. Long before the self-help movement, Shinn contended that clearly stated personal intentions could direct outcomes in a random universe by connecting with an inner power she called the superconscious. Basically, *The Game of Life* acknowledged the immense influence of the spirit and the divine without attaching it to a particular religion. Mostly by word-of-mouth, the book became wildly successful.

Just how all of this philosophy translated to Leon Bingham's face-to-face discussions with the people who walked through his door is unclear. *The Game of Life* is filled with inspirational stories of personal challenges with health, relationships, and finances met successfully by, as Dr. Norman Vincent Peale would later refer to it, the power of positive thinking. Placed in this context, Leon's role at 324 North 4th was probably a combination of spiritual counselor and life coach, pointing each client toward a personal belief system based on awareness and empowerment. Various stories were used for illustration: taken from literature, ancient cultures, and perhaps Leon's own life experience.

We know little else about Leon Bingaman's life in 1927. He was married at the time to Mary (Mayme) Bingaman, who was about 25 years his junior, a fact which may explain the age he gave to the visiting census taker. Leon and Mayme were living between Eagle and Chestnut Streets. The address was on the eastern edge of what was considered Terre Haute's Red Light District.

So metaphysics apparently became just another service available in the neighborhood. As far as Leon Bingaman saw it, whatever particular complaints folks arrived with, they were essentially responding to a strange feeling arising from an unfamiliar place inside. Perhaps Leon hung that shingle hoping to suggest possibilities, not necessarily provide pat answers. After all, if you leave a metaphysician with more questions than you arrived with, that might not be such a bad thing.

THE BIRD CAGE (Beatrice Shassere)—*pet store*—627 Cherry

In 1926, a census from the U.S. Department of Agriculture estimated that there were 22,000,000 bluebirds in the lower 48, or roughly one bluebird for every five Americans. You might think this would have led Americans to take the presence of songbirds for granted, but actually the opposite was true, at least in Terre Haute, Indiana. An article in the *Saturday Spectator* claimed that over 40 percent of all the households in the city contained a caged bird. Most of them, it seems, were canaries.

Keeping a canary in a home with a gas oven served a practical function. The birds had been used extensively in World War I to detect poison gas, and in a mining community like Terre Haute their practical value was widely recognized.

But beyond the matter of life and death, there was that heavenly song. In 1927, most of the canaries in Terre Haute, Indiana, had come from the Hartz Mountains in Germany. Five million canaries had been shipped abroad that year alone.

The price of the more common variety of canary sold in Terre Haute's pet stores was in the $4–$6 range, and Beatrice absolutely guaranteed hers to be singers. Their song, she might add, was perhaps less refined than that of the St. Andreasburg Roller. This particular canary could actually sing with its beak closed. The song was so distinctive that it was actually known as the canary aria. Elderly Germans from small mountain villages along the Swiss border had painstakingly trained each St. Andreasburg Roller with the help of a small pipe organ. Mrs. Frances Boyer had paid $50 for one of these special birds. It joined 92 other canaries that she and her husband Frank kept in their home at 1601 South Center Street.

But there was perhaps an even more unique canary living somewhere in North Terre Haute. Beatrice might even have been able to direct you. It was said that this bird could actually whistle "Yankee Doodle." Maybe it had been trained that way to serve in the trenches, and somehow had survived to sing about it.

(N) Cinderella Blade (spouse of Leonard—*porter*, Goldberg Company)—h 2531 N. 16th

Charles Bligh—County Poor Farm

Jessie Blocksom—County Poor Farm

Raymond E. Bohn (Beulah)—*sign painter*—h 2420 N. 10th

A vanishing job title by 1927. Printed billboards and posters and painted advertisements on the sides of brick buildings had been well-established for business promotion in Terre Haute for decades. Numerous individuals are listed in the 1927 Polk Directory as bill posters and sign writers. This particular job title refers to a specialized handicraft that would have still provided steady work for a sole proprietor in 1927, perhaps to the end of Raymond's productive years. Painting a detailed advertisement on the side of a building brought good money but it also involved work on a high ladder. Better to work indoors at eye level with fewer colors and smaller letters.

On the upstairs levels of almost every downtown building and grand edifice in Terre Haute were long hallways filled with various doorways. The doors themselves were generally solid oak with brass doorknobs and milky translucent glass window panes. On this door glass, you'd find the name of the business or the person within that had been hand-painted by someone like Raymond E. Bohn. That craft would flourish until the virulent spread of decalcomania, better known as decals. First developed in Germany in the late 1800s to decorate dinner plates, decals were already being introduced for letters and numerals. It was a development that would soon eliminate the need for the skilled service Raymond provided.

For as long as it remained a viable occupation, sign painting required an exceptionally steady hand, a sure ability to calculate and measure spaces, and at the upper levels of the profession, a modest artistic flair. Consider an all-night diner that might request the profile of an American Indian in full headdress on its plate glass window. Since all painting on exterior windows was done from the inside, Raymond might find himself facing the street and whatever pedestrians might stop and comment on his progress. While painting from the inside made a job on a fourth floor window less challenging, creating each word always demanded careful attention to detail. You might say when it came to painting letters, Raymond E. Bohn had the alphabet memorized backwards and forwards.

BON TON PASTRY SHOP (**Dorel L. Beal**)—*bakery*—705 Ohio and 666 Wabash

The business name comes from a 1920s term for the elite classes. These days, a proprietor would probably have opted for Upper Crust Bakery instead. The Bon Ton Pastry Shop would eventually become one of the most revered businesses in the history of Terre Haute, Indiana. And since it continued in operation until the early 1970s, there are still quite a few people living in Terre Haute whose mouths water at the mere mention of the name.

In 1927, the Bon Ton Pastry Shop had just completed the process of moving one city block from Ohio Boulevard to Wabash Avenue. The Bon Ton was a family business, Dorel having inherited the bakery from his father. In addition, Dorel L. Beal was a co-owner of the City Sanitary Market at 121 South Third Street. This business was fashioned after the public markets and bazaars of Europe and the Middle East. It contained space for well over a dozen vendors, who offered everything from dressed poultry to Chesapeake oysters to Mississippi green beans to warm-weather fruit shipped in colorfully labeled crates from California.

The Bon Ton Pastry Shop would also span the globe. It employed 14 bakers, who specialized in French, Danish, and Swedish pastries; this in addition to their fresh baked cakes, pies, and cookies. One popular feature at the Bon Ton was an automatic donut-making machine with glass sides where fascinated children could watch every step of the process all the while taking in the wonderful aroma.

Our modern perspective as consumers increasingly regards oven-fresh, hand-decorated pastry as both a luxury and an anomaly. In Terre Haute in 1927, it was still pretty much of a necessity. Air-tight cellophane, which would soon be used to prolong the freshness of baked goods and allow their shipment over long distances, had just been introduced for food preservation that year. Wax paper, one of Thomas Edison's many inventions, lined the bottom of the

The Bon Ton Pastry Shop on Wabash Avenue
Martin Collection, Indiana Historical Society

white cardboard boxes that had "Bon Ton Pastry Shop" in gothic script on the lid. Day-old pastries were discounted for quick sale and barring that, were sent home with grateful employees.

But here too, there were changes in the air. Social commentators were already becoming aware of the increasing loss of thrift in American life. Novelist Kathleen Norris wrote in 1927 that "if the American home has one outstanding characteristic, it is that of utter and incessant and undeviating wastefulness." The examples she cited? Electric lights that burned in the daytime, the unwillingness of homemakers to slice away a small piece of rotted potato, and finally, the inability of bakers to establish a market for day-old bread, even at two loaves for the price of one.

Clarence Bose—*boxer*—r 607 N. 12th

He was just 19 years old in 1927. No stats are available on his height or his weight but in Terre Haute, Indiana, at least, he didn't even have to aspire to the national male average. Charles "Bud" Taylor, born on the 2200 block of Tippecanoe in 1903, had already established a national reputation boxing in the bantamweight division at 5'6" and 118 pounds.

This reputation was not entirely based on his numerous victories. In 1924, Bud Taylor knocked out Frankie Jerome in a bout at Madison Square Garden. Jerome would later die from severe head trauma. Two years later in Milwaukee, Bud Taylor fought an undefeated 22-year-old boxer from the Philippines named Clever Sensio. It was a brutal ten-round match. A ringside reporter stated that several times it appeared that the challenger would drop from the constant blows he was receiving. Nevertheless, when the final bell sounded, Clever Sensio was still on his feet.

Some hours later, a window washer discovered Clever Sensio lying in a pool of blood in his hotel room. The post-mortem revealed that the young boxer had died from a massive cerebral hemorrhage, and also had apparently lied about his age. Ausensio Moldez, it turned out, was only 18 years old. The Milwaukee district attorney Eugene Wingert concluded the death was "just one of those unfortunate things that could happen in any sport."

So it was a vicious business that young Clarence Bose had chosen. This was true even for the victors. In the prime earning years of his professional career, Bud Taylor fought between 15 and 20 matches annually. He faced his best competition, and presumably his greatest punishment, over a ten-year period from 1921 to 1931, before he finally retired. Include all those early bouts in smoky athletic clubs and lodge auditoriums, and you're easily looking at 200 competitive boxing matches and all the body blows that went with them. The profits and interest in boxing had risen exponentially with the passage of the Walker Act in 1920, which legalized prize fighting. Plenty of money to be made. Plenty of men eager to make it. Many would come to regard the following decade as the Golden Age of Boxing.

Boxers from those years tended to pay with their lives; either sooner like Clever Sensio and Frankie Jerome, or later like Bud Taylor, who died from a heart attack before he reached 60. Boxing wasn't the stated cause of Clarence

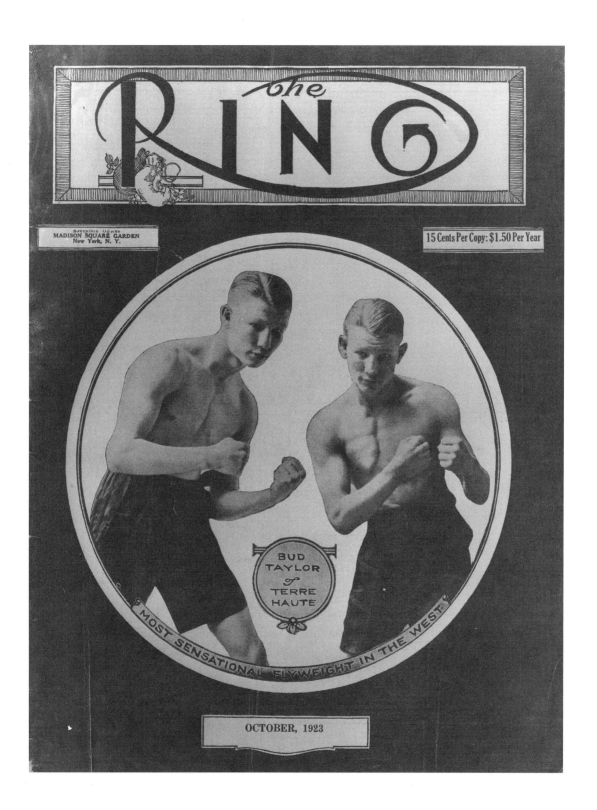

Bud Taylor on the Cover
of *Ring* Magazine

Bose's death, but it still came way too soon. On the night of September 13, 1937, a car flipped over into a ditch outside of Hymera, Indiana. Clarence suffered a fractured skull and a broken left arm and leg. The front page story in the *Terre Haute Tribune* reported he died at the scene. He was 29.

Clarence had probably figured his days of severe bodily injury were well behind him. At the time of the accident, he had been working as a gas station attendant in Hymera. So in the end, the name Clarence Bose did make it into the Terre Haute paper, just not on the sports page.

(N) **Godlove Bossert**—r 1822 S. 26th

Ezra Braden—County Poor Farm

Harley Brashear (Alice)—*manager*, Hotel Deming Garage—h 217 Monterey

In 1927, the Hotel Deming Garage at 621 Cherry Street was a lovely brick building whose elegance belied its everyday purpose. It featured leaded glass, skylight dormers, carriage lanterns, and café curtains in the front windows with fan lights above the entrance doors. The beauty of the exterior reflected the gleam on the Packards and Auburns that were stored inside.

Theodore Dreiser, a Terre Haute native, mentions commercial garages like the Deming frequently in his journal of the open road, *A Hoosier Holiday*. In the first decades of the 1900s, as cars gradually became practical for long-distance travel, auto garages at regular mileage intervals proved essential. In a sense, they were like watering stops for horses. Besides storage, the garage would monitor fuel, oil, and radiator levels; check tire patches; and provide what was called an "auto laundry" to deal with the daily effects of unpaved roads. Often, wealthy drivers and their passengers would linger around the garage as the job was done, accounting for the eye toward décor amidst all the grease and grit.

The Deming Garage was not the only building in Terre Haute whose appearance seemed inconsistent with its actual function. The Terre Haute Water Works at Tippecanoe and Water Streets incorporated arched windows, a majestic hip roof, and hanging ivy into a gentle park-like setting. Inside, the purpose was to pump in the filthy water of the Wabash River and somehow transform it into something fit for human consumption. That may be why the Water Works was built to resemble a church.

Ella A. Broom—*housekeeper*, Nurses Home—r 1912 N. 7th

Frank S. Broome (Bernice)—*janitor*, Garfield High School—h 2600 N. 12th

The two-word job résumé; like a florist named Rose or a barber named Harry.

Frank Brown—County Poor Farm

Bonnie Bryant—*bookkeeper*, Kleeman Dry Goods Company—r YWCA

Kleeman's was one of Terre Haute's major department stores in 1927, founded by Samuel Kleeman in 1890. Sam had died four years earlier but Bonnie still found herself working for the immediate family in the person of surviving brother Phil.

The Kleeman store at the corner of 6th and Wabash employed more than 150 people. Being a dry goods company, its inventory focused primarily on products that were woven: everything from rugs to draperies, bedding to corsetry (*see* Alma Niebrugge), art needlework to silk handkerchiefs.

In 1927, Bonnie Bryant apparently lived a tidy life in Terre Haute. Columns of neat handwritten numbers along with one small room at the YWCA at 121 North 7th Street, just a five-minute walk from her workplace. Even as early as 1927, Bonnie may not have been telling Phil exactly what he wanted to hear, but it's likely the changing face of American retail spoke a little louder. By 1929, Kleeman's had been replaced by a five-and-dime store, the third one on that 600 block of Wabash.

(N) Azalia Buchanan—(spouse of Ernest R.—*conductor*)—h 1410 N. 7th

Edward Bundy—County Poor Farm

John Burch—County Poor Farm

The Deming Garage
Martin Collection, Indiana
Historical Society

The YWCA

George D. Burns—*laborer*—h 502 4th Ave.

No telling whether this George Burns was enticed to see his namesake when the young vaudeville performer and his bride finally hit the Hippodrome with their stage act. If he did, it was due to false pretenses. George Burns the entertainer was actually born Nathan Birnbaum in New York City. He was struggling in vaudeville as a comedian until he met Gracie Allen, whom he married in 1925.

John Burton—County Poor Farm

Butler Sisters (Helen B. and Jeane A.)—*cigars*—Filbeck Hotel

We should start our story about this curious little family business with the Filbeck itself. The hotel, on the northeast corner of 5th and Cherry Streets, had been opened in 1869 by a disabled Civil War veteran, Nicholas Philbeck. Encouraged by the results, he built a four-story brick hotel at the same site in August of 1894.

Women didn't often travel alone in those days and so most of the amenities at the Filbeck were oriented toward the traveling man. Ergo, a billiard parlor, a barber shop, and a cigar stand in the lobby.

The first individual to lease the cigar stand at the Filbeck was one Ed McElfresh. Sometime in the mid-1920s, the lease fell to Helen and Jeane Butler. By that time, the Filbeck Hotel had lost both its original elegance and its singular purpose. It had evolved into a commercial hotel, a nice way of saying that the toilets for many of the rooms were down at the end of the hall. Its curious motto: "Fine enough for everybody, not too fine for anybody."

Filbeck Hotel, Terre Haute, Ind.

Filbeck Hotel

The Butler sisters were living together only a short stroll away from the Filbeck, at 304 North 5th Street. They were two unmarried women whose business, indeed whose entire work environment, revolved around men. Not just their customers, either. Many of the cigar brands that they sold at their stand featured a man's face on the box, characters that ranged from Robert Burns to King Edward, Wolfgang Amadeus Mozart to Abe Lincoln. Perhaps the most engaging cigar portrait belonged to an Indiana icon who had been memorialized 20 years earlier in a stained glass portrait on the rotunda of the Terre Haute Public Library (*see* Mrs. Cora K. Wood). The name on the box was Hoosier Poet, the name of the poet was James Whitcomb Riley. As for the draw on the cigar itself and whether it was worth the asking price of three for a quarter? Well, if you were standing in the lobby of the Filbeck Hotel in 1927 considering a purchase, you could ask Helen or Jeane Butler, who likely would have an answer based on their actual experience smoking one.

(N) Birdie Byrd—r 1331 Sycamore

Roxie Byrd—*musician*—h 110 S. 7th

Roxie Byrd, it appears, was naturally provided a good stage name. One suspects that for Birdie Byrd all the world was a stage.

C

Barden Calloway—*miner*—r 1018 Harding

Henry Calloway (Vina)—*miner*—r 2448 N. 18th

Jack Calloway (Hanna Belle)—*miner*—h 223 Eagle

James Calloway—*miner*—h 2428 N. 17th

James Calloway Jr.—*miner*—h 2428 N. 17th

In 1927, this one occupation apparently took care of all the Calloways in Terre Haute, Indiana, and that seemed to be true however you spelled it. Frank Callaway, who lived with his wife, Rachel, at 2924 North 15th Street, was also a miner.

It's interesting to note that even though the miners listed in the 1927 Polk Directory worked for various companies like Walter Bledsoe & Company or Coal Creek, the employer is never mentioned. It might be a union preference or perhaps they just considered the earth to be their boss.

An added bonus here is the name of Jack's beloved: Hanna Belle Calloway.

George Calvert (Ruth)—*laborer*, J.W. Davis Gardens—r 2406 S. 3rd St.

James W. Davis operated a truck farm in Terre Haute that cultivated mushrooms, cucumbers, tomatoes, lilacs, chrysanthemums, ferns, and pandanus under 35 sprawling acres of glass. Davis Gardens, as it came to be known, boasted the largest greenhouse in the world. During winter months, crates of hothouse tomatoes were shipped to expensive restaurants in Chicago for ten times the price of the local summer crop. It's likely that George Calvert was employed primarily to lift those heavy crates. Davis Gardens generally trusted the tending and picking of their produce to the more delicate hands of women.

Benjamin Camello—*peddler*—h 1520 N. 29th St.

Peddlers and traveling salesmen were listed separately in the Terre Haute 1927 Polk Directory. One distinction between them was the presence of a business sponsor. Peddlers were sole proprietors and usually the only source for whatever products or services they sold. Traveling salesmen usually answered to a particular product manufacturer which processed payments and provided their representatives with the goods they sold.

Occasionally, the products were the peddler's own invention, neither patented nor trademarked. The product's continued availability was dependent on the sale of the existing inventory, minus one sample commonly set aside for demonstration.

Today, we picture the door-to-door salesman as being the classic American itinerant, but peddlers would frequently cover a wide territory if they had happened upon a lucrative route or a receptive market. By and large though, peddlers were local merchants, limited by the constraints of a day-to-day livelihood. Peddlers generally carried their entire operation right to their customers—in a suitcase, in a pushcart, in a horse-drawn wagon. By the 1920s, more sophisticated retailing and advertising practices had begun to erode the regional customer base that peddlers relied on. Rural Free Delivery, which had been extended throughout the United States in 1917, brought mail orders directly to the outlying farms that peddlers had often included on their routes.

One characteristic common among peddlers was their unpredictability. Although peddlers relied on the face-to-face for customer contact and their sales, the cycle of these encounters tended to be erratic, often guided by the seasons or by a perpetual wanderlust. Many peddlers were just a step ahead of local authorities who often demanded that they procure daily licenses for their activities. In 1927, the municipal fee in Terre Haute, Indiana, was $1.00 per day for foot peddlers or $10.00 for a six-month permit to sell from a wagon. It was a cost of doing business many peddlers tried to avoid. Peddlers had no telephones, no storefronts, no fixed hours of business. In fact, a peddler's prolonged absence over time might be the only indication to long-time customers that he'd given up the territory or even the trade.

Workers at Davis Gardens
Martin Collection, Indiana
Historical Society

An article in a February 1921 issue of the *Saturday Spectator* remarked on the abrupt disappearance of a popular neighborhood peddler known as the Polish Lace Man. For years, he had offered a wide variety of fine hand-woven embroidery and tatting; from tablecloths to piano scarves. Apparently, this had been a full-time endeavor for both himself and his wife.

Around the same time, households along South Center Street were sorely missing a woman who had once sold them a mysterious concoction she had created herself: a thick paste that reportedly cleaned white woodwork and kid gloves more effectively than anything available on the market.

Whether Benjamin Camello peddled a product or a personal skill remains unknown, but a record survives of his background. Benetto Camello originally arrived in the United States in 1908 from a small village near Naples. His regular customers may not have even been familiar with his full Anglicized name. Benjamin Camello might have been better known to them as the Licorice Man or Benny the Knife Grinder. Today, the truly romantic among us might imagine that he sang a Puccini aria to announce his arrival in a neighborhood.

James C. Campbell—*bellman*, Hotel Deming—r 2411 3rd Ave.

There were actually six James Campbells listed in the Terre Haute Polk Directory in 1927. As a bellhop in Terre Haute's most elegant hotel, James C. Campbell would have been more than likely called Jimmy. The Hotel Deming was located at the corner of Sixth and Cherry Streets. It had 250 rooms, leather chairs in the lobby, a barber shop, a billiard parlor, a private garage, and fireproof construction throughout. The hotel restaurant was called the Gourmet Room. The main ballroom and banquet hall was the Cotillion Room. An orchestra played for dancing on Saturday nights, bringing in customers after the theater performances downtown. A steep admission of 75 cents was charged.

Every bellman at the Hotel Deming was uniformed, of course. The outfit was later popularized by Johnny Roventini, the diminutive spokesperson for Phillip Morris Cigarettes ("Call for Phillip Morris"). Standard issue for a hotel bellman was a double-breasted waist jacket with matching slacks and a pill-box hat with chin strap. A minimal salary plus the occasional tip for hauling heavy pieces of luggage, delivering telegrams, or lighting cigars was apparently enough for James/Jimmy to afford a small room on Terre Haute's north side, just enough space for him to lie on his bed after a long shift and gradually forget the crisp ring of the desk clerk's bell.

Jerry Campbell—*manicurist*, Terre Haute House Barber Shop—h 220 N. 6th

That's right, males' nails.

Amanda Carp—County Poor Farm

Joseph Carpenter—County Poor Farm

Ella Carter—County Poor Farm

Geneva Carter—*janitress*, Lincoln School—r 2241 Tippecanoe

The Lincoln School was located on the northeast corner of 16th and Elm, within easy walking distance of Geneva Carter's residence, which she shared with her husband, Morris, and six children. The Lincoln School was one of two public elementary schools operating in Terre Haute in 1927 that were exclusively African American. Both Lincoln and the Booker T. Washington School were constructed in the years after the Plessy v. Ferguson Supreme Court decision of 1894, which allowed for the concept of "separate but equal" in public accommodations and services. Writing for the majority in that decision, Justice Henry Billings Brown cited separate schools for the races as "to have been held to be a valid exercise of the legislative power even by courts of States where the political rights of the colored race have been the longest and most earnestly enforced."

To all outward appearances, Lincoln and Booker T. Washington looked like any other neighborhood elementary schools in Terre Haute. The brick construction reflected the broad public perception that segregation in public education and housing would endure for generations. Some residents in Terre Haute resented this continued exclusion, others resented what they saw as frivolous accommodation.

The Lincoln School
Martin Collection, Indiana
Historical Society

As it happened, the Lincoln School was located only a short distance from the headquarters of the Vigo County Chapter of the Ku Klux Klan at 1501 North 13th Street. Just about three blocks, in fact. It would have been Geneva Carter's job to sweep up any broken glass.

Phillip Carter—County Poor Farm

Harvey Cartwright (Kazia)—h 1611 S. 10th St.—*president*, UMW

By the early years of the twentieth century, Terre Haute had acquired a reputation as a strong union town. This reputation was either laudable or regrettable depending on which side of the labor divide you stood.

Campaign to Secure Debs'
Release from Federal
Prison, 1921
Martin Collection, Indiana
Historical Society

The city's union sympathies actually dated back to the beginnings of organized labor in America. On August 2, 1881, delegates from 13 craft unions representing more than 40,000 workers from across the United States convened at a former Presbyterian church on the corner of 5th and Ohio in Terre Haute, Indiana. The proclamation issued from this conference later proved to be the foundation for the American Federation of Labor, the nation's first successful confederation of trade unions.

Over the next two decades, the visibility of hometown resident Eugene Debs, national labor icon and Socialist candidate for president, further enhanced Terre Haute's working-class reputation. In 1902, another famous union organizer, Mary "Mother" Jones, was invited to Terre Haute to rally strikers during a bitter local transit strike. At the appointed time, "Mother" Jones arrived at the union meeting hall via a side window, dressed entirely in men's clothes.

The strong presence of unions in Terre Haute was symbolized in 1927 by the Labor Temple which stood at the corner of 5th and Walnut Streets downtown, just one block south of that hallowed meeting ground at 5th and Ohio. This imposing three-story brick structure had been purchased just four years earlier from the Phoenix Club, a Jewish social organization. (*See* Phoenix Club.) The Labor Temple served as the headquarters for the Central Labor Union, which organized 47 separate locals, from film projectionists to hod carriers.

The Labor Temple housed union offices, meeting halls, and a reading room. In October of 1926, the Temple had been chosen as the site of Eugene Debs's public wake when his coffin arrived back home from Chicago.

Terre Haute's working community was also served in 1927 by the *Advocate,* a labor newspaper that had been published weekly since 1919. Harvey Cartwright would have been a long-time subscriber and occasional contributor. The United Mine Workers, District 11 represented most of the estimated 5,000 miners who labored in the seven active coal fields surrounding the city. Many of these miners were actually city dwellers and shuttled back and forth to the mines in specially designated railroad cars nicknamed "doodlebugs."

Under the decades-long leadership of Samuel Gompers, the American Federation of Labor had gradually evolved into a mainstream labor organization. The city where it had been founded, though, maintained a stubborn radical edge. In December 1921, an estimated 10,000 people had greeted Eugene Debs upon his return to Terre Haute after nearly three years in a federal prison. His crime had been to deliver a speech in Canton, Ohio, opposing America's involvement in World War I. It was late on a cold winter night when the train arrived at Union Station. The massive crowd roared when the locomotive's lamplight appeared down the tracks. Faces shone bright in the glow of the torchlights, and Harvey Cartwright was almost certainly among them. Harvey's predecessor as UMW District 11 president, W. D. Van Horn, had been, like Eugene Debs, an avowed and outspoken Socialist.

After waving his hat to the cheering crowd and descending onto the train platform, Eugene Debs was hoisted onto the shoulders of a few strong men in the crowd and then escorted to the porch of his home at 451 North 8th Street. Pictures of Harvey Cartwright from the time show him to have the classic union countenance: four-square and lantern-jawed, the type of man accustomed to carrying a burden and making sure it arrived safely at its destination.

Frank L. Cassel (Catherine)—914 N. 15th St.—billiards h do

The cross-reference for 915 North 15th Street in the Polk Directory is listed as follows: Frank L. Cassel—cigars. The small pool room operated by Frank and Catherine Cassel was located amidst a bakery, a hardware store, and a doctor's office in a predominantly residential area of modest detached homes. The Cassels apparently lived adjacent to their small business. In 1927, pool rooms selling nothing stronger than a cheap cigar were quite common in Terre Haute. With the introduction of Prohibition seven years earlier, pool rooms had become popular gathering places for men, whether or not they actually ever chalked up a cue.

During the day, pool rooms were commonly a stop for truant officers in search of school-age boys who were playing hooky in addition to eight ball. Hoagy Carmichael and Johnny Mercer's song "Small Fry" contains this perceptive couplet:

> Small Fry, hanging 'round the pool room
> Small Fry, should be in the school room

All the long hours aside, the fact that Frank Cassel actually lived right next to a pool hall offered him a clear opportunity to improve his skills on the table. But Frank Cassel's approach to billiards may have resembled Casey Stengel's approach to baseball, where knowledge of the game is translated into observation and the occasional suggestion; content to provide opportunities for players rather than actually participate in the sport itself. Our assumption might be that any owner of a pool hall could easily run the table in a game of eight ball. But one never knows: Maybe Catherine actually had the best break in the family.

CATHOLIC SUPPLY STORE—(Loretta Kelly)—15 S. 6th

In 1927, Catholics maintained a very strong presence in Terre Haute. There were six parishes operating in the city: St. Joseph's, St. Ann's, St. Patrick's, St. Benedict's, St. Margaret Mary's, and Sacred Heart. St. Margaret Mary's and Sacred Heart had only been formed in the previous six years.

Each of these six parishes supported their own elementary schools. St. Patrick's and St. Joseph's also provided secondary education. Now here's the twist: The two high schools were for girls only. The Sisters of Providence was the teaching order that staffed all of the parish schools in Terre Haute. The order had always exhibited a deep commitment to the education and well-being of young girls. (*See* St. Joseph's Academy.) They had run St. Ann's Orphanage for Girls until its closing in 1919. The large brick building at the corner of 13th Street and 6th Avenue then stood empty until it was finally demolished in 1927, a considerable relief to the neighborhood children who had walked past it at night. In addition to the churches and schools, the Catholic Archdiocese also operated one of Terre Haute's two hospitals. St Anthony's was a 175-bed hospital and nursing school located at 1015 South 6th Street.

With all of this fervent activity around town, a Catholic supply store would have certainly been in order, and perhaps it was only appropriate that it be owned by a woman. The stock at Loretta Kelly's shop included rosaries, scapulas, small bottles of holy water, and copies of the New Baltimore Catechism. Fancy candlesticks were available for the deeply devout. And in response to that very special day in a Catholic girl's life, communion veils were made to order.

(N) Bessie Cauliflower—*seamstress*, Stahl-Urban Company—h 1520 S. 20th

John Chalos (Kathleen)—*shoe shiner*—r 1120 Poplar

John Chalos began his journey to America in Piraeus, Greece, departing from Constantinople, and was processed through Ellis Island in December of 1922. Like many immigrants he saw his new home as a land of boundless opportunity, both for himself and the children he had yet to see. On June 25, 1927, a son would be born to John Chalos and Kathleen Katrissiosis. In 1980, Pete Chalos would be elected mayor of Terre Haute, Indiana, and serve four consecutive terms.

Elizabeth Chambers—*principal*, Collett School—201 S. 9th St.

Children at Collett School
Community Archives, Vigo
County Public Library

Collett School was a public elementary school located in Terre Haute's Twelve Points neighborhood on the northwest corner of 12th and Linden. The building was a formidable brick and limestone structure with huge banks of classroom windows, heavy wooden doors, and milky globe lights to illuminate those rainy Mondays. There was no cafeteria at Collett School. Since its students were all drawn from the immediate neighborhood, it was expected that they would walk home for lunch.

Elizabeth Chambers also lived within walking distance of Collett School. From our perspective today, it might be interesting to consider how this woman's dual identity as neighbor and school principal affected the attitudes of nearby residents who did not have children in the public school system. Perhaps it reinforced the shared sense of community and a willingness to support the resources identified with it. In 1927, taxpayer support of public education was apparently vigorous enough to maintain a greater number of schools at the elementary and secondary level than exist in Terre Haute today.

Virgil Champ—County Poor Farm

Laura Chandler—*boxmaker*, Wabash Fibre Box Co.—r 1127 Tippecanoe

Like Bonnie Bryant, Geneva Carter, and Elizabeth Chambers, Laura Chandler lived within walking distance of her job. For most people in urban America, this proved to be more necessity than opportunity. While the modestly

The Wabash Fibre Box
Company
Martin Collection, Indiana
Historical Society

priced Model A Ford would be introduced to consumers in 1927, less than half of American households actually owned automobiles. In any event, Laura's address was less than a mile from her place of employment. A network of public transportation options already blanketed the city. (*See* Forrest B. Arnold/ Joseph E. Asay.) From the standpoint of both its daily utility and its monthly maintenance, Laura's prospective purchase of an automobile would have been an unwarranted expense. Today, it is estimated that over three-quarters of American workers commute to their place of employment by driving alone in their car. Less than 3 percent walk to work.

The Wabash Fibre Box Company, which manufactured cardboard boxes, was located at 19th and Buckeye. The 1100 block of Tippecanoe sat right alongside the railroad tracks, just two blocks from the Big Four Train Station and not very far from Union Station and the Vandalia Railroad Yards. Whatever Laura Chandler might have dreamed about at night, she certainly heard trains.

John Chervenko (Clara)—*confectioner*—h 2100 N. 21st h do

John Chervenko and his father first immigrated to the United States from Austria-Hungary with the plan of earning enough money to return to their native country as far wealthier men. They determined that this plan would take no more than a year. They soon found jobs at Terre Haute Malleable, which manufactured castings for heavy machine parts. A Hungarian neighborhood was just beginning to take shape in the area east of the plant. (*See* First Terre Haute Hungarian Society.)

Once that year had passed, there were two developments: John met Clara and decided to remain in America. John's father, meanwhile, returned to Hungary. The couple purchased a small storefront at the corner of 21st and Linden, and stocked it with varieties of penny candy, ice cream, and cigarettes. Since this was a neighborhood business in the truest sense, the Chervenkos didn't bother to hang a sign with the name of their confectionary. It was known to all of their customers that the Chervenkos owned it. They ran it. They lived in back. What else would you call it?

Actually, it was Clara Chervenko who ran the store on weekdays. John continued to draw wages working a day shift at Terre Haute Malleable. Meanwhile, their son, John Jr., 8 years old in 1927, got to live the childhood dream of growing up in a candy store. Not surprisingly, he remained in the neighborhood well into the next century—long after the storefront had been demolished, long after Terre Haute Malleable had closed, and long after those who once referred to the Hungarian neighborhood as "Hunkietown" had passed on.

Christopher Chies—*sausage maker*, Scheidel and Company—h 334 N. 16th

The old saw is that people are better off not knowing how legislation and sausage are actually created. Scheidel and Company was a family-owned meat company located at 300 North 13th Street. George did the butchering, George Jr. did the cutting, and Christopher Chies stuffed sausage casings with what was pushed off the chopping block. The most reassuring assumption would be that most all of it came from a slaughtered animal.

Christopher Chies used a hand-cranked industrial-strength meat grinder for hours on end, so you'd expect some evidence of his job to show up in the strength of one of his arms, much like it does for a major league pitcher or a professional bowler.

Herbert Church (Louise)—*dancer*, 720 Wabash—r 2204 S. 9th St.

In 1927, 720 Wabash Avenue was the location of the Orpheum Dance Palace. The Orpheum had originated as a 600-seat vaudeville theater, similar to the Lyric, which sat directly across the street. But by 1927, the Lyric had changed its name to the Liberty. And although the Liberty still featured a live orchestra, its theatrical performances were now presented on screen instead of on stage.

The Orpheum had made a similar transition during the 1920s. It became a dance hall six days a week featuring Bud Cromwell and his Kings of Rhythm. This provided work for Herbert Church as a dance instructor and an occasional partner. But as with vaudeville, Herbert's job didn't quite survive the Depression. By 1936, Herbert Church would be selling cars. At least one can hope that by the end of his life, Herbert might have spent more time dancing with Louise than he had with strangers.

On a note of pure speculation: The Marx Brothers were on the Orpheum vaudeville circuit that provided stage entertainment to various venues throughout Indiana. In his autobiography, Groucho Marx mentions a poorly attended show in Indianapolis and a risky romantic encounter in Muncie. Apparently, the brothers also did a brief tour of colleges in the state that included stops at

Purdue and Notre Dame. Based on the city's prominence alone, it's very likely the Marx Brothers performed on a Terre Haute stage just as Will Rogers, Jack Benny, Swain's Rats and Cats, and every other vaudeville act traveling the Midwest did. Years later, a crackdown on an illegal sports gambling ring in Terre Haute revealed that Zeppo Marx had been an occasional client.

CITIZENS MARKET—**Ernest L. Zwerner,** *proprietor*—Groceries, Meats, Fruits, and Vegetables—1244 Lafayette—Phone: Wabash 1825

Perhaps more than any other symbol of urban life, the corner grocery evokes the image of the traditional neighborhood—houses set along tree-lined streets within easy walking distance to retail stores and other public services. In 1927, there were more than 400 groceries doing business in Terre Haute, Indiana. The overwhelming majority of these were locally owned, with the name on the sign generally belonging to the face behind the counter. (*See* Charles M. Mooney.)

Thirty-four of these groceries were Oakley Economy Stores, a local chain founded in Terre Haute by Hollie N. Oakley. Hollie Oakley had opened his first store in 1909 at the corner of Wabash and 11th. The company's main office and warehouse continued to be located right in the heart of town. By 1927, Hollie and his wife, Anna, had taken to spending their winters in Florida. Even so, their home phone number for their residence at 1503 South 7th Street could still be found in the 1927 Polk Directory.

Throughout the 1920s, national grocery chains were expanding their presence all across America. The Great Atlantic and Pacific Tea Company, A&P for short, would be operating more than 15,000 stores nationwide by the end of the decade. In 1927, A&P had 14 stores located in Terre Haute. Within the next three years, a large manufacturing and distribution center for all A&P stores in the Midwest would be built on Fruitridge Avenue. Olives from Spain and coffee from South America would arrive in boxcars and leave the plant bearing the Ann Page, Rajah, and Bokar brand names. (See photos of A&P stores in Terre Haute at www.hometown.indiana.edu/1927.)

Citizens Market was just one of dozens of grocery stores competing for customers throughout the Twelve Points neighborhood. A&P had located two of its Terre Haute stores on Lafayette Avenue, one virtually next door to Citizens Market, at 1228. The fundamental distinctions between Citizens Market and the national grocery chains went far beyond price and selection. It wasn't simply that Citizens Market was locally owned. Citizens Market was also family owned. And that family—siblings, spouses, and offspring—worked together at Citizens Market every day. Regular customers got to know them by their first names and the Zwerner family often returned the favor.

Ernest L. Zwerner was the second son of German immigrants who had initially arrived in America through Baltimore in 1888. Well into his 50s, Ernest had dark, neatly parted hair and an impressive bearing. At Citizens Market, he always wore a crisp buttoned shirt and necktie beneath his shop apron. His genial face, framed by wire-rimmed spectacles, made him appear almost professorial. Indeed, he was regarded by those who knew him as a man of plainspoken wisdom and integrity.

Within the Twelve Points community, Ernest Zwerner maintained a role as both shopkeeper and neighbor. The Zwerner family home was located at 2420 North 8th Street, a short walk to and from the Market. At work, Ernest Zwerner kept a sharpened pencil behind his ear. He rewarded children who accompanied their mothers while shopping with a small sweet treat. And every New Year's Day, without fail, he personally undertook the task of documenting the store's inventory.

For bookkeeping, Ernest relied on his wife, Florence, who also supervised the store's customer accounts. In 1927, the couple had three sons ranging in age from 7 to 15 who each took on various chores around the store after school and over the summer.

Two of Ernest's younger brothers also became involved with the business. Fritz, or Fred as he was known to friends, had an affable and engaging nature, perfectly suited for the Market's many home deliveries. Meanwhile younger brother Leonard would eventually take on the onerous job of butcher. The family patriarch, George Sr., was listed as the meat cutter in 1927, which meant he did the coarse work on huge slabs of beef and pork originating from area farms and dressed at the local meat processor. Perhaps not surprisingly, George would soon retire, leaving all that bloody work to Leonard.

Leonard was somewhat of a myth-making character himself. In childhood, he'd been given the nickname he answered to thereafter: Skinny. From hack saws to heavy cleavers to filet knives, Skinny was surrounded by razor-sharp edges all day. The butcher's work at Citizens Market required a steady, conscious awareness. Just a moment's inattention or impatience could result in a serious injury.

Skinny apparently made his peace with this inherent danger. Whereas Ernest's interactions with small children generally took the form of a reward, Skinny was fond of performing a theatrical sleight of hand with a meat cleaver that appeared to sever a part of his left index finger, which had actually been previously amputated. Apparently, he'd overcome the trauma about the accident that caused it.

Almost all of the work around Citizens Market in 1927 was done by hand, only occasionally aided by simple tools: a box picker for merchandise located on the uppermost shelves, a feather duster for the rows of stationary cans, a crude hand truck to move heavy bags or boxes. Sometimes, the work task would simply require a steady almost Zen-like patience. The two window displays at Citizens Market consisted of carefully stacked pyramids of cans or boxes which would be changed weekly depending on the featured sale item. For those who window-shopped on Lafayette Avenue after store hours, the higher the pyramid, the more impressive and eye-catching the display.

This consistent daily effort was at the heart of every neighborhood business: attracting customer notice, re-enforcing their trust, and thereby earning their continued trade. Customer relationships are notoriously fickle in retail, constantly responding to shifts in packaging, marketing, or personal taste. In 1927, the growing competition from chain stores was just one aspect of the grocery business that required the Zwerners' attention. Another was the changing nature of food itself, including how and where food was being grown, how it was being presented at point of sale, and just who was providing it to the grocer.

The years following World War I saw a tremendous upsurge in the popularity of canned foods. Between 1918 and 1935, American consumption of commercially canned fruits, vegetables, and meats increased fourfold. Today, using the perspective of history, it's easy to see how a longstanding relationship between local farm and local grocery would be compromised by this change. But in Terre Haute, Indiana, as rural an American city as existed in 1927, the shattering of this bond still seemed unthinkable.

During this time, Terre Haute was home to a number of local food processors who produced a wide variety of canned goods. One wholesaler, Hulman and Company, marketed three distinct brands featuring a vast selection of food products and kitchen items ranging from canned gooseberries to stick matches. The Hulman Company was prominent enough to have earned a trusted status among independent grocers throughout the Midwest. Essential to this reputation was the knowledge that the company purchased its fruits and vegetables directly from area farmers. So the chain that stretched from the family farm to the locally owned grocery had not yet been broken here—it had merely added another hometown link with local processing.

Sensibly enough, the pyramid of cans displayed in the window of Citizens Market usually bore the Hulman and Company label. One of the brands was appropriately named Farmer's Pride. Even the cookies Ernest Zwerner offered to children were of local origin. They were produced by Miller-Parrott, a large commercial bakery located downtown on the 1400 block of Wabash Avenue.

Nearly all of the fresh produce at Citizens Market was supplied through trusted longstanding agreements with individual farmers or through vendors from the pre-dawn farmers' market on North 2nd Street and Mulberry. In 1927, the total distance from farm field to kitchen table was still a matter of a few miles, unlike today when the average bite of food in America travels more than 1,200 miles.

The chain of personal relationships which characterized food production and distribution continued with the customers of Citizens Market, primarily the residents of the Twelve Points neighborhood. If a customer arrived at the Market to shop, it was generally after a short walk from home or work. Otherwise, a delivery was made in a small pickup truck with Citizens Market proudly painted on the door. In 1927, the Zwerners had hired John Carney of 1536 2nd Avenue to help with these deliveries.

Personal credit was commonly extended at Citizens to regular customers. Occasionally, this credit had to be adapted to meet a personal crisis. Florence Zwerner was known to be very precise with both her record-keeping and her ability to judge human character. In the self-contained universe that was Twelve Points in the year 1927, much was accomplished on the simple strength of personal reputation and face-to-face contact. (*See* Baker A. Bannon.)

This system of mutual reliance extending from harvest to household was still functioning effectively and efficiently in 1927. Citizens Market maintained profitability based on its local network of suppliers and a loyal customer base.

Ernest Zwerner behind the Citizens Market Counter
Martin Collection, Indiana Historical Society

But within a single generation, the entire support system began to weaken and break apart. This would happen concurrently in cities and neighborhoods all over the United States. By 1940, the number of grocery stores in Terre Haute had been reduced by half.

The causes for all of this have commonly been ascribed to the increased use of the automobile, the rise of the self-service supermarket, and the decline of family farms and core urban neighborhoods. But one of the reasons for the decline of Citizens Market lies beyond the usual suspects. It arose from the personal philosophy of one Ernest L. Zwerner.

The Interurban
Terminal Building

In 1923, Clarence Birdseye successfully developed a process for flash-freezing perishable foods. For Ernest, who had already watched the preservation of food migrate from the family root cellar to the grocery shelf, this may have been a bridge too far. He adamantly refused to install freezer compartments in his store. By the 1940s, Ernest's daughter-in-law, newly arrived in Terre Haute and married to the son who had grown up making home deliveries with his Uncle Fred, soon indulged her curiosity and quietly patronized the A&P downtown.

Ever since its founding, Citizens Market had been rooted in family: one family's farm, one family's business, one family's credit. The fact that over time these families became consumers, or wholesalers, or hourly employees meant simply, and sadly, that they would eventually become strangers too.

John Clark—*porter*, Terminal Smoke House—r 641 Cherry

He emptied ash trays. He swept up cigar butts. He cleaned out spittoons with a filthy rag. He lived about two blocks from work. John Clark was part of a loose confederation of porters who worked along the 800 block of Wabash Avenue, where the Terminal Smoke House was located. In 1927, there were no less than six establishments on that one block of Wabash Avenue that sold cigars, tobacco, chewing gum, and minor league baseball tickets.

Situated above the tobacco shops and other businesses along the 800 block of Wabash were various gambling operations, all-night card games, and dimly lit pool halls. The address for the Terminal Smoke House was listed as 806½ Wabash, which opens the question of whether the proprietor, David Shorter,

might have been running a little side business in an adjacent room. If so, there would have been plenty to keep John Clark busy any hour of the night or day.

It should be mentioned that the word "terminal" here refers to the nearby Interurban Terminal, though from our perspective today it might seem like an apt name for a tobacco business.

May Clark—*waitress*, Sullivan Hotel—r 202 S. 4th St.

May Clark's life in 1927 would be a very easy one to overlook. The Sullivan Hotel went out of business sometime in 1928, converted by the owner, William Rogers, into furnished rooms. By 1932, the buildings that housed the Sullivan Hotel and the Oakley Grocery on the corner were demolished for a Cities Service gas station. There are no surviving records from the business; the hotel apparently printed neither postcards nor stationery. Until recently, no existing photographs of the hotel had been located. This photograph, which includes the sign for the Sullivan, gives us a sense of how marginal the accommodations likely were.

We do know that the Sullivan Hotel had just 50 rooms. Most of those registered there were probably living on the raw edges of daily existence and either wound up being there a lot longer than one night or just an hour or two at a time. The Sullivan probably made a fairly natural transition to a residence hotel.

The Oakley Grocery with Sullivan Hotel at Right

The Sullivan actually began as a "farmer's hotel," catering to rural merchants who brought their harvests into town. Initially, the hotel was known as the Boston House. At one point, someone must have thought that changing the name might attract farmers from Sullivan County to the south.

In 1927, the Sullivan Hotel offered what was grandly called a European Plan: room and board tallied separately for the length of the stay. This meant that the Sullivan also provided what was grandly called a restaurant. In the absence of frequent county health inspections, rodents in the kitchens of certain hotels could be as common as the bedbugs in their mattresses. The management's fervent hope was that a mouse scurrying under a table would be less bothersome to someone raised on a farm.

The Polk listing for 1927 tells us that May Clark lived and also worked at the Sullivan Hotel. Unlike the residential arrangements for single women existing in Terre Haute's red light district, May's situation was legitimate, sanctioned by both society and the law. But this really doesn't illuminate her situation any more clearly for us. We can only imagine the circumstances under which she spent much of her life that year. As both a waitress and a resident, she likely ate at the hotel and so was in a position to know about, and perhaps joke about, the rodents in the kitchen.

The surviving snapshot and the few facts we do know about the Sullivan Hotel begin to reveal how challenging any part of a life spent at 202 South 4th Street must have been; individuals in a daily struggle with a modest environment that was both their living space and their workplace. Those personal struggles, like the hotel and building that housed it, have been buried with time. All that remains is the struggle to recover them. For now, we begin and end with this: in 1927, May Clark was a waitress at the Sullivan Hotel in Terre Haute, Indiana.

Mrs. Stella Clark—*matron*, Friendly Inn—h 912 Chestnut

The Friendly Inn was established in 1921 to provide meals and temporary shelter to individuals stranded in Terre Haute without any discernable means of support. These were families with all their possessions piled into a vehicle that had broken down, newly pregnant women who had spent whatever they'd saved on a train ticket to go as far as they could, the destitute, the aimless, and the confused. At the Friendly Inn, the thread that bound them all together was that they had somehow arrived in Terre Haute, Indiana, as a stranger to everyone.

One typical case at the Friendly Inn involved an elderly couple, Joe and Sarah Watson, who had left their home in Detroit traveling in a light spring wagon. Their eventual destination was Jackson, Mississippi, where they had agreed to keep house for a nephew whose wife had died suddenly. With both their funds and their horse exhausted, they came to the Friendly Inn requesting food so they could reach friends in Clinton, Indiana.

Nineteen twenty-seven stood just a few years away from the start of the Great Depression. Comprehensive public assistance programs on the federal and state level had not yet been instituted. In Terre Haute, 21 churches listed themselves as missions. The Friendly Inn had been founded by a local philanthropist and was supported through a combination of charitable donations and a monthly stipend from the city, administered through the Society for Organized Charity. Over a three-month period, the Friendly Inn served more than 5,000 meals to 127 transients, 55 of whom were children.

Stella Clark lived at the Friendly Inn and, as the individual responsible for all intakes, became personally aware of the circumstances for each of the occupants in the Inn's 40 rooms. There's a temptation to think that a job like Stella's would be well worth it for the amazing stories of human resilience you'd hear every day; but that's just the nostalgia talking.

Mrs. William Clark—*president*, Women's Department Club—1334 S. Center

In 1927, Mrs. William (Carrie) Clark, like Mrs. Stella Clark, was supervising an organization devoted to the general welfare of a particular group, albeit one with considerably more material resources than the occupants of the Friendly Inn. The Women's Department Club was founded in 1922 by combining the membership and treasuries of 11 existing women's clubs in Terre Haute. Yet even after this merger, dozens of active organizations for women remained: the Atheneum Club, the Bayview Reading Club, the Tuesday Literary Club, and the Daughters of the American Revolution among them. In addition, practically every fraternal organization maintained its own women's auxiliary.

The Women's Department Club was unique for its time. The club maintained its own headquarters, where women could experience the same sense of personal domain as the male members of the Elks, the Oddfellows, or the Knights of Columbus. Initially, the membership rented a former residence at 654 Cherry Street, and opened up a savings account with hopes of someday purchasing a meeting space outright.

The ratification of the Nineteenth Amendment in 1920, granting the right to vote regardless of gender, had empowered women nationwide. The various departments in the club emerged from the idea that women might have interests that extended beyond housekeeping and motherhood. The club offered lectures, discussions, and field trips in art, drama, literature, music, current affairs, French, nature studies, and social science. By 1927, the membership of the Women's Department Club was approaching 900, with 200 still on the waiting list. It was by far the largest women's club in the state. For the most part, the membership consisted of upper-middleclass homemakers.

To help cover the expenses that dues alone could not, the women established a thrift store in the basement to sell used clothing and furniture: bargains for the upwardly mobile. The membership also considered a proposal to lease space to one Virginia Nosler. Miss Nosler had graduated from the Leland Powers School of the Spoken Word in Boston. Her intention was to conduct both private and group instruction at the club in proper diction, dramatic interpretation, and play reading. The resolution to rent Miss Nosler space at 654 Cherry Street was passed with overwhelming approval.

Around this time, the music department at the club was planning its first field trip of the year. A recording had been purchased downtown and previewed on the club's Victor Victrola for the group's assessment. A powerful bass-baritone filled the meeting room singing a mournful ballad that moved more than a few of the club members to tears. It was then announced that the singer would be giving a recital at Caleb Mills Hall in Indianapolis on Wednesday night, January 20. The women made their plans to travel from Terre Haute on the Interurban, a trip that was 70 miles each way, returning late at night. They quietly hoped the weather would cooperate.

Past this point, very little is known about the group's experiences in Indianapolis. Paul Robeson did perform at Caleb Mills Hall that Wednesday night. It is likely that he sang "Motherless Child" as beautifully as he had on the department club's Victor Victrola. What is unknown is whether any of the women were surprised to discover that Paul Robeson was, in fact, Black. In any event, the members' subsequent conversation on the train ride back home, as well as the minutes of the music department's next meeting are unfortunately lost to history.

John Cluxton—County Poor Farm

Emmet J. Cody (Mary E., Cody Hat Company)—h 1228 S. Center

CODY HAT COMPANY—**Emmet J. Cody,** *proprietor*—715 Wabash

Dress hats for men were popular in the United States until the early 1960s. It's often said that John Kennedy's refusal to wear a hat at his inauguration in 1960 was a fashion statement that soon reverberated throughout popular culture. And although what the new president actually disdained was wearing a formal top hat, the choice impacted the popularity of all styles, from homburgs to felt fedoras.

A man's hat served a practical function as well as expressed personal style. It was useful to individuals who needed shade for their eyes, a barrier for their sweat, and went more than a couple of days between shampoos. Ultimately, the style of hat a man wore was as distinctive as the pattern on his suit. Hats were sized numerically, with fractions of inches separating each fit. The individual features of the hat were included as well: the width of the brim and the height of the crown. At Cody Hat Company, these considerations were guided by the shape of the customer's face, the cut of his jaw, the slope of his nose.

With precision comes protocol. From Labor Day to early spring, it was a felt hat. The seasonal transition fell on May 15, or as Emmet J. Cody's print ads proclaimed: Straw Hat Day. This was the day when Panamas, Leghorns, and Straw Boaters made their first appearance of the season, as sure a sign of warmer weather as cloth awnings and irises. Annual maintenance for a straw hat might include a new hat ribbon (or hat band) to address the previous summer's sweat stains. Cody Hat Company featured a large and colorful selection.

Emmet actually went by the nickname "Bill," an allusion to William Frederick Cody, alias Buffalo Bill. Like many shopkeepers throughout Terre Haute, Bill Cody considered a catchy store motto to be essential in attracting business. His invitation to prospective customers: "Meet me bareheaded."

In life, pure coincidence will often trump symbolism. That said, John F. Kennedy was the last president elected in Bill Cody's lifetime.

James A. Colescott (Louise)—*veterinary surgeon*—1032 N. 4th h do

In 1939, James A. Colescott was described in national news accounts as a bald and bespectacled Terre Haute veterinarian. This was by way of introducing him to the general public as the newest Imperial Wizard of the Ku Klux Klan of America.

In 1927, James A. Colescott and his wife, Louise, were living with his parents, Frank and Minnie. Dr. Colescott's veterinary office was located at the same address. At this point in time, he had been a member of the local Ku Klux Klan chapter in Vigo County for about four years.

Surely, James must have exhibited real compassion toward animals. So there was what he practiced professionally, and what he believed personally. Twelve years later, they were still unable to find each other.

Edith Collins—County Poor Farm

Henry Collins (Cynthia)—*hod carrier*—h 1301 S. 13th

A hod carrier assisted bricklayers by carrying heavy loads of bricks and mortar to the worksite. In 1927, there was a hod carriers union local in Terre Haute which met the first and third Mondays of every month at the Labor Temple.

Henry and Cynthia Collins's address places them in Baghdad, which was the name given to Terre Haute's African American neighborhood. (*See* William Laffoon.)

The very existence of a union local representing hod carriers along with the fact that, given his race, Henry Collins could never have become a member, provides a small indication of just how far we've come in the years since.

Mrs. Nellie Cook—*physiognomist*—r 334 N. 13th

Physiognomist: Defined as the practice of judging human character by the presence of certain physical features. Considered by many academicians to be a pseudo-science, physiognomy actually came from ancient Greek traditions. Aristotle wrote about it. So did one Johann Kaspar Lavater. In the late eighteenth century, Johann Lavater began to observe his friends and study the portraits of famous individuals. From this, he made conclusions as to how the shape of the nose or the thickness of the eyebrows or the cleft of the chin determined various personality traits, like sensitivity to others or the willingness to display courage. According to Johann Lavater, the French philosopher Voltaire had a face that perfectly mirrored his extraordinary wit.

There was a nice little trick to all of this, one that Nellie Cook might have picked up along the way. You establish the personality first, maybe by talking to your eager subject about whatever. Mix in a little speculation with your observation and you're off. Since Aristotle's time, the physiognomy field had broadened to include hair color, foot size, and voice pitch. Nellie no doubt enhanced her presentation with a shelf of bound reference works, a medical chart on the wall, maybe some calipers for skull measurements.

You can speculate on the how-to easily enough. While studying the hands of a male client, Nellie might notice chewed fingernails by which she could then conclude that the long thin nose and protruding Adam's apple and high-pitched voice represented clear signs of chronic anxiety.

Ultimately, Nellie Cook had to rely on her powers of observation and her ability to listen as key components of her business. Not much different, really, than a high school counselor dealing with a surly teen or a bona fide physician during a seven-minute patient visit.

In 1927, Nellie Cook was the only professional physiognomist operating in Terre Haute, Indiana, and most likely the last. Strange, though, how physiognomy has declined in status even as we continue to obsessively scrutinize each other's personal appearance and make judgments. In a sense, we've all become amateur physiognomists, probably because now there isn't any other kind.

Emma Cory (widow, Oliver)—*elevator operator*—h 1905 6th Ave.

In 1927, only a handful of Terre Haute buildings of more than three stories had electric elevators. If they did they would have required the presence of a trained operator. Training and skill were apparently relative terms within various occupations, though. Unlike motion picture projectionists or laundry workers, the elevator operators of Terre Haute were not represented by a union local.

Most elevator operators, however, did tend to identify their workplace; William Brown in the elevator of the Grand Opera House downtown being an example. Emma Cory was one of the few who did not, one reason why her situation begs notice.

Emma's work day wouldn't be too hard to imagine: jerky stops, a sinking feeling in the stomach, constant enclosure in a very small space among strangers. Actually, being a widow in 1927 would have been a good qualification for the job.

Alvah Cottrell—County Poor Farm

Herbert Cox—County Poor Farm

Albert Creasey (Margaret)—*laborer*, Terre Haute Artificial Ice Company—h 501 S. 12th

Dorothy S. Creasey—*bookkeeper*—r 501 S. 12th

Floyd S. Creasey—*bookkeeper*, Terre Haute Artificial Ice Company—r 501 S. 12th

A common enough situation in 1927; son follows father into a small business the family doesn't actually own. But the name of the business is what resonates here. By the 1920s, refrigeration had developed to allow ice to be produced commercially using mechanical compression and the refrigerant Freon 12. This as opposed to using ammonia and salt brine to create ice, which in the late nineteenth century had supplanted the time-honored practice of cutting and storing ice naturally produced in the winter months, which the Chinese had been doing as early as 1000 BC. Thus the name of Mr. Dean

McLauglin's business at 925 Poplar Street, which apparently understood its proper relationship to nature.

(N) Oliver Cromwell—*musician*—r 715 Mulberry

Oliver Cromwell was born in Terre Haute in 1899. That same year, Hoagland "Hoagy" Carmichael would be born in Bloomington, Indiana, just 60 miles away. By 1927, both young men would have occupations as musicians.

Just a few years earlier, while attending Indiana University, Hoagy had assembled a small dance combo that played up in Terre Haute on occasion. Even then, he was experimenting with jazzy chord progressions on piano and giving them fanciful titles. One composition, never to see either lyrics or a formal copyright, was dubbed "Nice Fresh Halibut Fish."

Hoagy would actually begin the year 1927 working as a law clerk in West Palm Beach, Florida. It was there that he heard a Red Nichols recording of his composition "Washboard Blues" being played on a sidewalk phonograph. By summer, he had returned to Bloomington intent on devoting his life to music. In October of 1927, Hoagy assembled a group of musicians at the Gennett studios in Richmond, Indiana, to record an instrumental composition he had seen fit to copyright. Mitchell Parish would later add lyrics to the melody Hoagy had simply entitled "Stardust."

"Stardust" would become one of the most performed and recorded songs of the twentieth century. We don't know Oliver Cromwell's instrument of choice. But as a working musician in Indiana bent on fielding his listeners' requests, he probably learned how to play it at some point.

John Crowe—County Poor Farm

D

DAPHNE CONFECTIONARY—671 Wabash—**(John Kostavetes)**

Like so many of the single-proprietor businesses in Terre Haute, Indiana, in 1927, the Daphne Confectionary was perceived as inseparable from the life of its owner, so much so that one newspaper account of the time would actually refer to him as John Daphne. John Kostavetes personally created every one of the candies he sold at the Daphne. They all came from traditional family recipes he guarded vigilantly, never writing them down where they might actually be read. John employed Madison Avenue advertising jargon to name the Daphne's most popular candy, the Fig-O-Nut, which was actually a traditional Greek confection. This was assimilation in its purest form: a modest symbol of the transition taking place every day from ancient to modern culture.

John Kostavetes served lunch and dinner at the Daphne seven days a week. On Sundays, he tried his best to emulate a popular American tradition: the after-church sit-down dining room spread. For 85 cents, your choice of chicken served any one of five ways: boiled, fried, stewed, garnished, or à la king. For 55 cents on a Sunday, you could choose from veal cutlets, roast beef, roast pork, or get way down home with Virginia ham and sweet potatoes.

In 1927, these Sunday dinners at the Daphne were served in a cozy setting one flight up from Terre Haute's busiest downtown street. The white walls and the checkered mosaic floor were illuminated by a huge skylight overhead. Down the center of the room stood a row of tables spread with yellow linen tablecloths trimmed in black. Intimate wooden booths lit with small tea lamps lined the opposite walls. Each lamp had a parchment shade with the image of a stout leafy tree. If you happened to inquire about its meaning, John Kostavetes would respond with this ancient tale:

> The daughter of the river god Peneus was walking
> alone in the forest one day when she met Apollo.
> Her father, fearing his daughter was in danger,
> instantly changed her into a laurel tree.

The daughter was named Daphne. The story had originated in Greek mythology. One suspects that it provided the name for John's business so he could retell this ancient myth over and over again to his newest customers.

(N) Arizona Daugherty—h 1306 Chestnut

(N) Arizona Davenport—(spouse of Beverly F.—*laborer*) h 1833 S. 3rd

Earl Dean—*glassworker*, Root Glass—h 2211 S. 8th St.

In November of 1915, Earl Dean submitted a design for a small bottle to his company supervisor, Alexander Samuelson. The design was in response to an open competition being held by one of Root's customers. A soft drink manufacturer had been in search of a distinctive design for its 8 oz. bottle.

Earl Dean's initial design copied the shape of a cocoa bean, the product's signature ingredient. The problem, he quickly discovered, was that the bottle's convex shape was subject to excessive breakage during shipment.

Earl Dean determined that he could address the problem and still retain the distinctive look of the bottle by making it concave in the middle, like the shape of an hourglass. Earl Dean's unique design was ultimately selected, resulting in a royalty of 5 cents for every gross of bottles shipped by the grateful manufacturer, the Coca Cola Company of Atlanta, Georgia. That royalty was paid directly to Earl Dean's employer, Root Glass, or more specifically, to the company's owner, Chapman Root.

Apparently, what Earl Dean received for this now legendary design was a hearty handclasp and a measure of job security—but only a measure. In 1932, following the death of his only child, William, in a plane crash, Chapman Root sold his company to Owens-Corning Glass. By 1937, Earl Dean had lost his position as mold maker at the factory and thereafter found work as a common laborer. He and his wife, Gertrude, had left Terre Haute by 1940. It didn't matter where they wound up, really; that ubiquitous green glass bottle would likely have preceded them.

Reba Deardorf—*factory worker*, Mewhinney Candy Co.—r 314 S. 17th

The A.B. Mewhinney Candy Company, which in 1927 employed about 200 people in addition to Reba Deardorf, was truly a family business. Omar Mewhinney, the son of a Polish immigrant, was the company president. His eldest son, Donald, all of 24, was the vice-president. Charles Mewhinney, Omar's younger brother, was the secretary-treasurer, and Donald's younger brother Fred was the sales manager. Omar's youngest son, Hubert, was a salesman, but for Charles W. Bauermeister, a wholesale grocery in town. Therein lies an interesting family dynamic that's so far been lost to history.

Throughout the 1920s, Mewhinney Candy Company of Terre Haute, Indiana, produced large heart-shaped boxes of chocolates, the kind that you'd imagine Popeye might have presented to Olive Oyl on a date. The company was quite creative in devising names for its candies. One variety was called "Paris Mint," another "Soul Kiss."

Omar Mewhinney could honestly claim that his family ran a global operation out of Terre Haute, wherever his candies wound up. The company imported its chocolate from Brazil. Fancy nuts were shipped from Spain and Italy. Exotic spices came from India and raw sugar from Cuba. Elegant silk ribbons were shipped across the Pacific from Japan.

These far-flung contributions were then assembled inside the Mewhinneys' small brick factory at 123 North 9th Street. It may seem incredible in an age when one or two manufacturers supply a single product that's distributed under dozens of different brand names, but the entire manufacturing process for the company's product was conducted at this one address located in this one Indiana town. It included the many varieties of candies with hidden chocolate centers; butterscotch, coconut, cherry, and cream; and extended all the way to the production of the heart-shaped cardboard boxes with the embossed names and fancy ribbons.

Near the close of the twentieth century, long after A.B. Mewhinney's had ceased operations, a self-proclaimed chocolate connoisseur and lifetime resident of Terre Haute contended that the only impressive thing about Mewhinney's was the elegant box and that the chocolates themselves were singularly unimpressive. It could be that the Mewhinney family had long ago concluded that when it comes to gifts of the heart, it's the thought that counts. Either that, or they believed there was really no such thing as bad chocolate candy.

In 1927, Reba Deardorf was a working mother in her mid-40s pulling a full shift at a factory. It is probable her closet smelled like chocolate-covered moth balls. Reba's husband, Clarence, was an auto mechanic. Their only child, daughter Dorothy, would have just been entering adolescence around this time. Hopefully, if Clarence was looking for a pleasant surprise to boost his wife's spirits on occasion, he was smart enough to bring home a bouquet of flowers.

Laura M. Devees (widow, W.M.)—*barber*—206 S. 3rd h do

No evidence that she had an actual business before 1927, so it's likely W.M.'s head was her only training. Maybe he'd received enough random compliments that she felt confident in choosing haircuts and shaves as her livelihood after he passed. As a barber, relying on tips, she no doubt discovered that her own flattering compliments proved more valuable to her male customers than the latest joke.

Laura M. Devees and Ada Clark were the only female barbers in Terre Haute at a time when the city also had only one female physician. Rare birds, in any case. In 1927, there were at least 130 barbers practicing the trade in Terre Haute, along with about 100 physicians. Turnabout being fair play, William Scherr was the proprietor of a beauty shop on South 6th Street.

John Devine—County Poor Farm

Ellis Dickerson—*barber*, Hotel Deming—r 809 N. 5th St.

Ellis Dickerson's position at the Hotel Deming was similar in many ways to his fellow employee James/Jimmy Campbell: a clean uniform, modest pay, and the occasional coin pressed in his palm for excellent service.

Barbers in 1927 provided more than just haircuts to their customers. Although they had passed the era when they could legally remove moles, most barbers did offer face massage with a hot towel wrap. They also styled and waxed moustaches, clipped nose and ear hair, and provided a stropped straight razor shave with a practiced stream of conversation that covered everything from the latest neighborhood obituary to city politics.

There were 112 barber shops listed in Terre Haute in 1927. Many of these shops had multiple chairs. Like pool halls and fraternal organizations, barber shops were exclusively male domains. Most of them carried a subscription to the *Police Gazette Magazine*, a lurid tabloid that graphically described sensational crimes and deviant behavior. While a position at the Hotel Deming or the nearby Terre Haute House might be considered the peak of the barbering profession in Terre Haute, there was not a great disparity in the fee for services rendered across town. Most barbers in this city were dues-paying members of the union local, which set fees for a shave and a haircut and met the first Wednesday of every month at the Labor Temple. The cost of a shave in Terre Haute, Indiana, would not exceed a quarter until after World War II.

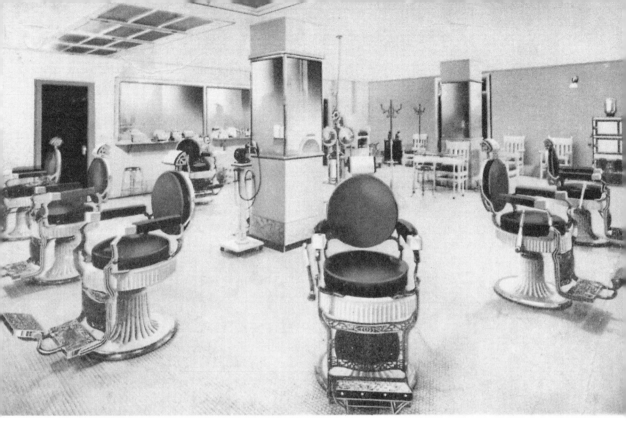

The Deming Hotel
Barber Shop

THE DIEKHOFF MUSIC HOUSE—1214 Lafayette Ave.

Augusta Diekhoff—*stenographer*—r 513 N. 14th St.

Herman Diekhoff (Avis)—h 515 N. 14th St.

Ignatz Diekhoff (Freda)—*teacher*—h 513 N. 14th St.

The very name of the business sounds melodic: The Diekhoff Music House. One can almost picture it as a small Bavarian music box—lift the lid and the music plays back in perfect intonation, just the way Ignatz hoped to hear his students play their lessons after a week of solid practice.

The Diekhoff brothers offered all things musical in their shop. They provided music instruction, sold band and orchestra instruments, and were able to repair those instruments. They also sold player pianos and piano rolls as well as phonographs and records. Apparently, there were enough aspiring and accomplished musicians within walking distance to support the business.

In 1927, one might understand a serious musician making a clear distinction between music performed live and music that was mechanically reproduced. Privately, the Diekhoffs might have harbored fears or prejudices similar to vaudevillians who were watching huge movie screens take over the very stages they had dominated just a season before. During this time, all throughout the entertainment industry, live presentations were making way for recorded performances. In February of 1928, star vaudevillian Al Jolson performed a song in a theater in downtown Terre Haute and the audience in attendance applauded. The difference was he sang on the screen, in the nation's first talkie, *The Jazz Singer*.

Amidst this monumental change in popular culture, one could have posed the question: Why learn to play a musical instrument for the entertainment of family, friends, or even the public at large when a piano roll or a phonograph or a movie soundtrack could easily present a more accomplished performance?

The Diekhoff brothers may have simply been convinced that any reason to put music out into the world was a good one. Since it was the music itself that made people joyful, or tearful, or got their bodies swaying to the beat, why argue the relative merits of how it got there? Why wouldn't you just spend your time enjoying the music instead?

And so the Diekhoffs continued to offer both music lessons and phonograph records at the Music House. One surmises that in their respective homes next door to each other at 515 and 513 North 14th Street, the brothers made room for both a piano and a phonograph in the living room. On summer evenings when the windows were wide open, perhaps one household played, and one listened.

Within a few years, when it came to music outside the home, the brothers Diekhoff would still be listening and watching, but the Diekhoff Music House would close its doors. Ignatz would be teaching exclusively at Sam Sterchi's downtown music store. Herman would move up the block and up a floor to 1265½ Lafayette. There he would open the Apollo Dance Hall in 1932. It became a place where dancers could face the daily rigors of the Depression by holding each other tight with their eyes closed.

DIXIE BEE GARAGE ([*owner/proprietor*,] **Arthur Johnson**)—2804 S. 7th St.

This interesting name for an auto repair business was derived from its location on U.S. Route 41. Route 41 ran from Chicago to Miami and formed the north-south axis of the Crossroads of America at 7th and Wabash in downtown Terre Haute.

In the years before its numerical designation in 1926, the road had been popularly known as the Dixie Highway. Its nickname among truckers, hitch-hikers, and snowbirds was the Dixie Bee Line.

Arthur Johnson was listed as living with his wife, Maud, right next door to the garage at 2802. While servicing a car engine had become an increasingly complex task by 1927, much could still be accomplished with a flat head screwdriver, an oil can, and two skillful hands.

(N) Florida Dodson—*domestic*—r 1220 S. 13th

James Donaldson—*manager*, United Cigar Store—h 2030 S. 8th St.

In 1927, the United Cigar Store stood on the southwest corner of the Crossroads of America at 7th and Wabash. United Cigar Store was a national chain that had grown enormously during the 1920s. In 1921, there were 2,000 United Cigar Store locations. By 1929, that number would nearly double to 3,700.

But throughout this period, the overwhelming majority of cigar dealers in Terre Haute were, like the grocers and the druggists, sole proprietors. There were 23 cigar and tobacco retailers listed in the Polk Directory, along with five wholesalers. This impressive total did not include the numerous cigar stands located at train stations or various hotels around town (*see* Helen and Jeane Butler). In addition to that, practically every drugstore and pool room in the city sold cigars. It was an Indiana native after all, Vice-President Thomas R. Marshall, who first uttered the phrase: "What this country needs is a good five cent cigar."

It also would have been easy to underestimate the true number of cigar wholesalers operating in Terre Haute at this time. Emory Daschiell, a recent transplant from Madison, Indiana, roomed at Edith Sonier's boardinghouse on 722 Walnut. Emory apparently sold his cigars to dealers out of a suitcase. Incidentally, in 1927, those cigars still could have legally come from Cuba.

Darrell D. Donham (Kath)—*general contractor*—465 Barton Ave. h do

In 1912, Darrell D. Donham built his first residence: a modest wood frame house at the northwest corner of Barton and Oak Streets. Initially, he shared the house with his widowed mother, Eve. But this new construction was a testament to his faith in the future. For although Darrell would not see the birth of his first child for another eight years, the completed house was one and a half stories tall with two small bedrooms located upstairs. And even though Darrell had just begun to establish his construction business, he had already made provisions for a first floor office and a detached garage to shelter his yet unpurchased pickup truck. Darrell installed lovely hardwood wainscoting in the dining room and affixed an elegant chandelier to the 12' living room ceiling. While waiting for the eventual extension of the municipal sewer line, Darrell also dug an outhouse in the backyard.

By the time the above listing appeared in the Polk Directory in 1927, the toilet at 465 Barton had been moved indoors. Darrell had begun by then to see the manifestation of his earlier dreams. With his wife, Katherine, he had brought four children into the world: three boys and a girl.

Darrell's business had grown significantly as well. Despite the modest layout of his own home, Darrell had begun to cultivate a local reputation as a builder of large, exclusive dwellings. A few years earlier, he had constructed a home at 2204 Ohio Boulevard for Carl R. Stahl. With the death of his father on February 4, 1927, Carl R. Stahl had become the co-owner of the city's largest clothing manufacturer, the Stahl-Urban Company, located on the northeast corner of 9½ Street and Ohio.

Capitalizing perhaps on Terre Haute's reputation as a factory town, the Stahl-Urban Company produced heavy-duty worker's overalls. By 1927, the company had acquired the Samuel Frank and Sons plant on North 14th Street, supplementing existing operations at its main facility. In keeping with the four-square nature of their overalls, the Stahl home on Ohio Boulevard was a sturdy brick structure constructed on a corner lot. The windows featured large cloth awnings to protect furniture from fading in the southern exposure. While the home itself was large, sitting on a generous lot, it still remained within easy walking distance of schools, churches, retail shops, and in Mr. Stahl's case, his place of business.

Darrell Donham would also be one of the contractors constructing homes in Allendale, a very exclusive suburban community located approximately four miles south of the city limits. In 1921, the Terre Haute Country Club moved to Allendale from its earlier location east on Route 40. More and more of the club's membership would follow.

The houses in Allendale were grand and luxurious, built on large plots of land that separated them from neighbors. It would not have been inaccurate to call most of the homes there mansions. The properties were platted on idyllic wooded acreage with a small creek. Unlike the residential neighborhoods that had been developed in Terre Haute up until that time, there were no businesses, schools, churches, or jobs within walking distance. Accordingly, the hilly, winding roads of Allendale had no sidewalks. Most of the houses were designed without front porches since, in the absence of sidewalks, there were no neighbors passing by to wave to or converse with.

The Allendale development would probably have been inconceivable just ten years earlier. But since every household in Allendale already had access to an automobile and a telephone, all the elements that had traditionally supported the functioning of a neighborhood could be located a good distance away or dispensed with entirely. Groceries could be delivered, after all, especially if a generous tip was waiting.

The Allendale homes showcased the lifestyles of Terre Haute's most affluent citizens. In a post-industrial society, they came to represent the aspirations of many who lived in the city's core neighborhoods. The area combined the best features of the city and the country, and residents had both the leisure and the location to stroll over to the Terre Haute Country Club and enjoy life. It wasn't as if the homeowners in Allendale had to punch a time clock the next day.

Allendale was located far enough away from the city that in 1927 the tide of residential and commercial development was still decades away from reaching it. Anyway, there simply weren't enough households in this secluded exclusive neighborhood to sustain the presence of services and businesses nearby. Ultimately, a corner grocery or a neighborhood drugstore would only have existed for the convenience of domestic help. One notable convenience was extended, however. Allendale was located along the interurban mass transit line that ran from Terre Haute to Sullivan. It just involved a long walk up a steep hill.

The Allendale development would also anticipate another trend in American housing: the increased size of the home itself. Prior to 1940, only 20 percent of the houses in America had more rooms than people. Within a generation, this ratio had been almost completely inverted. After 1970, over 90 percent of American homes were spacious enough to provide more than one room per person.

For 20 years after Darrell Donham built his own home at 465 Barton, he had very few neighbors. This changed in the mid-1920s as the small platted lots south of Poplar and Oak Streets began to fill up with new residential construction.

These homes would be classic Hoosier-style bungalows. Their functional design was a variation on the one-story shotgun home popular in cities throughout the South. A broad front porch led directly to a living room which was often connected by an open archway to the family dining room. A kitchen, a small bathroom, and a bedroom completed the floor plan.

The bungalows on 22nd Street south of Oak were each positioned a mere 12 feet from the sidewalk, with scarcely that much space between the houses themselves. The lots were just large enough to accommodate a small detached garage. The size of the backyards allowed for a fruit tree and an ample garden plot. But if the neighborhood kids decided to play baseball, the playgrounds at Davis Park School or Thompson Park at South 17th and Oak clearly offered a better alternative.

Playgrounds, schools, and churches were all within a short walking distance of the houses in this new neighborhood. Retail stores were just as accessible. In 1927, Katherine Donham shopped at Cahill's Market on the corner of 17th and Poplar. Much like Ernest Zwerner (*see* Citizens Market), Joe Cahill was a classic neighborhood grocer. Joe's residence at 438 South 17th was just four blocks from his store. Within ten years, Joe Cahill would offer an after-school job to the Donham's eldest son, Richard, which marked the start of Richard's long career in the grocery business.

At first glance, the neighborhood surrounding the Donham house might appear to be the precursor to subdivisions that would later dominate the American landscape. Suburban sprawl developments commonly maximize housing density to an extent that the narrow lawns between the homes are in perpetual shade. The exterior and interior design of the units are virtual clones of one another, since the proscribed covenants within the subdivisions prohibit any design variations.

The philosophy that guides much of the current residential development in America borrows from the Oak Street neighborhood and Allendale in ways that Darrell Donham could not have projected. The Allendale development was designed to allow for an almost complete reliance on the automobile. Similarly, after World War II retail stores, schools, churches, and public services were seldom made available within walking distance of new residential construction. These days, most walking in America's suburbs is done across gigantic parking lots. By 1960, few suburban housing developers even bothered to include sidewalks in their plans.

In 1927, the residents who lived in the new neighborhoods to either side of Oak Street reflected the modest sustainable design of their homes. Living west of the Donham family on the 400 block of 22nd Street were three city firemen, two printers, two factory foremen, a clerk, and a policeman.

The residences to the south of Oak Street on 22nd Street were home to yet another printer, another clerk, and a day laborer. Mayme Ellis lived in a house midway down the block on the west side. Mayme was the cook at the Union Station Restaurant. Terre Haute's Union Station was a massive red stone structure that served both the Pennsylvania and the Chicago and Eastern Illinois Railroads. (*See* Union Depot.) Most of the 75 passenger trains that arrived in Terre Haute every day ran through Union Station. Door-to-door salesmen, vaudevillians, and kids fresh off the farm would step down onto the station platform, envisioning this seemingly commonplace Midwestern city as a welcoming place to be. Almost invariably, sometime during her workday, Mayme

Ellis would cook the very first or the very last meal someone would ever eat in Terre Haute.

Terre Haute's Union Station was located at 9th and Sycamore Streets, quite a distance for Mayme to walk, especially in the wee hours. But in 1927, Mayme would have had the option of riding the city trolley back and forth. There were 25 miles of streetcar track running throughout Terre Haute. The first cars emerged at 5:42 every morning and carried passengers until 1:04 AM. Mayme Ellis lived just a short walk from the Crawford Street trolley stop at the corner of 17th Street. She would have been able to ride that one trolley car to within a couple of blocks of her workplace.

William and Elizabeth Holler lived right across the street from Mayme Ellis. William Holler could actually walk to work if he so desired and, depending on his route, he might even run into his boss. William was employed as a pattern maker at Stahl-Urban. The patterns he created were for thick 16-weight denim overalls. The sunlight streaming through the large windows at the Stahl-Urban factory found his drafting table during the day.

The neighborhood that grew up around the Donham house in the 1920s represents the last blush of a sustainable working-class community in urban America. Each home had a backyard for growing, a basement for canning, and a sunny kitchen to bring it all together. The open front porches with their brick or hardwood pillars were among the largest floor spaces in each home. With their proximity to the sidewalk, to the house next door, even to the house across the street, these open front porches created an easy connection between neighbors on lazy summer evenings.

Occasionally, the connection between neighbors would extend beyond the home. Victor Meagher owned the Dawson Drug Store at the corner of 13th and Poplar. And in 1927, just across the street from his house lived Paul Rausch, who was a salesman for E. H. Bindley—Wholesale Drugs. Many of the homes on South 22nd Street took their morning milk delivery from Terre Haute Pure Milk and Ice Cream Company. Their neighbor, George Packer, had a daily route.

This commitment to job, neighborhood, and hometown would be severely tested by the onset of the Great Depression. By 1930, Terre Haute's population, and with it the city's self-image, would register its first decline from a previous census. For the residents who lived on South 22nd Street as well as some who lived in Allendale, this was their first real indication that their relationship to the American dream might include years of hardship.

For the Donham family, the upheaval would be far more personal. In 1931, Darrell Donham would die of lingering complications from an automobile accident. Katherine and four children, ranging in age from 6 to 11, continued to live in the home Darrell had built 20 years earlier. The original lighting fixtures, the hand-forged brass doorknobs, and the mahogany bedstead that Darrell died in would remain in the house, and the house would remain with the family.

Over the course of his life, Darrell and Katherine's eldest son, Richard, would not only stay in the grocery business, he would stay in the family home as well. Richard and his wife, Grace, would raise their children at 465 Barton, and then continue to live there together after the children had grown and moved away. Today, the home originally constructed by Darrell Donham remains tidy, well-maintained, and unpretentious in an urban environment that is by its very nature dynamic and unpredictable. Remarkably, the Donham family would continue to occupy their modest home on Barton Avenue for more than 95 years, until shortly after Richard's death in 2006.

Charles Douglas—County Poor Farm

William B. Drain (Bertha)—*actor*—r 2044 Park

As one of six professional actors living in Terre Haute in 1927, William B. Drain was witnessing the transformation, some might say the extinction, of who he was and what he did. Just 20 years before, there had been hundreds of small stock companies traveling regional circuits across America, performing everything from slapstick to Shakespeare. Indoor stage venues included vaudeville theaters in large cities and opera houses in small towns while the summer months offered opportunities ranging from the Chautauqua circuit to seasonal resorts. Around this time, a young actor out of Chicago named Ralph Bellamy would form a small theatrical troupe. One of his stops would be at the Hippodrome in downtown Terre Haute.

Ralph Bellamy was part of that same transformation. Prior to forming his own stock company, Ralph Bellamy had been a set designer, prop master, and a director with 15 different stage troupes. In 1929, with the Depression looming, he finally made it to Broadway. It was like catching the last train out of Johnstown before the dam burst; the Hippodrome in Terre Haute would close that same year.

For regional actors and performers operating on the margins of solvency, the next few years would prove devastating. Sound movies, radio, and the Depression would combine to provide an almost perfect scenario for their complete elimination. Vaudeville was declared dead when the venerable Palace Theater in New York City closed in 1932. Just south of Terre Haute, the Merom Chautauqua had been presenting a wide variety of live performances since the summer of 1905. After the 1936 season, it decided to cease operations.

The following year, Ralph Bellamy starred with Cary Grant and Irene Dunne in *The Awful Truth,* playing the spurned boyfriend. By then, when most Americans entered a theater they expected to see a film, not a stage performance. By 1938, there were more movie theaters in the United States than there were banks.

As for William Drain, he had been gone from Terre Haute for ten years by then, in search of better prospects that involved getting paid rather than getting roles (list of actors at www.hometown.indiana.edu/1927).

Mary Draper—County Poor Farm

Otis Duck (Ruth)—*manager*, Hotel Deming Billiard Parlor—h 1101 S. 7th St.

Terre Haute, Indiana, in 1927 was both a river town and a railroad town, attracting a broad and diverse ethnic base. This resulted in some very unique

The Deming Hotel
Billiard Parlor

surnames, many of which would eventually be Anglicized or shortened right out of existence.

Otis Duck was born in 1893 and it probably wouldn't surprise you to learn that there were quite a few other Ducks living in and around Terre Haute when Otis was growing up. Perhaps the most glorious phonetic creation in this lineage was Perry's widow, Basheba Duck. Most of the Ducks were handed fairly benign first names to deal with, like Ray, James, and William. Fortunately for the male children of Otis's generation, there were no Donalds.

One can imagine that Otis Duck was emerging into his full glory when this core sample was taken in 1927. He was in his mid-30s and getting paid to manage the most elegant pool room in town. Let us also acknowledge the obvious suitability of the man's no-nonsense name here, especially set amidst the late-night click of billiard balls and thick cigar smoke. Nostalgia might dictate that Otis's story conveniently resolve itself in the basement of the Hotel Deming, but that wasn't the case.

Billiard rooms and pool halls would begin to vanish from river and railroad towns once Prohibition ended in 1933 and bars started reasserting themselves as the de facto gathering place for men. By 1944, Otis was living with his second wife, Julia, in a small flat above a shoe repair store at 692½ Lafayette in Twelve Points. That year, Otis reported that he was working as a laborer. Just what that job would have entailed for a man in his 50s remains unclear to us today. Likely this was low-skilled, short-term employment borrowing from Otis's network of social contacts around town. All indications are that it was a spare and challenging existence. Otis Duck would die just four years later in late February 1948. The obituary in the *Tribune* referred to him by his nickname, Duckie.

(N) Lemon H. Dunn—*fisherman*—h 11 Pearl

There were eight fish dealers listed in Terre Haute in 1927 and just like vendors who sold fruit or flowers, they relied on the freshly harvested. Though this did not always mean local, it almost always meant variety.

For example, while Harry Woods Fish Market at 1301 Wabash carried Baltimore Oysters, it also sold fresh catches from inland waters: Yellow and Blue Pike, Logoe Smelt, Lake Trout, and River Buffalo. Fresh and local in the fish market meant that what was available on a Tuesday would not necessarily return on a Friday, either to Harry's counter or Lemon's fishing line.

E

Tilatha East—r foot of Cherry

That lovely first name immediately draws you in, but there's also that vague address. In 1927, she was a single woman with no reported occupation living in a poor part of town. No numbers on the houses. Probably wasn't too tough to find her, though. Follow Cherry Street west to the river. Just ask for her by name.

Ephraim Eastham (Mary)—*piano tuner*—h 2651 S. Center

He carried it all in his ear, aided by a simple set of tuning forks and some replacement felt hammers ordered from the Schaff Piano Supply Company. And then there was the piano Ephraim and Mary kept in their home. Hopefully in tune, but it's hard to say how much playing actually got done. After a busy week, the sound of notes being struck must have felt like a busman's holiday.

C. M. Eaton—Mother's Dining Room—208 N. 8th h do

Teressa Eaton—Mother's Dining Room—208 N. 8th h do

A business striving to imitate life itself. Terre Haute still had an ample supply of boarding houses in 1927, designated by the Polk Directory as furnished rooms. (*See* Pauline Karns.) These were generally large private homes whose owners, often widows, had claimed the houses as their sole financial asset. For a young man or woman fresh off the farm, this residential setting, the home-cooked meals, even the shared bathroom helped to make them feel more grounded in a strange city.

Which leads us to the curious endeavor that was Mother's Dining Room. 208 North 8th Street was a large clapboard house two blocks south of where Eugene Debs and his wife, Katherine, lived and two blocks north of Wabash Avenue and the heart of downtown. Terre Haute's elegant Masonic Temple, constructed just ten years before, stood just footsteps away. Two homes similar to 208 had been demolished for that project. Even in 1927, it wasn't too hard to see where this formerly residential street was headed.

Clarence M. Eaton had come to the big city from Sullivan, Indiana. In 1920, he lost his first wife to childbirth. The man had the right last name for running a restaurant, at least. Beyond that, the skills lay with his sister Teressa and her ability to create a little slice of home in the front parlor of this house in downtown Terre Haute. It would prove to be a successful venture, at least in terms of establishing Teressa's reputation around town. When she died in June of 1940, the obituary in the *Tribune* referred to her as "Mother" Eaton.

EDGEWOOD GROVE CLUB—226 S. Adams

The Edgewood Grove neighborhood first emerged around 1912 and was among the very first suburban residential developments in the United States. It predates Levittown, New York, by a generation. Edgewood Grove is often overlooked as a true suburb because the amenities it offered stood in stark contrast to those in postwar subdivisions.

The enormous expansion of suburban housing developments in America after World War II matched a parallel growth in automobile registrations. But in 1912, the developers of Edgewood Grove perceived the family car as more a luxury than a necessity, and regarded its presence in their planned neighborhood as simply a four-wheeled vehicle absent a horse; literally a horseless carriage. The paved streets within the subdivision were winding avenues that led to broad boulevards with grassy medians in between. It was thought that any automobile would travel at a speed that would allow the driver to recognize a neighbor sitting on a front porch and easily greet them with a wave.

If Edgewood Grove had any contingency plan for urban transit, it was found in the neighborhood's location along Terre Haute Municipal Trolley Line #3 which ran on National Road west to the downtown and east to Highland Lawn Cemetery. The larger interurban system, which connected Terre Haute with Indianapolis, also ran along this route. Walking was how most daily distances were covered within the subdivision, so there were sidewalks and street trees providing shade throughout the development, this in spite of the fact that Edgewood Grove was itself surrounded by open fields and cow ponds.

In every sense, Edgewood Grove was a true suburb. It was also an oasis of sorts. Initially, it stood apart from any established residential neighborhood. Although city utilities had been extended to the development, Edgewood Grove was nearly a half mile east of the acknowledged edge of the city, 25th and National Road, where the Rose Orphan Home sat on the northeast corner.

The homes within Edgewood Grove were each distinctive in their design, with multiple levels, generous rooms, and high ceilings, more than double the space of the 750 square feet later offered in the average Levittown house. Each home in Edgewood Grove stood on a spacious lot and was constructed a minimum of 20 feet back from the front property line. Covenants required that the minimum cost of each home exceed $3,000. Within ten years, 80 homes had been constructed in the neighborhood.

There were two other factors which identified Edgewood Grove as a true American suburb. First, the overwhelming majority of homes were owner-occupied. It was estimated in 1920 that of the 71 homes occupied in the subdivision, fewer than a dozen were rentals. Within the decade though, the neighborhood would respond to the growing market for one- and two-bedroom flats. In July of 1924, a charming brick apartment building, Edgewood Grove Apartments, was dedicated along Wabash Avenue at the eastern edge of the development.

Another factor distinctive to Edgewood Grove was a covenant almost unheard of in urban neighborhoods up until that time, although it would eventually become the recognized standard for new residential subdivisions across America: Advertisements for Edgewood Grove touted the fact that no retail or commercial development would be allowed within the planned neighborhood. The projected incentive for homeowners was that long-term property values would be protected from the vagaries of urban growth as Terre Haute expanded eastward. Ten years later, the upscale Allendale development south of the city would also be devoid of retail and commercial services.

The unintended consequences of this particular policy would become evident in the coming decades. Segregating commercial services apart from residential areas, a policy enabled by the unlimited daily use of the automobile,

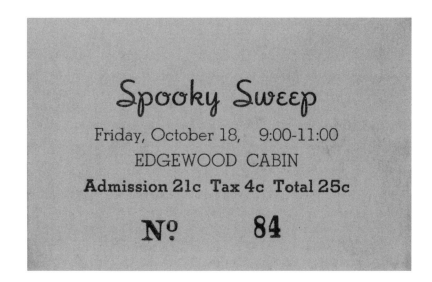

Spooky Sweep

Friday, October 18,   9:00-11:00

EDGEWOOD CABIN

Admission 21c Tax 4c Total 25c

№   **84**

Halloween Party at the
Edgewood Grove Clubhouse

defined the character of most post-war neighborhoods. By attempting to insulate housing developments from the dynamics of city growth, restrictive zoning policies created static, featureless residential neighborhoods that would wholly rely on clusters of big-box and strip-mall commercial centers for their retail services.

The residents of Edgewood Grove, having ensured that urban diversity and transition would be strictly regulated in their neighborhood, moved to monitor compliance through the establishment of the Edgewood Grove Planning Club in 1917. The club soon constructed a homey one-story log cabin for their headquarters. The property at 226 South Adams featured a meeting room large enough for social events. The adjacent grounds included two tennis courts.

The existence of this clubhouse, it was thought, would encourage Edgewood Grove residents to connect with each other and thus strengthen the identity and character of the neighborhood. It was hoped that the strong sense of community that infused Terre Haute neighborhoods like Twelve Points would be more purely distilled within this small planned community. These 80 households, whose children played together, who waved to each other from porches and sidewalks, could now further deepen their connection by playing tennis together, attending the neighborhood Christmas party, or joining the separate women's auxiliary. Birthday celebrations and wakes for longstanding residents were on the horizon: everyone bringing a covered dish, the men retiring outside the clubhouse for cigars afterward.

The deeper intention behind the clubhouse and the club itself was a shared premise that life in Edgewood Grove was ultimately an improvement upon traditional neighborhoods. It was accompanied by the lifelong resolution from each resident and club member to keep their close-knit community and its way of life intact. Beginning each day by bounding down a birdseye maple staircase into a broad foyer with the aroma of fried eggs and hot coffee in the air. The sunlight radiant through the white window lace on the front door. The day ahead set to unwind as gently as a pocket watch.

Ulysses Edwards (Ida)—*waiter*, Hotel Deming—h 504 Harding

The Hotel Deming, the city's most elegant hotel, featured a restaurant for its guests called the Gourmet Room: sturdy china with the hotel's seal, linen napkins, and small cream pitchers as part of each table setting. Ulysses Edwards was 45 years old in 1927. He had been born in Louisville, Kentucky, and like many African Americans of his generation, he'd migrated north—albeit only 164 miles.

Despite his nominal title as waiter, Ulysses's function in the Gourmet Room was to quickly clear dirty plates, keep coffee cups filled, and empty trays. This would have been accomplished with as much deference to white patrons as his silence or a soft response could muster. Casual disdain or outright verbal abuse would often accompany customer requests. White hotel guests had often traveled in the same direction Ulysses had, only from a greater distance south.

In 1927, an African American holding a position in an elegant hotel might be seen by both whites and blacks as having achieved an admirable status. But any job for blacks that dealt with the expressed needs of whites involved a substantial daily risk.

An incident had occurred just ten years earlier that clarified this. Likely, Ulysses Edwards could have recounted the story. In downtown Indianapolis, a disagreement had arisen in one particular hotel restaurant over the amount of sugar in a bowl. In response, the white customer, one Danny Shay, shot and killed his waiter. During the subsequent trial, Mr. Shay pleaded self-defense, contending that his "colored waiter" had called him a bad name and had also threatened to assault him.

Following jury deliberation, the defendant was acquitted.

Sarah E. Ehrenhardt (widow, Henry)—Auto Storage, Day and Night Service, Automobile Garage, and Feed Farm—27–31 S. 1st h do

By 1927, she had been a widow for seven years and was already well into her 60s. Henry had left behind a few parcels and a house, albeit in the poorer section of town. The outbuildings had once accommodated the feed farm, but Sarah apparently saw an opportunity for change. Or, given the declining presence of rural businesses in Terre Haute, maybe it was simply the necessity of day-to-day survival. At any rate, Sarah E. Ehrenhardt would have four years of life left in 1927. This is how she spent it.

The key phrase here would be "Day and Night Service." Roads between destinations in the United States were still somewhat unreliable in 1927, as the vast majority remained unpaved as late as 1920. The entire length of U.S. Route 40, a national highway, was only completely paved in 1926. Any regional motor trip involving rural routes would inevitably have involved rutted roads and unexpected detours, which added hours to an itinerary.

Sarah's modest auto garage, little more than a stable for cars, was located right along the river, a short distance south from the Wabash Bridge. She would have been a lone light and a welcome sight for travelers in search of a place to service or store their cars after hours. A bright star shining in the east.

In 1927, automobiles seeking out inexpensive overnight storage would likely be of a vintage that would require constant maintenance for long-distance trips: tires patched, fluids checked, parts lubricated. The lines from "Back Home Again in Indiana" come to mind here:

> And I think that I can see
> That little candlelight
> Still shining bright
> Through the sycamores for me

Sarah's feed farm included free-range poultry, and that would have presented an added challenge for her visitors. Her chickens would have been slow to respond to approaching vehicles. Fatalities were probably quite common. Whether it was from compensation for the fresh eggs or for the occasional accident, Sarah just might have kept some hens pecking in the yard as a way to fatten a customer's invoice.

James Elliot (Elsie)—*ball player*—r 1311 S. 16th

Terre Haute's other major leaguer-in-residence (*see* Victor Aldridge) was one big man: 6'3" and 240 lbs. To put it into the context of the sport: Babe Ruth, considered gargantuan among baseball players of the time, was one inch shorter and 25 pounds lighter. So you might say our local hero came by his nickname, "Jumbo," honestly.

Nineteen twenty-seven would prove to be a break-out season of sorts for Jumbo Elliot in that he somehow established himself as a reliable major league pitcher without having a very good season. He would win only six games for the Brooklyn Dodgers that year, while losing 13. His best years were ahead of him, it turned out. In 1931, he'd win 19 games for the Philadelphia Phillies. Three years later, he'd be out of baseball. Terre Haute, Indiana, was still home, though, and would be until his death in January 1970.

John Emil—County Poor Farm

George E. Endres—*general manager*, Little Wonder Light Company—r 319 S. 5th

A tender, almost innocent name for any business that wasn't manufacturing toys. Perhaps it's appropriate then that the Little Wonder Light Company operated on a fair amount of blind faith. In 1927, the company was manufacturing gasoline lights. And while gas-powered lamps had initially dominated home and business lighting across urban America, the introduction of Thomas Edison's incandescent electric light bulb had changed all that. By the late 1920s, gas-powered lights were primarily relegated to work and road construction sites—places where electric power was either unavailable or impractical. Actually, the broader market was just waiting for electric battery technology to become efficient enough to render what the Little Wonder Light Company made completely unnecessary.

The patent for the first battery-powered light dates to 1903. That was about a quarter-century behind Edison's invention, so there was still a little time left for George and his cohorts. The company's operations were located at 130 South 5th Street, just a couple of blocks from George's home. There was a very serious intent behind it all. The Little Wonder Light Company had a president, a vice-president, and a treasurer. Within a few years, the treasurer, Gertrude Van Slyke, would assume control of the company. For the most part, the Great Depression eliminated any business that was gasping for air and sometime in the mid-1930s, the Little Wonder Light Company would cease operations.

Thomas Alva Edison himself would die in 1931, secure in the knowledge that his invention had become the future of powered illumination. But exactly how much would only be revealed with his passing. As a fitting tribute to the man and his invention, President Herbert Hoover wished to have all electric lights in the United States dimmed for one minute. Hoover's advisors quickly persuaded him that his proposal would cause enormous disruptions. Apparently, Edison's "Little Wonder" had completed its transition from novelty to necessity.

Andrew A. Engstrom (Nannie)—*saw filer*—h 2005 Buckeye

One of the many jobs in Terre Haute devoted to the periodic maintenance of products that were built to be sturdy and simple enough to encourage ongoing care. Andrew A. Engstrom's was a job that had to be done by hand, took whatever time it took, and demanded his constant personal attention throughout: delicacy for a coping or keyhole saw, more vigor for a lumberman's two-handed crosscut saw.

This was apparently Andrew's full-time job in 1927. Work done that allowed other work to be done. By the way, a sweet poetic justice that he lived on the street he did. In the early twentieth century, the yellow buckeyes found in the Wabash Valley were only considered suitable for cheap furniture and kitchen implements. Not much reason to bother them with a saw.

Clara B. Enyart—*butter wrapper*—Armour Creamery—r 609 S. 13½ St.

Imagine it: a freshly sliced one-pound block of hard fresh butter, a sheet of wax paper torn from a roll, printed company name facing up, fold tightly and neatly—almost like a Christmas gift. Then repeat.

It's pretty obvious that a machine would be doing this task within a few years, but not at the Armour Creamery. Small dairies and creameries thrived throughout America in the 1920s, pasteurizing milk from local farms, investing in a mixture of simple machinery and muscle to produce products for a strictly local market, relying on returned glass bottles from steady customers for their daily supply. In many ways, this was an early model for a sustainable business. (*See* Edward C. Bell.)

There were many reasons why these small manufacturers would fail in the coming decade: tighter credit from the Depression, changing regulations for product manufacturing and hygiene, and perhaps in Armour Creamery's case, the necessity of investing in new equipment that could do Clara's job faster and perhaps more precisely than she could.

But to what end, if the task was simply to wrap the butter made from whatever milk had been delivered that morning? In 1927, this was apparently

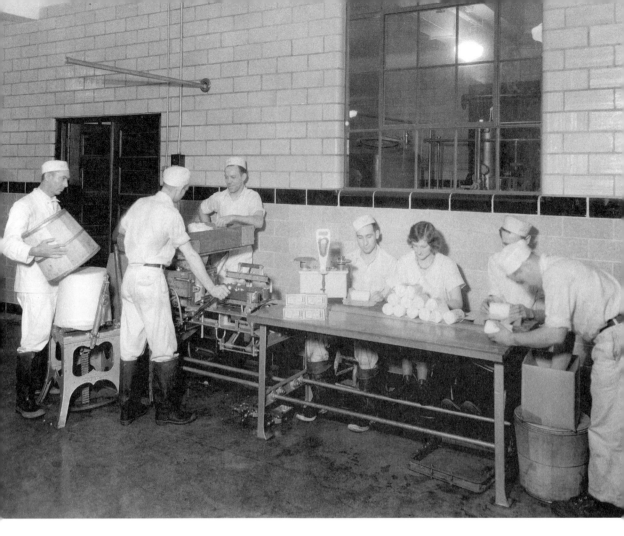

Creamery Workers Cut and
Wrap Butter
Martin Collection, Indiana
Historical Society

a job Clara could accomplish within the confines of her personal skills and her working day at Armour Creamery. This was consistent with the conscious human effort present throughout the process, beginning with two hands milking a cow.

It wouldn't just be the advent of wrapping machinery that would force this change. It was also the recent developments that would allow companies to store and preserve milk for longer periods before it was processed which gave them the ability to acquire the milk from regional, not just local producers, and then finally led to the investments they would make to have butter measured, cut, weighed, and wrapped mechanically—resulting in at least one more machine, at least one less worker, and in many cases one less company.

Eugene A. Esker—*teller*, McKeen National Bank—r 410 S. 21st

The McKeen National Bank stood on a prominent corner of downtown at the northwest corner of Sixth and Wabash. At the top of the bank's domed cupola stood a statue of Mercury, one of many references around town to ancient cultures. The Orpheum Dance Hall, the Hippodrome, the label on Dauntless canned fruits and vegetables which featured an illustration of a gladiator; all of these might have stirred curious questions from a child. And if the adult who was listening happened to be a graduate of Terre Haute's Municipal High Schools, it's likely they would provide an informed answer. Wiley and Garfield each featured four years of Latin in their curricula. In the 1920s, it was estimated that a quarter of all high school students had studied Latin.

So it's very possible that young Mr. Esker himself could have informed customers that the statue above the bank represented the ancient Roman god of commerce. Two other conversation starters may have eluded him, though.

John Dillinger, who would eventually be listed by the F.B.I. as Public Enemy Number One, was an Indiana native. During the 1920s, he built his national reputation with brazen bank robberies throughout the state where he would often leap over a teller's cage to collect the available cash. But actually, whatever fears Eugene Esker may have harbored for his own safety would have proven unfounded. John Dillinger believed that robbing banks in Terre Haute was too risky a proposition due to the busy railroad lines which crisscrossed the city, any of which might delay his speedy getaway.

Then there was the popular comic strip *Our Boarding House,* which featured Major Hoople and his cast of wisecracking boarders. In the spring of 1927, writer Gene Ahern featured a visit to the boardinghouse by the Major's ne'er-do-well brother Jake from Chicago. After hearing secondhand about one of his shady financial proposals, one boarder observed: "Bus, you sure are a simple and trusting soul. I could make you believe the banks of the Wabash pay 15 per cent."

Sanford Ethington—County Poor Farm

Mary Euriga—*clerk*, Peoples Bakery—r 2009 Maple Ave.

One of three Twelve Points businesses in 1927 with similarly themed names: Persons Hardware and Furniture, Citizens Market, and Peoples Bakery.

F

Mrs. Ethel Failing—*teacher*, McKeen School—h 1107 N. 4th

Frances Failing—*teacher*, McKeen School—r 1900 N. 13th

Lena Failing (widow, Charles H.)—h 1900 N. 13th

Nellie Failing—*teacher*, Davis Park School—r 1900 N. 13th

How they ever eluded Robert Ripley and his popular news feature is a mystery unto itself. After all, the coroner of Will County, Illinois, a Mr. Blood, was featured in *Ripley's Believe It Or Not,* as was Mr. Barber, a barber from Punxsutawney, Pennsylvania, and Miss Toombs and Miss Coffin, employed by Parklawn Cemetery in Rockville, Maryland.

Shedding their maiden name would have presented a different challenge for the Failings. During the 1920s, married women were not allowed to teach in Terre Haute public schools.

WALTER E. FAILING (Ann)—Furniture, Rugs, Domestic and Oriental; Bric-a-brac, Interior Decorations, Carpets and Upholstery, 441 N. 7th, Phone: Wabash 7225

What would emerge as fine antiques much later on would have been sold as new in 1927 at Walter Failing's tiny shop. Like many other locally owned specialty shops in Terre Haute at this time, the proprietor's personal taste determined the existing inventory. In this case, the choices were made by a cultured individual in his early 60s who had been born in New York City and had married a woman nearly 20 years younger. Apparently, American rustic furniture appealed to Walter. He carried Old Hickory: tables and chairs fashioned from the finished branches of the tree itself, manufactured in nearby Martinsville, Indiana. Imports and exotic curios were also featured at the shop, likely the result of his extensive travels. Trips back and forth from work, however, did not contribute much to this total since Walter and Ann lived at 459 North 7th Street, just footsteps from the shop.

The Failings seem to have been as discerning in their personal acquisitions as they were in their professional taste. 459 North 7th Street was a small brick apartment building, where the couple occupied apartment #6. With these space limitations, any bric-a-brac would be set out for appreciation and not just for dusting.

There was an ongoing need for more exotic treasures to acquire for the shop, though. Walter may have been enticed by an advertisement appearing in the *Saturday Spectator:* an Around the World Cruise for $1,250. The cost in 1927 would have discouraged a lot of people. But perhaps Walter saw the vast opportunity that lay ahead of the vast sum of money. While the linear distance from Terre Haute to the Far East, India, the Holy Land, and the Mediterranean was the same in 1927 as it would be 80 years later, the separation between cultures was certainly far greater. Perhaps Walter knew, even then, that the world they were advertising would only become smaller.

FAIRVIEW ANNEX—Rose Home—25th and Wabash Ave.

There was a small brick school building on the grounds of the Rose Orphan Home. In 1927, it had two teachers, two classes, and provided the only opportunity for girls and boys at the Home to interact, albeit within the rigid confines of a classroom.

In 1925, Terre Haute school superintendent J. O. Engleman announced that the district would no longer furnish teachers to the Rose Orphan Home, which was, after all, a private facility. To ease the transition, Ernest Alden, the director of the Home, decided to personally fill two of the three positions affected. The youngest children at the Home would immediately begin attending first grade at Fairview School at 25th and Chase. The older children at Rose had already been registered at the city's junior and senior high schools: Woodrow Wilson and Wiley.

For each of them, it became an opportunity to experience the world that lay beyond the 20 acres at the Orphan Home. With it went the reminder of all that they were missing by being there.

(N) Dovey Fallowfield (spouse of Edward—*shoe repairman*)—h 2322 Garfield Ave.

FARMERS HOTEL—**(George L. Woodsmall)**—128 S. 4th St.

Operating at the end of a long, if not a particularly grand tradition. The Farmers Hotel had begun its life as the Market Hotel, one of four modest establishments near the site of the former City Market. They provided lodging to farmers who traveled into Terre Haute to sell their produce. The Sullivan Hotel, at 202 South 4th had been one of these, as had the Henderson Hotel further down the street at 209, and the Arlington Hotel at 329 Walnut.

In years past, these establishments often referred to themselves as "House" rather than "Hotel." The thought was that The Henderson House might sound more appealing to someone for whom a visit to the city rivaled a tooth extraction for all the fear it caused. The Farmers Hotel offered a generous farm-style breakfast served very early in the morning on long communal tables on the first floor. Upstairs, a narrow hallway led to a series of tiny sleeping rooms on the left. A thin mattress, a bare hanging light bulb, and a washstand with a used towel were what passed for overnight accommodations. A cell in a cloistered convent would be an apt comparison.

By the late 1920s, the whole purpose of these establishments was breaking down very quickly. While the early morning farmers' market was still in operation, it had long since moved from its original location at 4th and Walnut north to 2nd and Mulberry. By 1927, it featured rows of trucks instead of horse-drawn farm wagons. This change had made arriving the night before unnecessary for local farmers.

There were also changes made in the job itself. The number of farms in Indiana had declined by nearly 10,000 between 1920 and 1925, and nearly 2,000,000 acres of cultivated land had been lost. As for the future? Well, in 1920 there were more than 50,000 farms in the state with fewer than 50 acres, while just barely 1,000 farms exceeded 500 acres. Just add 50 years to that and do the math.

The Farmers Hotel would be gone within the decade; the site was sold in 1935 to a family-run business, Shahadey's Grocery—which one day would also be among the last of its kind in Terre Haute.

(N) Ignatz Felawich—*miner*—r rear 1444 Beech

Bituminous coal is relatively soft in comparison to anthracite coal and produces a fine dust that's easily carried back to a miner's home on clothing and skin.

Ignatz Felawich lived alone in a small detached structure set behind the Roumania Hall, a social club for recent immigrants who worked the heavy northside industries like Highland Iron and Steel, Terre Haute Malleable, and Columbian Stamping and Enameling. Each of these factories emitted massive clouds of thick grey smoke that quickly dirtied shirt collars, window curtains, and wallpaper.

This thick grey smoke was yet another byproduct of the bituminous coal that Ignatz Felawich extracted from the ground every day by hand. So as he noticed black particles floating in soapy water or on the tip of his jackknife as he cleaned his fingernails, Ignatz Felawich might have briefly contemplated the burden he carried. Much like shepherds permanently stained by the ferrous livestock-dye reddle, Ignatz Felawich was left with a daily reminder that no one ever leaves this earth alive.

Denzil M. Ferguson (Margaret)—*sanitarium*—126–128 S. 6th—h 2201 S. 8th

In 1927, Terre Haute, Indiana, continued to maintain a complex relationship with the natural world. On the most basic level, there was the food that was consumed: locally grown for the most part with every harvest dependent on the climate for that area. Local deposits of bituminous coal provided heat. Limestone pits provided tombstones.

Canaries in cages, horses in harness: Each furnished their caretakers with a practical benefit as well as an ongoing connection with a living creature. Then there was the mythic reverence shown the Wabash River, which had been celebrated in song, referenced in product names, and navigated by small excursion boats headed for picnic grounds and a leisurely day in the country.

The beneficial role that nature might have in restoring physical balance was recognized throughout the medical community. Even in the heart of the city, people relied on natural treatments for everyday injuries and illnesses. Some home remedies arose from years of observation and tradition. Lean raw meat was said to soothe bee stings. It was believed that wet tea leaves could effectively stanch bleeding. A mixture of mayweed blossoms and alcohol was considered to be a strong liniment for sore muscles.

Natural compounds, herbs, and minerals were prominently displayed on the shelves of local drugstores throughout Terre Haute in the 1920s. Flaxseed, Licorice Compound, Oil of Sassafrass, Coconut Oil, and Chamomile were sold in bulk at Hook's Drug Store on the corner of 7th and Wabash. Gillis's Drugs featured 26 varieties of natural tonics, including Nuxated Iron and a mystical concoction called Swamproot. Buntin's Drug Store featured Dr. Bell's Pine Tar Honey for coughs, Syrup of Figs for neuralgia, and Pluto Water, a popular local remedy taken for irregularity.

Pluto Water originated from the natural springs located in French Lick and West Baden Springs, Indiana, about 75 miles south of Terre Haute. Buntin's sold a bottle of Pluto Water for 39 cents, but many folks preferred to take the cure by taking the train to the two famous spas or to nearby Trinity Springs in Martin County. (*See* James W. Thompson.) A ladle of this sulfur-infused water taken directly from the spring was said to be good for what ailed you, while smelling foul enough to convince you it could kill or cure most anything.

In 1927, Pluto Water actually had a very famous and faithful customer who nevertheless would never have been put forth as a company spokesman. Louis Armstrong would have probably taken advantage of the Buntin's sale had he been playing in town with his Hot Five. It was said he seldom left Chicago without at least one bottle of Pluto Water in his satchel.

Throughout the 1920s, sulfur was considered to be an effective treatment for many illnesses. One popular home cure recommended a dose of powdered sulfur quickly followed by a spoonful of either sugar or kerosene for treatment of a sore throat. Denzil M. Ferguson maintained that the external absorption of sulfur through the skin was helpful in the treatment of everything from rheumatism to kidney disease. He offered nurse-assisted sulfur sweat baths at his sanitarium located on South 6th Street. The nurse in question was a Miss Effie Infange.

The poet Max Ehrmann kept an apartment directly above the sanitarium in 1927. Hard to say if the sweat treatments or the foul odor proved inspirational for him, but at some point during that year, Max Ehrmann would write his most enduring work, the poem "Desiderata."

(N) Osceola R. Ferguson (Musa)—*salesman*, Fred C. Foltz Co.—h 640 Barbour

(N) Ardmore Fernsel (Mamie)—r 445 N. 5th

Eli Fielding (Elizabeth)—*miner*—h 2405 N. 15th

Eli Fielding (Ilena)—*miner*—h 1907 N. 12th

George Fielding—*miner*—r 2405 N. 15th

James Fielding (Catherine)—*miner*—h 2411 N. 15th

Nora Fielding—r 2405 N. 15th

Thomas Fielding (Lena)—*miner*—h 1343 Lafayette Ave.

Five men, four separate households. Remarkably, it's the only occupation for the only Fieldings listed in the Polk Directory (*see* Barden Calloway).

Albert Fiess (Amelia)—*harness maker*, John Zachman—h 1131 S. 4th

There were still three harness makers in business in 1927, all located within a block of each other right in the heart of downtown. The Froeb Brothers were located at 19 South 5th Street. Fisbeck Harness Company at 21 South 4th was owned by Harry Kliptasch and Louis Graff. Then there was John Zachman's at 112 South 4th. They all made and sold leather harnesses, realizing that for most of their customers and their customers' horses this next harness might be their last.

Each of these businesses stood in close proximity to the four original farmer's hotels and the Quinlan Seed Store, just footsteps from the old City Market. It wasn't a convenience that amounted to very much in 1927, since the farmers' horses rarely came in to town anymore. Moving to another location at this late date was unlikely to improve anyone's prospects. And so they all huddled together in the ship's hold as the water came pouring in.

Albert Fiess had originally learned his craft as a young man, back when having a horseless carriage meant it didn't move. By 1927, Albert was 70 years old. Interesting to contemplate his situation: working downtown, still drawing a paycheck as a harness maker, hearing the steady din of motor vehicles as he stitched leather.

The situation over at 19 South 5th Street was also moving toward a final resolution. There were actually three Froeb brothers connected with the business. In 1927, the co-owners were the two eldest Froeb brothers, Emil and Herman.

Their baby brother Henry would turn 53 in 1927. A bachelor, he lived with Herman and sister Rose in a tidy home at 1018 South Center Street. Lo these many years, Henry had been working as a clerk for his two older brothers, hoping perhaps that at 73, Emil might be contemplating retirement soon. That would then open the way for Henry to become co-owner of Froeb Brothers Harness Company. Henry stared at the books, he stared at the dusty harnesses hung on the wall, he stared at the traffic outside. At some point, he must've smiled at the irony of it all. If not, it's doubtful he would have made it all the way to age 94.

(N) **Milwada Finnegan**—*clerk*—r 1356 1st Ave.

FIRST TERRE HAUTE HUNGARIAN SOCIETY—southeast corner of 22nd and Linden

In 1927, the Society's headquarters was a modest clapboard building that provided a gathering place for wedding receptions, ethnic holidays, and religious feast days. It symbolized community created by individuals in transition. Like John Chervenko, each of them had arrived in Terre Haute, Indiana, with a dream that would soon collide with reality. They had been required to learn a new language. They had worked at the lowest-paid, most physically demanding jobs. Gradually, they would begin to look to their children for the fulfillment of their dreams because as adults, they simply didn't have enough time left to realize them.

The intersection of 22nd and Linden on Terre Haute's north side was at the heart of the Hungarian neighborhood. George Gaul's grocery stood on the northwest corner, diagonal to the Society's headquarters. The owner stocked fresh ground paprika and poppy seeds, essential in numerous Hungarian recipes.

Downtown, a fine prepared meal could be had at the Little Hungarian Restaurant, upstairs at 677½ Wabash—just a flight up off the street, marked by a small red sign. The owners, Harry and Sadie Heller, had come to Terre Haute from Chicago. Sadie, described as an artist in her profession, steadfastly refused to employ helpers in her kitchen or use anything but creamery butter in her recipes. Every morning, she would first bake bread, cake, or cookies before devoting herself to the main course: Chicken Paprikash or a goulash served alongside fresh beet soup.

Unlike many restaurants in the downtown area, Harry and Sadie's expressly welcomed vaudeville performers and traveling salesmen and encouraged them to make the Little Hungarian their dining room when in Terre Haute. Likely these visits left them with few tips and many tall tales. Still, Harry and Sadie resolved to make the encounter satisfying for both sides. The slogan they chose for their restaurant was "The Place of No Regrets."

The potential for lasting regret threatened every immigrant experience in America like a dark cloud holding rain. These were adventurous souls who had left their homelands and crossed an ocean and then half a continent to reach Terre Haute, Indiana. There, a simple folksong strummed on a zither could instantly remind them of an early experience from their small mountain village. Along with it might come the realization that they would likely never get to see their homeland again. This was the painful ecstasy that the First Hungarian Society offered to its members. They invited this feeling, all the while hoping that time would ease its effects.

Membership in the Society also had a practical purpose. In fact, practicality was the reason for the founding of the Society. It had all started with one man's untimely death. He had arrived from Hungary without family. Whatever other circumstances Terre Haute had changed for him, that situation remained constant. Ultimately, he had taken this great risk, worked himself unto death, and died alone. The Hungarian neighborhood that settled around 22nd and Linden numbered about 40 families in 1909. Realizing that this man had no money for a funeral, no plot for burial, not even friends for pallbearers, the community decided to respond. The First Terre Haute Hungarian Society actually marked its beginning with a photograph of a small group of men surrounding a casket they themselves had paid for. They had already determined among themselves that this situation should not be allowed to happen again. At the same time, they were aware that if a debilitating injury or illness ever prevented them from working, it just might.

The organization they set up operated like an annuity. Society members would pay an initiation fee based on their age: $2.00 for working individuals from 16 to 20 ranging up to $5.00 for those 45 to 50. Monthly dues were fixed at 75 cents a month. After ten years of dues-paying membership, a Society member or his family would be eligible for a death benefit of $100.00, plus a lump sum resulting from a $1 contribution by each remaining member of the Society. In case of illness or injury, the Society would pay out $6.00 a week for a maximum of five weeks in a calendar year. Childbirth and the added expenses it might entail were compensated by a flat payment of $15.00.

A Feast Day Commemoration at the First Hungarian Club Archives of the Vigo County Historical Society, Terre Haute, Indiana

The payments stood as a guarantee in a largely unpredictable world. There were few occupational safety standards and no system of unemployment insurance. Early in the twentieth century, even in a labor town like Terre Haute, little thought was given to organizing unskilled workers or accepting immigrant workers into existing unions. This produced a constant dread that had surely been felt by every immigrant who had arrived in Terre Haute with little more than immigration papers in their pockets. After all, who would look out for their interests if their ability to work for low wages for long hours in difficult and dangerous conditions were somehow compromised? Not their employers, not their government, and certainly not the surrounding community. Much of the reason for the neighborhood's existence and its name, "Hunkietown," was that the new immigrants were unwelcome in this city they now called home.

By 1923, when the building housing the Society was finally constructed, the First Hungarian Workingman's Sick and Death Benefit Society had 103 members. The following year, the total for death benefits was $766.00. The need remained, and so the membership grew. In 1928, it would stand at 133 paying members.

By then, the original members who had surrounded that casket in 1909 were thinking about their own mortality. The Society would continue to pay benefits and eventually survive all of them. In the first year of the new century, the Hungarian Society fund distributed $648.00 in benefits to its members.

Meanwhile, the building on the southeast corner of 22nd and Linden would continue to function as a meeting hall and Society headquarters, keeping the presence of Hungarian culture alive even though the immigrant population had virtually disappeared from the neighborhood surrounding it.

Joseph Fischer (Mary)—*shoemaker*—h 1469 Chestnut

Joseph Fischer apparently worked at home. Didn't advertise either. This would lead you to believe he got by on local reputation. He is listed as a shoemaker, as opposed to doing shoe repair, for which there was no shortage of business. (*See* Max Frank.) In 1927, Terre Haute had 47 shoe repair businesses, 247 miles of sidewalks, and an urban culture that understood the value of a fresh set of rubber heels applied to a comfortable pair of shoes.

Careful attention was also being paid to the foot inside. Four licensed chiropodists were practicing downtown within a block of each other, the principal distinction for prospective clients being their gender. Drugstores throughout the city prominently listed foot remedies in their newspaper ads. With all those miles being walked every day, somebody was suffering somewhere.

The depth of this pain was reflected in the products advertised, with a clear distinction made between Blue Jay Corn Plasters and Blue Jay Bunion Plasters, and a clear preference expressed between liquids, creams, powders, and soaps.

Joseph might tell you that a pair of his shoes would ultimately save you money on foot care since most foot ailments arose not from walking but from a poor fit or shoddy workmanship with the shoe itself. Still, by 1927 there were only a few shoemakers left in town to compete with local retailers selling the mass-produced brands. It all seems planets away from where we find ourselves now. Today, a pair of handmade shoes are regarded as an extravagant luxury. Meanwhile, most mass-market footwear is currently being manufactured outside the United States, even though it might still bear the familiar nameplate of an American company.

After a visit to Terre Haute by Buster Brown in 1925, Joseph Fischer had probably given up on the next generation anyway. On September 16 of that year, a promotional campaign brought the popular shoe spokesman and his little dog, Tige, to the Grand Opera House downtown. Buster Brown had initially been created by the Brown Shoe Company of St. Louis to promote their line of children's shoes. Inside every shoe was an illustration of a boy dressed in a sailor's suit with a smiling Boston terrier at his side.

The Brown Shoe Company had first employed an actor to portray Buster Brown at the St. Louis World Exposition in 1904. Ever since that time, Buster and his faithful companion had made select regional appearances. Considering that Terre Haute was only 169 miles by train from St. Louis, a visit seemed in order. Local shoe dealer Ben Becker made free tickets available at his store at 525 Wabash. The event was scheduled for a Wednesday at 3:30 PM, right after the schools let out.

Hard to say whether it was the shoes, the free pencils, or Buster's trademark wink that drew them in, but that afternoon an estimated 3,000 kids gathered outside the Grand. The theater's total capacity was about half that.

On stage that day, Buster Brown told some amusing stories, got Tige to roll over, and showed the audience slides of the Brown Company factory in St. Louis; a factory that would close in 1995 as the company shifted its manufacturing operations overseas in response to market pressures.

FISK TIRE SERVICE—(Harley E. Mace)—Fisk Tires, Tubes and Service, Vulcanizing, Road Service, Complete Line of Tire Accessories—20 S. 5th, Phone: Wabash 4619

Like the Brown Shoe Company, Fisk Tires also relied on the illustration of a child to promote its products in national print ads. In this case, a yawning boy about 3 years old appeared dressed in a nightshirt holding a candle and carrying a Fisk tire over his right shoulder. The company's slogan printed underneath: "Time to Re-tire." The question of what a 3-year-old was doing carrying a lighted candle hangs in the balance.

Jerry Fitzgerald (Mary)—*president*, Jerry's Bakery—r 1826 Ohio

Like John Kostavetes and Ernest Zwerner, Jeremiah Fitzgerald's presence in Terre Haute was defined by his business. In 1927, his gregarious personality combined with his business name made him instantly familiar to people who wouldn't have recognized him on the street.

He was pretty hard to miss, though. A big, voluble Irishman born in Tralle in County Kerry, Jerry Fitzgerald had come to the United States at age 19, his brogue set firmly in place. In 1910, he decided to open a bakery in Terre Haute and leased a building at 207 Ohio Street. Initially, the entire operation was Jerry, his brother John, and one other employee to bake and deliver bread each day. Jerry's family of four lived in a small apartment just above the bakery.

Jerry's business grew rapidly, both in the number of employees and the variety of breads produced. In 1927, the standard one-pound white flour loaf was called "Kew-Bee." Then there was Jerry's Rye, Jerry's Bran, Jerry's Whole Wheat, Jerry's Raisin, and, of course, Jerry's Irish Bread, a hearth bread with a shamrock on the wax paper wrapper.

All throughout the 1920s, commercial bakeries were trying to convince homemakers that bread taken off a conveyor belt could be just as fresh and flavorful as the home-baked loaves that women had traditionally labored over. Certainly, there were residents in Terre Haute for whom fresh baked bread had an overwhelming sensory appeal: its soft texture, the aroma filling the house, the way creamery butter would melt in those first moments after the bread was taken from the oven. Many households in Terre Haute also canned preserves and relishes created from backyard fruits and vegetables. The question for them was why anyone would even consider using cold store-bought bread for that first jar from the root cellar.

In 1927, there were plenty of bakeries willing to engage the argument. The Vigo Bread Company, local producers of Hoosier Maid bread, had hired Mrs. Florence Eakes, a graduate of the Home Economics Department at Columbia University to supervise a clubroom that the company made available to various women's groups. The clubroom featured a spotless kitchen where Florence would prepare sandwiches for her guests made with slices of Hoosier Maid.

Her implied message to the assembled gathering: This was less time better spent than all those hours required to bake bread at home.

The manager of the Vigo Bread Company, E. T. Norton, was more direct: "We believe there is no more reason for a housewife to be burdened with bread baking than there is for her to weave the cloth for clothing worn by her family."

Jerry Fitzgerald, who likely learned baking at his mother's side in County Kerry, was a little more measured in his message. His company slogan: "Jerry's Bread is as good as mother's and better than others." Either way, commercial bakeries were intent on converting an apparently stubborn minority. In the 1920s, one in four housewives were still baking bread at home.

In July of 1925, Jeremiah Fitzgerald joined with a partner to infuse his bakery business with more than $150,000 in capital. It was the immigrant's dream writ large: hard work bringing success. But even so, Jerry was both aware of the opportunity provided him and respectful of the struggle it involved. From the first ballot he cast, he voted in every election as a registered Democrat from the Third Ward. During Fourth of July parades through the downtown, Jerry would hand out tiny American flags to bystanders.

Jerry Fitzgerald Presented with a Birthday Cake
Martin Collection, Indiana Historical Society

Jerry's Bakery had always been a union shop. The business was prominently featured among advertisers in the annual Labor Day program. In 1912, when local miners went on strike, Jerry sent two wagonloads of bread every day to commissaries set up in West Terre Haute and Twelve Points.

His clear sympathies probably cost him as many customers as he ever gained, but perhaps that was the whole point. Jerry Fitzgerald simply wanted the town he lived in to get to know him better. He obviously worked very hard to make that happen, even for those who would never purchase a loaf of bread with his name on it.

Joseph Fivecoat—*boxmaker*, Wabash Fibre Box Company—r 34 S. 10½ St.

The Miami nation occupied settlements along the Wabash River before the arrival of the Europeans. Early French explorers described the tribe as mild-mannered and polite. Soon after the War of 1812, the Miami were scattered westward along with the neighboring Illinois tribes. Those that survived the forced trek eventually settled in the Oklahoma Territory.

A little over a century had passed since the Miami had last occupied the wilderness surrounding Terre Haute. Joseph Fivecoat's life in 1927 is a small measure of how much can possibly change in that amount of time. Joseph lived alone and spent his days indoors with a mechanized din as his constant companion. He would have been 17 years old.

One tiny consolation: The origin of the word "Wabash" is from the Miami word pronounced *oubach*. It means "white," a reference to the countless mollusks and limestone deposits found on the riverbed.

Lenora Fogg—*mappist*—r 1428 N. Center

Emigrated from England to the United States when she was 2, but apparently still preferred the British term for her chosen profession. Turns out she was right. It sounds a lot better than cartographer.

August Fokosski—County Poor Farm

(N) Fostoria Fortwendell—(spouse of Oscar—*highway patrolman*)—h 733 Harding

FOULKES BROS. (George C. and Harry J.)—Hatters, Haberdashers and Merchant Tailors—11 N. 6th—Phone: Wabash 44

In 1927, the first block of North 6th Street in downtown Terre Haute might have drawn comparison to Fifth Avenue in New York City or Savile Row in London. Many of the shops located there offered the elegant and the expensive to their customers.

J. M. Bigwood, a high-end jeweler at 20 North 6th, had been established in business for half a century. Among the finer things gently handled there: Doulton china and Gruen watches. Steiger's Fur Shop at 23 North 6th offered a broad assortment of slaughtered animals, some with their facial features still intact. These included sable, mink, and silver fox. Jacob, Saul, and Irving Steiger also provided customers an airless vault to protect their pelts from the ravages of creatures still alive and thriving.

At 22 North 6th, Miss Rose Schavloske offered stylish women's fashions at the Polly Ann Shop. Rose was living with her brother and sister at 2315 2nd Avenue. In 1927, sister Wilhelmina was working as a forewoman at the Miller Parrott Baking Company, proving that while the apple doesn't fall far from the tree, it may roll a bit once it hits the ground.

Harry and George Foulkes had been serving the well-dressed man since 1890. As hatters, they carried only the finest brands: Stetson and Knox. For late spring and summer, they introduced the Hopkins line of English and Italian straw hats.

Then when the weather turned, the Foulkes brothers stood ready with the finest cashmere topcoats, Harris tweed overcoats, and Ulsters, a loose-fitting coat made of heavy Celtic fabric. Like the Steigers' furs, these were outer garments made to squarely engage the natural elements by enlisting the aid of nature itself. It's just that these didn't involve stopping a beating heart.

Jennie France—County Poor Farm

Max Frank (Edith)—The Sole Saver, Expert Shoe Repair—Northwest corner of Cherry and 7th—Phone: Wabash 1995—h 1470 S. 10th—Phone: Wabash 2887

As his title implies, Max Frank was a man on a mission. Appropriate perhaps that he set up his shop just a few footsteps away from the Crossroads of America. The Sole Saver represented a particular choice of direction. An ad for the business in the *Saturday Spectator* featured an illustration of a boot with closed eyes and its tongue hanging out. The caption: "Don't let your shoes die in the prime of life."

Max would find a devoted response to his message from the people living in Terre Haute in 1927. (*See* Joseph Fischer.) In the absence of cars, they walked city blocks. In the absence of escalators, they walked up and down staircases. And in the absence of television and radio, they walked after dinner. Dispensing with fashion concerns for more practical ones, they employed galoshes and gumboots to protect their leather shoes. Eight businesses were formally listed in the Polk Directory as shoe shiners—a fraction of the actual total. Often, it was a job faithfully done by amateurs at home.

Max turned 64 in 1927. He would not live to see the next decade. You might say he got out just in time. For as we now know, far fewer people would be walking to work, to school, or to shop in the coming years. And if they were walking at all through the Crossroads of America, it was in the opposite direction from Max Frank and what he represented.

In 1927, shoes were made by a process called lockstitching, which firmly secured the insole and the welt to the shoe's upper. At the factory, the heel was then attached to the shoe in what was called the making room.

Max Frank had acquired the skill to basically replicate any of these steps, allowing a customer's shoe to be repaired and maintained over time. Increasingly, shoe repair shops have been prevented from doing this by the manufacturing process itself. Today, shoes are often hot-glued rather than stitched. Current designs frequently combine the heel and the insole. The end result is that shoes have come to join pens, razors, and small appliances in abandoning the possibility of any maintenance, leaving the user no other recourse but their premature disposal.

Eunice Frankes—County Poor Farm

Harry Fredericks (Cecile)—*shade maker*, Kleeman's Dry Goods Co.—h 323 S. 13th

These would be lampshades, not window shades. A lovely hand-painted landscape or floral design, enhanced by soft light passing through silk fabric.

Kleeman's also offered classes to the general public in making lampshades, fashioning paper flowers, and decorating pottery. Harry likely taught at least one of these. By displaying samples of his own work he probably created customers as often as he encouraged students.

Martha Ann Fritz—County Poor Farm

William C. Fuchs—*laborer*, Whistle Bottling Works—h 224 S. 17th

William C. Fuchs Jr.—*musician*—r 224 S. 17th

Considering the name of the employer, you might guess that music was a family tradition at the Fuchs household. And who knows? Maybe blowing into an empty bottle was exactly how Junior got started.

(N) Rodalia Fulwider (spouse of William—*blacksmith*)—h 1410 N. 6th

Emma Fyfe—County Poor Farm

James H. Gallian (Violet)—*detective*—h 2929 Schaal

The 1927 Polk Directory makes a clear distinction between city detectives in the Terre Haute Police Department (Guy Bowsher, Scott Delbert) and private gumshoes like James Gallian.

In the late 1920s, writers like Dashiell Hammett and James M. Cain began to create what would become the popular image of the private investigator: small upstairs office, slouch fedora, a bottle of whiskey stashed in the desk drawer. Terre Haute during the 1920s could have provided real inspiration for this genre, even if James Gallian himself didn't. The city was rife with illegal activity, most prominently gambling, prostitution, and bootleg whiskey. Perhaps even more enticing was the fact that so much of this activity operated openly with only selective enforcement from the police. When the authorities finally decided to take action, though, it often resulted in violence. Between 1922 and 1924, four of Terre Haute's finest were killed in the line of duty.

One of the most notable and notorious speakeasies in the area was a farmhouse out on Canal Road called George and Anne's. Sunday afternoons were devoted to cockfights in the barn. Occasionally, speakeasies would rely on music as a draw. A blues musician named Big Ione Williams sang and played barrelhouse piano into the wee hours in a blind tiger near Fort Harrison. Her signature song was a risqué version of what would eventually become a rock 'n roll classic, "Reelin and Rockin" ("Looked up at the clock and it was quarter to three . . ."). Big Ione apparently had a particular fondness for port wine, which frequently accompanied requests for songs and information.

(N) Fern Garden—*pianist*—Rex Theater—r 1720 N. 3rd

That's right, Harry Bennett's little endeavor on North 6th Street. A small movie theater is where Hoagy Carmichael's mother, Lida, did most of her playing in the 1920s as she accompanied silent films on piano down in Bloomington, Indiana.

A little closer to home was the Alhambra Theater at 1472 Locust Street, where Miss Ada Campbell, a colleague of Fern's, also improvised soundtracks for the silent features on piano. Ada Campbell was known around town as "the girl with the merry smile." She was talented enough to front her own ensemble, Ada Campbell's Wabash Serenaders. The orchestra featured the requisite female vocalist, but it wasn't Ada. She would stroll onto the stage after the band played an opening number, greeting the audience with her cheery trademark, "Oh, hello folks!"

On Sunday, February 27, 1927, after the last film at the Alhambra, Ada headed out to the Trianon, a popular dance hall on the 2700 block of Wabash Avenue. (*See* Dorothy Stuckwish.) She was riding in a brand new Ford Coupe driven by Max Rukes, who had recently moved to Montezuma, Indiana, to sell them. On their way back home, the car struck a trolley head on. Ada and Max both died from their injuries the following day.

Four vehicles were needed to transport all the flowers that were sent to the Campbell family residence. The floral arrangement from the Alhambra Theater contained fresh roses and lilies fashioned into the shape of a harp with one broken string.

Fern Garden was likely standing at the gravesite in Calvary Cemetery that week and then back playing at the Rex on Friday night. Her job required that she focus on the action up on the screen and synchronize her music accordingly. But maybe she stole a glance at her busy hands at some point during the evening. For now, there she was, still making music.

Emeline Gardner—County Poor Farm

Buck Gargas—*watchman*—r 423 N. 4th

Whatever he was watching, I'll bet the owner of it slept peacefully.

Ross S. Garver (Jennie L.)—*manager*—h 216 S. Adams

Ross Garver, if asked, just so happened to have a lovely Christmas story to share. It occurred back in 1919 when he was managing the Hippodrome Theater. The mid-level vaudevillians from the Keith and Orpheum circuits who performed there did not often spend holidays at home. For all practical purposes, family had become the other acts of their traveling troupe.

After the last performance of the last show on that Christmas night, a large banquet table was set up behind the closed curtain. In attendance, the actors and performers, the members of the Hippodrome pit orchestra, the stage hands, and the theater manager: 38 in all.

There was Dancing Davy from Chicago; the Murray Sisters from Wichita; Grant and Wallace, two saxophone players from San Francisco; and F. F. Stevens, the animal trainer and his son Stanley, who had come all the way from France to spend this Christmas in Terre Haute, Indiana. The Stevenses had decided to bring the third member of their act along for the celebration that night: a trained bear named Jim.

Earlier in the day, Katherine and Evangeline Murray had received a long-distance telephone call from Kansas. A Christmas present had arrived safely at the Deming Hotel, a beautiful silk kimono.

On the Hippodrome stage, the banquet table was spread with a magnificent feast: turkey and chicken, oyster dressing, potato salad, cranberry sauce, baked beans, olives, pickles, and celery, with ice cream and cake for dessert. Afterward, as everyone basked in the warm glow of a meal well-eaten, cigars and toasts made their way around the table. Not only was this the last Christmas of the decade, it was also the last Christmas before Prohibition went into effect. The out-of-town visitors were introduced to a local favorite: Champagne Velvet Beer. This included Jim the trained bear who, after downing a few bottles of CV, demonstrated why he had been billed as "The Shimmy King." Later on, enough chairs, enough people, and enough alcohol produced a few rounds of "Marching to Jerusalem," known to a more secular world as Musical Chairs.

The party finally broke up around 3:30 in the morning. The Murray Sisters returned to the Deming Hotel and eventually to Wichita. The Shimmy King returned to his cage, and Ross Garver locked up for the night. No gifts had been exchanged at the Christmas party that night, possibly because the story of that evening had sufficed for everyone.

Harry Gauger—*coatmaker*, Wm. C. Mitchell—r 1304 Wabash

In 1927, William Mitchell was listed as running a tailor shop at 921 Wabash Avenue. Coatmaker was a specialty within a specialty. Creating a three-piece men's suit from whole cloth involves a variety of skills. Maybe Bill handled the pants and he and Harry drew straws from the whisk broom for the vest.

Unless you're talking about a war uniform or a wedding gown, clothing of this vintage was seldom preserved for posterity. One small consolation for Harry was that his work was often displayed in open caskets, literally the last suit its owner ever wore.

Mrs. Harriet Gay—*Christian Science Practitioner*—216 N. 6th h do

Just to get our bearings here: In 1927, the Church of Christian Science was less than 50 years old. The philosophy of Christian Science bases physical healing on personal faith. The founder of the movement, Mary Baker Eddy, believed she had recovered from serious bodily injury by reading Matthew 9:1–8.

In 1927, there was a Christian Science Reading Room located on the third floor of the Citizens Trust Building in downtown Terre Haute. The Citizens Trust Building was the city's first skyscraper. From 1920 to 1921, the 12-story brick structure had been under construction at 19 South 6th Street, supplanting Pop's Lunch Room. Upon completion, the building would rise 140 feet from the ground.

The blueprints called for 80 offices, an observation roof that was open to the public, and two high-speed elevators. This last feature would prove particularly important to one Peter Holmes, described in news accounts of the day as "a colored man with but one eye." Peter was employed as a laborer on the upper floors of the building. One day in July 1921, he mistakenly stepped into an open elevator shaft just after the car had descended. For a few eternal moments, he was in freefall; then he miraculously landed feet first on the elevator's roof at about the 9th floor. He then rode the high-speed car all the way to the bottom. Peter's statement to the press that day: "Gentlemen, both of us was sure goin' some." A long trip, a quick prayer, and it would seem, a good place for the Christian Science Reading Room to locate.

(N) Gottliebe Geckler (widow of Gottlieb)—h 2121 S. 8th

OK, just like married couples who happen to be named Roberta and Robert or Patrick and Patricia. Sort of. Anyway, they both liked what they shared. Their son, working in Terre Haute at the time, was also named Gottlieb.

John Gibbs (Martha)—*medicine manufacturer*—604 S. 3rd h do

His place of business was listed as his home, so he was literally mixing something up in the basement. Not as far-fetched or illegal as it sounds, since in 1927 many so-called patent medicines contained purely natural ingredients based on traditional recipes.

The Sycamore Building
Martin Collection, Indiana
Historical Society

Elsewhere in the city, at North 16th Street at the Vandalia Railroad, the Bear Manufacturing Company was manufacturing a camphor-based remedy, a creamy salve called Jack Frost. Like whatever John Gibbs turned out, Jack Frost was advertised as good for what ailed you, including cold, whooping cough, sunburn, windburn, and insect bites. A jar at Gillis Drug Store downtown sold for 29 cents.

According to a Chamber of Commerce survey in 1927, Bear Manufacturing produced Jack Frost with a workforce of five employees. Working together at 604 South 3rd, John and Martha Gibbs were almost halfway there.

James Gibson—County Poor Farm

Lawrence Gladish—*chiropodist*—r 430 N. 14½

No office, so it's probable that he often traveled to see his clients. The various tools of a chiropodist's trade, like those for a piano tuner, could be easily carried in a small samples case. Often a necessity, since someone with a painful plantar wart can be encouraged to move about as easily as a baby grand.

Margaret B. Glick—*tailoress*—67 S. 15th h do

Sarah J. Glick—*tailoress*—67 S. 15th h do

Let's consider the job titles they chose for themselves. They certainly must have discussed it seriously at some point; and don't you wish you'd been there when they did. Had Margaret and Sarah been making and altering women's apparel, they would have likely opted for the title of seamstress or dressmaker, both of which were common designations for a female skilled with fabric and thread. Tailoress stands apart, proudly. It advertises to all a woman who's intent on making men's clothing.

In 1927, just measuring the inseam for a pair of men's pants while they were being worn was a leap of faith for a woman, even if she did consider herself a professional. The carpenter's adage of "measure twice, cut once" might not have proven either appropriate or practical. Just another reminder, as if Margaret or Sarah needed one, to get it right the first time.

Globe Realty Company (Samuel S. Gobin)—25½ S. 5th, Rms. 1–2

Again with the name. Presumably chosen by Samuel Gobin as a reflection of his aspirations; projecting how his enterprise would grow from its modest beginnings in two upstairs rooms on a side street in Terre Haute, Indiana.

When you think about it, Globe Realty Company turns out to be a perfect manifestation of that ageless realtor's mantra: location, location, location.

(N) Goldie Gooch (spouse of Emmett—*grocer*)—h 1840 N. 3rd

Minnie Gore—*dishwasher*—Sullivan Hotel r do

Both co-worker and co-occupant at the Sullivan with May Clark, so it's very likely they spoke on occasion. This might have included a final goodbye. The hotel's conversion to furnished rooms was about a year away.

Richard J. Grace (Grace M.)—*rug weaver*, 663½ Wabash—h 1423 S. 12th

For a moment, we'll overlook the obvious splendor of Grace's married name to relate Richard's story. He worked on a large hand loom in a small upstairs room located footsteps from the Crossroads of America at 7th and Wabash. Those footsteps, when he made them, would have been mindful ones since Richard Grace was blind.

He had developed quite a reputation around Terre Haute by 1927. The Women's Department Club scheduled a field trip to his upstairs studio and then proceeded on to the home of Walter Gregory, who did chair caning along the river. Mr. Gregory was also blind so apparently there was a theme here.

Richard Grace died in Terre Haute in September of 1948. By then, maybe he'd woven enough rugs to transcend his particular distinction. We can hope that somewhere someone might have simply marveled at his work without ever knowing it had been created by a person who was sightless.

Lydia Grafe—County Poor Farm

Frank M. Graham (Agnes W.)—*boatman*—h 1423 S. 3rd

Frank Graham was one of the last individuals in Terre Haute to have a business relationship with the Wabash River. The reasons to access the river and its resources were clearly starting to disappear by 1927. For years, individuals had harvested the tiny mussels that were found on the riverbed. The mother of pearl was purchased by a factory in Sullivan that manufactured dress and collar buttons. There were also numerous rustic houseboats floating on the river, mostly along the west bank at Taylorville. It was at best a marginal existence for families there. Lots of fish in the diet.

Then there were the excursion boats. This is where Frank came in. He operated a wooden passenger boat that ferried people of all ages to the picnic grounds north to a place near Montezuma, Indiana. The boat actually consisted of two vessels, the *Reliance* and the *Reliable*. The *Reliance* held the engine house and pushed the *Reliable* against the river current. On the return trip, the rudder did most of the work.

The 1920s witnessed an enormous transition for the excursion business on the Wabash. In the summer of 1926, two smaller passenger barges operating in Terre Haute, the *Defiance* and the *Rainbow,* were sold to a man from Merom, Indiana, for use during the popular Chautauqua there. Frank Graham's remaining competitor in Terre Haute, a Mr. Bert Brown, had sent two of his excursion boats to Vincennes. He replaced them with the *Sunshine 1* and the *Sunshine 2.* Each featured a Victor Victrola on board for the entertainment of passengers.

On this count at least, Frank Graham believed he had a decided advantage. When the *Reliable* and the *Reliance* left the dock at the foot of Ohio Street, the barge usually carried a small musical ensemble—generally a trio. The band would get some work in at the picnic grounds, but the musicians' true purpose came on those lazy summer nights floating downriver on the return trip.

Frank had strung the barge with colored lights and, though dancing was encouraged, one could simply stand on the starboard side and watch the sunset. The perfect time to do this, of course, was right after someone had made a request for "On the Banks of the Wabash."

Between the picnic grounds, the river, and the sunset, city residents experienced a healthy dose of nature. It might have seemed unthinkable for a conscious society to turn away from all of this. But the *Reliance,* the *Reliable,* the *Sunshine 1* and *Sunshine 2*—in fact, all barges navigating the Wabash—would soon reach the end of their voyage. The Army Corps of Engineers, which had regularly dredged the river to ensure adequate draft, would decide in 1930 to permanently discontinue this activity. From then on, only small boats would regularly ply the waters of the Wabash. Fewer boats and fewer people who did much more than glance at the river as they crossed over it in their cars.

Edward Gray (Mary B.)—*hide buyer*—h 1034 N. 9th

Yet another endeavor in Terre Haute that was directly connected to the cycles of nature. Native Americans had been making leather from wild deer for

centuries. They tanned the hides by pounding the animal's brain into the skins and then smoked the hides to create the soft, supple leather we've come to know as buckskin.

Most of Edward Gray's purchases involved animals that had been domesticated. The local farms that he had formed relationships with were a reliable source for horses, cows, calves, pigs, sheep, and even goats.

Unlike the furs sold at Steiger's on North 6th Street, these hides came from animals that were otherwise productive during their lives. The animals had not been raised or killed with the intention to harvest their hides.

But when they became available, there were practical uses found for every one of them. Although sheepskin had become simply a term for parchment diplomas, footballs were still actually made out of pigskin. And the covering of every baseball was white horsehide.

William Gray—County Poor Farm

GREAT NORTHERN HOTEL (Charles J. Dressler), Hot and Cold Water in Every Room, Opposite Big 4 Depot, 7th and Tippecanoe, Phone: Wabash 91

In half of the rooms at the Great Northern, this would have meant a small sink. The other half included a private bath and a toilet.

The Riverbarge *Reliable* with a Picnic Group
Martin Collection, Indiana Historical Society

Joseph Green—County Poor Farm

Cora Greggs—*stenographer*—r 1401 S. 11th

Sarah Greggs—*stenographer*, Milks Emulsion Co.—r 1401 S. 11th

John Robert Gregg wrote his manual of stenography in 1888, borrowing liberally from a system devised by one Isaac Pitman 50 years before. Due to his tireless promotion in the United States, Gregg's method became the standard for business and law transcription by the 1920s. It is almost certainly what the Greggs sisters used daily in their work.

All things considered, not enough of a coincidence to pass muster for Ripley's, but still . . .

Jack Griffith (Minnie)—*farmer*, Rose Orphan's [*sic*] Home

Nearly all of the daily operations on the farm at the Rose Orphan Home involved Jack's supervision of a workforce of young boys. Together, they successfully raised beets, tomatoes, corn, beans, lettuce, onion, peas, cucumbers, and radishes. Every morning, the boys milked cows in a barn located just west of the main building. All of the milk and vegetables they produced were consumed at the Rose Home. The longstanding policy at the Home required every child to drink three glasses of whole milk a day.

Evidently, it had a noticeable effect. It was reported in the *Saturday Spectator* that every boy who had been at the Rose Home for a year or more was 11 percent above the average weight for boys his age. No one expressed the slightest concern, however, that the boys were in danger of becoming overweight.

Lydia Grindell—County Poor Farm

Charles F. Grosjean (Ninetta)—*assistant superintendent*, City Schools—h 1929 N. 11th

Mary E. Grosjean—*teacher*, Wiley High School—h 1312 S. Center

Robert B. Grosjean—*student*—r 1929 N. 11th

Thomas H. Grosjean (Nellie L.)—*teacher*, Wiley High School—h 1312 S. Center

The commitment to education by the residents of Terre Haute, Indiana, in 1927 looks very impressive today. This community of a little over 60,000 people supported four public secondary schools (Wiley, Garfield, State High School, and Gertsmeyer Tech), three private secondary schools (St. Patrick's, St. Joseph's Academy, and King Classical), 25 public elementary schools, and six parish elementary schools. Thomas and Mary Grosjean were among the 457 teachers working in the Terre Haute school system.

In 1927, that system included two public elementary schools, Lincoln and Booker T. Washington, that were segregated by race. (*See* Geneva Carter.) It's also notable that in 1927 Catholic parents were required to send their children to their parish school. That said, these numbers reflect an extraordinary community support for childhood education at a time when only half of adolescent children continued to attend school.

Flora Gulick
Martin Collection, Indiana
Historical Society

The Grosjeans, like the Barrymores, the Kennedys, or the Andrettis, was a family that loomed large in their chosen field. Their particular and unheralded dedication was to the everyday education of children in the Terre Haute public school system. The devotion of this family and their community now shines particularly bright for a society that now struggles mightily to emulate it. Today, the clear majority of retiring public school teachers say that, were they to do it again, they would have chosen another profession.

Flora G. Gulick—*supervisor*, Flora Gulick Boys Club—r 421 Osborne

Flora Gulick began her extraordinary odyssey as an employee at the Terre Haute Post Office, working at the money order window. Every day, she would find herself making change for newsboys who hawked the daily headlines on downtown streets. Flora soon became a trusted and reliable adult for these boys, who ranged in age from 8 to 13.

Flora soon realized that the boys were not attending school. By gently asking questions over time, she came to discover that some of the boys were homeless as well. A few of the older ones had been sleeping outside in empty wooden barrels stored in alleyways. They were, as Flora would later describe them, boys that no one else wanted around.

From day to day, Flora responded the way any responsible adult would and addressed the immediate need. She would offer a piece of fruit, bind up a nasty cut or scrape, smile with sympathy or understanding. In January of 1908, she began to teach five of the boys to write the alphabet. Five months later, at a gathering attended by some of Terre Haute's most prominent business leaders, each of the boys wrote their names on a slate. Flora was soon able to solicit a promise of a dollar a month donation from 50 merchants. She then used the money to rent some upstairs rooms at 611½ Ohio Boulevard. Into these rooms, Flora moved a piano, eight drums, four bugles, some tools for manual training, and some used exercise equipment. For the boys she had in mind, books would have to wait until later. Flora then opened the doors. Within a year, the Flora Gulick Boys Club had more than 900 members.

Flora's charitable venture nearly went broke when a salaried superintendent from Boston was hired at the club. The years during World War I were also a challenge. Laws restricted solicitation from charities that were not directly related to the war effort and the Boys Club had to make do with a $25 monthly allotment from the city.

By 1925, the club had obtained a permanent home, a two-story clapboard house with a big wraparound porch. The mission of the club had never really changed; 220 North 3rd Street would be a place that boys that no one else wanted could feel safe, accepted, and hopeful about how the world was treating them. For many of the boys who came there, Flora Gulick's club was the only welcome home they had ever experienced and Flora the only adult they had ever really trusted.

Flora Gulick died on Wednesday, July 30, 1941, at age 79. By then, she had outlived her husband, Frank, and her two daughters. The only immediate family surviving at the time of her death was a son-in-law in Mississippi. Then there was her extended family. She had continued to teach Sunday school classes at the Boys Club up until her death, adding to the enormous number of young lives influenced by her presence. The boys that she began her journey with had since grown into adults, something that was not at all certain when she first entered their lives. A century later, the Terre Haute Boys Club still operates at 220 North 3rd Street in Terre Haute.

Joseph A. Haddox—*window cleaner*—h rear 534 S. 5th

A fertile yet frustrating market for his skills, considering the fact that the soot and smoke from bituminous coal would have made any window in Terre Haute, Indiana, dingy almost as soon as it was cleaned. In 1927, Joseph still probably relied on the popular standard for the task at hand: a bucket of hot water mixed with a half cup of vinegar. Old newspapers were used to dry the surface. No streaks, no lint.

A sobering thought for someone in the profession might have been the increasing height of some of those windows. The Terre Haute Trust Building, constructed at the southeast corner of Seventh and Wabash in 1911, was eight stories tall. The Citizens Trust Building on South 6th Street was four stories taller. (*See* Mrs. Harriet Gay.) Somebody had to clean those top-floor windows from the outside. No adjustable safety scaffolding as yet. Often, it was just sit on the sill with your feet dangling inside, maybe with a canvas strap attached to keep you upright. Oops! Missed that spot in the upper left corner there.

Charles P. Haley—*pin setter*—r 2004 Washington

The likely place for his employment would have been the Central Academy at 823 Wabash which featured 12 bowling alleys, with one or two lanes devoted to duck pins. In the absence of legalized bars and taverns, the Central Academy was a sanctioned gathering place for men. There were 18 billiard tables. Cigars, chewing gum, and baseball tickets were sold over the counter.

Ladies were only invited to bowl at the Academy. Charles would be there for each nervous frame, perched on the low wall behind the pins. Too noisy for him to offer any encouragement. They'd probably have stared right through him anyway.

Harry Hamby (Frances C.)—*reporter*, Terre Haute *Tribune*—h 1216 S. 25th

In the summer of 1926, Harry Hamby began a weekly series in the Terre Haute *Tribune* entitled "The Other Fellow's Shoes." Terre Haute was still a city whose residents depended on each other for the basics of everyday life: food, transportation, news and information, communication, and entertainment. Harry Hamby looked to strengthen the fabric of his hometown by increasing the shared sense of what each contribution involved. He gave these contributions a name and a face and in the process provided a perspective and comparison to other jobs, other lives. He outlined his purpose for the series in an early article:

> You see, I'm still in search of that other fellow's
> job, one that would be more of a snap than mine
> because I have been long convinced, and you have
> too, that we have about the worse jobs on the face
> of the universe and that if we only had "the other
> fellow's job" how happy we would be. But somehow,
> I haven't been able to find that right job yet.

And every week he would continue to try. In his first installment, Harry accompanied motorman John Snoddy on an interurban run from Terre Haute

Harry Hamby Interviews
Himself
Martin Collection, Indiana
Historical Society

to Indianapolis, a trip covering 74 miles in just over two hours. The following week, Harry joined mail carrier C. C. Thompson on his twice-daily routes along North 6th Street. The discoveries he made and shared in his articles reveal to us, as they revealed to readers back then, the enormous effort and skill required for everyday blue-collar jobs. For instance, how an interurban that was traveling between 40 and 60 miles an hour was constantly being endangered by automobiles whose drivers lacked both patience and perspective at rail crossings. Or how a mail carrier's daily load amounted to 150 pounds hauled over ten miles. In subsequent weeks, Harry Hamby would visit a coal miner, a milkman, a city police detective, and a telephone company lineman.

At the very least, this front-page recognition provided a means of introduction between strangers and a topic of conversation between friends; a down payment perhaps on that 15 minutes of fame that Andy Warhol later referred to. Harry Hamby might have realized that this type of recognition had far greater resonance inside a community where people spoke to each other face to face. Back then, that 15 minutes was like a nickel in your pocket: spending it closer to home meant it went a whole lot further.

Harry Hamersley—*salesman*—r 1135 Eagle

Harry C. Hamersley (Myrtle)—*salesman*—h 1250 Beech

Harry C. Hamersley (Lorraine)—*manager*—h 1441 Liberty

The Rose Orphan Home
Dining Room
Martin Collection, Indiana
Historical Society

In considering these three individuals with two occupations and one name, one might ask if Harry 1 and 2 sold the same product or, to make things even more confusing, two similar but competing products. Added to this is the possibility that Harry 3 had recently, and mercifully, been elevated from sales.

Cora J. Hamilton—*cook*—Rose Orphan Home

Cora was under an extraordinary amount of pressure, most all of it unspoken. Criticism or even suggestions from the dining room never reached her. Nevertheless, every meal that came from Cora's kitchen became comfort food for someone. For many of the residents at the Rose Home, it would have marked the first time in their young lives they had reliably received three meals a day. (*See* Anna Asher.) But among the rest, there would have been those who had left real home cooking behind; that is to say food prepared as an act of love with aromas that would forever conjure up a favorite meal or a soothing image. Some of the orphans might have remembered smelling fried eggs through the bedroom floor or home-baked rolls steaming on the dining room table.

A memory for at least a few of the children at the Rose Home: being drawn to a lighted kitchen after coming home from school, where a woman is facing the stove, stirring a pot. She turns as her child's footsteps cross the floor. And then, her smile.

Daniel Hamz—County Poor Farm

Fred J. Haneline (Lora)—*carnival road man*—h 308 Eagle

His occupation suggests he was either searching for something or running away from it. Apparently, he met up with whatever it was further down the road. In 1930, Fred J. Haneline was listed as an inmate at Leavenworth Federal Prison in Kansas.

(N) Minnie Hanker (widow, Henry)—h 93 S. 19th

Charles D. Hansel (Della)—*miller*—h 2401 N. 9th

One of the many jobs in Terre Haute attuned to nature and so in imminent danger of extinction by 1927.

Charles Hansel operated Markle Mill, a large stone mill on Otter Creek that had been operating since 1816. The mill ground harvested wheat and corn without the motorized assistance of whatever technologies had been developed in the interim. Two heavy limestone burrs, fed by the natural power of water and gravity, ground up the grain into flour, meal, and feed. Just a few ancient mechanical principles that a schoolchild could understand. The true complexity here was reserved for nature.

Charles Hansel had first leased the mill property in 1911. Even then, the future of milling had been apparent. By 1927, most mills were being driven by engines. That said, Markle Mill had been in continuous operation for over a century and the fuel that ran it was free. Charles proudly marketed his own wheat cereal: "Fresh from the Mill." The illustration of that mill on the package looked like an oil painting.

So the burrstones would continue to turn along with the cycle of sun and seasons, moving toward an inevitable resolution. On September 20, 1938, Markle Mill was ravaged by fire. It became just one more local example of nature receding as technology advanced. The oldest and largest mill in the area had been destroyed by fire and there was no serious consideration given to ever bringing it back into operation—even though that free fuel—the water in Otter Creek—was still flowing just fine.

Howard C. Harkness (Jessie)—*barber*, Woodsie D. Fuqua—h 714 N. 9th

You play on this team, pal, you better bring game. Howard Harkness was 40 years old in 1927; still a relative novice in his trade learning at the elbow of the master. Woodsie D. Fuqua's barber shop was located at 671 Tippecanoe, right next door to the Great Northern Hotel and right across from the Big Four

Railroad Terminal. This prime location guaranteed that a steady supply of rumors, jokes, and off-hand wisdom would be arriving at the shop every day. This in addition to whatever quips might emanate from a character named Woodsie D. Fuqua. As they say, the rich just get richer.

In the basement of the Great Northern Hotel, next to the huge mangles that pressed the hotel's linens, sat a room devoted to various card games. A thick cloud of smoke, a harsh lightbulb suspended from the ceiling, four tables covered with checkered oilcloth. Always enough hands and antes to keep the games going in perpetual motion, 24/7. The room was known informally as the Rathskeller.

The Rathskeller's location would have been quietly recommended to new customers apart from tips on the best lunch wagon or the most receptive neighborhood for a Bible salesman. You never delivered word of the Rathskeller or the nearest speakeasy to a full barbershop, even if it was likely that everyone there knew all about it. This type of knowledge and how to handle it discreetly would be among the first lessons Howard would have learned from the master. The best barbers can tell you: A pair of sharp ears beats a pair of sharp scissors anytime.

Frank Harper—*laborer*, Vigo Ice and Cold Storage Company—r Sullivan Hotel

From November to April, he was always cold.

Markle Mill
Community Archives, Vigo
County Public Library

Happy Harris (Sue)—*coal*—700 N. 3rd St. h do

This was a time and place that even gave interesting names to lumps of coal. Included among Mr. Harris's inventory: Jackson Hill and Old Glory. Dead serious about the name Happy, by the way. The listing in the 1927 Polk Directory carries no quotation marks.

(N) Anastasia Hart—*stenographer*—r 1444 Elm

James B. Harvell—*tamales*—h 2319 Spruce

James Harvell had originally come to Terre Haute from Middleton, Tennessee. His tamales were tasty, yet simple: spiced ground beef seasoned with peppers, wrapped in a dried corn husk. James was well known to Terre Haute residents in 1927 as the "Hot Tamale Man." Every evening at 9:00, one could find his small vending cart at the Crossroads of America, Seventh and Wabash. From there, James would roam north to Chestnut Street, where he'd go east one block to North 6th, and then south to Wabash to complete the circuit, bellowing his wares all the way. By the late 1920s, tamale vendors had actually become a common sight on America's streets. In 1931, a Hollywood film entitled *The Tamale Vendor* would be released. The director of that film: William Goodrich, a pseudonym for Roscoe "Fatty" Arbuckle. (*See* Will G. Hays.)

Mexican food in Terre Haute, Indiana, in 1927 was much like the Chinese food: popular and generic. Chop Suey and Egg Foo Yung were the staples at the King Lem Inn on the 700 block of Wabash Avenue. Just around the corner at 26 South 7th, within hailing distance of the "Hot Tamale Man," Archie Chambers had affixed his name to a small café that bore the slogan: "Good chili—That's all."

The alliteration offered by his name served Archie very well over the long run. Fifty years after his death in 1947, both the business and the man would be remembered as Chili Chambers.

(N) Clarence W. Hawhee (Grace H.)—*restaurant*—609 N. 4th h do

The Hawhees ran their modest operation in a residential area not far from the Vandalia railroad tracks. The only other competition on that block was a restaurant run by a man named Ordie Lewis. One might dream of a sign out front that read "The Hawhee Café," but this far from the downtown many retail businesses dispensed with signage altogether, since those businesses had no need for actual names. (*See* John Chervenko.) Being that Clarence and Grace lived and worked at 609, there was little reason to announce it to their customers, most of whom were also their neighbors. Look through the window. Check for smoke from the stovepipe. Yup, they're open.

This business approach would seem to invert the logic of using exposure to build market share in the face of direct competition. But it was like this: The decision to eat at Ordie's or the Hawhees' was often based on who greeted you by name when you sat down or which lunch was a shorter walk.

An old joke from the comic strip *Moon Mullins* seems appropriate here. An old fellow advises Moon on the available lodgings in his town: "Well, there's some that prefers the Railroad Hotel and some that prefers the Eureka House. But which ever one of the two you take, you'll lie awake all night wishin you'd went to the other."

Thomas Hayden—County Poor Farm

Will G. Hays (Margaret)—*Postmaster*—h 700 S. 17th—Phone: Wabash 3446

Ships passing in the night. Will Hays was a famous name throughout America in 1927. It was challenging enough for an average everyday individual to share that name. Add a few more similarities with your namesake and you might find yourself moving from coincidence to an outright curiosity.

Will G. Hays was the younger of the two by 12 years. At age 33, he became the postmaster of Terre Haute's Main Post Office downtown. As a member of the Zorah Shrine Temple, he soon had his name added to an elegant framed roster located in the lobby of the Shriners' new headquarters on North 7th Street. The building was completed in 1927 and included among its many features a 1,700-seat auditorium.

The second and more famous Will Hays was in a Masonic order at the same time, albeit a chapter located in Los Angeles. He also had strong Hoosier roots, having begun his life in nearby Sullivan, Indiana. Like his younger counterpart, Will H. Hays had ascended the ranks of leadership quickly. By age 39, he was National Chairman of the Republican Party. After Warren G. Harding's successful campaign for the White House in 1920, Will H. Hays was given the job of Postmaster General. He was only in the position for a year. His abrupt relocation to the West Coast was occasioned by a very attractive job offer: President of the Motion Picture Producers and Distributors of America.

The appointment garnered a lot of national attention. Like major league baseball two years before, the movie industry had found itself reeling from a succession of scandals. One February morning in 1922, film director William Desmond Taylor was found shot to death in his study. A few months earlier, popular comedy star Roscoe "Fatty" Arbuckle had been arrested in San Francisco following the death of a young actress at a hotel party he had hosted. In both cases, the press uncovered evidence of rampant drug and alcohol use. There was speculation in the Arbuckle case that Virginia Rappe had died from injuries suffered in a sexual assault.

The selection of Will H. Hays, like that of the new baseball commissioner Kenesaw Landis, was designed to reassure the public that the lost integrity of their two favorite pastimes would be swiftly restored. In 1927, Will H. Hays devised a long list of production standards that would later form the basis of censorship for most every commercial film exhibited in the United States. It subsequently became the responsibility of Will H. Hays to enforce this set of rules once it was made public in 1930. Mindful of the man's ultimate power over their films, studio heads began to refer to the rules as the Hays Code.

The various restrictions in the Code were broadly worded, which ultimately gave Will H. Hays a great deal of latitude with enforcing them. The Hays Code prohibited the onscreen portrayal of drug trafficking, the dynamiting of trains, and interracial marriage. Presenting sexual activity in film was expressly forbidden, as was the frequent outcome of that activity, childbirth. Nudity had been a constant in visual art for centuries, so Will H. Hays provided a brief explanation for enforcing an absolute ban. To wit: "The fact that a nude or semi-nude body may be beautiful does not make its use in the films moral." Such is the curse of the newborn baby.

Some might say that these standards simply reflected the pervasive attitudes of the time. Others contend that the Hays Code actually went a long way toward dictating them. In 1930, the U.S. population stood at about 123 million. The weekly sale of movie tickets was about three quarters of that. At any rate, it was a great deal of power for one man to have his name on and that does tend to make a fellow comfortable in his job. Will H. Hays held the post of president for the Motion Picture Producers and Distributors for 23 years.

As it turned out, the task of scrutinizing the public's behavior appealed to both men. Just before he was appointed Terre Haute's postmaster, Will G. Hays had held another position in town. He was the group chief of the Federal Prohibition Office, responsible for regulating the sale and consumption of alcohol in Terre Haute under the Volstead Act. Unlike his namesake, Will G. apparently proved capable of occasionally turning a blind eye.

(N) Saphronia Heady (spouse of Linus H.)—h 915 S. 10th

Dorothy Heath—County Poor Farm

Patrick F. Heavey (Bell)—*house manager*, Hippodrome Theater—h 425 S. 7th St., Apt. 4

The Hippodrome, at the corner of 8th and Ohio, was Terre Haute's premiere vaudeville theater in 1927. Designed by the famed theater architect John Eberson, the Hippodrome opened to great fanfare on the night of February 15, 1915. The governor of Indiana was in attendance. On stage, a magnificent hand-painted fire curtain depicted a Roman chariot race in the original Hippodrome.

Al Jolson would appear at the Hippodrome, singing live onstage instead of being viewed onscreen. Unlike the other vaudeville venues in Terre Haute, such as the Liberty, the Indiana, and the Grand, the Hippodrome had steadfastly resisted the trend of exhibiting movies in competition with its live presentations. The Hippodrome was purely a stage venue, accommodating everyone from magician Harry Blackstone to the Paul Whiteman Orchestra. Somewhere in between fell Jack Wyatt and his Scotch Lads and Lassies performing "Hoot Mon."

The natural acoustics of the Hippodrome produced a sound from the stage that was unamplified by microphones or speakers. The audience experienced the pure singing voice, the firm landing of an acrobat, the flapping wings of trained doves, the percussive click of tap dance. It would all be absorbed into the floorboards of the stage to resonate long after the curtain fell.

The hundreds of vaudeville acts that performed at the Hippodrome were engaged in what was called the "two-a-day." At the Hippodrome, this meant weekday performances at 2:30 and 8:15 of about ten minutes in duration. There was a great lore and language surrounding vaudeville life. This included a vast store of superstition that would accompany every sparse crown or uneven

performance. Seasoned vaudevillians would never count the total attendance in a small audience, or the numbers would surely follow them to the next venue. One would never cross in front of another vaudevillian who was about to go on stage. If that happened, the offending party was asked to immediately return to his or her dressing room and close the door. That would supposedly break the curse.

The Hippodrome

Patrick Heavey was probably aware of a few superstitions his fellow theater managers had cultivated over the years. For instance, it was thought that a box office should never allow someone to enter the theater on a complimentary pass before the first ticket had been sold. Like whistling in a dressing room, this would surely result in poor attendance. In 1927, Patrick was probably searching for some rituals that led to a full house instead. By then, vaudeville was clearly dying and the Hippodrome in Terre Haute was just two years from closing down. (*See* Ross S. Garver.)

HEBREW CEMETERY AT HIGHLAND LAWN

Sanborn maps from 1912 show it to be set apart on the cemetery's western edge.

Carl A. Heckelsburg (Anna)—*medicine manufacturer*—1227 S. 17th—h 1229½

Carl provided a pretty fair advertisement for the product, whatever it was. He was born in 1858 and lived to be 73. Anna made it to 84. Not too many of their contemporaries were able to claim that.

The 1920s would see some landmark discoveries in the field of medical research. In 1928, Alexander Fleming would discover a mold growing on a culture that inhibited the growth of some common germs. He named the germicide penicillin. At the same time, the use of unsynthesized natural remedies was declining steadily. Science was quickly replacing nature as the primary healer of human ailments.

The practitioners of natural medicine were dying off. The source of the knowledge they held was becoming more remote and inaccessible. In a few cases, the remedies had been gathered and written down, but increasingly the volumes had fallen out of print. By 1927, uncovering this timeless wisdom almost involved an expedition.

Middlebury, Indiana, was a day-long excursion from Terre Haute in the 1920s. In this small town of 600, located about ten miles from Goshen, there was a natural apothecary called the Herb and Root Medicine Company. What was on the shelves? Which remedies for what ailments? How did the proprietors assemble all their knowledge? Today, it is wisdom lost much like the volumes inside the ancient library in Alexandria. We are left to imagine what was there inside that small shop in Middlebury. It's amazing enough just to imagine what it must have smelled like when you walked through the door. (*See* John Gibbs.)

John Hellman—County Poor Farm

William Helmstettler—County Poor Farm

Noah Hendrickson (Kate)—*butcher*, Earl Harkness—h 220 Lockport Rd.

A butcher named Noah. Somebody at work probably had fun with that.

Gottfried Herman—County Poor Farm

Edgar P. Herrin (Abbey)—*musician*, American Theater—r 623 S. 7th

His instrument was the violin. Ran a side business in two upstairs rooms at 612 Ohio Street where he taught, repaired, and sold them.

In 1927, the Liberty, American, Hippodrome, and Grand Theaters in Terre Haute all still maintained house orchestras. The American at 817 Wabash was the smallest of these with a total capacity of 900. It was also the first of these venues to make the complete transition from vaudeville to showing movies exclusively. These were still silent pictures in 1927, so Edgar still had a steady gig.

Not to say it wasn't a hard work day. The American was an exclusive Paramount theater and had seven daily showings; the first at 12:30 in the afternoon, then every hour and a half until the last screening at 9:30. Even so, when sound pictures finally came to town the following year, it probably wasn't a relief for Edgar. Between the recorded music being played on phonographs, radios, and movies, and its increasing presence and popularity across America, Edgar might have wondered if he'd ever be paid to perform as a musician again. (*See* Diekhoff Music House.)

The addition of a movie soundtrack also resulted in a noticeable change in theater decorum. Observers reported that the viewing public went from being a vocal and expressive audience in silent movies to being a mostly silent one once sound had been added.

The A. Herz Department Store

Charles Herz—County Poor Farm

Milton E. Herz (Helen)—*President*, A. Herz—h E. Wabash Ave. RD E

Pauline H. Herz (widow, Adolph)—r 309 S. 6th

In 1927, these were the only three listings under the Herz name in Terre Haute. Milton E. Herz was the president of the A. Herz store, located at 646 Wabash. A. Herz was a Terre Haute tradition, the most elegant department store in town. The various store departments included Draperies, Rugs and Curtains, Jewelry and Silverware, Books, Art Needle Work, and Stationery. The Herz Tea Room drew in white-gloved ladies to lunch.

A. Herz had been founded by Milton's father, Adolph. When Adolph died in 1917, a number of stores in the downtown area closed in tribute. His widow, Pauline, was still residing at the family homestead in 1927. During the summer months, the family spent considerable time at the Herz Family retreat near Culver, Indiana.

The third listing here is for Charles, who was 83 years old in 1927 and apparently living his final years in supervised poverty.

(N) Rufus Higgenbotham (Emagean)—*boxmaker*, Wabash Fibre Box Company—h 2139 Tippecanoe

Rufus and Emagean Higgenbotham had a baby daughter in 1927. They chose to name her Mary, in case you're wondering.

Buford Hills (Mable)—*salesman*, Owsley's Apparel Shop—h 2715 Garfield

Chester Hills (Lulu)—*collector*, Owsley's Apparel Shop—h 1719 Liberty

Eugene Owsley's clothing store at 905 Wabash Avenue advertised itself as "out of the high rent district" or, put another way, "we're spending well within our means so you won't have to."

In-store charge accounts were not only accepted at Owsley's but actively solicited, which is where Buford came in. Chester would come in later after the payments had fallen due on the children's school clothes, or the groom's suit, or the dress that mother was buried in.

Chester was not your typical repo man, since literally giving him the shirt off your back was not an acceptable resolution to the incurred debt. Both Buford and Chester's money came from commissions, so to some degree they were working at cross-purposes. Buford would convince you to buy whatever you wanted, while Chester had to convince you to pay whatever you owed.

As owner, Eugene Owsley made out regardless. But just to be absolutely sure, he installed his daughter Doris as the store's bookkeeper.

Carl Hogue—*lather*—r 1446 8th Ave.

Charles E. Hogue (Maggie)—*lather*—h 1446 8th Ave.

Fredrick Hogue (Mary)—*lather*—h 2131 7th Ave.

Gilbert Hogue—*lather*—r 1463 Plum

Roy Hogue (Clara M.)—*lather*—h 1463 Plum

Well, I guess you'd call the Hogues for that. Hire them all at once and you'd have a houseful of walls set up in no time. The family legacy from three brothers and two sons can still be found all over Terre Haute. You'd just have to tear out a lot of cheap paneling and old plaster to get at it.

George G. Holloway (Leora)—*photographer*, 26½ S. 7th—h 206 Kent Ave.

There were actually two photographers sharing the upstairs studio at 26½ South 7th Street. The other was Hiroshi Nakamura, married to Mitsuko and living at 48 South 17th Street.

The two photographers lived within a few blocks of each other. It was a pretty long walk to work, but company would have made it go faster. Lying at the root of this partnership were all the photographs we've never seen. Certainly there were plenty of wedding and family portraits shot at the studio. But the soul would be shining through images taken on the off-hours: landscapes, loved ones—all informed by the rare experience of this Japanese American living in Terre Haute, Indiana, in 1927, and the rare experience of a white man who actually got to know him.

HOOSIER CAFÉ (James B. Nichols)—Good Steaks and Good Coffee, Private Booths, No Extra Charge, Sunday Dinner a Specialty, Open All the Time, 807 Wabash, Phone: Wabash 1597

You might imagine the 800 block of Wabash in 1927 to be a pretty active place on Saturday nights. what with the Central Academy—"A Gentleman's Place of Recreation," 9:30 movie screenings at the American Theater, half a dozen cigar stores, a couple of billiard parlors, and all the gambling going on upstairs on both sides of the street. Gambling was already flouting the law, so you can bet that much of what went on was fueled by bootleg alcohol. You can also rely on the fact the Hoosier Café would have been serving meals into the wee hours. Right around 3:00 AM, it probably resembled Edward Hopper's *Nighthawks at the Diner* when seen from across the street.

Sunday morning would have been an opportunity for everyone to recover; the porters sweeping up, the card dealers squinting at the sunlight. A man standing in front of a door was either locking up for the day or fumbling with his keys to open it.

The businesses essential to this gradual recovery would count the Sabbath as just another working day. The Hoosier Café would serve a Sunday dinner like Mama used to make before her boy went astray. One should always make the effort to be presentable, though, even for strangers. So the Metropolitan Bath Parlor in the basement of the Interurban Terminal Building opened promptly at 8:00 AM on Sundays. First, a hot springs bath to open up the pores and cleanse the liver. This would be followed by a fierce massage from Fred Standau. Then, a clean shirt, a splash of bay rum, and a shoeshine upstairs in the Terminal lobby.

Nothing like those Sunday morning rituals to convince you life ain't that bad and surely bound to get better.

Adolph O. Hornung (Rickey)—h 24 13½ St.

He had recently retired from the post office, having walked the same route for 32 years. Mr. Hornung covered the area north of town from 1st to 5th Street above the Big Four Railroad Bridge as far as 8th Avenue.

This was one of 40 designated mail routes operating in Terre Haute in 1927. The U.S. Post Office Department provided for two residential deliveries a day. Mail carriers left the main post office building downtown at 7:15 AM and 1:15 PM. (*See* Harry Hamby.) This meant that if you wished to invite someone in town to dinner on a Friday evening, you could mail a postcard on Wednesday with complete confidence that they would have ample time to respond by mail.

By 1927, telephone calls were already starting to change this custom. As with so many aspects of daily life, faster with less effort was being balanced against elegant and more personal with technology providing the weight that would forever tip the scales.

John Howard—*paperhanger*—H. Stuckwish and Co.—r 128 S. 5th

Even though he spent most of his work day in other people's homes, John could easily walk to his place of employment. H. Stuckwish and Company was prominently located on the corner of 5th and Ohio Streets downtown. Henry Stuckwish was the high-end wallpaper dealer in town, offering his customers both domestic and imported selections.

During the nineteenth century, wallpaper became popular in the home for practical as well as decorative reasons. Red and brown wallpaper tended to hide the soot emitted by coal heat and gas jet lighting. But by the 1920s, as steam heat and electric lights became the standard for newer homes, wallpaper sample books became more colorful and more festive. Often, the floral designs selected for patterns provided another gentle reminder of nature. This was at a time when many foyers and living rooms already featured vases of freshly cut flowers.

Tillman Howard—County Poor Farm

Frances Hughes—*reporter,* Terre Haute *Star*—r 521 S. 7th

In 1927, Frances Hughes was just beginning a career in journalism that would extend over the next half century. Very impressive that it would all be spent reporting on Terre Haute, Indiana. Almost as impressive as the fact that Frances accomplished it all as a single woman.

Frances Hughes wrote a style column on the inner pages of the *Star,* entitled "A Glimpse at the Fashions." She was only a couple of years beyond finishing school, having graduated in a class of seven from King Classical in 1924. The King Classical School, located on the southwest corner of 6th and Park Streets, had been founded in 1906 by Bertha Pratt King. The school provided co-ed elementary education, K–8. Its secondary school curriculum was exclusively for girls. Class sizes never exceeded the single digits.

As you might expect from the school's name, education and refinement went hand in hand. Seven years of Latin were required and French was taught to every child at every grade level every day. The French teacher, Mrs. Olga Peters, had been educated entirely in French schools.

King Classical was literally a schoolhouse. Bertha Pratt King lived in a modest apartment at 6th and Park and taught English classes in her sitting room. Having extended this invitation into her home, Miss King demanded the utmost in etiquette and decorum. Students were to stop and make way for any faculty member passing them on staircases and in hallways. Classes were instructed to stand until the teacher was seated.

The King Classical School was meant to be an exclusive experience, but Bertha Pratt King was determined that it not be a sheltered one. All of the girls in their final year were required to do settlement work somewhere in Terre Haute. Furthermore, a private invitation was to be extended once a month to an impoverished girl for a luncheon at the student's home.

With tuition at the school running to $100.00 annually, those homes were at least solidly middle class. Frances's parents ran a confectionary and luncheonette at 127 South 7th Street in the new Indiana Theater Building. Elegant

Miss Frances Hughes
Martin Collection, Indiana
Historical Society

candies from Bunty and Cynthia Sweets were arrayed in a lighted display case in the front of the store. The newspaper offices where Frances wrote her fashion column were located just a block away. Frances would be celebrating her 20th birthday in 1927. All this, and fine chocolate, too.

Frances's father, Harry, died in 1928. The luncheonette closed immediately and as the only child, Frances became the sole support for her mother, Mary. She would continue to provide that support until Mary's death 34 years later.

It is impossible for anyone besides Frances Hughes to know how she truly felt about her unexpected role in life or just how her long career in journalism factored into it. In the end, her own longevity at least afforded her some time to come to terms with it. Frances Hughes would publish her writing over a span of nine consecutive decades. And like any writer who's seen far more than they'll ever put into words, Frances Hughes was talking about finishing her next piece when she died at age 95.

I

(N) Josephine Ice (spouse of John A.—*carpenter*, Commercial Solvents Corp.)—h 1516 S. 18th

INDIANA THEATER—southwest corner of 7th and Ohio

The Indiana Theater turned out to be the last commercial theater built in the twentieth century in downtown Terre Haute. Both its construction features and the date of its completion reveal a great deal about where the city was in the 1920s, especially how it imagined itself moving into the future.

The Indiana was one of many grand movie palaces constructed in American cities during the twenties. The scale and design of these showcase theaters were meant to impress. Spacious lobbies with sweeping staircases led up to the balcony, lit by ornate crystal chandeliers. The films exhibited were still all silent, so it was necessary to provide live musical accompaniment. House orchestras were an ongoing expense. To avoid this, many of the theaters relied on huge pipe organs whose multiple keyboards could mimic the presence of an orchestra. The organ for the Fisher Theater in Detroit was constructed by the Wurlitzer Company at a cost of $80,000.

It was deemed essential that the daily attendance in these theaters match the enormous investment. The Lowe's Paradise in the Bronx was able to accommodate 4,000 moviegoers; the Fox in downtown Detroit almost 5,000. With the breathtaking splendor that surrounded them, patrons were transported to another reality long before the lights went down.

The Indiana Theater was constructed in 1921. The developer, Theodore Barhydt, was familiar with the Terre Haute vaudeville circuit. He had initially arrived in the city from Illinois to manage the Grand Opera House on North 7th Street. Subsequently, he had promoted live performance in three other venues downtown, all the while conscious of the quick ascension of movies as an entertainment medium.

Theodore's Barhydt's stated intention was to offer "more than a theater, more than a picture show, more than a great orchestra, more than a building of architectural beauty and comfort." The designer for this dream would be John Eberson, whose theaters literally spanned the globe, from the magnificent El Robie in Mexico City to the Rex Theater in Paris. Six years before, he had designed the Hippodrome in Terre Haute, which stood just one block east of the proposed site for the new theater.

On the night of January 27, 1922, Theodore Barhydt held a sneak preview in the new Indiana Theater for 1,000 invited guests. It was an extraordinary event. Like many other movie palaces, the décor of the Indiana Theater followed an exotic theme. The motif at the Fisher Theater in Detroit had been Mayan, the exterior of its mighty Wurlitzer made to resemble a pre-Columbian temple. For the Indiana Theater, John Eberson turned to the Moors of Spain for inspiration. Tall windows in the outer lobby flooded the space with dazzling natural light, reminiscent of the bright Andalusian sun. The design for the main ceiling was borrowed from a Moorish blanket pattern. The lobby floors were laid in mosaic tile. At the landing of the balcony staircase, John Eberson placed an exquisite marble fountain. Each of the 2,000 seats in the theater and promenade lobby was upholstered in genuine Spanish leather.

The premiere featured a 30-piece symphonic orchestra although subsequent film screenings would be accompanied by a Hope-Jones Wurlitzer organ with 13 ranks of pipes.

The Stag Hotel

On the night of the preview, waiters and valets were dressed as toreadors, the female ushers in the lacy dress of the senorita. Standing on a pedestal in the outer lobby was yet another senorita holding an ornate fan; a living statue who posed throughout the evening for curious onlookers. Also welcoming arrivals that night was a 14-foot peacock. Constructing the Indiana had been a huge undertaking: more than a million and a half bricks, more than 200 tons of steel. But perhaps most astonishing were the 3,000 lightbulbs used to illuminate the enormous peacock hanging outside the theater. Its brilliance at night almost substituted for the Andalusian sunshine.

But as Theodore Barhydt would soon learn, there is no substitute for good luck. The 14-foot peacock was the corporate symbol for Paramount Pictures, who had agreed to be the exclusive source for the feature films shown at the Indiana. At the preview, Theodore Barhydt had even arranged to rent live peacocks to roam the lobby. In doing so, he chose to ignore a long-standing vaudeville superstition regarding the presence of a peacock in a theater, convinced perhaps that the undeniable power of this new entertainment medium, not to mention a theater costing three quarters of a million dollars, could overcome mere folklore.

Folklore or not, these things are known for sure. The following year, Theodore Barhydt's venture with Paramount Pictures abruptly ended and the Indiana Theater closed. The 14-foot peacock, with its 3,000 lightbulbs, was quietly removed before the theater re-opened under new management.

INDOIS HOTEL—Samuel M. Young, *proprietor*—204 Wabash

These days, any blending of Illinois and Indiana is generally referred to as "Illiana." The word "Indois" has a more exotic air to it. This might have been why Samuel Young considered the name a refinement over the hotel's previous incarnation as the Stag. Samuel Young was apparently a man who appreciated words. He was a playwright in his spare time.

Though no photographs of the original lobby survive, you'd have to think a mounted eight-point buck on the wall was part of the décor. There were 80 rooms available at the Indois. The hotel took tiny ads in the back pages of the newspaper advertising good rates.

Oddly enough, the one thing that did survive into the twenty-first century was the hotel's barber shop. After urban renewal decimated the entire 200 block of Wabash in 1969, the hotel's barbers set up in a small building at 317 Locust Avenue. The shop was down to one chair by the year 2000; a framed postcard of the old hotel and a selection of cheap toupees serving as acknowledgments of a long-lost past.

Abe Issac, The Tailor, Cleaning, Pressing and Repairing, Ladies' and Gents' Garments, Uncalled for and Used Clothes for Sale, 801 N. 13th, Phone: Wabash 8084-L, h do

The difference from a thrift store would be that Abe had a story for every piece of clothing he sold.

Mary Jackman—County Poor Farm

Guy G. Jackson—*meats*—101 N. 4th and stands 7–8 City Market—h 101½ N. 4th

J

In 1906, Upton Sinclair wrote *The Jungle,* an expose of unsanitary conditions in the Chicago meat-packing industry. The resulting public outcry led to the speedy passage of the Pure Food and Drug Act, which provided for routine federal inspections of meat slaughtered and sold commercially. At the time, Americans per capita were eating in excess of 70 pounds of beef annually.

The culture of meat eating in America in the early part of the twentieth century was very different from today. This was especially true in Terre Haute, a city that stood close to nature. Like fruits, vegetables, and dairy products, much of the meat being consumed in Terre Haute originated on area farms. In addition, many rural residents hunted for game, which made greasier meats like venison and opossum commercially available in the city. For the uninitiated, all it took was a tasty recipe and a kept secret to make the meat of these animals palatable.

The daily consumption of beef, pork, and lamb in the 1920s extended beyond actual cuts of meat to what was known collectively as variety meats, or basically whatever animal organs could be retrieved by a butcher's knife. This effort by local butchers like Guy Jackson met the frequent requests for brains, tongue, the second stomach (known as tripe), and even the thymus glands (more delicately referred to as sweetbreads).

Guy Jackson was conversant with every bit of it and obviously proud that both the animals and their slaughtering were local. The slogan at Guy Jackson's meat market was "Home-killed Meats," followed by the assurance that daily operations on the corner of 4th and Cherry Streets were completely sanitary. Every week, customer demand at Guy Jackson's required the slaughtering of 50 cattle, 40 to 50 calves, and 80 to 100 hogs. Apparently, this was not quite enough spilled blood for the owner. Guy Jackson was a front-row regular for the local prize fights held at the Knights of Columbus. (*See* Clarence Bose.)

The result of all this feverish activity was a wide assortment of cuts: pork, lamb, mutton, and veal chops, mutton and veal roasts, sugar-cured bacon and ham. Most every beef cut was available, from boiling beef and pot roast to pinbone sirloin and porterhouse steaks. And if lard could possibly be described as pure, Guy Jackson sold it to customers by the 5-lb. pail.

By the mid-1920s, Upton Sinclair had focused on another perceived danger from America's processors: canned food, which he described as being "denatured." He was hoping to be half as persuasive as he had been 20 years earlier. Though it's difficult to know how many Americans swore off eating meat forever after reading *The Jungle,* the average consumption of beef during that time had fallen off by about a quarter.

You might assume the two positions would have produced sworn enemies, but like Upton Sinclair, Guy Jackson was eager to let folks know how he stood right up front; which for him meant right out in front of his store. When customers entered Guy Jackson's establishment on North 4th Street, they were confronted by two stag heads mounted on the wall above the meat counter.

Perhaps here, the two crusaders might have shaken hands across the table. In his own way, each of them was saying: Let's be very clear about where this food came from and how it got here. Simply put, it was an effort to achieve the same feeling before you began to eat as you hopefully had before you dropped off to sleep at night: no apologies, no regrets.

Harriet Jackson—County Poor Farm

George Jacob (Lenna)—*teacher of violin*—207–209–211 Rea Building, Phone: Wabash 2180—r 202 S. 8th

He had originally come to America from Germany in 1908. When he descended the gangplank of the H.M.S. *Finland,* he was likely carrying a violin. George was already accomplished enough on his instrument to tackle a piece like "May Breezes," arranged by the virtuoso Fritz Kreisler larghetto. But upon reaching Terre Haute and assuming the position of manager at the Grand Opera House, George Jacob began to imagine other pieces being played by other musicians.

He decided to present an annual series of classical performances at the Grand featuring the finest artists and orchestras of the time. It was a decision that involved a great deal of risk. The Grand was a 1,500-seat venue in a town that was, by and large, unfamiliar with classical music. George Jacob's intention was to change all that.

On October 18, 1920, George Jacob brought John Phillip Sousa and his band to town for two shows at the Grand. Matinee tickets could be purchased for 50 cents. The highest-priced evening ticket was $2.00. John Phillip Sousa was enormously popular as both a composer and conductor. It was hoped this performance would build a bridge to the concerts that would follow.

The first All Star Artists Course premiered on December 15, 1920, with Anna Pavlova and her Russian Dancers. For most stage performers at the time, touring the American Midwest involved stops at the three largest cities in the region: Chicago, Detroit, and St. Louis. George Jacob quickly realized that Terre Haute, Indiana, was almost equidistant from Chicago and St. Louis: roughly 170 track miles. Terre Haute, it seemed, would be a logical stopover.

In 1920, Anna Pavlova was acknowledged as the greatest ballerina of her generation. So inspiring were her graceful movements that composer Michel Fokine wrote "The Swan" expressly for her. Since 1907, Anna Pavlova had been appearing to great acclaim in all the capitals of Europe. She was 39 years old that December, but the beauty of her artistry was treasured as timeless by individuals who knew and appreciated classical performance. It became George Jacob's job to find enough of those individuals in Terre Haute, Indiana.

And oh, how he tried. The following month, a personal dream was realized when Fritz Kreisler appeared on stage at the Grand. He was followed by Ernestine Schumann-Heink, the famous contralto, who presented a program of lieder, German art songs. Early the following year, a performance by the Cincinnati Symphony Orchestra ushered in an ambitious schedule. The young Russian violinist Jascha Heifitz would appear a month later. In October, Mischa Elman gave a recital at the Grand just a few months before becoming an American citizen.

GEORGE JACOB

Presents

The Second All Star Artist Course

(1922-23)

——OF——

TERRE HAUTE, IND.

GRAND OPERA HOUSE

At 8:15

Thursday, October 26, 1922
MISCHA ELMAN
The Violinist

Thursday, November 2, 1922
FRANCES ALDA
The Soprano

Tuesday, December 12, 1922
SERGIUS RACHMANINOFF
The Pianist

Thursday, January 11, 1923
ALBERTO SALVI
The Harpist
And Assisting Artist

Monday, February 5, 1923
PABLO CASALS
The Cellist

Tuesday, February 20, 1923
JOHN McCORMACK
The Tenor

Thursday, March 15, 1923
THE CLEVELAND SYMPHONY ORCHESTRA

A Program for the
Artist Series at the
Grand Opera House
Archives of the Vigo
County Historical Society,
Terre Haute, Indiana

Then on December 12, 1922, George Jacob brought the legendary Sergei Rachmaninoff to Terre Haute, Indiana. It was a Tuesday night. The Grand Opera House had been described the year before as being "out of date in seating and decorations" to the point where "everything about the place is in bad taste." So on to the stage strode this very tall man; the great Rachmaninoff, internationally acclaimed composer and pianist. He bowed stiffly to the audience, sat down at the piano, and instantly the shabby theater in downtown Terre Haute was transformed.

A few weeks later, on a Monday night in February 1923, Pablo Casals played his cello in recital. Later that same month, John McCormack, the greatest Irish tenor of all time, sang to the furthest seat in the Grand without the aid of a microphone. Then in March, a concert by the legendary Cleveland Symphony Orchestra concluded the season.

For all practical purposes, that performance would conclude the artist series as well. In 1924, George Jacob announced that the combination of high performance fees and inconsistent ticket sales had forced him to suspend the Artists Course indefinitely. But apparently, George weighed the money he lost against the joy he'd experienced and decided to try yet again. Later that year, Anna Pavlova returned to the Grand Opera House. She arrived in Terre Haute with a full orchestra to perform two ballets: "The Magic Flute" and "Amarilla."

In 1925, Fritz Kreisler also returned to the Grand Opera House. Soon after, George Jacob would leave his position at the newly renamed Grand Theater with stories for his students and fresh inspiration for his musical duets with Lenna, a gifted pianist. One can imagine George standing in the wings that night during Fritz Kreisler's final selection, anticipating the motion that would draw the bow across the violin to rest at his side. That one last note, a flash of light on the horizon just after the sun has set.

Elsie Jared—baths @ 9 N. 14th, Room 5—r 2406 Arleth

Providing a service we now expect to find in every American home. There were many personal indicators of poverty in place in 1927: frayed clothing, missing teeth, and excessive body odor among them. If you lived in a cold-water flat, as many adults did in Terre Haute, you might come to see Elsie once or twice a week. Gender preference might dictate a trip instead to visit Charles Taylor on Ohio Street.

These were not the mineral baths of the Ferguson Sanitarium or the Sulfur Vapor Bath Institute on the 1300 block of Wabash. This involved a porcelain or metal tub, a used bar of soap, and a fresh towel. Considering the Wabash River water that filled the tub and the likely condition of the clothes hung on the wall hook, that towel might have been the only clean thing some customers would feel against their skin all week.

Thomas (Lilly) Jeffers—h foot of Cherry

The answer to the Tilatha East mystery found here. Surely, one of them could have pointed to her home.

Charles Jensen—*umpire*—r 2150 Crawford

His seasonal employment was courtesy of the Three I League, a Class B minor league whose seven teams included the Terre Haute Tots. In 1927, umpiring baseball was a day job. The first official night game in the major leagues would not occur for another eight years.

Over the course of their season, the Tots played 63 games at home. Home in this case was Memorial Stadium, a 16,000-seat venue that had been constructed only two years before. Memorial Stadium had been designed as a multi-use facility. Accordingly, one of the first major events scheduled there had nothing to do with baseball or even sports.

On May 16, 1925, in an effort to raise money for the construction of their new temple on North 7th Street, the Zorah Shrine announced what can only be described as an exotic extravaganza. Over the course of three days during the upcoming July 4th weekend, Memorial Stadium would be transformed into a scene from pre-colonial India. Sixty-foot-high hand-painted murals suspended across the outfield depicted the ancient city of Delhi. The pageant was simply entitled "India." The show, produced by a fireworks exhibitor from Chicago, carried a cast of 400, although with the exception of a large herd of elephants, few of the participants had ever actually set foot in their advertised country of origin.

After a half-hour of entertainment by the Zorah Shrine's brass band, the spectacle opened with a brilliant lighting display set against the scenic backdrops: an attempt to portray the city of Delhi at dawn. This was followed by a re-enactment of various religious rituals, among them the ancient Hindu practice of suttee, when a widow casts herself upon the flaming funeral pyre of her husband. Soon after, three of the Indian elephants, "Mary," "Wilma," and "Sidnie," were selected to perform intricate steps and stunts. This opened up a circus segment familiar to most of those in attendance. Billy Hill and his trained pony, Frisco, convinced many in the crowd that Frisco could really count and distinguish colors on command. The Fisher Sisters, known professionally as "The Human Butterflies," performed in midair while hanging by their teeth. Then, the Flying Valentinos and the Rebras Duo executed a thrilling aerial ballet on the trapeze.

Besides Mary, Wilma, and Sidnie, the only indigenous act on the bill was the Hadji Troupe of Tumbling Arabs. The troupe performed their amazing flips and balances without the aid of props, finishing their performance with a spectacular feat: two of the members held up the remaining ten in an inverted pyramid.

Then it was on to the show's spectacular finale, an explosives and fireworks display featuring a re-enactment of the battle for Delhi in September 1803 when British colonial forces captured the city. This segued into an enormous fireworks display that culminated in a huge American flag twinkling in the sky.

Tickets to the India pageant had been set at $1.00 for general admission and $1.50 for the stadium's box seats. The officers at the Zorah Shrine had already paid out $7,500 to cover the cost of the elephant herd, Billy Hill's dog-and-pony show, and the installation of 30,000 square feet of painted scenery. Beyond the fervent prayers for clear skies in the days leading up to the event, there was a growing feeling of anxiety over the expected attendance. Just a week before, at the formal dedication of Memorial Stadium, a baseball game between the Tots and the Peoria Tractors had attracted about 9,000 people. An optimist might say the stadium was half full.

The public's response to "India" was impressive, if not particularly lucrative. After an opening night crowd of 5,000, attendance over the two following nights dwindled. The Shriners counted 1,200 cars parked outside the stadium; their occupants were content to enjoy the fireworks without paying admission. The following week it was announced that the venture had broken even. In the end, the risk was seen by the Zorah Shrine as more of a close shave than a first step.

Actually, Memorial Stadium had been struggling with public expectation from its inception. The initial plans for the old four-cornered harness track at Brown and Wabash called for an enormous indoor coliseum to be built in front of the stadium. The proposed coliseum would be constructed of Bedford, Indiana, limestone. It would include a 6,000-seat auditorium, a ballroom large enough to accommodate 700, and a meeting room for 500. The blueprints commissioned by the American Legion, the Chamber of Commerce, and the Merchant's Association provided for the Legion's headquarters, as well as offices for the county extension agent and the humane officer. This last proposal was designed to entice the Vigo County Commissioners into approving a bond issue for the project. Ultimately, they didn't, so the $5,000 cost of the initial design was borne entirely by the sponsors.

The early designs for Memorial Stadium also reflected an expansive vision of the city's future. Along with its 16,000-seat capacity, which was after all a quarter of the city's population, local architects Shourds and Stoner had proposed a towering array of water fountains positioned just beyond the center-field fence. The positioning of the center-field fence was quite extraordinary in itself. It sat 546 feet from home plate. In the entire history of major league baseball, no home run has ever been hit that far. And the teams that would be playing baseball in Memorial Stadium were a long way from the major leagues.

But one day in 1926, the Terre Haute Tots would actually get within hailing distance of the bigs. On Wednesday, April 26, the St. Louis Cardinals, en route to Pittsburgh to play the Pirates the next day, arrived in Terre Haute at 12:45 in the afternoon. An arrangement had been made for an exhibition game with the Tots to be played in Memorial Stadium at 3:00. The Cardinals would then return to Union Station, sleep on the overnight train, and arrive at Forbes Field in Pittsburgh fresh and ready to play.

That at least was how the team owner Sam Breadon envisioned it. The players, led by veteran second baseman Rogers Hornsby, may have had a slightly different perspective on the day's activities. But this Cardinal team had just been shut out at home by the Chicago Cubs the day before. Whatever resentment they might have had about their employer or the working conditions he imposed, they were not about to let a bunch of Class B minor leaguers extend their losing streak.

In the other dugout, the Tots clearly saw this as their opportunity to shine. Early on, they kept the game close. The game was tied 2–2 after three innings. The Cardinals slowly extended their lead in the middle innings and as the shadows began to lengthen across Memorial Stadium, the Cardinal players began thinking about a nice steak in the club car. They had a big lead—just one more inning to play.

It became apparent to some observers, including a local reporter for the *Star,* that the major leaguers were not bearing down. Suddenly, in their final at-bat, the Tots came alive. Three doubles, two singles, four runs scored, and suddenly the tying run stood on second base.

This would be the climax to the story when former Tots like Paul Wolf and Roy Witcraft would later relate the events of that fine spring day. To put it all in context, the St. Louis Cardinals had fielded a team that included two future Hall-of-Famers: Rogers Hornsby and Jim Bottomley. Later that year, these very same St. Louis Cardinals would win the World Series against the legendary New York Yankees of Babe Ruth and Lou Gehrig. So for a moment, let's just hold that memory there and admire it. This all happened one day in April 1926

Terre Haute Tots Team
Archives of the Vigo
County Historical Society,
Terre Haute, Indiana

in Terre Haute, Indiana. The game itself lasted a total of 3 hours and 16 minutes but it resonated over many lifetimes. The fact that the pitch-hitter for the Tots struck out to end the game is little more than a footnote.

The box score in the Terre Haute *Star* the next day indicates that one umpire called the entire game. Charles Jensen is the only professional umpire listed in the Polk Directory. So it's very likely that particular Wednesday in April became his memory too.

(N) Pansy Jewell—*dipper*, Columbian Stamping and Enameling Co.—r 615 8th

A. Jackson Jewett—(A.J. Jewett Printing Company)—r 934 N. 5th

Charles T. Jewett (Grace)—*newspaper reporter*—h 934 N. 5th

Publications known as "Tijuana Bibles" were a curious form of expression that had become very popular, or at least very saleable, in the early 1920s. They involved re-drawing popular characters from the comic pages and putting them in lewd situations. The illustrations were then printed in limited editions and sold surreptitiously. It's not entirely clear whether this form was chosen because it was funnier or more innocent or less explicit than actual pornography. But like pornography, possessing or manufacturing the material was certainly considered illegal.

In the summer of 1926, Charles Timothy Jewett and his son Jackson Jewett were arrested in Terre Haute on charges of "printing vulgar pamphlets based on national comic strips." Their distributor in town was one Stanley B. Watt, who owned a drugstore at 660 North 6th Street and lived at 827 North 5th, a block away from the Jewetts. Stanley was the distributor in the sense that the vulgar pamphlets were kept in brown paper wrappers under his drugstore counter or in the back room.

Ultimately, the offending material was discovered in a high school locker and arrests were made. There was a second Jewett son who may have formed a missing piece to the puzzle even though he wasn't included in the original arrest warrants. Charles M. Jewett was also living at 934 North 5th Street in 1927. His occupation was listed as a commercial artist. Maybe he claimed the drawings were artistic.

James John—County Poor Farm

Julia Johnson—County Poor Farm

Paul D. Johnson (Lillian F.)—*musician*, American Theater—h 1534 1st Ave.

Actually, Paul was the director of the American Theater Band in 1927. He was in his mid-30s and had been a professional musician in Terre Haute for more than ten years. It's unknown whether Paul and Lillian actually attended the premiere of *The Jazz Singer* at the Grand the following February. It was an opportunity to see Al Jolson projected on a screen and making music for a theater audience, just like Paul.

Throughout the early 1900s, the performances of visual vaudeville acts like jugglers, dancers, contortionists, strongmen, and trained animals were filmed by major studios. The images were often kept out of circulation, as if they were blackmail photographs. After all, once the studios had a good take of these acts in the can, they could always threaten to exhibit them at the very theaters that continued to present vaudeville acts between movie features. Once film soundtracks arrived in 1927, the studios performed a similar disservice for comedians and musical acts.

Herbert Jones—*stage hand*—r 2102 Locust

This was a union job in 1927. The local chapter of the International Alliance of Theatrical Stage Employees had been founded on Christmas Day, 1897. The original chapter had 12 members.

A stage hand's job is comprised of actions taken at very specific, prearranged times during a performance or production. No surprise then that the union local met at the Knights of Pythias Hall on the first Tuesday following the first Sunday of every month.

Lydia Jones—*waitress*, Sullivan Hotel—r 202 S. 4th

Apparently, May Clark had a roommate.

William R. Joyce (Esther)—*musician*—h 2110 S. 7th

That old joke about the three best reasons to become a schoolteacher (June, July, and August) also applied to vaudeville in the 1920s. Except in the largest cities, the indoor performance season ended in early June as windowless, unventilated venues suspended operations in face of the summer heat and the competition from the outdoors. Not surprisingly, theaters were among the first commercial buildings to be air-conditioned in the early 1930s; just around the time vaudeville died.

Billy Joyce was a drummer with the Hippodrome Orchestra. With the theater's closing in the first week of June, Billy announced his plans to head off to either Cuba or Canada for three months. The orchestra played "Auld Lang Syne" after the final show. A cymbal crash at the end, and then he was gone.

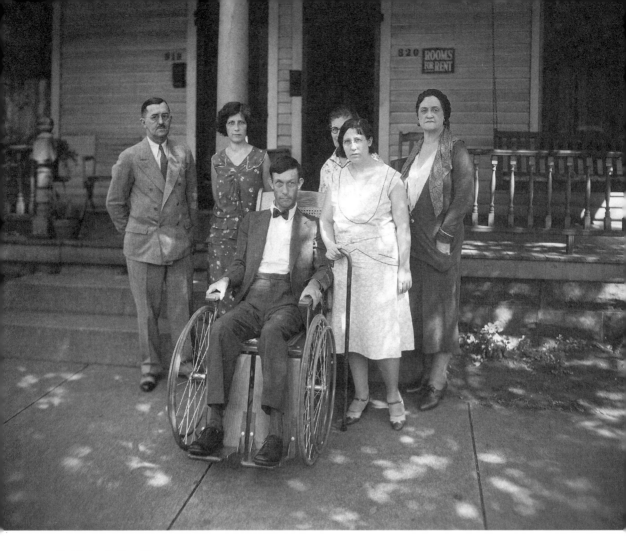

Residents of a Terre Haute
Boarding House
Martin Collection, Indiana
Historical Society

Albert Kaeling—County Poor Farm

Pauline Karns (widow, James)—*furnished rooms*—418 N. 9th h do

Behold the classic boardinghouse, which would be gradually phased out of existence by a combination of permit renewals, zoning regulations, occupancy restrictions, and insurance requirements. The need for cheap room and board never went away in America's cities. Witness the long waiting list for Katherine House, a boardinghouse for young women in New York City that provides a modest private room and two squares for $135.00 a week in the twenty-first century.

Elsewhere in America though, boarding and rooming houses continue to disappear. Nationwide, there are only about 1,600 operating currently and the 1927 model on exhibit here: landlady in residence to cook and clean three bedrooms rented by separate boarders has almost completely vanished. The average boardinghouse these days has five employees.

Reverend Timothy Kavanaugh—*pastor*, Sacred Heart Church—h 2271 N. 13th

Father Timothy Kavanaugh was the second pastor of Sacred Heart Church; one of six Catholic parishes operating in Terre Haute in 1927. The first pastor and the founder of Sacred Heart, Father Aloysius B. Duffy, had been extremely popular with his parishioners. Young, handsome, and personable, Father Duffy could easily have provided the inspiration for later Hollywood priests like Spencer Tracy, Pat O'Brien, and Bing Crosby.

It was Father Duffy who laid the cornerstone to the brick structure that would serve as the parish's church and school. In March 1924, with the building still under construction, Father Duffy celebrated Sacred Heart's first Mass in the basement. Ultimately, it may have been impossible for parishioners to imagine a Sacred Heart without Father Duffy. But suddenly, on June 6, 1926, they realized they would have to try. At Mass that Sunday, Father Duffy announced that he had been transferred by the archdiocese to St. Malachi's Catholic Church in Brownsburg, Indiana. A farewell party was hastily planned for the following Wednesday.

That night, approximately 450 families gathered on the church property. A brass band from the First Hungarian Workingman's Society led the procession. After a full night of toasts and tears, Father Duffy departed Terre Haute for his new assignment.

Northwest of Center Point, Indiana, just about 20 miles from Terre Haute, Father Duffy's car left the road. The young priest suffered severe cuts to his face and head. He had lost a great deal of blood by the time help arrived. He was immediately transported to St. Anthony's Hospital. Among his many well-wishers were those convinced that God had intended the accident as a sign that the beloved priest was meant to stay at Sacred Heart. Nevertheless, after his recuperation Father Aloysius Duffy moved on to his next assignment.

His replacement was Father Timothy Kavanaugh, who would soon discover the enormous size of the black shoes he'd been assigned to fill. For reassurance in this hour of trial, Father Kavanaugh turned to the power of prayer and good

Garfield High School

home cooking. Margaret Kavanaugh is listed as a housekeeper at the church rectory on North 13th Street.

Time moves on, but memories can cast a very long shadow. As it turned out, Father Kavanaugh and Father Duffy would each remain at their new parishes for about a year.

Mrs. Ethel Keedy—*cake icer*—h 326 McKeen

Today, the task of professional cake icing involves many of the same implements and about the same amount of time as it did for Ethel in 1927. It probably wouldn't be anybody's sole job title in Terre Haute, though.

To put an even finer point on the value of the skill itself, Ethel apparently freelanced.

George Kellar—County Poor Farm

Inez Kelley—*teacher*, Garfield High School—r 1619 Locust

She taught mathematics. Pictures from the 1927 Garfield yearbook show a willowy young woman of 33 who must have inspired student fantasies even as they struggled with the concept of cosines.

Garfield High School was established as the city's third municipal secondary school just in time for the 1912 school year. The quality of the education provided to the students at Garfield was reflected in the education provided to their teachers. In 1926, there were 42 faculty positions at Garfield High School, including those for Assistant Athletic Director, Manual Training, and Home Economics. Among the remaining 39 teachers, nine had attended Columbia

University and nine had studied at the University of Chicago. (*See* Charles Zimmerman.)

Louise Lammers had studied the classics at both institutions and supervised a Latin Club at Garfield that had 44 student members. Adele Schwedes, who taught English and was Dean of Girls, had also matriculated at the University of Chicago and had continued her studies at the University of Marlburg in Germany. Each woman had then chosen to return to Terre Haute, Indiana, and teach in the public school system.

The 1927 school year at Garfield High School would hold some very sad memories. Miss Elsie Gilkison, who had been Adele's colleague in the English Department over the previous four years, would die suddenly in late February. Inez Kelley and Elsie Gilkison had attended both Indiana State Normal School and Columbia University together. On March 2, 1927, the entire school was dismissed for the funeral. The next day was a Thursday. Inez Kelley stood before her class, took a deep breath, and somehow began to talk about numbers.

KERMAN GROTTO MYSTIC ORDER OF VEILED PROPHETS OF THE ENCHANTED REALM—502½ Wabash—3rd Floor

They were referred to in the 1927 Polk Directory as "Secret Organizations." What bound them together was an exclusive membership, ritual practices in meetings and initiations, and a reliance on interpersonal, face-to-face connections. For all their enforced secrecy, these fraternal and social organizations reveal a great deal about America at the time. Actually, these revelations are precisely why those bent on nostalgia prefer that they remain secret.

In 1927, secret organizations in Terre Haute were strictly segregated along lines of class, gender, and race. The major fraternal groups like the Masonic orders, the Oddfellows and the Knights of Pythias all had what were described as "colored auxiliaries." They met at separate times in separate places. The women's auxiliaries, like the Daughters of Job or the Hyacinth Temple, were at least permitted to enter the main meeting halls. But there was no pretense as to who occupied the superior facilities or the most elevated position within the group. The original membership requirements for many of these fraternal groups specified "white" and "male."

Still, the names of the many fraternal groups operating in Terre Haute at the time offer at least the illusion of diversity. Meeting somewhere in town every week were the Modern Woodmen of America, the Independent Order of Foresters, the Order of Scottish Clans, the Knights of the Macabees, and, presumably in tribute to Indiana author and Freemason Lew Wallace, the Tribe of Ben Hur.

The mysterious origins and rituals of these groups were all part of their innate secrecy. But despite all the ancient biblical and tribal references, most of these organizations had fairly contemporary Western roots. The Masonic order was the oldest, having been founded by a consortium of four lodges in London in 1717. Freemasonry was a common bond among America's founding fathers. George Washington, Benjamin Franklin, and James Monroe were all Masons, as were 18 signers of the Declaration of Independence and 13 signers of the U.S. Constitution. Over the course of America's history, 13 presidents would hold membership in their local Masonic lodge. Beethoven, Winston Churchill, Mark Twain, and Terre Haute's own Mordechai "Three Finger" Brown were also among those to have taken the oath.

Groups like the Independent Order of the Oddfellows, the Benevolent Order of the Elks, and the Loyal Order of the Moose were subsequently founded in the United States during the nineteenth century. By the early twentieth century, these groups had established functional chapters in practically every mid-sized town in America. The 13 separate chapters, councils, and lodges of the Masonic order operating in Terre Haute had a membership of approximately 2,000 during the 1920s. The Independent Order of the Oddfellows, consisting of 12 various lodges or encampments around town, was estimated to have about 3,000 members. The Knights of Pythias met at the Pythian Temple on 121 South 8th Street next to the Hippodrome. Their membership rolls reportedly reached 2,000. Every year, these tallies provided these fraternal groups the rare occasion to acknowledge and include their colored auxiliaries.

The names of these groups were often misleading. One might imagine that the Independent Order of Foresters or the Modern Woodmen of America were founded with a mission of ecology, dedicating their time to exploring forests, re-planting trees, or advocating for the long-term preservation of wilderness areas. Actually, the primary legacy of the Modern Woodmen over the course of the twentieth century was an insurance program for its members and a tuberculosis retreat in Colorado that closed in 1947. How much time the Tribe of Ben Hur actually spent delving into ancient Roman culture every third Wednesday remains open to speculation. No minutes from the local chapter of the Bismarck Court, No. 134 survive. Frank Oberbacher was the group's designated scribe, and apparently Frank chose to take those secrets with him.

Aside from the Mystic Order of the Veiled Prophets, maybe the most intriguing fraternal name in Terre Haute belonged to the Improved Order of Redmen. The Redmen, who only admitted "free white males of good moral character standing of the full age of 21 great suns," organized themselves into tribes and councils, much like the Native Americans they clearly felt superior to. The membership was distributed among the Tacomas, the Paconda, the Sagwa, the Ionia, the Ute, the Nocatawa, the Coquesey, the Wenonah, and the Wawahtosee. The four latter councils were women's auxiliaries, led by a singular figure known as the Grand Pocohontas. In Terre Haute during much of the 1920s, Lulu Little held this esteemed honor.

Each meeting of the Redmen and women opened with the singing of "America." This was followed by a confidential report from the Mystery Committee. In 1927, all of these proceedings took place in the group's main meeting hall on the northeast corner of 12th and Mulberry. The building had been purchased just two years earlier. Up until that time, it had been an Orthodox Jewish Synagogue, B'nai Abraham. Once the deed had been transferred, the Redmen formally renamed B'nai Abraham "The Wigwam."

From our perspective today, these efforts to create community can seem stodgy and archaic. Since they also represent the prevailing social attitudes of the time, we often see them as racist and sexist, as well. The Mystic Order of the

Veiled Prophets of the Enchanted Realm met every Monday night at 7:30. The content of those meetings was fraught with formal ritual, ornate garments, and ceremonial initiations. But as difficult as it is to understand these arcane practices and their overall purpose, perhaps the most challenging aspect remains the methods employed to determine inclusion into these various groups.

Individuals were evaluated for membership strictly on the personal testimony of existing members. The subsequent discussion of the applicant's character inevitably included a fair amount of hearsay, innuendo, and rumor. That was followed by a vote.

Most secret organizations utilized a secret ballot, involving a series of small wooden balls dropped into a large ornate box. Each standing member was given two wooden balls of contrasting colors. This was the origin for the term "blackball." If even one black ball was found in the final tally, the proposed candidate was rejected.

The Great Depression drastically reduced the pool of proposed candidates as well as much of the dues-paying membership for these fraternal groups. The Zorah Shrine, which opened a new meeting hall in 1926 with a membership of 2,200, would dwindle to 175 members in 1932. Like the Zorah Shrine, the

Members of the Zorah Shrine Temple in Costume
Martin Collection, Indiana Historical Society

Mystic Order of the Veiled Prophets maintained a fine brass band. In 1927, the band rehearsed twice a week, on Thursday nights and Sunday mornings, perhaps never considering the likelihood that in five years the only qualification they'd look for in a new member would be the ability to play the tuba.

So in the end, the dissolution of many of these lodges became a great loss for the individuals involved as well as a great loss for the parades down Wabash Avenue. Some of the losses would remain forever hidden, if only because they would simply be forgotten with time. All throughout the 1920s, the Kerman Grotto sponsored a Christmas party for the children at the Rose Orphan Home. Each child received a wrapped gift, the only ones they were actually permitted to receive. The commitment continued from 1927 on throughout the Depression, though eventually it would become a challenge to find any member fat enough to be Santa.

Alma Kickler—*clerk*, Meis Brothers—r 1502 Poplar

Earl W. Kickler—*teller*, First National Bank—r 1502 Poplar

Fred Kickler—*laborer*, Turner Brothers Company—h 1502 Poplar

It was a common situation throughout Terre Haute in 1927: two adult children living with a parent. The mother, Louise Kickler, died in May of 1914. Earl had graduated from Wiley High School with the Class of 1919 and almost immediately found himself working full time at the five-story menagerie that was Levin Brothers.

Levin Brothers, which occupied the upper floors of the building on the southwest corner of Ohio and Sixth, was one of the most fascinating businesses in Terre Haute, Indiana. Levin Brothers was a product wholesaler, which is about as precise a description as one could come up with after perusing their catalog. Abe Levin and his brothers Max, Meyer, Morris, and Isaac sold everything from handguns to handkerchiefs, bibles to baseball bats, pillowcases to playing cards, teaspoons to toilet paper.

Each of the five stories at Levin's was home to an odd collection of merchandise. Earl's assignment was in the Toy and Novelty Department, known within the company as the Faker Department. The novelties consisted of the cheap dolls, bamboo canes, and Japanese fans that were handed out as consolation prizes at carnival booths. The department was also the storehouse for practical jokes carrying an ample supply of dribble glasses, sneezing powder, and rubber pencils. If fun could not be found with those, then maybe with a Hohner Marine Band harmonica or a Wabash coaster wagon.

The annual catalog of Levin Brothers was called "The Hustler." The product catalog had been given a title probably because like any inspirational work in print, it deserved one. Just consider all the poetic names to be found inside: Engineer's Friend overalls, Indiana Belle hair nets, Grey Goose golf balls, Old Glory spinning tops, Old Faithful chalk, Thistle Lawn envelopes, Lady Falcon steel pens, Shotwell's Jelly Puff candy, Henry's Triumph straight razors, and finally, two items likely to confuse rather than tempt the tastebuds: Bloodberry Gum and Sauerkraut Fudge.

The Levin Brothers Building

As of 1927, Meyer Levin had been serving as president of B'nai Abraham, Terre Haute's Orthodox Jewish Congregation, for more than 30 years. This devout practice apparently did not prevent Levin Brothers from offering the King James Bible as well as a few less savory titles: *The Lover's Manual, Anecdotes of Life on a Pullman Car,* and *From Dance Hall to White Slavery.*

After five years at Levin Brothers, Earl's legible handwriting was noticed by Robert Nitsche, the assistant vice-president and cashier at First National Bank. Soon the call came to move on up to the 500 block of Wabash. Earl would work at the bank for the next 47 years, eventually ascending to the position of the man who had originally hired him.

Earl would leave Levin Brothers having acquired a most valuable skill: an expansive view of life. Without apology, he drove fast cars, smoked strong cigars, played piano in a jazz combo, and somehow lived to be 102 years old.

Noah T. Kincade—*butcher*—h 113 N. 14th

So the combination of first name and job wasn't so unusual, after all. (*See* Noah Hendrickson.) Maybe his argument might have been that the Ark had saved them so that we could eat them.

Charles I. King (Zola O.)—*salesman*, Royal Ice Cream Company—h 314 N. 23rd

In 1927, ice cream represented the concepts of local and sustainable as well as any other food produced in Terre Haute; this despite the fact that often not all the ingredients used were local in origin. Pearl Ice Cream, manufactured by Terre Haute Pure Milk and Ice Cream Company, featured Orange Ice Cream that was made with "heaps of sliced oranges," presumably from Florida, as well as locally produced milk and cream. The only preservative involved was the actual ice it took to freeze the mixture.

This frozen state, coupled with the immediacy of processing all dairy products meant that you made it and then sold it very quickly. Storing ice cream on a grocery shelf, even a very cold one, was not only impractical in 1927, it was prohibitively expensive. (*See* Citizens Market.)

This immediacy, which translated easily to presence in the moment, perfectly suited the experience of eating an ice cream cone: quick before it melts. It also resulted in a rich diversity similar to what was found in local fruits, vegetables, meat, and cultivated plants. Witness the various flavors of ice cream available in Terre Haute during the summer of 1927—flavors that have somehow vanished with time.

Losing a flavor of ice cream almost seems like a color becoming extinct. What possible rationale would there be to explain it? In 1927, the Model Ice Cream Company at 915 Eagle Street in Terre Haute offered the following flavors: Diplemont Vanilla, Parker House, and Tutti-Frutti. Somehow, somewhere, you might find a long-lost recipe for these selections; but likely you'd have to settle for a description from someone with a sweet summer memory.

Magic and sheer delight surround the entire concept of ice cream. So, one imagines that within the family partnership between Irving and Isaac King that founded Royal Ice Cream Company, Isaac got the best of the deal. His brother was left to administer King Brothers Dairy at 2501 North 10th—milk, butter, and cream; whereas Isaac had a two-story brick building along the Wabash River with ten employees devoted to the daily production of 1,000 gallons of ice cream. So where would you like to head off to work every morning?

Ten employees and 1,000 gallons came down to just one flavor. Believe it or not, some of the potential choices were actually preferable to others. It must have been a hard decision. What Isaac H. King settled on and Charles I. King sold was Orange-Pineapple.

The big windows at the Royal Ice Cream factory overlooked the Wabash River. The fresh pineapples came from even further away than the oranges, well beyond the far bank of the river. All day spent making ice cream and then you got to bring your work home with you. In May of 1925, the ten employees and the four delivery trucks of the Royal Ice Cream Company gathered for a group portrait. Relaxed in the pose, knowing the only thing more temporary than ice cream is the image captured by a snapshot.

John Kinkade—County Poor Farm

Nellie M. Koch—*Spiritualistic Medium* @ 334 N. 13th—r 1308 S. 11th

Walter Koch—*tailor*, Joseph's and Sons—h 1308 S. 11th

Nellie M. Koch was born Nellie Roberts and had been married and divorced twice before she wed Valentine Walter Koch in 1920. At the time, being a twice-divorced and thrice-married woman would have far exceeded the rarity of being a spiritualist medium. In fact, you might gauge the popular acceptance of her chosen profession by the fact that she actually hung out a shingle in an Indiana town. In 1927, she shared her office with a chiropractor.

Hard to say whether that office contained a large circular table for late-night séances or whether Nellie conducted her sessions one-on-one, or rather one-on-two, as the case may be. Ultimately, whatever you might think of her ability to contact and channel the dead, her work as a spiritualist medium was about comforting the living. Just as baby food is manufactured to match a parent's impression of what would taste good to a baby, so too spiritual mediums provide an interpretation meant to reassure whoever's paying.

From their little corner of time, Nellie and her clients sought communication with the departed before finally joining them. Nellie herself passed over on Saturday, April 27, 1946. Seems at this point she'd be very willing to talk with anyone who sought her out.

Here's an intriguing little fact: In 1930, Walter and Nellie Koch were sharing their home with one Eliza Savage. Eliza was listed in the U.S. census as a servant, even though at 63 she was the oldest one living in the house. As it turns out the chiropractor who'd shared Nellie's office three years before was named James A. Savage.

Sam Korshak—Fur and Hide Dealer, Auto Accessories, New and Used, Buyer of Junk of All Kinds, 18–20 N. 3rd, Phone: Wabash 7513; r YMCA

KRAH BOX COMPANY (E. Silverberg), Barrels Recoopered and Prepared for Any Purpose, Secondhand Barrels and Boxes of All Kinds, 1447 Tippecanoe, Phone: Wabash 3736-J

Louis H. Kuhlman (Florence)—*handle maker*—h 122 S. 14th

Lillian Kuhn—*spotter*, Powers Cleaning Company—r 45 S. 14th

In Terre Haute, much of what we would now define as sustainable activity was simply part of the day-to-day effort for survival. There was still an active market for secondhand barrels in 1927 and, despite the busy production schedule

YMCA

at the Wabash Fibre Box Company, the largest shipping containers were still made from solid wood. Once they'd reached their destination you could break them down and burn them for heat or maybe make a tree house, but if the crowbar used for unpacking hadn't splintered the wood too badly, the crates were generally worth reconditioning. Here's where one E. Silverberg saw an opportunity.

As for Louis Kuhlman, his profession involved repairing the ravages of hard work with a wheelbarrow, a hammer, an axe, or a garden spade. Shy of a solid hickory handle, it was assumed that the forged part of a tool would always last the longest, outlast the owner in most cases. Louis Kuhlman was one of many amateur and professional craftsmen in Terre Haute who refurbished clothing, footwear, dull edges, and stopped watches. The steady mantra in this pre-consumer society went as follows: Repair before you replace. To put Louis's particular skill in a larger context: There was also a small manufacturing plant called the Terre Haute Handle Company operating in 1927 at the corner of Oak and Water Street.

Lillian Kuhn rescued treasured items of clothing for customers with far smaller closets and maybe one Sunday suit. In lieu of complex chemicals: salt and distilled water to remove bloodstains from a shirt. A stick of chalk kept handy to absorb oil from fabric. A drop of eucalyptus oil to treat a lipstick smudge. Kerosene for grass and ink. Talcum powder on silk.

Sam Korshak deserves our attention not only for recycling everything from carcasses to carburetors but also for his modest address. At the end of his work day, Sam retired to one rented room located in an old converted mansion at

644 Ohio. Not enough space to mess up or save up much of anything. His tidy living arrangement formed a counterpoint to the noise, grime, and clutter of 18–20 North 3rd Street while remaining perfectly aligned with the business's humble purpose.

One measure of a sustainable society is its ability to repair and retain that which has already been manufactured for its use. Currently, two-thirds of the economy relies on consumer spending. A substantive change in direction would mean Americans owning less that is brand new; which over time may lead to Americans simply owning less.

L

Minnie Mayme Lacy—(Sulfur Vapor Bath Institute)—h 1319 S. 9th

Much like Leon Bingham, Minnie would swipe a good ten years off her age when the U.S. census takers came calling in 1930. Turns out her 1958 obituary, over which she had considerably less control, lists her as being 76. The potential health benefits of sulfur spring therapy notwithstanding, the census taker apparently had no trouble believing her. (*See* Denzil M. Ferguson.)

Bruce K. Ladd (Gustava)—*janitor*, The Women's Department Club—h 518 N. 23rd

Ernest Ladd (Matilda)—*janitor*, Mary Stewart Apartments—h 410 N. 6th

Henry Ladd (Lena)—*janitor*—h 1433 N 25th

Marcellus C. Ladd (Hattie L.)—*porter*, SS Kresge Co.—h 2217 Tippecanoe

Might have been an impressive family tradition had they all been related. As it stands: a unique little quirk in the community. The only other Ladd in Terre Haute who held a job in 1927 was also engaged in a form of property management: rentals and real estate.

410 North 6th Street was one of Terre Haute's largest apartment buildings in 1927, with 28 units, including Ernest and Matilda's in the basement. Like the Walden and Bement Flats, the Mary Stewart Apartments offered sedate rental units for individuals with steady employment in the downtown area. Bertha Byerly in Apartment B was a bank teller alongside Earl Kickler at First National. Benjamin Blumenthal in Apartment I was the manager at Brown's Smart Shop, a high-end women's clothing store on the 600 block of Wabash Avenue. His walls were shared with Joseph Flaig, a watchmaker in Apartment J and Joseph Traum, a tailor living in Apartment H.

The Mary Stewart Apartments had the requisite share of salesmen-in-residence, including the ultimate door-to-door icon, Terre Haute's Fuller Brush Man: Dewey F. Harmon. The sheer number of tenants suggests that Ernest and Matilda's Christmas envelope from the residents might have been fairly generous.

Then there was Mr. Bruce Ladd's situation: male janitor for the state's largest women's club, certainly regarded as sacred space. Here, the janitor would have been practically guaranteed a substantial Christmas bonus from the ladies, having undoubtedly earned it during the year (*see* Mrs. William Clark).

(N) Leefronia Laffoon—*domestic*—r 1111 S. 6th

William Laffoon (Viola)—*barber* @ 1532 Wabash h do

Terre Haute, Indiana, in 1927 was a segregated city. There were separate public elementary schools for African Americans, a separate municipal swimming pool, a separate day nursery for toddlers and infants, separate seating in theaters and public transit, as well as a separate newspaper column inside the Terre Haute *Star* called "News from the Colored People." At the very same time, the Terre Haute *Tribune* ran a column of jokes, entitled "Dinner Stories." The columns for June 27 and August 15, 1926, included the word "nigger," apparently assuming the slur would provoke some coarse laughter among its readers.

The largest African American neighborhood in Terre Haute was commonly referred to as Baghdad. Like the red light district, downtown, or Terre Haute's various ethnic enclaves, Baghdad's boundaries were imprecise. It is believed that Baghdad's southern edges reached to the cross streets of Hulman or Deming. 13th Street formed the neighborhood's western border, extending to Crawford or even Ohio Boulevard to the north and then east as far as 16th or maybe 18th.

This neighborhood provided a refuge from the suspicion, indifference, and exclusion that African Americans faced every day of their lives. In 1927, there were not only former slaves still living, but former slaveholders as well. Just four years earlier, a march by 2,000 African American women prevented an effort by southern lawmakers to erect a statue in the U.S. Capitol honoring the "Black Mammy of the South." Meanwhile, Alvira Washington, who had been born into slavery in Virginia, entered her 85th year at 621 South 3rd Street in Terre Haute.

Various other addresses across the city offered safe havens for African Americans. The so-called colored lodges met on the upper floors of two buildings along 3rd Street. There was a small African American neighborhood near Lincoln School at 16th and Elm. But the Baghdad neighborhood was, by and large, the place for non-white residents to go if they were in need of a meal, some medicine, or burial arrangements for a family member.

Baghdad was not without its dangers. At night, street gangs like the Crow Janes and the Bulldogs roamed the neighborhood. If there was any violence or property damage, city police were reluctant or, at best, slow to respond.

In many ways, Baghdad was structured like other neighborhoods in Terre Haute. Schools, churches, and businesses were all within walking distance for residents. John and Lovenia Edwards's grocery at 1424 South 13½ Street was literally next door to Elijah and Hattie Parks's grocery at 1428. Willis West and Henry Morton ran restaurants on opposite corners of Dean Avenue. Saulter's M. E. Chapel was on the corner of 13½ and Franklin. John and Terra Barbee ran a popular eatery at 1417 South 13th.

And then there was Laffoon's on the corner of 16th and Wabash, more than holding its own among the white-owned businesses that dominated the downtown. Upstairs, above the barber shop, William and Viola Laffoon had made meeting space available to the auxiliaries of the Oddfellows and Knights of Pythias. In addition to the barber shop, the Laffoons operated a small lunch counter.

The daily banter around Laffoons helped to sustain and enrich the African American community in Terre Haute. And the large windows facing the street proudly displayed it on Wabash Avenue, the city's main commercial thoroughfare.

Significant, it turns out, because throughout the mid-1920s, the local chapters of the Ku Klux Klan marched down Wabash Avenue every Saturday night. (*See* Rev. Orval W. Baylor.) They announced their marches and proclaimed their policies through fliers posted on lamp poles. The notices never seemed to stay up very long on the poles near 16th Street.

Marily J. Lamb—County Poor Farm

Hugh M. Larrance (Miriam F.)—*Manager*, Furnas Ice Cream Company— h 336 Potomac "Edgewood Grove," Phone: Wabash 4526

Every kid playing in the neighborhood on those long summer nights must have known where he lived. (*See* Edgewood Grove Club.)

(N) Narcissus Lash (spouse of Homer—*laborer*)—h 2629 Jackson

James V. Layman (Lara E.)—*watchman*, Mewhinney Candy Company— r 1135 8th Ave.

Suitable employment for a man who would turn 73 in 1927. In the absence of Social Security, one could also call it necessary employment. (*See* Reba Deardorf.)

LEVI DRY GOODS COMPANY—504–506 Wabash—Phone: Wabash 571— Dry Goods, Notions, Men's and Women's Furnishings—**Joseph V. Moore,** *president*—**Phillip H. Kadel,** *vice-president*, **Samuel E. Balch,** *secretary and treasurer*

In 1927, synthetic fabrics were only beginning to find practical usage in manufacturing and the marketplace. The first synthetic fibers were actually simple combinations of natural materials. One early synthetic was produced by mixing fresh cotton and spruce wood chips to produce a pulp that was then treated with the basic chemical compound sodium hydroxide. The inventor of this process, Hillare Chardonnet, initially called his discovery artificial silk. Honesty would have dictated that it stay that way. Instead, in 1924 the name of the material was changed to rayon.

Most of what was sold at Levi Dry Goods in 1927 were fabrics that had been spun out of natural fibers. This direct connection with nature created a vast array of woven fabrics that in the years since have been displaced by the successful mass marketing of chemistry and convenience.

At Levi Dry Goods, the high walls were lined with bolts of fabric that excited the senses of touch and sight with their dazzling and subtle beauty. Elegant English broadcloth, diaphanous rajah silk from India, the soft knotty weave of pongee silk from Japan, and light zephyr gingham from America's heartland, perfect for creating bright kitchen curtains or a breezy summer dress.

And in Terre Haute, in 1927, there were plenty of people who were capable of doing just that (*see* Minnie G. Allen). The connection that resulted with these natural materials and the distant lands that produced them became an intimate one. With a shirt, a bed sheet, or a foundation garment, you could feel the texture of the natural fabric on your skin. The rays of the sun might shine through a light fabric igniting the colors of natural dye and inspiring the imagination.

Over time, as fabrics became more chemical and synthetic, this intimate sensory connection became obscured. Scientific processes would soon supersede the presence of nature as more convenient polyester blends were introduced to consumers. Whatever their utility, these synthetic fabrics simply could not reward human touch. Their colors, however extreme and insistent, were somehow dull and artificial to the eye.

In 1927, the shop windows at 504–506 Wabash Avenue could immediately command the attention of passersby with their display of bright colors and patterns. Inside the store, the purchase of even one thimble set in motion a process that delighted the children fortunate enough to go shopping with their mothers. From the elevated offices at the rear of Levi's, a small wire basket ran on a pulley all the way to the front counter. Once the bill of sale had been drawn up, it was placed in the basket along with the payment and then sent back to the office where change was counted out and the transaction entered in the store's ledger.

Even in 1927, this ritual was slower than a cash register. In years to come, it would have proven far slower than processing a debit card. But within the surroundings of Levi Dry Goods, it could be compared favorably to the speed of a silk worm.

Daisy Lewis—*chicken picker*—r 1326 S. 1st

Technically, chicken plucker—although that wouldn't sound nearly as good. The job was necessitated by the fact that live chickens were often delivered to local groceries in Terre Haute, which processed them in-house. In 1927, most any farm girl raised in Indiana could break a chicken's neck in one smooth motion. Then she could start in on the feathers.

Two sidebars here: Chicken picking is the name of a distinct style of guitar playing that became popular when the electric guitar emerged in country music in the early 1950s. Think of the clucking sound a cartoon hen makes.

Also, the local shochet was another skilled professional who was comfortable with the challenge of a live chicken. In 1927, Orthodox Jews who followed a strict kosher diet could engage the services of a shochet, or kosher butcher for home visits twice a week. A monthly fee of $2.00 was charged with an additional 5 cents for each fowl killed.

The rules of the Talmud dictate that all slaughter be done without inflicting pain on the animal. The animal's neck is thought to be the area where the least suffering will be felt. For reasons of efficiency rather than religious observance, this is pretty much what Daisy had in mind every time she grabbed hold of a squawking hen.

Reverend Melrose E. Lewis (Nellie)—*traveling evangelist*—h 421 S. 16th

He stood in the fabled tradition of regional itinerants, a vocation that was beginning to disappear throughout America during the 1920s as broader sources of communication and marketing emerged. (*See* Benjamin Camello.) And what radio or chain stores didn't kill, the Great Depression soon would. Although many of the working population were itinerants in 1933, they would be moving meal to meal instead of town to town.

The good Reverend Lewis spoke at any church or tent revival that would have him, relying on the offerings and hospitality of the multitude. If one sermon didn't cover the fare back home, it was off in search of the busiest street corner, just like any other peddler hoping to attract a crowd.

Harry M. Lindley (Hilda)—*film operator*—h 1511 Poplar

In 1915, the Motion Picture Machine Operators Union No. 273 was chartered in Terre Haute. Ten years later, it had 25 members. Unlike vaudevillians and theater pit orchestras, the projectionists in town would ride the transition to sound movies successfully; at least for as long as Harry would be threading film. The highly flammable cellulose nitrate film stock he worked with would prove to be an occupational hazard until 1950.

William H. Lockhart—*soft drinks*—131 N. 3rd h do

If you go by the 1927 Polk Directory, selling soft drinks appears to have been a pretty popular calling in Terre Haute. There were six other vendors operating within a block of 131 North 3rd.

William H. Lockhart's business was located on the corner of 3rd and Mulberry Streets, in the heart of Terre Haute's red light district. There's little doubt that he actually sold soft drinks to his customers, who very soon after would pull a flask of White Mule or Cherry Bounce from an inner pocket and begin mixing. And if they happened to empty the flask, a quick trip to the back room might address the problem.

Actually, much of what went on in Terre Haute with regard to prostitution, gambling, and alcohol consumption was conducted with the implied consent of law enforcement. The German American residents had an old world term for this: "mit a vink" (with a wink), allowing illegal activity in the face of the law or a desist order. (*See* James H. Gallian.)

Louis G. Lockwood (Elizabeth)—*Artificial Limbs*—651½ Wabash Avenue, Phone: Wabash 6943; h 1019 N. 6th, Phone: Wabash 6769

Always a steady demand for the products he serviced and sold. His clients would have included veterans from the recent world war, though it's possible they reached back even further. In 1925, there were still 367,819 Hoosiers collecting pensions from the Civil War. More than a few of them were amputees.

In a factory, farming, and mining town like Terre Haute, severe injuries were also occurring every day on the job. Each year during the 1920s, 100,000 Americans were permanently disabled by an accident at their workplace; 25,000 were killed. Compensating a worker to pay for an adequate prosthesis was rare.

On balance, you might say the combination of wars and working conditions conspired to create a steady need for Louis's little business, much like the passage of time does for roofing and undertaking. Curious though, that he chose to locate it on the second floor of a building without an elevator.

Archie Long (Erma)—*musician*—r 111½ S. 13½

In the 1920s, the occupation of musician or entertainer was one of the few positions for which African Americans could receive actual respect from the whites who paid them. By 1927, two African American entertainers had become nationally popular with mixed audiences: Louis Armstrong and Bessie Smith. Around this time, there were also a handful of regional musicians like Blind Lemon Jefferson, Lonnie Johnson, and Charlie Patton who occasionally played and sang the blues at speakeasies or house parties frequented by whites. Throughout Indiana and down south into Covington, Kentucky, blues pianist Leroy Carr and guitarist Scrapper Blackwell were well-known and decently paid as performers.

We don't know anything about Archie's chosen instrument or the style of music he played. Unlike Big Ione Williams, there's no indication that he shared what he did with white audiences in speakeasies. (*See* James H. Gallian.) We do know that Archie lived in Baghdad. And even if he never left the neighborhood to play out, he would've found plenty of illegal revelry going on right there to keep him busy.

Herbert Long—*pugilist*—r 1013 7th Ave.

Truthfully, the sport hadn't produced a pugilist since John L. Sullivan fought Jack Kilrain for the last bare-knuckled championship in 1889. Though the term "prize fighter" sounds far less respectable, that's pretty much what the job amounted to in 1927. Fights of a few rounds held on a Friday night in a smoke-filled armory for a modest purse. Win the bout quick enough and you'd be in good shape physically for next week's undercard. As for being in good shape financially; well, that was something else again. (*See* Clarence Bose.)

THE LOUDON PACKING COMPANY—2101 S. 3rd—Charles F. Loudon, *president-treasurer*—Stewart Rose, *vice president–secretary*

Since its inception in Terre Haute in 1905, the Loudon Packing Company had been somewhat of a rarity, a factory that remained responsive to the cycle of the seasons. Specifically, the local growing season for tomatoes; which Charles F. Loudon processed and then bottled into a variety of tomato products including catsup, chili sauce, and relish.

This yearly process began through individual agreements reached with various local farmers to grow the crop. Charles Loudon contracted for a certain number of acres with each provider, furnishing the seeds for the spring planting. If the seedling stayed relatively free of cutworms and tomato wilt, then the inevitable bumper crop would result. When that crop was ready for harvest in late summer, the real work at Loudon's began.

All of the 2,800 acres that Charles Loudon had under cultivation were located within a 45-mile radius of Terre Haute, with 300 acres being grown right around the city. Tons of tomatoes were picked by hand, placed in wooden crates, and delivered by boxcar to the siding of a 200' × 100' brick building on South 3rd Street. From late August to the middle of November in 1927, the Loudon Packing Company employed 500 workers and kept operating around the clock. Workers were able to produce 100,000 bottles of catsup and 40,000 bottles of chili sauce a day.

Laborers Picking Tomatoes
for Loudon Packing Company
Martin Collection, Indiana
Historical Society

Although Loudon Catsup made far-flung appearances in London, Glasgow, and Capetown, South Africa, the primary market, just like the primary ingredient, was local. There were more than 400 grocery stores in Terre Haute in 1927. Since the vast majority of them were locally owned with the proprietor literally standing behind the counter, it gave Charles Loudon a genuine opportunity to compete for the store's limited shelf space. Only one brand of catsup would be carried by these groceries and if Loudon Catsup could be that brand, maybe Charles could speak to the owner later on about his chili sauce.

By 1927, Loudon Catsup faced some very serious competition. The R.J. Heinz Company of Pittsburgh, Pennsylvania, had already established a market for its food products worldwide. As its labels promised, the company literally offered 57 varieties. Heinz Catsup was Number 48. Heinz Fig Pudding was Number 13. Heinz India Relish was Number 50. A full-page ad which ran in the *Ladies Home Journal* displayed all of the company's products listed alongside a map of the world.

And if that wasn't enough, there were other hometown brands of catsup in Terre Haute for Charles Loudon to contend with. The Hulman Company with its Farmer's Pride line of food products and the Bement-Rea Company with its Keystone Catsup each had a legitimate claim on the Terre Haute market. In addition, individuals who grew and canned tomatoes every year often employed their own personal recipes for making catsup at home.

Mrs. Bertha Moorhead, living with her husband, James, at 1457 Ohio Boulevard, was just one of these many home producers. Bertha was confident enough to share her recipe with readers of the weekly *Saturday Spectator.* Her implied message: Since almost anybody can grow a tomato, almost anybody can make catsup, too.

Squeezed as he was from all sides, Charles Loudon might have been eager to find another use for all of those tomatoes sitting on all those boxcars. Ten years later, his former vice-president, Stewart Rose, who by then had purchased the company, would actually find one. A home producer from Illinois named W. G. Peacock had come up with a zesty tomato juice which included hand-cleaned carrots, celery, parsley, and beets. Mr. Peacock initially decided to call his concoction "Vege-Min."

One day after counting up the number of ingredients, Mr. Peacock decided on a new name for his juice. Then, after counting up the growing number of orders, he decided his juice should have a new owner as well. The Loudon Packing Company would soon begin to produce and market "V-8 Juice." In 1948, when the Campbell Soup Company finally purchased the brand, gross sales were approaching $5,000,000. By then, that farm wagon of tomatoes harvested from a few acres near Terre Haute, Indiana, had begun to look very small indeed.

Franklin Lowe—County Poor Farm

Harry Luckens—County Poor Farm

Frank E. Lutes—*branch manager*, Piggly Wiggly—r 434 N. 6th

Quite serious, despite the name of the business. In 1916, Clarence Saunders opened the first Piggly Wiggly store in Memphis, Tennessee, introducing an innovative approach to grocery shopping. The concept was touted as "Scientific Merchandising." Clarence Saunders created self-service shopping that followed a specific traffic pattern down long aisles with shelved products stacked to either side. Initially, Piggly Wiggly stores were called "cafeteria-style groceries" or grocerterias. It took a little time for the name "supermarket" to catch on.

The first Piggly Wiggly grocerteria in Terre Haute opened in June of 1922. Within 18 months, four other locations had been established throughout the city. The company had begun the decade with 515 stores nationally. By 1929, it would have five times that many.

From the outset, Piggly Wiggly stores stocked national brands to the exclusion of local food processors. An ad running in the Terre Haute *Tribune* on October 25, 1925, offered Del Monte canned pineapple, Domino sugar, and Heinz fig pudding. The ambition for all this was made clear in the company motto, written in script under the store's name: "All Over the World."

Today it's apparent that even if Clarence Saunders's store locations didn't fulfill that prophecy, his concept certainly did. But almost unintentionally, self-service shopping began to place increasing burdens on the shopper it was meant to serve. An individual shopper's responsibility gradually moved beyond simply selecting products for purchase and transporting them to the check-out aisle. Now it often includes processing the purchases, as well. Also, while eliminating a system in which the grocer retrieved goods stacked on shelves behind a counter, the self-service concept quietly discarded home-delivery of those groceries as well.

Initially, the idea of letting shoppers choose which brand of cereal to buy seemed like democracy in action, until the process turned in on itself. While the number of brands increased exponentially, the number of actual product manufacturers gradually decreased. The unforeseen result is that grocery shoppers spend more time considering various brands that are actually originating from a single food processor. Meat and bakery departments in many supermarkets are now often limited to stocking pre-packaged selections originating from a central manufacturer and distributor.

Meanwhile, accompanying the exponential growth in supermarket square footage has been the increased time spent navigating long product aisles and enormous parking lots. This makes one wonder whether, 80 years on, time and energy is actually being saved driving to a supermarket as opposed to walking to the corner grocery.

The concept of self-service has now been completely realized, though it's unlikely Clarence Saunders would recognize it. Today, grocery shopping, like banking or dining out, can be accomplished without interacting with anyone who might assist or advise in the process. In the end, the concept of scientific merchandising has left us planets away from the idea of one business with somebody's name on the sign. Those answers that Clarence Saunders initially came up with in 1916 have over time eliminated the possibility of even hearing a once-familiar question: "Can I help you?"

John W. Lyda (Lena B.)—*teacher*, Booker T. Washington School—h 462 S. 16th

Mrs. Lena B. Lyda—*teacher*, Lincoln School—r 462 S. 16th

Two careers dedicated to public education while teaching in segregated schools. John and Lena Lyda grew where they were planted and in the process enriched and inspired countless young lives for the critical years ahead.

A personal challenge involved in creating change is that the final results often go unseen by those who struggle mightily to achieve them. The teachers of young children must constantly trust their efforts in the present, knowing that the future may not be revealed to them. John Lyda died in 1951, the same year that the state of Indiana decided to end its policy of segregation in the public schools. Just before his death, John had completed a comprehensive history of the African American experience in his home state. The book, entitled *The Negro in the History of Indiana,* was finally published in 1953.

But one important dream was not deferred. When John and Lena's son, Wesley, graduated with high honors from Wiley High School in 1930, the school arranged for a full scholarship to DePauw University. It was a complete surprise to everyone when the award was announced at the graduation ceremony. For John and Lena, it was a rare opportunity to see great expectations in life manifest while they were still living.

M

Albert McBride—County Poor Farm

David McCarter (Nettie)—*barber* @ 1716 N. 15th—h 1462 Plum

James McCarter—*barber* @ 1518 N. 13th—h 1462 Plum

Moses McCarter—*barber*, James McCarter—r 1462 Plum

Viola McCarter—r 1462 Plum

By 1927, it had become the family profession and possibly a source of pride. David McCarter began the tradition, having left the family farm in Seymour, Indiana, where he had been born on New Year's Day in 1870. Like many Indiana farm boys of his generation, David migrated to the nearest big city and learned a trade. By age 57, he had settled into a comfortable daily ritual. 1462 Plum was just two buildings away from his barber shop on the corner of Plum and North 15th. Three adult children were living with him and Nettie. The two sons were trying to follow in daddy's footsteps, opening up a barber shop within a short walking distance of home.

Track these footsteps just a little further and the McCarter family can tell you something about what happened in Terre Haute and in America generally in the following decade. Between 1920 and 1940, Terre Haute's population would decline by more than 4,000 people. Eldest son James would be one of those who left. Just packed up his scissors one day and moved on.

The Great Depression would come down hard on the small self-proprietor businesses so common in Terre Haute during the first years of the twentieth century. In 1927, there were 112 barber shops in Terre Haute. A dozen years later, the number had dropped by 15 percent and would continue to fall. By 1936, Moses had put away his scissors altogether. That year, he reported his job as janitor—skills probably acquired during his time sweeping up hair for his dad and older brother. Moses was 33 years old by then, and still living with his parents.

By the beginning of the next decade, Nettie McCarter had died, Moses had married, and James and Viola had long since left town. Nothing for David to do but call for the next customer. By then, he had kept a barber shop for so long, it's likely he still had a rack of personalized shaving mugs for customers as old as he was. It was a tradition worth continuing if only to invert another mug with news of the latest passing. On January 18, 1942, two weeks after his 72nd birthday, David McCarter remarried. On his courthouse marriage application, he listed his occupation as barber. Standing behind the next chair was his youngest son, Tom, who hadn't even been cutting hair in 1927. Just a few more years and David could leave the shop in good hands, or at least die believing that Tom would keep the family tradition going.

Jean McCormick (Irene)—*musician*, American Theater—h 728 8th Ave.

Yet another member of the band, along with Edgar Herrin and Paul D. Johnson. In 1931, after the double-whammy of the Depression and talkies, he would still survive somehow as a musician in Terre Haute, Indiana.

Frank McCrocklin—*livery stable*—208 S. 3rd

Fred McFall (Myrtle)—*livery stable* @ 209–11 S. 3rd—h 1329 S. 8th

In 1874, an impressive brick building was constructed on the northwest corner of Fourth and Walnut to house the City Market, where area farmers could sell their produce directly to merchants.

Within three years, the City Market had become Terre Haute City Hall. The Farmer's Market, as it was now known, had relocated to the other side of Wabash Avenue on North 2nd Street and Mulberry. This was a bad break for the stables, farmer's hotels, and harness makers that had initially located near the Market, but not nearly as bad a break as the arrival of the internal combustion engine.

Fifty years later, these two competitors were still in business right across the street from one another. Frank actually lived on site, taking advantage of those wee hours when a farm wagon might be arriving in town. The previous summer, an outdoor produce market sponsored by the Terre Haute Truck and Fruit Growers Association had opened at Third and Walnut Streets near the City Sanitary Market at 121 South 3rd Street. Just like the old days. The hours of 4:00 to 8:00 AM open exclusively to grocers and restaurants, followed by business with the general public. Everything there except the horses.

(N) Ebbie McFate (Ella)—*musician*—r 621 N. 7th.

The total package here. Born in Illinois in 1886. Ebbie and Ella were living in Clinton, Indiana, in 1920. It seems Ebbie was attracted to Terre Haute by the opportunities in his field. The name suggests an untrained folk or blues musician but apparently he had enough training to teach alongside Ignatz Diekhoff at the Terre Haute Conservatory of Music.

Even so, like Leadbelly or Lightning Hopkins, Ebbie McFate could have earned a listen purely on the sound of his name. There's still hope that some fledgling rock band will make use of it and hit big. Lynyrd Skynyrd permanently memorialized the rock band's high school teacher that way.

William McGlean—*stone cutter*—h 1232 N. 7th

During the 1920s, over half a million tons of limestone was quarried annually in Indiana, by far the largest output of any state in the lower 48. Limestone is a perfect stone for sculptors and engravers since it can be chiseled easily in any direction without splitting. The carved results were often used as capstones on buildings and headstones in cemeteries. Ralph Tucker, who would serve five terms as Terre Haute mayor, actually wound up using one for the other. He rescued a carved limestone angel from Cottage Number 2 at the Rose Orphan Home when it was demolished and arranged to have the angel placed at his gravesite. As a child, Ralph Tucker had resided in Cottage Number 2 for five years. (*See* Anna Asher.)

Edward McGowan—County Poor Farm

The St. Nicholas Hotel and Restaurant

(N) Rosebud McGrew (spouse of Harold—*advertising manager*, Oakley's Economy Store)—h 2338 Hulman

She might have gotten away with claiming to be the love child of Dan McGrew and the lady that's known as Lou; that is, if they hadn't been fictional characters and she hadn't married into the name.

Hugh McGurty (Dona)—*proprietor*, St. Nicholas Hotel—h 625 N. 9th

One of the many "drummer" hotels that sat across from Union Station. On the 400 block of 9th Street there was the Albert Hotel and the Brinkham. Just across Sycamore Street, you'd find the Plaza, Ryder's Hotel, and Miss Lottie Sandison's European Hotel.

Actually, there was more than just the shared bath and the meal plan that gave these lodgings a European air. For one thing, most everything about these hotels was small: their staff, their restaurants, the number of rooms they had, the size of the rooms themselves. The largest hotel, the Plaza, had a little over 100 rooms. The others were more the size of Miss Lottie's place, which had only 25.

And if you look closely at the photograph of the St. Nicholas, you get a sense of how these hotels might have made this small section of Terre Haute feel European. Shady trees, with residences and small restaurants sharing the block. No indication that the cafés at St. Nicholas, the Sandison, or the Plaza had sidewalk tables, but space, not sensibility, probably dictated that.

McMillan Sporting Goods
Martin Collection, Indiana
Historical Society

Also, in the interests of illuminating one of the more interesting jobs in town: The desk clerk at Lottie Sandison's European Hotel in 1927 was a Mr. George Kizer. His position included both lodging and meals.

Mary McKiey—County Poor Farm

Fanny McKinney—*chef*, Sullivan Hotel—r do

Apparently Fanny thought she should be called a chef and who knows, maybe that was the difference keeping a restaurant operating in a marginal hotel that would disappear completely in a year or so.

Nice to imagine May Clark, Minnie Gore, Lydia Jones, and Fanny sitting down after-hours to a lovely meal. A little magic from the kitchen could have made it the best part of their day.

Vernon R. McMillan (Frances; McMillan Athletic Goods Company)—
h 2207 N. 10th

Became a larger-than-life character by living it to the fullest. In 1927, he had put his name on a sporting goods store at 832 Wabash, located amidst the cigar shops, billiard parlors, and gambling dens that graced the most masculine block in town. During the 1940s, Vern would also serve one term as Terre Haute's mayor. But the foundation of his local legend was a stunt he pulled as a young man of 22. In 1915, Vern McMillan gunned the V-Twin engine on his Indian motorcycle and rode straight up the steep stone steps of the Vigo County Court House. Whoa.

Keeping this in mind 30 years later, you might have overlooked his party affiliation and given him your vote anyway. And in 1927, if you were living right, you might have been buying a fishing rod or a tennis racquet when Vern happened to be at the counter. You just know he'd have to demonstrate.

John R. McNew—County Poor Farm

Herbert Mading—County Poor Farm

John Mago—County Poor Farm

Leonard Mahan—*orchardist*—h east side of 17th; 2 parcels south of Hulman

The job title is significant by its present-day absence. In 1927, Terre Haute actually had two orchardists in practice. The location here is also significant. Two blocks east of these carefully tended trees, just south of Hulman, stood Henley Brothers Florists. It was inadequately described in print as "an acre of greenhouse flowers"—it was 60,000 square feet of potted plants, cut flowers, and floral arrangements under glass.

Many of the professional growers working in Terre Haute in 1927 were located on the periphery of the city: the north side of Hulman west of Fruitridge, the south side of College east of Brown, the south side of Margaret east of 25th. In many urban areas, such parcels have since been swallowed by sprawl. But one of the side benefits of Terre Haute's stagnation over the course of the twentieth century is that many of these parcels remained underdeveloped. Even so, they were no longer orchards, gardens, or truck farms by the end of the century; which tells us as much about the trajectory of progress in America as sprawl ever could. (*See* Robert Axlander.)

Elizabeth Malone—County Poor Farm

Bert Manwaring (Marie)—*casketmaker*—h 1936 Monterey

Confronting death daily. On a larger but not necessarily loftier scale, this was also being done at the Terre Haute Casket Company at 560 North 9th Street, which described itself as a "Mail and Telephone Order House." Bert probably dealt face to face with the grieving more often. The concept of a rush order, in both cases, was relative.

Bert Manwaring's death would occur on June 16, 1961, at age 70. Plenty of time for him to contemplate both the inevitability and the circumstances. Wonder how close he came?

Forrest W. Marts (Ferne)—*bartender*, John Boyd—h 926 S. 1st

Well, the jig is up. The Polk Directory lists John Boyd as a soft drink dealer at 131 2nd Street, living upstairs with wife Mary. But while such euphemisms protected the owners of illegal establishments during Prohibition, a title hadn't yet surfaced to cover the man behind the counter. Protocol required Forrest to keep a straight face when adults continued to ask for ginger ale. (*See* William H. Lockhart.) In 1927, Ross Landers was listed as a soda dispenser at Shandy's Courthouse Pharmacy, but obviously that job description wouldn't accurately fit the position at 121 2nd Street.

James W. May—County Poor Farm

Sarah Maynard—County Poor Farm

Reuben A. Meek (Catherine L.)—*taxicab*—1400 N. 4th

A gypsy cab—one driver, one vehicle, and ideally, multiple passengers every time it moved forward.

In the walkable neighborhoods of Terre Haute in 1927, served by convenient public transit with most local grocers making home deliveries, it was still possible to get along fine from day to day without an automobile, and only place an occasional call for a cab. Reuben and Catherine's number in 1927 was Wabash 131, probably penciled on the wall of a phone booth or two on the northside.

After dropping off a passenger, Reuben was not above pulling up to a crowded trolley or bus stop and negotiating a fare for his return trip home. (*See* Forrest B. Arnold / Joseph E. Asay.)

(N) Minnie C. Meneely (Millard B.)—*employee*, Turner Brothers Co.— h 511½ N. 13½

Helen L. Meyer—*nurse*, Public Health Nursing Association—r 500 2nd Ave.

In the absence of Medicaid or Aid to Dependent Children, Helen Meyer represented one of the few resources for health and recovery available to poor families in Terre Haute. St. Anthony's Hospital, which had initially been established through a grant by Terre Haute businessman Herman Hulman in 1882, described itself as a hospital "where the poor could go." To that end, the Sisters of St. Francis offered 57 charity ward beds. In addition, the Rose Dispensary on the northeast corner of 7th and Cherry had been providing Terre Haute's poor with free dental care, eye care, and prescriptions since 1895. This too was a privately funded healthcare facility. The clinic operated off an endowment by local philanthropist Chauncey Rose, who had also founded the Rose Orphan Home.

Every day, Helen Meyer visited the indigent in their homes and usually discovered the root causes for the illnesses she confronted—causes she was often powerless to address. Some of the poorest sections of Terre Haute were located along the riverbank. The dwellings of Taylorville, on the west bank of the Wabash, lacked even basic amenities, drawing constant pleas for improved sanitary conditions. A local Chamber of Commerce report from 1926 delicately described the community as an "unsavory suburb." Writer Frank Tannenbaum had given an outsider's perspective in the *Century Magazine* in November 1925. His article, entitled "Two Towns That Are One," described Taylorville's "dirty and unkempt" shacks as being "built of tin cans, old sacks, and odd pieces of wood." As was so often the case with Helen Meyer's work, wherever her help was summoned, she always seemed to find children there needing it the most.

The Converted Home of
Milks Emulsion
Martin Collection, Indiana
Historical Society

MILKS EMULSION COMPANY—507 N. 13½ St.—**James Milks,** *president*—**Frank Brinkman,** *vice-president*—**Buena Marshall,** *secretary*

A nod to the company secretary, whose middle name was Vista.

Let's begin with a policy statement from the company president: "Nature never intended that we should use artificial digesters to digest our food." A rare perspective, even for 1927. There's something both knowing and respectful in the way that nature is referenced here.

Milks Emulsion, which was recommended for constipation, had been on the market since 1902. Ninety percent of it was pure unadulterated petroleum oil compounded with glycerin, vegetable oils, and wild cherry extract. No specific dosing instructions other than to "eat it as you would ice cream." You might be tempted to laugh or even retch. But there's evidence that at least a few folks back then found it effective. By 1927, more than 13,600,000 bottles of Milks's emulsion had been sold across the country.

Milks Emulsion was a family company with two brothers at the fore: James Milks and Charles, who was listed as the company salesman. Just like Abel's, Milks supported about two dozen employees. (*See* Sarah Greggs.) They manufactured the product, they bottled it, and they shipped it all from one address north of downtown.

Now that we've established some reasons why Milks Emulsion Company couldn't possibly exist in America today, let's revisit that initial policy statement. It seems to imply that if people continued to relieve their constipation using artificial means, the supposed remedy might actually create a chronic condition. Eventually, the result would be consumers purchasing more and more of these artificial means to relieve these aggravated symptoms. Boy, it's a good thing we've been able to avoid all that.

Frank H. Miller (Mary)—*chief*, Terre Haute Fire Department—h 1459 Ohio—Phone: Wabash 7850

In 1927, the City of Terre Haute, Indiana, maintained nine separate fire stations to help protect an area of ten square miles. In addition, there were 465 fire alarm boxes which were connected directly to the nearest firehouse. These boxes were located on prominent corners in every residential neighborhood, like Number 81 at Lafayette and Buckeye or Number 261 at Barton and Seabury. Many of the larger buildings and businesses also had fire boxes: Root Glass, Miller-Parrott Baking Company, and the A. Herz department store among them.

The reason for this dedicated effort was twofold. First, the majority of structures in Terre Haute were built of wood. Secondly, American cities had a long history of devastating fires. In 1903, a fire at the Iroquois Theater in Chicago killed 600 people. New York City's Triangle Shirtwaist Factory Fire in 1911, which killed 147 people, was especially tragic because fire exits in the building had been blocked by management to prevent workers from smuggling out merchandise. Most all of those victims were young women, many of whom jumped together to their death from the ninth and tenth floors.

There were still firefighters working within Chief Miller's department who had responded to the Havens and Geddes store fire on December 19, 1898. A short circuit had ignited cotton being used to decorate a Christmas window display. The fire quickly spread, trapping a number of people inside. Many were children who had come to the toy department in the store's basement to visit Santa.

The man wearing the white beard that night was only 18 years old. In the minutes following the fire's discovery, Claude Herbert directed 30 children up the stairs to safety and then went back into the store, hoping to rescue shoppers on the upper floors.

Claude Herbert would not return. He left behind a widowed mother. A small fountain was soon placed at the site of the fire as a memorial, not that anybody who was living in Terre Haute that Christmas would ever forget. The story of the Havens and Geddes fire was so heartbreaking that even the retelling of it a century later would reduce men in their 90s to tears. The story had been told to them as young boys. For some of them, it was the only time they would ever see their fathers cry. The various details in these individual accounts would become selective with age, but inevitably every memory would begin and end with Claude Herbert's name.

Oliver E. Miller (Martha)—*farmer*—h 233 N. 5th

Oddly enough, he and Martha lived two blocks from downtown in a residential neighborhood. You might call Oliver's daily trip to work the complete opposite of a suburban commute.

William C. Miller (Mary)—*miner*—h 3102 N. 15th St.

He was known as "Dusty" to friends and neighbors. Likely more than a few of them first learned that William was his given name when they read his obituary in the Terre Haute *Tribune* in November of 1945. Being that Dusty was 85 at the time, this may have been the only surprise his passing afforded them.

Dusty Miller was born just prior to the Confederate attack on Fort Sumner and lived long enough to hear about the attack on Hiroshima. This particular lifespan allowed him to bear witness to some extraordinary passages in human history. By 1927, Dusty could have regaled a child with memories of the first time he listened to recorded music, switched on an electric light, or answered a telephone. Like many adults who've transcended youthful awe and amazement, he simply might have shrugged off the emergence of motion pictures and airplanes. It's very likely he never saw the need to obtain a driver's license.

But throughout the course of his long life, there was one significant event that William "Dusty" Miller bore witness to and may have participated in personally. He was in his early 40s at the time, living on North 15th Street, the same address he occupied nearly half a century later. In 1927, many of the surviving participants to this event were still living in Terre Haute. When asked, however, some witnesses might have recalled their memories in a halting whisper. For others, it was a tale they'd already shared many a time, more than eager to display a well-worn souvenir while recounting their own experiences that day.

Any thorough account of the event would have described two days in late February 1901. The first character introduced to the listener would have been a young schoolteacher at Elm Creek School, a Miss Ida Finklestein. The Finklestein family had endured enormous hardship. Ida's father, Solomon, had been killed during a confrontation at the Alum Mine, leaving behind his widow, Bess, and eight children.

In the months that followed, despite tireless efforts, the family was simply unable to sustain itself. Bess made the wrenching decision to place her three youngest children in an orphanage located in Ohio. Meanwhile, she and four older children moved north to Chicago. Ida, the eldest, was able to stay in Terre Haute. She was a bright and ambitious young woman and soon after beginning classes at Indiana State Normal, accepted a teaching position at Elm Creek, a one-room schoolhouse east of town.

Ida's plan all along was to help support the remnants of her family in Chicago. The small Jewish community in Terre Haute immediately became involved in this effort, ensuring that Ida could send almost all of her pay directly to her mother. Ida was provided a room at the home of Max and Theresa Blumberg on South 5th Street. From there, Ida could catch the trolley that ran east along National Road and walk to Elm Creek School. It was a rural area, with paths rather than paved roads, and very challenging to navigate in inclement weather. But here too, assistance was extended to Ida. She knew she could always find shelter whenever it was needed at the Herman Vaughn household, north of the Country Club property.

It was just before 5:00 PM on Monday, February 25, 1901, when Ida left the Vaughn household to catch the westbound trolley back to her room at the Blumbergs'.

Ida Finklestein never reached her destination. Two hours after she'd set out, Ida crawled onto the porch of the Walter Nicholson home just south of National Road and weakly asked for help. She was bleeding profusely from wounds inflicted by a shotgun blast and a crude penknife. It would be another hour before medical help arrived and another hour still before Ida could be transferred to Union Hospital on the city's north side. Four hours of intense suffering would finally end at 11:25 that night when, despite the efforts of three doctors, Ida Finklestein died.

Before she slipped away, however, Ida was able to provide a description of her assailant; in her words, "a colored man dressed in hunting clothes." The employees of the westbound trolley were contacted and in fact, someone matching the description had boarded the trolley in the early hours of that evening and gotten off at a stop between 18th and 13th Streets.

It was just a matter of hours before the suspect was identified. When police finally located George Ward, he was at work. The motorman on the trolley had accompanied detectives and immediately confirmed his identity. In George Ward's pocket, a penknife was found with a missing blade, matching the one that had broken off during the assault.

At this point, word was spreading in every direction at a breathless rate of speed, much like a grass fire or a plague. It had been fueled first by news of a young schoolteacher's assault, then her painful death, and now her suspect's capture. This communication was engaged like most transactions in Terre Haute at the time: face to face. As the story spread, it gathered up the rumor and speculation that always embellish a tale spoken then heard, then spoken again. Some stories spoke of Ida's orphan siblings and her murdered father. Of George Ward polishing his shotgun in silence every night or a mysterious head injury he had suffered at work some months before. These and other details might have made it into the version that was passed along. But two elements to the story were consistent throughout: a white 20-year-old woman walking alone in a remote area and a colored man with a gun and a knife. The motive for the attack had apparently been robbery. Three dollars had been surrendered by the victim. No evidence of a sexual assault, although its likelihood was probably claimed or inferred as the story made its appointed rounds.

The Vigo County Sheriff, Daniel Fasig, suspected that mob violence was likely to occur. An angry crowd had begun to gather outside the county jail demanding the prisoner. In response, Sheriff Fasig dispatched jailer Lawrence O'Donnell to fire one warning shot into the air and alerted the local National Guard for possible support. In the meantime, he arranged to transport George Ward by train to Indianapolis. The train was scheduled to depart Terre Haute that afternoon at 12:59.

At 11:50 AM, a crowd that had grown to about 1,000 people laid siege to the Vigo County jail. Using a 25-foot-long tree trunk tipped with steel, the mob broke in a side door, overpowered the jailers, and removed the terrified suspect from his cell. George Ward's screams were loud enough to reach clear to the margins of the mob. Perhaps someone in the crowd reckoned this might create some sleepless nights for the perpetrators, so a sledgehammer was used. George Ward's final words, according to one witness: "For God's sake, please don't take me down."

As a black man living in early-twentieth-century America, George Ward must have known where he was bound. The actual lynching would now be for show, since the blow from the sledgehammer had already killed him. In any event, the mob would not have far to go with their captive. A sturdy length of sea rope was found at Joe Chisler's wagon yard nearby and used to drag the prisoner's corpse to the Wabash River bridge. A cheer went up from the mob as George Ward's body dropped and swayed from the crosstimbers.

But even with this terrifying spectacle, the mob's collective rage was far from spent. George Ward's lifeless body was soon cut free and fell down onto the west bank of the river. There a bonfire was built around the corpse. The bonfire was fed with oil and wooden crates from a nearby poultry house until it could be seen by city policemen gathered on the opposite bank. The body burned steadily for the next two hours. When the fuel and flames finally gave out, it was discovered that the victim's feet had not burned completely. Someone on the riverbank offered a dollar for one of the toes and a young boy with a jack-knife quickly responded. This initial offer was soon followed by others. Finally, amidst the smoldering ashes and the mutilated body, someone located a few bits of charred metal. These turned out to be hobnails from George Ward's boots. They were quickly gathered as souvenirs.

Only so many hobnails to go around, though. Not nearly enough to satisfy all those wishing to commemorate the event. This provided a clear opportunity for an ambitious man with a camera. The photographer in question processed three shots from that afternoon. One from the riverbank showed George Ward's body hanging from the Wabash River bridge. The second was a picture of the bonfire as it raged. Finally, a shot of an open field, perhaps known to some in the crowd as the place where George Ward's burned body was finally buried. It was common at the time for postcards of lynchings to be printed and sold publicly. But in this case, the real profits lay with a professionally matted photograph, a set of three actually, with a straight-edged line added to the photograph of the bridge. The sea rope, it turned out, could not be captured on camera, due to the distance from which the shot was taken.

These were not the kind of photographs that would be prominently displayed in the home. Maybe kept in a drawer of the dining room buffet instead, reserved for occasions where a few too many had led to the story being shared. It's possible that Dusty Miller had wearied of relating his own version over the years. It's also possible that Dusty still kept a blackened hobnail to display near the story's end. In any event, three photographs of the lynching of George Ward matted on decorative pasteboard wound up being donated to a paper

The Lynching of George Ward

drive during World War II. Maybe Dusty tried out the well-worn story one last time on the neighborhood kid who went door-to-door collecting paper that day. After 40 years, Dusty Miller's three commemorative photographs would be sacrificed in support of a noble cause, which finally completed a cycle in a sense since something once perceived as a noble cause was why those pictures had been taken in the first place.

Hard to say how much of a burden Dusty had carried personally or whether he felt relieved of it with his donation. In any event, he got pretty far carrying it: 85 years old when he died on November 16, 1945. Yet there is some evidence that a kind of final reckoning was waiting for him. The obituary on page 2 of the *Tribune* made a point of mentioning he died at midnight.

Mrs. Jennie Milligan—*cook*, Clara Fairbanks Home for Aged Women—r 721 8th Ave.

This elite retirement facility had been constructed just three years before with a $150,000 grant from local philanthropist Crawford Fairbanks. It actually looked like a home: a Georgian-style two-story with French doors, a sun porch, and a fireplace in the living room. Each resident of the home had her own room furnished with a mahogany bed, a dresser, a writing table, a sewing

CLARA FAIRBANKS HOME Terre Haute, Ind.

The Clara Fairbanks
Home for Aged Women

table, and a large, deep closet to accommodate the wardrobe of a longstanding lady of means.

And you thought Bruce Ladd had a tough gig at the Women's Department Club. Rest assured that Jennie heard about the quality of every single meal. The Clara Fairbanks Home would stay in operation for the next 62 years. A good bet would be that the turnover rate for the position of cook was higher than it was for the residents.

E. Clair Montgomery—*musician*, American Theater—r 112 N. 7th, Apt. 6

Yet another member of the band. He came from a musical household, or actually in this case, a musical apartment. His widowed mother, Tenie, also lived in Apartment 6, and offered music lessons. 112 N. 7th was located just a block from the Crossroads of America. It might actually be a stretch to call Number 6 an apartment. The Paddock Building seems to have been a commercial space, although Alice Jaques, a chiropractor in Number 1, apparently lived at her place of business, as well.

It's an accepted fact that when it came to square footage, adult Americans were able to get by on far less in 1927. That said, daily music lessons can make for a very small home indeed. For E. Clair Montgomery, that movie theater might have really been an escape from reality.

Charles M. Mooney (Gertha E.; Mooney Grocery Co.)—h 620 Walnut

MOONEY GROCERY CO. (Charles M. Mooney)—204 S. 4th and Stands 3–6, City Market

A true believer in what would never come to pass.

Charles M. Mooney, the sole proprietor of one of Terre Haute's many locally owned groceries, clearly saw himself pitted against the growing national chains like A&P and Piggly Wiggly. Witness this call to action printed in an ad in the Terre Haute *Star* in April 1926:

Notice—Food Buyers!
Use our service—Save your gas—Phone your order—We cut the price
and deliver your order free.
Stop and think what it means to you to patronize
"Hometown Groceries," namely service in the way of delivery
and in most cases charge accounts; it also gives you the advantage of
personal contact with the real owner and proprietor of a hometown
grocery. Last but not least, these merchants are citizens of our city.
Mooney's grocery is a hometown food store. If not convenient
to patronize us, you can find one in your neighborhood.
Watch for the red sign. It signifies Hometown Grocery.
Patronize us and receive the service you're entitled to.

Just six months earlier, in an essay entitled "The Open Hand," Mooney anticipated the challenges facing Terre Haute as hometown pride slowly drifted into apathy:

We are proud of our city. Let us all boost. Don't be
a quitter. Don't be a knocker. Don't backslide. Let's
all put our feet on the gas. All stay in Terre Haute
where we have sunshine, rain, and flowers, friends
and neighbors, no grafters, plenty of cheap homegrown food, cheap fuel, and no get-rich overnight
real estate booms.

Charles Mooney's inventory at his store on South 4th Street reflected his philosophy of local sustainability. Regional produce was presented along-side the daily supplies necessary for home cooking, home baking, and home canning.

A short shopping list:

Cornfield beans—6 pounds @ 25 cents
New comb of Pure Bee Honey—25 cents per rack
Pure Buckwheat Flour—7 cents a pound
Horseradish Root—17 cents a pound
New Vermont Maple Syrup—70 cents a quart
Pinhead Gunpowder Tea—75 cents
White Michigan Celery—10 cents a stalk

Taken together, the products, the sentiments, and the pleadings that now seem so prescient (save your gas, plenty of cheap homegrown food, the advantage of personal contact), all present themselves as lost artifacts of a

The Mooney Grocery
Building

once-sustainable society. This sustainability and local focus was borne out of necessity rather than intention or design. But you can classify the benefits as you would those of increased physical activity. Those benefits to the individual and the community were real, however they were arrived at. Let us add at this juncture: Charles Mooney likely walked to work every day.

The rising tide would soon overtake him. By 1933, Charles Mooney had sold his operation to the local grocery chain H. N. Oakley, which in turn would sell out in 1939 to a regional grocery chain based in Cincinnati, Kroger. Charles Mooney's hometown would continue to lose population from its peak of 66,083 in 1920. In 2007, the population of Terre Haute, Indiana, was estimated to be 57,259.

By then, most of what Mooney Grocery represented was regarded as inconvenient, inefficient, or unnecessary—any adjective to just get it out of the way.

Martha Moss—*clerk*, Butler Sisters—r 304 N. 5th

Apparently, she lived with them as well as worked with them. Martha was 26 years old that year; a former teacher recovering from a failed marriage to an auto mechanic. So now we have three women running a cigar stand in the lobby of the Filbeck Hotel in Terre Haute, Indiana, in 1927. It's like contemplating smoke rings as they float in the air.

MUNICIPAL SWIMMING POOL—1st and Park

Actually located in Fairbanks Park. Many municipalities built large public pools in the early part of the twentieth century to help keep their residents cool during the summer months. Terre Haute's pool was typical. It had a water area that could accommodate 1,500 people with 1,600 lockers to hold a change of clothing.

Since the pool was a public accommodation in 1924, it was deemed essential that every one of those bathers had to be white. After acknowledging that African American residents in the city were helping to pay for this pool with their tax dollars, the city council approved the construction of a smaller, separate pool in the Baghdad neighborhood. It was summarily referred to by whites as "The Inkwell."

Many cities like Baltimore and St. Louis maintained large municipal swimming pools and a segregated policy for their use up through the 1950s. When federal laws requiring the integration of public facilities were finally enacted, white bathers opted to abandon these pools almost completely. Rather than continue to provide public services to residents who had previously been denied their use, the cities decided to close these mammoth pools entirely.

This awkward situation was avoided in Terre Haute 30 years earlier when, literally, the earth moved. In 1934, the Municipal Swimming Pool at Fairbanks Park was abruptly closed after a large crack developed. The pool was never re-opened. After becoming aware of the potential response if it actually were, the city decided to demolish the facility in 1964. A new strategy emerged. Wait about 20 years for social changes to take hold, then try again with smaller pools in other city parks.

The Municipal Swimming Pool at Fairbanks Park

ERNESTINE MYERS DANCING ACADEMY—634½ Wabash

When it came to Terre Haute, Indiana, in the 1920s, Ernestine was regarded as the greatest dancer of her generation.

As is so often the case with dancers, she started quite early. Accompanied by her mother, she traveled to Los Angeles at age 14 to study with Ruth St. Denis and Ted Shawn. A few years later, she was appearing at the Winter Garden and the Palace Theater with partner Clyde Randall.

She had a promising career far beyond the Broadway chorus line by now; for some a little too far. Performing in "Silks and Satins" at the George M. Cohan Theater, Ernestine received mixed reviews. Critics complained about her barefoot dancing and her exotic mix of classical ballet, Creole, and Oriental dance styles. This was territory that dance pioneer Isadora Duncan had been exploring. But then, she was from San Francisco, not Terre Haute.

In 1922, Ernestine Myers was ready to embark on a European tour. A sensible career move, since it was in Europe that Isadora Duncan had experienced the greatest reception to her innovative work. But on the eve of Ernestine's departure, her business manager died suddenly. Ernestine Myers decided to cancel her bookings and return to her hometown to start a dancing school.

And in 1927, there it was: a large sunlit room on an upper floor overlooking the busiest street in town. Perhaps fittingly, one of Ernestine's neighbors was a chiropodist. Isadora Duncan was in Europe that year. As she was riding through France seated in a sleek roadster, her long silk scarf became entangled in the spokes of the rear wheel. Isadora was killed instantly. Meanwhile back at 634½ Wabash Avenue, Ernestine Myers had 64 years of life ahead of her with nothing left to do but dance.

Agnes Nairn—*welder*, Columbian Enameling and Stamping Company—r 2031 N. 12th

Elizabeth Nairn—*welder*, Columbian Enameling and Stamping Company—r 2031 N. 12th

Charles W. Napier—*furnaceman*, Columbian Enameling and Stamping Company—h 2038 Plum

Dona Napier—*sorter*, Columbian Enameling and Stamping Company—r 3236 N. 15th

Roy Napier—*clerk*, Columbian Enameling and Stamping Company—r 1526 6th Ave.

S. Anna Napier (widow, Charles)—h 1526 6th Ave.

William R. Napier (Amy L.)—*laborer*, Columbian Enameling and Stamping Company—r 2714 N. 18th

The Columbian Enameling and Stamping Company was the largest single employer in Terre Haute in 1927 with about 950 employees. The massive facility covered 13 acres. Like many of the industries operating in Terre Haute around this time, the company marketed an iconic piece of Americana: the white enameled coffee pot commonly found in campsites, cabooses, and kitchens all over the country. The perfect cup from this pot called for coffee grounds with bits of dried eggshell or chicory root mixed in.

In 1927 most all of that coffee would be harvested in Brazil. Upon its arrival in Terre Haute it was ground and marketed by local food processors like the Hulman Company and Bement-Rea. Just by itself, Hulman produced Rex, Dauntless, and Old Plantation brand coffee, just part of an entirely local breakfast consisting of bacon from the Home Packing Company, hominy made with cornmeal from C. D. Hansel's mill, and eggs from a neighbor's backyard coop. In 1927, thousands of Terre Haute residents started the day firmly grounded in the place where they woke up. The Nairn sisters might have done exactly this before walking over to their shifts at the Columbian plant.

The initials C E S C O were painted on the side of Columbian's tall brick smokestack rising above Terre Haute's north side. The company had been operating there since 1902. At its peak in 1920, the company employed more than 1,200 workers. A quality product was produced, profits were made, wages were paid, the shift whistle blew, workers washed up and headed home. You might think a cooperative relationship like this would cycle through the days as naturally as the tides or the seasons. Unfortunately, where the volatile passions of human beings are involved, this is rarely the case. It might have been difficult to predict in 1927, but within ten years the workers and the management at Columbian would engage in a fierce struggle resulting in violence and destruction. Whatever good feeling once existed between them would evaporate almost overnight.

There were more than 22,600 strikes called in the United States over the course of the 1930s. One of the most memorable would occur at the Columbian Enameling and Stamping Company plant on March 23, 1935. The conflict had actually started the year before with an effort to unionize the workers. In the wake of federal legislation that facilitated labor organizing, the United Garment Workers Union negotiated a one-year agreement with the management at Columbian. The agreement outlined grievance procedures, a seniority system, and an arbitration process to resolve any serious differences that might lead to strikes. Over the course of this initial contract, it was agreed that union membership would be entirely voluntary.

Almost from the outset, there were serious disagreements. First, the management claimed it was unable to institute an automatic deduction of union dues from the paychecks it issued. This was despite the fact that it was already processing a similar deduction for company-sponsored insurance premiums. The company then established an athletic club exclusively for non-union employees and followed that up with other preferential benefits and promotions.

The union soon realized that the only way to ensure its long-term survival at the company was to create a "closed shop," where all non-management positions at Columbian would be unionized. Negotiations between the company and the union began in November of 1934. Meanwhile, an interim report from Department of Labor mediator Robert Mythen concluded that given the conditions at Columbian, the union's request for a closed shop was reasonable.

Not surprisingly, negotiations dragged on over the course of the next five months with little change in company policy. The rank and file finally voted to strike and on Saturday, March 23, 1935, 450 workers at Columbian Enameling and Stamping Company walked off the job. In response, company president Charles Gorby closed the plant for an indefinite period. Now there was no turning back. It's as if everyone involved suddenly became convinced that wherever all this was leading, it would have to end badly.

On June 11, 1935, the company management announced that it would hold no further discussions with the union and if the plant did reopen, it would be with non-union labor. Four days later, armed uniformed guards hired by the company entered the plant.

The next day was a Sunday. Outside the company's offices on Beech Street, a large crowd began to assemble. In a very short time, the crowd became an angry mob. It attacked the offices where the guards had barricaded themselves, demolishing the telephone exchange, overturning desks, and tossing office equipment onto the floor. The private guards quickly retreated to await a police escort away from the plant.

The following weeks were filled with accusations, threats, and growing resentment, without any communication that resembled meaningful dialogue. The company management hired representatives to visit the homes of workers to convince them to abandon the union and return to work. A further escalation of tensions was almost inevitable. Finally, on Wednesday, July 17, a private security force of 50 men armed with shotguns and submachine guns entered the plant.

The response to this latest provocation was immediate. Much like the huge crowd that gathered at Union Station to welcome Eugene Debs home from federal prison, citizens amassed outside the county courthouse the following Sunday. The total number has been the subject of speculation ever since. A

fair estimate would be about 3,000 people. Were it not for the actions taken that day, history would have been content to completely ignore the gathering, assuming those who attended simply returned to their daily lives.

But that afternoon, this crowd decided to organize a citywide labor holiday. It began at 1:00 the following morning when all public transit in the city was shut down. Terre Haute's factories, its retail stores, its movie theaters, and its barber shops were all informed that a general strike was in progress. By midday on Monday, July 22, 1935, the city of Terre Haute, Indiana, had virtually ground to a halt. By nightfall, the strike had been deemed 90 percent effective.

Starting on that Monday morning at 1:00 AM, Terre Haute, for all practical purposes, entered a dead zone, a place of paralysis where collective shock and outrage obscures the ability to manage a situation. This would be only the third general strike called in American history. The two others had occurred in much larger cities: San Francisco and Seattle. While this fact may have made Terre Haute's general strike less impressive, the actions taken within those ten square miles also made it more effective.

At 5:00 PM on Monday, July 22nd, Indiana governor Paul McNutt declared a state of emergency and ordered 7,000 National Guard troops to the city. Tear

A Crowd Masses at Columbian Enameling, 1935 Martin Collection, Indiana Historical Society gas and rifle butts were used on two separate occasions to disperse crowds gathered outside the Columbian plant. There were multiple injuries and more than 150 arrests. Suddenly, a local strike had become national news. Although Labor Secretary Frances Perkins issued a statement placing the primary responsibility for the conflict with the company, it carried neither the force of law nor sanction. On August 1st, the Columbian Enameling and Stamping Company plant announced its plans to resume operations with replacement workers and that it would no longer discuss the job action with union representatives, federal mediators, the press, or anyone else. Terre Haute, Indiana, would remain a military district until February 10, 1936, a period of more than six months.

The division and damage done to Terre Haute from that one long, painful year proved to be irreparable. It struck at the very heart of what made the city a hometown for its residents. Throughout the 1920s, individuals had relied every day on other people they knew or recognized for food, entertainment, news and information, as well as simple human connection. The Depression had already affected much of this interdependence as local grocery stores that had extended credit to steady customers went unpaid and small family businesses who had hired their neighbors cut payrolls. During the general strike, personal decisions divided families, boarders, barbershop customers, households living side by side. People began to avoid each other's glances on the sidewalk, glances that once led to a greeting and a moment of friendly conversation. Some residents turned inward, while others suddenly became frantic to get out of town.

The state of martial law declared by Governor Paul McNutt was the equivalent of a final divorce decree. People chose sides, hardened their positions, and drew thick lines around their friends as well as their enemies. That left a tacit agreement to be struck between the divided camps. This agreement was never actually signed by the warring parties since it was never an actual document, nor was it followed by any subsequent action or negotiation. It was simply an agreement to allow daily life to continue in Terre Haute by avoiding this painful chapter for as long as those who had lived through it were still alive. Seldom discussed, never revisited—not for now, anyway.

The last veterans from all of the nations who fought in World War I will finally die early in this century. It is thought that their passing may offer the first real opportunity to openly discuss and evaluate this crippling human event with some sense of perspective. Someday, after time does its work, perhaps that day will arrive in Terre Haute, Indiana. At last, no feelings left to hurt, no arguments left to have, all of that anger finally spent with the last breath and heartbeat of the very last witness.

(N) Minerva Nash (spouse of Wayne R.—*manager*, Nash Baking Company)

Nasser Brothers (Essa N. and Moses N.)—*grocers*—224 N. 2nd

In the 1920s, the Syrian population in Terre Haute, Indiana, was estimated to be between 400 and 500 individuals. Perhaps more than any other ethnic group living in the city, the Syrians would become identified with an occupation. A remarkable number represented the ancient tradition of street merchants first established in the bazaars of Damascus. It was estimated in 1922 that there were 66 Syrian groceries operating in Terre Haute. In the spirit of those ancient bazaars, many of these were clustered within footsteps of each other just north of downtown.

Essa and Moses Nasser not only ran one of the many Syrian groceries in Terre Haute, but also one of many groceries in Terre Haute run by grocers named Nasser. Incredibly, in 1927 there was a completely separate grocery store located at 302 North 1st Street operated by one Essa M. Nasser. In addition, on the 100 block of North 4th, there was Esseff Nasser's grocery, followed by the Nasser Brothers, then Essa N. Nasser's second location at 208, and finally Joseph Nasser's grocery at 231. Just up the street, there were two groceries on the 300 block: one owned by George Nasser on the corner of Eagle Street and one owned by Saleem Nasser at the corner of Chestnut. Down on the city's south side, Harding Avenue featured three separate groceries run by Faris, Kelly, and Thomas Nasser.

If you didn't happen to find the actual proprietor standing behind the counter, it's likely another Nasser would be there to help. Albert Nasser worked in the South 4th Street store that his father, Moses, owned. Charles Nasser worked for his father, Saleem, while Frank Nasser clerked for his father, Samuel.

The inevitable name confusion was often resolved by customers in ways that strengthened their neighborhood using the subtleties of place and name. It's fascinating to think of North 4th Street residents shopping with Joseph Nasser simply because they lived on the 200 block or with George or Saleem because they were living just a little further north—this Nasser because it's this part of North 4th Street. There were also the distinctive first names to establish a store's ownership and identity. After these names had been pronounced correctly and had come to be used every day by born Hoosiers, the North 4th Street neighborhood became just a little bit larger, while the world beyond it moved nearer.

(N) Williams Neal—County Poor Farm

Gladys Neill—*waitress*, Farmers Hotel—r 128 S. 4th

William F. Nelson—*clerk*, National Hotel—r do

Maude Newman—*furnished rooms*—20½ N. 4th h do

They were all modest commercial lodgings located up and down 4th Street.

Breakfast at the Farmers Hotel was served with the customer in mind: farm-style with big bowls and long tables. For Gladys, that made it early in the day and hard on the back. She apparently lived at the Farmers Hotel as well, though considering the amenities there you could hardly call this a fringe benefit.

The National was a hotel with only 65 rooms located in the heart of downtown at 17 North 4th Street, a half-block from Wabash Avenue. Probably the smallest hotel you could have found in Terre Haute with its own restaurant and barbershop. Across the street from the National and just upstairs from a grocery store, a few furnished rooms were offered by Maude Newman.

Each of these individuals took up one room out of a pretty small total. For a slightly different perspective on their presence in life: it's likely at least two of them faced a brick wall out their windows.

Raymond Niccum—*musician*, American Theater—r 623 S. 7th

The vocalist for Paul Johnson's American Theater Orchestra.

Alma Niebrugge (widow, George W.)—*corsetiere*—h 452 N. 6th

A necessary job back when corsets were popular, not only for their sale but also for their installation. The traditional corset was bound and secured from the back with long, strong strings. Over the years, mothers, sisters, and roommates had been enlisted to tighten the corset and then tie the knot. By 1927, this job was increasingly being done by a sympathetic daughter or maid. Girdles had pretty much taken over the foundation market for younger women, when such things were being worn at all. The primary advantage with girdles was that their elastic stays enabled them to be self-administered.

Alma was 59 years old in 1927. Her impressionable years had been during the 1880s, when Lillian Russell emerged as the American standard for female beauty. Lillian was a farm gal from Clinton, Iowa. Her full figure, made curvaceous by the tightest of corsets, encouraged more than a few young women of her day to pull their abdomen in and push their bosom out while lacing tightly to maximize the effect. An indication how much those standards had changed in the intervening generation: Lillian Russell weighed approximately 200 lbs.

Edward Noel—County Poor Farm

NORTH BALTIMORE BOTTLE GLASS COMPANY, north side of Maple Ave. at the Chicago and Eastern Illinois Railroad—Phone: Wabash 6520—Manufacturers of Beverage Bottles of All Kinds—**Albert J. Phau,** *president*—**E. D. Richardson,** *secretary-treasurer*

The North Baltimore Bottle Glass Company was part of a once-flourishing bottle-making industry in Terre Haute that had employed 2,500 workers back in 1912. Union Local 60 of the Glass Bottle Blowers Association had claimed 450 members, the second-largest total in the United States. The North Baltimore Bottle Glass Company was manufacturing bottles for Schlitz Brewing Company of Milwaukee and Anheuser-Busch of St. Louis. That year, Schlitz had introduced brown glass beer bottles to the market for the first time. The North Baltimore factory employed 800 workers. Times were good. It called for a toast.

Then came the passage of the Eighteenth Amendment to the Constitution, which prohibited the sale, manufacture, transport, and possession of alcoholic beverages. The law took effect on January 16, 1920. By 1921, the total number of workers employed by Terre Haute's bottle-making factories had fallen to 250. The North Baltimore Bottle Glass Company lost its lucrative contracts, laid off a quarter of its workforce, and finally suspended operations altogether. A dark decade lay ahead.

By the summer of 1926, Albert Phau had decided to re-open on a more limited scale. It was thought that bottling ginger ale might hold some promise for the company. In the meantime, Albert could find a sympathetic ear from

August Busch and the president of Schlitz Brewery, Joseph Uihlein. All of them would be weathering the same storm over the next seven years.

The three men shared a common heritage. The tradition in the German culture was to encourage beer consumption starting in early adolescence. This new and curious legislation passed in their adopted homeland must have made them shake their heads in wonder.

The North Baltimore Bottle
Glass Company
Community Archives, Vigo
County Public Library

(N) Harry E. Oaf (Leona)—*manager*—h 2528 S. 7th

Patrick F. O'Brien (Margaret)—*police*—h 732 N. 4th

Supposedly the answer to every Irish mother's prayer—that is, if her son hadn't chosen the priesthood instead. Well-worn stereotypes aside, many ethnic groups in America did gravitate toward particular occupations in the early decades of the twentieth century. A large number of grocers in Terre Haute came from the Syrian community. In New York City, much of the skyscraper and elevated bridge construction was accomplished by Mohawk Indians who possessed extraordinary ease and focus while working at great heights. Italian immigrants were commonly drawn to the barbering trade. Chinese Americans often opened hand-wash laundries.

This last association was so well fixed in the broad American consciousness that the Polk Directory for 1927 actually had a separate business listing for "Laundries—Chinese." There were six such operations in Terre Haute and the Moy family ran three of them. Jim Moy's laundry was located at 102 North 4th Street, right next door to Esseff Nasser's grocery.

Officer O'Brien might very well have checked the locks on both businesses during his appointed rounds. In 1927, foot patrolmen were common throughout Terre Haute: halting traffic at school crossings, rousting vagrants from park benches, enforcing the laws of the land. It was a privileged position in American life that the mothers of Jim Moy and Esseff Nasser had never even dared to pray for.

Carrie Oelgeschlager—h 825 S. 3rd

Edna Oelgeschlager—*teacher*, Hook School—r 825 S. 3rd

Mary E. Oelgeschlager—*seamstress*—r 825 S. 3rd

Sophia Oelgeschlager—r 825 S. 3rd

The German community had firmly established itself in Terre Haute by the 1870s. Oelgeschlager is one name from the old country that made it across intact. Not that it didn't meet with a few challenges upon arrival. When Henry F. Oelgeschlager married a doctor's daughter in September 1908, the courthouse clerk cropped his last name off at the second "g" on the license application. As it was, the space provided on the form just barely accommodated this abbreviation.

Over the years, easily as many young women married into the Oelgeschlager name as out of it, so that by 1927 Terre Haute had 15 adults carrying this 13-letter surname. Just to increase the confusion, this included two Henrys, two Katherines, and two Marys. Mary Frances Oelgeschlager had what many might consider the perfect maiden name, but she had to wait till she was 35 to marry Floyd Cooper. Mary Frances would squeeze her entire last name onto her marriage application, no doubt relieved that it would be the last time she'd ever have to write it.

The name Oelgeschlager was precisely the kind of distinctive ethnic identity that would get shortened and Anglicized right out of existence as America became more blended over the course of the twentieth century. From 1927 on,

The Hotel Deming
Gourmet Room

a dozen Oelgeschlagers would have their obits printed in Terre Haute newspapers. The last two, interestingly enough, were Edna and Sophia, who died within hours of each other in the first few days of 1969.

Both of these sisters had remained single and retained the family name throughout their entire life. So in a strange way, Edna's and Sophia's passing marked the formal end of the Oelgeschlager line in their community—a distinction not often bestowed upon a woman's life.

Jennie Olson—*helper*, Mother's Dining Room—r 223 N. 5th

Or, Mother's little helper. For a business looking to recreate the comforts of home for its customers, the job title of dishwasher didn't quite fit, even if the job description did. (*See* C. M. Eaton.)

(N) Alkarkadelphia Orr (spouse of Preston—*laborer*, Terre Haute Malleable and Manufacturing Co.)—h 829 Gilbert Ave.

George Osborne (Lula L.)—*doughnuts*—715 N. 8th h do

When it came time to make the doughnuts, at least he didn't have to travel far to do it. In 1927, we're talking the two basic varieties: plain or with a confectioner's sugar coating. This reflected the widespread belief that a doughnut's true purpose was for dunking in a hot cup of coffee. Clark Gable gives a good tutorial on it in the 1934 film *It Happened One Night*.

James Osler (Ellen T.)—*chef*, Hotel Deming—r 211 N. 5th

The title of chef was not as much of a stretch here as it was for the Sullivan Hotel and Fanny McKinney. The Hotel Deming's restaurant was named the

Gourmet Room. But this being Terre Haute, Indiana, Chef Osler had a continual challenge living up to his job title. The lunch crowd at the Deming was by and large middle-brow businessmen, so reinventing standard menu items had as much to do with the choice of words as it did the choice of ingredients. A bowl of soup became consommé. A standard dessert became shortcake. And faced with a seasonal demand for a popular Midwestern staple, the Gourmet Room discovered regional cuisine. And so, hot dogs were listed as Milwaukee Frankfurters with Horseradish on the menu. Diners at the Gourmet Room were greeted by a hostess. From noon to 1:30, the Fisher Ladies Trio on violin, cello, and piano would entertain the diners. All told, it was just barely enough class for the noon meal at the Hotel Deming to earn the title of luncheon.

Mabel P. Paine—*supervisor of penmanship*, Public Schools—r 1819 S. 8th

This was regarded as a fundamental skill in 1927. Like daily grooming and good grammar, neat penmanship was valued as a quality that enhanced an individual's status in a community. You don't need statistics to trace its declining importance over recent generations. Currently, many 80-year-olds still display the skill with proficiency while it's almost impossible to find a 20-year-old who has ever properly learned even the fundamentals. The importance of beautiful handwriting currently falls somewhere between whistling and gardening; while its presence is still noticed and admired, few people appreciate it enough to actually acquire the skill themselves.

Penmanship was once among the many forms of individual expression that helped to define identity, much like the kind of hat one chose to wear. Elementary school classes in America had been teaching penmanship as an essential component of childhood education since the eighteenth century. The Copperplate and Spencerian styles with their fluid sweeping curves and flourishes were seen as both artistic and practical. With time, someone's handwriting could help to define their overall identity—becoming as distinctive as the sound of their voice. It's little wonder that handwritten letters could often communicate and elicit the deepest emotions.

Ballpoint pens would not become widely available until the late 1940s. So any serious handwriting done under Mabel Paine's watch involved the use of a fountain pen or a metal nib dipped in an inkwell. This just added to the skill set. Children were first introduced to penmanship through manuscript or block letter printing using a thick graphite pencil. By the late second or early third grade, the switch would be made to cursive writing in ink on lined paper.

Like sewing or carpentry, the skill of handwriting required a mix of patience, dexterity, and attention to detail. Once handwriting was mastered, distinctive variations might emerge—especially with one's signature. But those were among the rewards of mastery. Like any apprentices to a craft, Mabel Paine's charges were encouraged to carefully copy examples and strictly follow directions.

In 1927, the eventual rewards for mastery in sewing or carpentry might include a professional career. But by this time, Mabel Paine was probably the only person in Terre Haute, Indiana, actually earning a living from the craft of penmanship. Sadly, no surviving samples of her work have yet surfaced.

PAITSON BROTHERS (Edward J. and R. Walter Paitson), Baking, Grocery, and Meat Market—1474 Locust—Phone: Wabash 6618

PAITSON BROTHERS (Robert C. and Stanley J. Paitson)—Hardware, Paints, Oils and Varnish, Hartford Batteries, Automobile Supplies, General Automobile Repairing, Storage, Gasoline, Oils and Greases—916–918 N. 15th—Phone: Wabash 4291

You'd have to wonder about their childhood: gravitating as they did toward specific shared interests early on. One imagines their spare time spent separately in the kitchen or at the tool bench. In 1927, Edward and Walter had been

The Paitson Brothers Grocery
Martin Collection, Indiana
Historical Society

operating their grocery on Locust Street for eight years. Each of them lived in the 1400 block, literally right across the street from one another. To give you a sense of their neighborhood, when the two brothers walked to their store every morning they passed by the home of a music teacher and the small movie theater where Ada Campbell played, the Alhambra.

Robert and Stanley were operating their hardware store, gas station, and auto repair shop just around the corner, between Locust and 1st Avenue. Right next door to Frank and Catherine Cassel's billiard room, in fact. Bob and Stan loved cars, obviously, so it's possible they drove to work instead.

More story to tell here. There was actually a fifth brother, Fred, who had learned baking. His business partnership was with George Martin, who lived with his wife, Edna, in the same building as the bakery. It was located right next to Max Frank's shoe repair shop at 106 North 7th Street.

From being quite common in 1927, local family businesses with brothers or fathers and sons had become fairly scarce by the end of the century. The Paitson brothers' grocery store finally closed in 1979. Robert and Stanley's business legacy, however, would actually survive the century. The Paitson name continued to thrive in the family's hometown, albeit from two separate locations, as both a hardware store and as contractors for heating and cooling.

John Parish—County Poor Farm

James P. Parks (Sarah J.—Parks Purity Pie Company)—h 323 N. 18th

The Paitson Brothers Hardware and Garage Martin Collection, Indiana Historical Society

The original heaven of pies. The company was founded and run by James and his brother Thurston. At the time, occupational cleanliness in food preparation was perceived as being extremely important to customers. It was common for small diners to name themselves "sanitary lunches," attempting to counter their popular reputation as "greasy spoons." Locally, the Terre Haute Pure Milk and Ice Cream Company operated alongside King's Sanitary Dairy.

The motto at Parks Purity Pie Company was "bakes nothing but pies." This singular focus would stand the company in good stead over the years. Parks Purity Pie Company was still operating in Terre Haute at the end of the twentieth century, though it would close soon after. A pity you can no longer call to place an order and hear someone navigate that mouthful of alliteration. It was a daily challenge that dated back to 1927, when the number to dial was Dresser 505.

(N) Millicent Parsley (spouse of Arthur, *station engineer*)—h 2504 N. 15th

PARSONS FIELD (Normal Athletic Field)—northeast corner of 1st and Sycamore

In the spring of 1927, a small group of committed female students from Indiana State Normal began practicing field hockey. The informal practice sessions had only been intended to last through the fall semester. But the women, led by senior Rosemary Draper, continued to refine their team game when the warm weather returned. No games against actual competition had been scheduled. This was due in no small part to the difficulty of finding other women's field hockey teams within a reasonable distance. Actually, in 1927 finding women playing any collegiate sport was a challenge. Even so, the women continued to practice together. Their male classmates would occasionally gather on the sidelines to watch and kibitz.

Then, as the end of the school year approached, an invitation was extended from St. Mary-of-the-Woods, an all-women's college located just across the river. One game. The Indiana State Normal field hockey team was quickly formed: 14 women athletes—11 position players and three substitutes—made the short road trip. The team featured the school's most avid female athletes. Rosemary Draper was also a guard on the women's basketball team. Center forward Florence Davis excelled in both basketball and track and field. One of the two inners, Beulah Watson, would win individual honors in tennis that spring. The other, Edith Johnson, was an accomplished dancer.

But beyond that one game, what then? Teaching careers, for some. Marriage and motherhood, for others. And what role would athletics or simply the joy of movement play in their daily lives? Something to contemplate as the small team bus crossed the Wabash River bridge. Some other thoughts might have focused on the game itself, especially on the trip back. The Indiana Normal Field Hockey team lost that day to St. Mary-of-the-Woods by a score of 8–2.

Tillman Payne—County Poor Farm

PEERLESS CLEANING COMPANY—(F. J. McGough)—A Mother's Care to the Clothes You Wear—Men's Suits Cleaned and Pressed—207–215 Hulman—Phone: Wabash 8000—Uptown office: 15 S. 6th—Phone: Wabash 263

Peter K. Peters (Mary; Fountain Theater)—h 622 N. 5th

Somewhere in the back of his mind, perhaps, some thanks that his parents hadn't chosen Robert. That name may have formed the basis for even more unrelenting taunts throughout his childhood, considering it's part of what was a popular off-color joke from the period:

> A man entering a barbershop: "Bob Peters here?"
> Barber: "No, I'm sorry. We just cut hair."

William Phinney—County Poor Farm

The presence of the Jewish community in Terre Haute reached its zenith sometime during the 1920s. It was a meteoric rise; one aligned with the life span of a particular generation. The story begins with a group of young entrepreneurs who set up businesses in Terre Haute's downtown and then gathered socially after they closed up shop. This has always been a potent formula for community building. If shared interests among various individuals can be established alongside their social interaction and an ongoing financial commitment, what generally results is a group whose influence far exceeds the sum of its parts.

In 1888, approximately 30 Jewish families were members of the B'nai Abraham Orthodox Synagogue in Terre Haute, Indiana. Just two years earlier, the Phoenix Club had been established. The club's existence was likely a response to the fraternal organizations in Terre Haute who would not admit Jews to their membership, but fundamentally it was just an excuse for people to get together and have some fun. By 1899, the Phoenix Club had established headquarters in the Cox-Froeb Building above the M. Joseph and Son clothing store at 512 Wabash. The space included a billiard room, a library, a card room, and a small dance hall.

The membership of the Phoenix Club continued to grow and soon a larger facility owned outright by the club seemed like a logical step. A large brick building at the corner of 5th and Walnut Streets became the club's new headquarters. Then in 1920, when the Terre Haute Country Club moved to Allendale, the Phoenix Club decided to lease their vacated site—55 acres just east of the city. Within a year, the membership had purchased the property outright for $70,000. The Phoenix Country Club opened on June 1st, 1921. Two years later, the building at 5th and Walnut was sold to the Central Labor Union and the club set up its downtown headquarters at 330 South 6th Street.

By then, the Phoenix Country Club had become a social oasis for Terre Haute's two distinct Jewish congregations. Temple Israel, the city's Reform synagogue, had been dedicated in 1911 at 549 South 6th Street. Within a dozen years, the membership had grown to 130. Temple Israel's rabbi at the time was Joseph L. Fink, a tenth generation rabbi who was serving as president of the local Community Chest. Soon after his appointment, Rabbi Fink had received a letter from the Vigo County Chapter of the Ku Klux Klan demanding his immediate resignation. To further this effort at intimidation, the letter called for the rabbi to appear at the weekly gathering of Klan members in Highland Lawn Cemetery.

Three hundred robed Klansmen were waiting. Rabbi Fink arrived at Highland Lawn alone. Addressing the Klansmen directly, he criticized them for hiding their faces and then told them that although the group prided itself as being "100% American," its actions were contrary to the Bill of Rights, which guaranteed freedom of religion. Because of this, Rabbi Fink concluded, the Klansmen were essentially un-American. He would walk away from Highland Lawn Cemetery that night unharmed.

In 1925, the B'nai Abraham Orthodox Congregation announced plans to build a new synagogue on the southeast corner of 5th and Poplar, just a block

The Phoenix Club Downtown

from the former site of the Phoenix Club. With the support of the 100 families in the congregation, the synagogue was finally dedicated on August 28, 1927. That year, there were 47 Jewish businesses operating on Wabash Avenue, including some of the most prominent names in Terre Haute's downtown: Herz, Kleeman, Lederer, Silberman, Goodman, Goldberg, and Silverstein. These businesses would be closed on significant Jewish holidays, including Yom Kippur. In a clear response to every Terre Haute resident who might avoid shopping at a store owned by a Jewish merchant, there was the committed support from congregations at both Temple Israel and B'nai Abraham. At the Tuesday evening bridge parties held in the Phoenix Club, the prizes included gift certificates from the stores of club members: men's clothing from Carl Wolf, women's clothing from Harry Jame, matching shoes from Ben Becker. The Phoenix Club hosted charity balls, wedding receptions, joke-a-stroke golf tourneys; basically, this was a community functioning.

Then gradually, almost imperceptibly at first, it started to fade away. In 1927, a fire at the country club would destroy the main clubhouse. In 1928, the Phoenix Club would close its downtown location on South 6th Street, focusing all of the club's activities at the eastside location. Then, with the onset of the Depression, the club's membership began to decline. Within a few years, it would affect far more than the community's social and leisure choices. In 1935, the Orthodox and Reform Jewish congregations in Terre Haute voted to merge. It became the first such merger completed in the United States. After a generation of growth, the Jewish community in Terre Haute was now starting to consolidate and constrict.

Over the course of generations, a common lament is heard among religious and ethnic groups as cultural assimilation changes personal values. Family businesses die because sons move away or choose to become doctors instead. Religious congregations and social clubs reflect their increasingly aging membership and find themselves unable or unwilling to attract new blood. Orthodox services would be conducted at Temple Israel until 1960. In 1979, the Phoenix Country Club formally disbanded. The site of the club would eventually become another type of community, attuned to the more impersonal realities of life in the late twentieth century. Within a few years, a residential subdivision would be built there.

Foursome at the Phoenix Country Club
Martin Collection, Indiana Historical Society

Howard Pierce—*coffee roaster helper*—r 629 Chestnut

Long before Starbucks, Howard Pierce was working in a high-growth industry. Between 1914 and 1937, coffee drinking in the United States increased 20 percent. In 1936, the Pan American Coffee Bureau was established to promote the practice even further. During the first four years of their advertising campaign, annual coffee consumption nationwide rose another 20 percent.

In Terre Haute, Indiana, a good place to learn the trade was Joseph Strong & Company. For years, the mills at 29 South 6th Street ground a wide variety spices, tea, and coffee and roasted the beans. Joseph Strong & Company also held the distinction of having installed one of the earliest telephones in the downtown area. Their phone number in 1927 was Wabash 34. But why would someone call them on the phone and miss out on that indescribable aroma?

(N) Commodore D. Pigg (Jennie)—*machine operator*, Indiana Consumer Gas and By Products Company—h 2959 S. 8th

Carl E. Plummer—*employee*, Wabash Cutlery Company—r 2320 1st Ave.

The factory was located at 811 North 22nd Street. Carl Plummer rented a room about three blocks away.

We'll begin with the hometown company name, the modest size of the factory itself, and the residential neighborhood that surrounded it. Combine all this with the product that was made there and what results is a small window into an America that was still flourishing in 1927, at least in Terre Haute, Indiana.

The Wabash Cutlery Company manufactured jackknives—to whittle a stick, clean a thumbnail, cut a fishing line, slice an apple, or mark the annual height of your child on a doorjamb. In other words, a tool essential to a life spent engaged with the natural world. The hometown, Terre Haute, Indiana, was imprinted right there on the blade.

And it was a pretty good-quality jackknife too. The starting price in online auctions for jackknives with the Wabash name today commonly exceeds $100.00.

Dominick Polvisitis—County Poor Farm

Mary Porter—County Poor Farm

J. Wood Posey (Gertrude T.—Twelve Points Bicycle Shop)—h 1315 S. 7th

Charles G. Pugh (Louise)—*bicycles* @ 607 Ohio—h 1107 S. 7th

When pneumatic tires were first invented in 1888, they were intended for bicycles, not automobiles. Within the next ten years, a string of improvements would be made to bicycle safety and comfort, including cushion seats, coaster brakes, and adjustable handle bars. Accordingly, the number of riders across the United States grew exponentially until by 1896 it was estimated that about 4,000,000 Americans rode bicycles regularly. That would have been over 5 percent of the total population. By the turn of the century, the nation had more than 300 bicycle factories producing a million bicycles a year.

Riding a bicycle represented a blending of the technical and the sensory that achieved a certain sublime balance. The bicycle itself was mechanical, the smoothness of the ride dependent on such innovations as rubber tires and paved surfaces. Even so, it was raw human power that moved it. The rider developed at least a subliminal consciousness of the natural surroundings: gradual changes in elevation, a cool summer breeze, the shade of a street tree. The experience was much like walking in the end, only faster.

By 1927, there were six bicycle dealers operating in Terre Haute, Indiana—a city of about 65,000 people and 16,000 automobiles. Although children rode bicycles to and from schools and playgrounds, the youth market was primarily served by hardware and department stores. Charles Pugh and J. Wood Posey focused on adult models, bicycles from 26" up. Like certain popular automobiles from this period, many bicycle brands, including Pierce, Yale, and Iver-Johnson, are no longer manufactured. This despite the fact that the basic technology of the sprocket-driven bicycle has changed very little in the intervening years. Then as always, the only oil required to operate a bicycle is for lubrication.

The Twelve Points Bicycle Shop run by J. Wood Posey was located in a classic urban neighborhood. The shop also sold and repaired motorcycles, thought to be a natural progression from a childhood spent balancing on two wheels. Every service in Twelve Points was within walking distance of home, but adding a bicycle, especially a motorized one, to your life would easily expand your range to the downtown area.

That's where you'd find Charles Pugh and his three competitors, two of whom were also located along Ohio Street. Each man had been in early

The Twelve Points
Bicycle Shop

adulthood during the bicycle revolution in America. Each had swooned under the spell, and through their businesses the old passions remained. Herman Nektar at 420 Ohio featured a brand of two-wheelers that would soon become legendary, although the Harley-Davidsons on his floor had no engines. J. E. Sayre and Son at 331 Ohio was the largest bicycle dealer in the city, featuring nine different brands.

Charles Pugh, operating further up the street, carried Cleveland and Wabash brand bicycles. The latter would presumably have been ideal for riding around Terre Haute. But there were other reasons to drop by Mr. Pugh's small shop. Every morning he was open, Charles Pugh stood on the sidewalk at the 600 block and fed the flocks of pigeons that made homes in nearby church steeples and building eaves.

The pigeon population on that stretch of Ohio had been decimated a few years before when a large flock roosting in the belfry of the Congregational church just across the street from the bicycle shop was mysteriously poisoned. Pigeons have a life expectancy that can reach up to 35 years. By the spring of 1927, the survivors and their new families had returned to the belfry and had grown to trust Charles Pugh. As he spread breadcrumbs on the sidewalk in front of his shop, a few of his friends would perch upon his shoulders.

The addresses for the Posey and Pugh households should be noted here. Apparently, it would have been possible for J. Wood and Charles to ride to work together, though both their advancing age and the growing temptation of automobiles would make this far less likely in a year or two.

(N) Arvella Pushback (spouse of John—*glassworker*)—h 2818 S. 13½

THE QUALITY SHOP—**Herb Leach,** *proprietor*—Haberdashers, Hatters, Tailors, and Shirt Makers, 523 Wabash Ave., Phone: Wabash 1113

The finer details of personal appearance have traditionally been the province of women, from polished nails to jewelry to perfume. But in 1927, men of average means gave enormous attention and spent a good bit of their resources on grooming and adornment. This effort might have occasionally gone to what we now consider extremes, in part because men today are simply unwilling to invest the necessary time or acquire the necessary skills to achieve a signature style. And in America, if adults become disinterested with something—it generally doesn't get done.

We're not necessarily talking about an elegant presentation here, but rather an individualized one. Accessories for this distinctiveness included hatbands, boutonnieres, pinky rings, cuff links, watch fobs, cravats, and monogrammed handkerchiefs. Any or all of these would be compared, selected, and applied before stepping out into the world. Maintaining this practice might require a generous assortment of each to match the daily whims of the man in question.

Ultimately, having a neat personalized attire served the same purpose as good grammar or a strong vocabulary. It placed solid intention behind one's presentation to the world. Since that presentation was primarily conducted face to face in 1927, it engaged all the senses. The thought was to appeal to the eye with color or to the nose with fragrance, much as one would appeal to the ear with words chosen in speech.

Along with Foulkes Brothers on North 6th Street, the Quality Shop was the fashionable choice for men in Terre Haute in 1927. Herb Leach had purchased the shop from Arthur Asbury. Along with the inventory, Herb received a small file drawer with customers' collar, waist, and inseam measurements. As the old saw goes: "Try to please all and you will wind up pleasing none." At the Quality Shop, Herb Leach and his salesmen helped customers to cultivate an awareness of subtle detail that is the foundation of personal style: selecting the suit pattern that enhanced or disguised the physique, favoring a color that matched the eyes or skin tone. Bowties for pointed chins, neckties for broad chins.

It made little sense to abandon personal style after shedding the suspenders and laying down the watch and chain for the night. Accordingly, the Quality Shop inquired of its customers in print ads: "Do you appreciate good pajamas?" If so, Manhattan Silk and Silk Weave Pajamas were available at the Quality Shop for $6.00 to $8.00—probably more money than a man of average means spent on his day clothes.

Louis B. Radcliffe (Alda)—*manager,* The Vim—h 395 N. 8th

It was a sporting goods store located at 423 Wabash. In 1927, only four businesses operating in Terre Haute actually listed themselves as dealers in sporting goods. One of these was a hardware store. Not that there was a lack of interest in physical activity or the sporting life. It was just that much of the time spent in movement or exertion was not considered leisure, but rather a necessary component of everyday life. You'd balance high up on a step ladder. You'd lift a wicker basket of wet clothes. You'd walk back home from the grocery store toting a sack of groceries. You'd sprint 20 yards to catch a trolley car. Maybe all of it in the course of one day. Still, no one at the time would have labeled this a workout regimen.

Whenever leisure time did combine with physical activity, it generally took on a different form than power walking or step aerobics. The Herz employee picnic was held every summer along the Wabash River. Excursion boats ferried 300 employees, their families, and an 18-piece band to a place called Kramer Landing. (*See* Frank M. Graham.) While many were content to relax beneath shade trees or play cards, the day offered strenuous physical activities. They included the requisite baseball game with a crooked umpire and a board walking contest. Long lengths of 2 × 4 were suspended 3 feet off the ground. Contestants balanced and walked as far as they could without falling. A young clerk, Zadah Baird, once won the competition by completing a distance of 70 feet. (See photo of Herz Picnic at www.hometown.indiana.edu/1927.)

There was another impressive athletic feat by a young woman that would be talked about around town in 1927, even though it had taken place the year before. On August 6, 1926, 19-year-old Gertrude Ederle became the first woman to swim the English Channel. What's often forgotten today is that her time of 14 hours and 31 minutes beat the existing men's record by nearly two hours.

Within the year, Gertrude's courageous achievement would be eclipsed by a man crossing another body of water. It's significant, perhaps, that Charles Lindbergh received far more adulation for relying on a machine to do it.

Charles Ragan (Evangeline)—*physician*—815 S. 5th h do

A physician in solo practice whose office was in his home, located in a residential neighborhood. And to further separate him from our modern reality of health care: the doctor also made house calls.

Claude M. Redman (Essie)—*mule buyer*—h 643 Chestnut

And if Claude just so happened to possess a stubborn streak in his negotiations; that was only to be expected, right? Actually, the inevitable decline in the use of mules during this time seems to have been somewhat grudging as well. While the number of horses in Indiana had shown a marked decline between 1920 and 1925, the number of mules in this same period rose by 3,000. Behavioral, historical, or statistical, just one contrary animal and that's all there is to it.

William Reedy—County Poor Farm

Effa Reeves—*seamstress*, Ehrmann Manufacturing Company—r 425 N. Center

Like the Stahl-Urban Company, Ehrmann Manufacturing produced work clothing at its plant at 929 Wabash Avenue. You might think this would suggest a certain empathy from the company for those they had hired to make a living with their hands. But this is like associating the impulse to manufacture canned stew with an appreciation of gourmet cooking. The manager of Ehrmann Manufacturing, Fredrick Reckert, had been at work on the evening of Tuesday,

May 27, 1913. Perhaps enough time had passed by 1927 that he might have been willing to share his particular version of the events from that evening.

For much of 1913, the 74 seamstresses working at Ehrmann had been on strike to protest a steep reduction in the piece-rate pay for their 11-hour shifts. The company had rejected offers of arbitration with representatives of the garment workers local and instead had decided to hire strike breakers. These actions immediately resulted in union pickets outside the factory. Interactions between strikers and the replacement workers had started to become confrontational during the 6:00 PM shift change.

That particular Tuesday evening, one of the replacement workers was being escorted from the building by her husband, a man by the name of Max Howard. Apparently, there had been an incident involving the Howards the night before. Cora Donham, one of the elected officers of the garment workers local had said something to Mrs. Howard which her husband took exception to. He responded by slapping Miss Donham in the face.

The following evening, Cora Donham again confronted the Howards and repeated the words she had said the night before. But this time, as Max Howard readied his response, a man named Edward Wade stepped between them. Edward Wade was a teamster and a union member, Local 144. His brief invitation to Max Howard was as follows: "Strike a man, not a woman."

At that moment the owner of the plant, Emil Ehrmann, who had been standing just inside the door fired a single shot from a 32-caliber Smith and Wesson revolver. It struck Edward Wade in the chest. Emil Ehrmann then pointed his gun at the stunned crowd and retreated with the Howards inside the building. Edward Wade was carried to a nearby drugstore where he died before medical help could reach him. Emil Ehrmann was arrested and charged with first-degree murder. Emil Ehrmann's brother-in-law Fredrick Reckert, who had also drawn a gun during the incident but not fired it, was initially charged as well.

Emil Ehrmann came from a respected Terre Haute family, which included Emil's brother, noted poet Max Ehrmann. (*See* Denzil M. Ferguson.) The Ehrmanns had extensive property holdings which included the building housing Kleeman Brothers on Wabash Avenue, a local summer retreat built with original timbers from Fort Harrison, and a vacation home in Jacksonville, Florida.

At the time of his death, Edward Wade had been the sole support of his family, earning $13.50 a week as a union teamster. He left behind a wife and a 10-year-old daughter.

More than 5,000 people accompanied Edward Wade's casket to the cemetery. Emil Ehrmann would spend five weeks in custody before being freed on bond. At the grand jury proceedings Harry Keife, a 19-year-old clerk at Hulman and Company, contended that he had seen a leather blackjack in Edward Wade's possession as he confronted Max Howard. Earlier testimony from Mr. Keife on the night of the incident had neglected to mention the weapon. He was, in fact, the only witness to refer to it. A witness later identified the object as a pair of leather teamster gloves.

After numerous postponements, the criminal case against Emil Ehrmann finally came to trial on September 29, 1914—almost a year and a half after the incident. A change of venue had shifted the proceedings to rural Parke County. Witnesses for the prosecution, mainly working people, faced the daunting task of traveling from Terre Haute to the courthouse in Rockville, a distance of 25 miles. Among the witnesses not attending the trial: Mary Wade, the widow of the victim.

Prospective jurors were questioned in the courtroom about their feelings on the right to organize and the right to strike. Throughout the trial, the defense characterized the fatal shooting as the actions of a man who was simply protecting his property. Final instructions to jury members from Circuit Judge Charles M. Fortune ordered them to consider the right of self-defense in reaching their verdict. The first ballot found 11 of 12 jurors in favor of acquittal. Lunch was served, after which the vote became unanimous. In total, the jury had been deliberating less than an hour.

Thirteen years later, in 1927, Harry Keife was operating the Keife Auto Laundry, which was conveniently located a short walk from the scene of the shooting. Perhaps not surprisingly, many of those who had witnessed the killing of Edward Wade that night would leave Terre Haute, Indiana, in the years to come. This included Cora Donham, the Howards, and, soon after his acquittal, Emil Ehrmann. Emil Ehrmann would die after a self-imposed exile in Jacksonville, Florida, on March 13, 1946. His body was then quietly shipped to Terre Haute for burial in the family plot. This offers up one final irony. Since it had arrived by train, Emil's casket would actually be borne by unionized railroad workers, even if it was only to unload him from that cold boxcar.

THE REXALL STORES—(**Charles H. and David C. Russell**)—Prescriptions Carefully Compounded, Soda Fountain, Candies, Cigars and Tobacco, Books and Magazines, Toilet Articles, Sick Room Necessities—333 Walnut—Phone: Wabash 354—7th and Seabury—Phone: Wabash 2616

In the early 1920s, the Rexall Drug Company, based in St. Louis, intended to establish drugstores carrying its name across the United States. By 1927, thousands of druggists were either managing stores owned outright by Rexall or had entered into marketing agreements whereby the company would supply them with a variety of retail products to stock their shelves.

Traditionally, many over-the-counter products sold in locally owned pharmacies had been processed from natural herbs and extracts. Shandy's Courthouse Pharmacy, which had the Rexall name added to its building, sold Ricker's Egyptian Henna, Sodium Phosphate, Casgara Sagrada tablets, and Oil of Coconut.

Gradually, the shift away from local drugstores and independent suppliers would accompany a shift away from relying on the natural world as an unsynthesized source for health remedies. But in the 1920s, standard pharmacology included herbs, natural minerals, and basic chemical compounds. Pharmacists were still operating as apothecaries and given the responsibility of creating a doctor's prescription using a scale, a mortar, and a pestle.

A Terre Haute Rexall
Store—the Shandy
Courthouse Pharmacy

So perhaps it was consistent with Rexall's day-to-day functioning, at least for the short term, to sponsor a national contest whose outcome would be determined by the whims of nature. Accordingly, it was announced that on a Saturday morning in late September two homing pigeons would be released from downtown Terre Haute. Their destination would be Rexall's national headquarters in St. Louis where more than 8,000 druggists had gathered for their national convention. It was expected that pigeons would be sent from Rexall's 2,500 stores within a 500-mile radius of the city. People in these various locations were encouraged to guess the flying time of their pigeons to St. Louis. Prizes included Kodak cameras, boxes of chocolates, and bottles of toilet water.

As we meditate on the complex connection that once existed between average individuals and the natural world, consider that this contest was actually dreamed up and then successfully conducted, which means that 5,000 homing pigeons and many more human contestants participated. Most of the pigeons arrived in St. Louis and multiple winners were announced. Some of those winners had precisely calculated their winning entries, based on their everyday knowledge of the flight of a bird.

Harry B. Rhoads (Mary S.)—*traveling salesman*—h 1842 N. 10th

The opening scene from *The Music Man* might come to mind with a group of town-to-town drummers sharing a railroad car.

There were still a fair number of traveling salesmen in the 1920s who lived out of one suitcase while living off of another. Terre Haute was as good a place as any for a home base as it was almost ideally positioned among major markets in the Midwest. Chicago was 178 rail miles away. St. Louis was 169. Louisville was 164 and Cincinnati was 182. This meant that you could grab the midnight train to any of these cities and arrive around dawn. (*See* Benjamin Camello.)

Return to a town enough times and you'd discover the cheapest, cleanest place to eat and sleep and get to know at least a few people by name, though it would be unlikely any of them would actually be customers. For Harry, home was the perfect counterweight: a relief to return to, a relief to leave again. He could always drop a postcard to Mary at North 10th Street if something good happened or something bad was anticipated.

Daniel Richards—County Poor Farm

James H. Richey (Annie F.)—*poultry dealer*—h Davis Ave. RD B Box 382

Throughout the 1920s, Terre Haute was an urban environment with a very strong rural presence, although the demarcation between the two was increasingly being drawn by public ordinances and zoning regulations. For the time being, though, there were plenty of city residents still blurring the lines and hopping the fence.

At their home on South 5th Street and Margaret Avenue, Charles and Belva Piepenbrink maintained an 18 × 40 foot chicken house, big enough to accommodate 250 birds. James Richey, who lived just a little further south, near Davis Gardens, would have been the man to see when those meat chickens reached about four pounds. Not much chance that a thief or predator would get to them

first. Neighbors reported a deep-chested, bench-legged bulldog keeping a close watch on all of those nervous Piepenbrink hens.

Reverend Rippetoe's 90th Birthday Celebration Martin Collection, Indiana Historical Society

Ethel Richie—*seamstress*, J. T. White—r 910 N. Center

One of the 12 employees working at J. T. White in 1927. The company, located at 919 Wabash Avenue, made women's aprons and housedresses for a regional market. This created an odd situation for the seamstresses there: working hard everyday to make something that they might later wear themselves to work hard at home. A pleasant diversion might involve imagining who would buy the blue apron with the flowers, or what her house might look like, never fantasizing once about all the work she'd have to do in it.

Cora Riley—County Poor Farm

Andrew Rinkas—County Poor Farm

E. Blanche Rippetoe—*music teacher*—h 1701 N. 9th, Apt. 2, h do

For many families, the music teacher would be the first expense they'd cut back on once the Depression hit. But over the years, if none of her students remembered their pieces, or even still played their instruments, it's pretty likely they'd still remember her, don't you think? A very musical name, E. Blanche Rippetoe; one that she enhanced beautifully by harvesting her middle name. In 1927, she was single, 37 years old—just about right for the work she did.

Add to that an apartment house on the corner and the presence of her 86-year-old father, a former pastor, and you'd probably have wound up with a good story or two out of all those lessons—at least as entertaining as the music you'd have learned.

Amelda Roberts—County Poor Farm

John R. Root—*paving bricks* @ 201 Arcade Bldg.—h 829 S. 6th

Street surfacing had achieved a relative balance by the middle of the decade. In 1925, 46.3 miles of Terre Haute streets were set in brick with 47.6 miles covered in concrete or asphalt. The tipping point came on May 23 of that year when the city undertook a major project to pave over the remaining brick surfaces. Apparently, an irregular road surface, however appealing to the eye or ear, offered what was at least a perceived obstacle to the optimum speed of automobiles. By then, every public effort was being made to make way, to step aside, to smooth the road ahead for the motor vehicle. Within a year, it would be announced that the lovely grass medians and catalpa trees on Ohio Boulevard would be removed east of 9th Street in order to improve traffic flow.

From his second floor window at 112 South 6th Street, John Root could contemplate the surfaces of the street and sidewalk outside. A new red brick sidewalk would make for a pleasant walk home. Outside of the occasional baby buggy, rubber tires seldom traveled the sidewalk and speed was never a consideration there. But ultimately, why bother? There's no use advocating for beauty once progress opts for efficiency.

Ludolph N. Rottman (Clara)—*cigars* @ 26 N. 6th—h 123 S. 20th

Ludolph Rottman had a tall, painted statue standing out in front of his shop. It was a real wooden Indian which, like the butcher's bloody apron, represents a classic image from America's retail culture. But since this was Terre Haute, Indiana, in 1927, not every cigar retailer opted for the obvious or the expected.

In 1927, Fred J. Biel also had an enormous wooden statue standing in front of his cigar shop at 322 Wabash Avenue. It was a 5'-tall carving of the popular pup-pet Punch, complete with a demonic grin and a tall stocking cap. Punch had been a silent spokesman for the Biel family business on Wabash Avenue since 1867, far enough back that it was still known as Main Street. One of his hands held cigars, the other chewing tobacco. After closing time at Biel's, Punch was moved inside presumably to serve as night watchman.

Mickels Rue—County Poor Farm

Joseph Rusbason—*finisher*, Martin Photo Shop—r 2019 N. 7th

Frank Martin opened Martin Photo Shop in 1906. Throughout its early years, the photo shop became the visual recorder of life in Terre Haute, Indiana. There

The Wooden Indian at L.N.
Rottman
Martin Collection, Indiana
Historical Society

were many cameras in operation across the city every day, but the vast majority of their photographs documented private intentions: a personal portrait whose significance was shared by the subject and the person to whom it was presented. The photographs seldom survived their subjects. The Martin Photo Shop also functioned as stringer for Terre Haute's daily newspapers, commercial photographer for Terre Haute's manufactured products, and the recorder of accident scenes for insurance claims. Their photographs not only included the posed images of thousands of individuals but the results of purely random events. The combination of the two can provide a fairly accurate reflection of life itself.

By 1927, Frank Martin could count on the able assistance of his two young sons, Kenneth and Willard. Together, over the course of two generations, the Martins would produce more than 300,000 photographs until the shop at 681½ Wabash Avenue closed in 1976.

The visual images that were taken by the Martin Photo Shop in the 1920s include photographs on a wide format banquet camera and motion pictures shot on a DeVry 35 mm. The movie footage would be assembled into local newsreels that were shown at the downtown Liberty Theater before every main attraction.

Joseph Rusbason was involved in processing all of the nitrate film stock shot by the Martins. A photographic still or a motion picture literally captures a moment in time. It is only the integrity of the processed image that guarantees its survival into the future. While the task of processing and preservation fell to Joseph, this responsibility was influenced in no small part by the fact that nitrate film physically deteriorates over time. It is estimated that about half of all major studio features shot prior to 1950 have been permanently lost. Today, nitrate negatives are considered hazardous materials. (*See* Harry M. Lindley.)

Among the vanished images initially shot by Martin Photo Shop during the 1920s are all of their 35 mm newsreel footage and the vast majority of their still photography. The entries in the log books from that period give us an indication of what's been lost:

> Neg. No. 2053—Mewhinney Company Gum Drops
> Neg. No. 2084—The Root's Department Store Tea Room Filled with
>   Employees
> Neg. No. 2423—The Stag Hotel
> Neg. No. 2492—Columbian Enameling Company Picnic
> Neg. No. 2657—Central Academy Crowd Waiting for World Series
>   Results
> Neg. No. 3024—Guy Jackson's Meat Market
> Neg. No. 3162—Laying the Sacred Heart Cornerstone

The subjects of these photographs—the people, the buildings, the artifacts—would vanish completely in the coming decades. And since these negatives seem to have vanished as well, we now have nothing but words to describe these particular occupants of place and time. What did Root's Tea Room, or the lobby of the Stag Hotel actually look like? These would have all been grainy black-and-white photographs. Not like being there, but certainly a sure step in that direction.

It's peculiar to find the power of words and imagination inadequate in the pages of a book. But when something from the past has been irretrievably lost, it invites us to consider the value of it having been there in the first place. Artifacts from a time and place are an imperfect substitute, but that's about the best one can hope for without actually being present to experience it fully. It can't be helped that time passes quickly while so much of it is being taken for granted.

Jacob Ryan—County Poor Farm

St. Joseph's Female Academy

ST. JOSEPH'S ACADEMY—129 S. 5th

The Sisters of Providence, who had first arrived in the wilderness west of Terre Haute in 1840, were fiercely dedicated to the cause of female education. Initially, their mission found expression through the establishment of St. Mary-of-the-Woods, located on the west bank of the Wabash River. By 1927, St. Mary-of-the-Woods was a fully accredited college, offering a four-year undergraduate degree program exclusively to young women.

By that time, St. Joseph's Academy had become one of two parochial high schools operating across the river in Terre Haute. While the archdiocese of Indianapolis had prevailed upon the Sisters to teach boys at the parish elementary schools, the Mother Superior was politely adamant concerning educational opportunities offered beyond the eighth grade. As the Sisters of Providence saw it, these resources weren't often available for girls to begin with and so, at least in Terre Haute, secondary education provided by the order would not merely include girls, it would be devoted to them exclusively.

The Sisters had opened their first female academy in Terre Haute in 1849 with 28 girls attending. For years, St. Vincent's Academy operated in various locations, including a converted mansion at 5th and Crawford. Meanwhile, the Franciscan order had constructed a graceful brick school building at 5th and Walnut for their all-boys school, the St. Bonaventure Lyceum. But by 1888, the property had been turned over to the Sisters and their prized students.

Initially, the classes at St. Joseph's Female Academy were attended by about a dozen local girls who had grown accustomed to watching their sisters, their cousins, and their friends leave school in adolescence to take factory jobs or get married. But once those girls entered the doors of the Academy, they were exposed to the radical belief that they could actually continue their education and in so doing nurture their deepest dreams. And the girls were given a further incentive for completing their studies at the Academy: St. Mary-of-the-Woods and a college education awaited them just across the river.

In 1927, the Sisters of Providence were dutifully providing teachers for the elementary levels in each of the city's six parish schools while living modestly in small convents located near St. Ann's, St. Benedict's, and St. Patrick's. In the previous school year, St. Joseph's Female Academy had graduated a senior class of 21 girls, 14 in the academic department and 7 in the commercial department. Over at St. Patrick's High School, which had opened in 1923 with a total enrollment of 27 students, the graduating class was all girls as well. The number of students was never large, but the opportunity provided to them was.

It would all last for another ten years. In 1937, St. Joseph's Female Academy and St. Patrick's High School would merge, giving up their separate identities and their tradition of gender-based education. The beautiful Academy building, which had housed the early aspirations of so many young girls as well as the daily encouragement dedicated to keeping them alive, was demolished in 1940. The prospectus developed for the property suggested that the site would be suitable for either a parking lot or a gas station.

SANDBURR HOLLOW—east side of Wabash River, north from First Ave.

This might sound like the ideal name for an exclusive subdivision; that is, unless you've actually had experience dealing with sandburs. In 1927, Sandburr Hollow was a community of modest homes populated by families living on the margins of existence; households supported by men getting work whenever and wherever they could find it. Although comparatively small, this section of town was recognized just like Baghdad or Twelve Points. Mention the name and most folks in Terre Haute could reliably direct you there.

Among the residents of Sandburr Hollow in 1927: Charles and Anna Farmer, Ebenezer Christenberry, Charles and Edith Kindred, Lyman Mavaney, and Clines and Hazel Rudy. They formed a close-knit community, if only because of the constant threat they all faced. The area apparently flooded quite often.

Burr Sanders (Edna)—*candy maker*, Betty Jane Company—h 10 S. 8th

Mrs. Edna Sanders—*chocolate dipper*, Betty Jane Company

The history of the Betty Jane Company in Terre Haute had only begun in 1925. Previous to that, the shop at the corner of 8th and Wabash had been a locally owned candy store known as Patsy Mehaney's. Throughout much of the 1920s, the proprietor's was a familiar name in the Terre Haute retail community. Like Jerry Fitzgerald, Ernest Zwerner, and John Kostavetes, Patsy Mehaney was more than just the face of his business, he radiated it from his very being. This devotion supplemented the excellent quality of the candy itself, which attracted children and adults alike.

Patsy Mehaney's candy store turned out 800 pounds of peanut fudge at a time. He also produced delicious taffy, even though Terre Haute itself stood hundreds of miles from any salt water. Despite all this effort, much of Patsy Mehaney's status in town came from his homespun quips and adages.

In the early part of the twentieth century, due to the popularity of humorists like James Whitcomb Riley, George Ade, and Kin Hubbard, Indiana developed a national reputation as a repository of rustic wisdom. The storyteller O. Henry remarked in his short story "The Higher Pragmatism" that "Aesop has been copyrighted by Indiana." (*See* William E. Williams.)

Borrowing off of this tradition, Patsy Mehaney filled his candy shop with his sage and cryptic observations:

> "Nowadays you don't realize how little you know until your children grow up."
> "A good start is about all some people ever get."
> "The world has plenty of good talkers but needs a few good thinkers."
> "When it rains—I just let it rain."
> "My milkman has a cow."

When Patsy wasn't dispensing his platitudes in print ads or on the walls of the shop, he'd deliver them to customers in person, which probably made the message even more memorable. It seems the man sported a mouthful of gold teeth.

Then unexpectedly, over a relatively short period of time, this distinctive hometown character whose name, personality, and front porch musings had created a solid and familiar presence decided to abandon the considerable currency he'd built up around town. The process began, curiously enough, with his signature smile. In May of 1921, Patsy Mehaney had a dentist extract every one of his gold teeth, which he then replaced with an everyday set of dentures. Patsy's print ads soon began to repeat a single line, a mantra that seemed to strike a note of sour desperation: "I dare you to talk about me."

Given this, it probably didn't come as that big a shock when Patsy announced in 1925 that he had sold his shop for $5,000 to the Betty Jane candy company, a regional chain that was already operating several stores in Indianapolis. Soon, the walls at 801 Wabash with all of Patsy's sayings were painted over.

So, plenty of rumors for Burr and Edna to discuss if they'd cared to. Patsy Mehaney himself had left town after the sale was completed and he never returned. Notice of his death out there somewhere never even appeared in the local papers. After that last piece of taffy was unwrapped, the only surviving trace was when someone in town recalled some old adage and wondered aloud if it might have come from Patsy.

The mystery of the man's disappearance lingered for a little while longer, as well. $5,000 was a lot of money in the 1920s. And then, there were all those leftover gold teeth. Taken together, it was more than enough to start over again someplace where they'd never heard your quips or tasted your candy.

(N) Philabaretta Sandoe (spouse of Charles)—h 213 Poplar

SATURDAY SPECTATOR (Weekly)—The Spectator Publishing Company— Publishers—51 Spectator Court—Phone: Wabash 1460

In 1925, there were 2,000 daily and 6,000 weekly newspapers operating across the United States. Terre Haute itself supported three daily newspapers in 1927. The *Star* was the city's morning paper. It claimed the largest circulation at 25,000 readers. The Terre Haute *Tribune* hit the streets in the late afternoon when its delivery boys returned home from school. The publishers of the *Tribune* figured that after a long day, readers might like to sit under the living room lamp or a porch light and take in whatever the world beyond had to offer. The 23,000 subscribers of the *Tribune* seemed to agree. The third Terre Haute daily was also being thrown onto front stoops just shy of dinner time. This was the Terre Haute *Post,* which got by with a circulation barely half that of its competitors.

Strong party affiliation was an accepted part of journalism in the 1920s. The *Star* reflected Republican sensibilities, the *Tribune* gave the Democratic perspective, while the *Post* considered itself to be independent and nonpartisan. All of the dailies, however, agreed on their shared responsibility to be tireless boosters for their hometown. This might lead to an occasional glossing-over of the facts, but no more so than the proud father who claims his only daughter is gorgeous. And while it was true that a recent U.S. Chamber of Commerce report had ranked Terre Haute, Indiana, as a city of the second class, hope for the future would spring eternal in the pages of Terre Haute's dailies.

In 1925, the *Tribune* estimated that the city's population had already reached 80,000, an increase of more than 20 percent in just five years. One year later, Fred Rakeman, secretary for the Terre Haute Chamber of Commerce, predicted that Terre Haute would surely have a population of 115,000 by 1950; pointing out that mining, manufacturing, and agriculture assured her of future growth.

Meanwhile, the Terre Haute *Star* was featuring another optimistic forecast from Lionell Edie, Director of the Bureau of Business Research for the Indiana University School of Commerce and Finance. In his front-page remarks, Lionell Edie sounded a note of impatient optimism. "There is no excuse," he contended, "for Terre Haute having a population of only 72,000 when many cities with only a fraction of her advantages have hundreds of thousands." All the while, it turns out that Terre Haute was experiencing its first economic contraction; one that would take its population of 66,084 in 1920 down to 62,810 with the 1930 census. So despite all the inflated rhetoric, the city was actually shrinking.

During this time, while Terre Haute's dailies aspired to have the city ascend to the prominence of a Chicago or a St. Louis, the weekly *Saturday Spectator* continued to imagine it as a small Midwestern hometown. The coverage in the *Spectator* was intensely, one would think uncomfortably, personal. Actions and events were thought to be of great interest simply because local people were involved. A child would visit home from college. A beloved neighborhood dog would suddenly die at age 16. The gladiolas were particularly stunning at a certain address on South Center Street.

All of the week's births, deaths, and marriages in town were duly noted in the *Spectator,* not only to address the need to know, but also to acknowledge that these events had real significance within the community. Each Saturday, the *Spectator* invited its readers to notice and attend to the smallest details of everyday life, if for no other reason that they were occurring right here, right now. Because of this, much of the paper's content reported on human interactions with the natural world.

For instance, there was the tale of Dickie's new bride. In the attic of the Templeton family home at 2409 North 10th Street, a tiny love bird had been discovered. Mrs. Nellie Templeton realized that the bird would not be able to find food in the wild and was also grieving to death from the loss of its mate. Immediately, Nellie Templeton purchased another love bird. A few days later, she read a story in the *Spectator* about Mrs. Inez Jett, whose two love birds had escaped from their cage. Around this same time, the *Spectator* office received word that Henrietta, Dickie's mate, had traveled to a home located south of town. Henrietta had died within an hour of being discovered, leaving Dickie a widower for a brief time. Happily, within the week, Dickie and his new bride had returned from their honeymoon abroad to the Jett household.

Another encounter with nature concerned a small patch of blue forget-me-nots growing near the outlet of the dam on the south lake of Highland Lawn

Cemetery. Based on this information alone, many readers would have been familiar with the flowers in question. The purpose of the *Spectator* article was to trace their history. Apparently, Mrs. Molly Kean of 504 S. 18th Street had received a small bouquet as a corsage for a ball given many years before and had planted them during a subsequent picnic at Highland Lawn. Blue forget-me-nots had flourished there ever since. (*See* Anthony J. Wilson.)

One popular feature in the *Spectator* was meant to encourage a small-town curiosity that was supposedly absent from big-city life. The feature was entitled "Bill Smith Wants to Know." Although Bill Smith was actually a fictional character, there seemed to be no occasion or occurrence too trivial to command his attention. So what did Bill Smith want to know this week? How John T. felt after that fourth piece of pie or whether Bill Jensen wasn't wearing a lovely black-and-blue spot where he caught a foul ball last Saturday or whether the new flagpole on the courthouse square should not be adorned with a handsome new flag in place of the faded one that floated there.

Taken together, the weekly observations found inside the *Saturday Spectator* evoked the simple hometown pleasures available to all who lived in Terre Haute, Indiana, with special attention being paid to childhood. An ad placed in mid-April would announce the formal start of the kite season. With a family's purchase of a 1-lb. can of Dauntless brand coffee and a signed certificate from one of the hometown grocers displaying the familiar red sign, a child could receive a new kite at Hulman Company headquarters at the corner of 9th and Wabash.

Then, as the weather warmed, the Hulman family would unwittingly provide another resource for outdoor fun. A large wooden sign that had been posted near the pond on Anton Hulman's property cautioned "NO SWIMMING." The *Spectator* reported that a gang of boys had not only gone skinny-dipping but had also removed the S and the G from the sign during their time there. The altered sign read "NO WIMMIN."

The *Saturday Spectator* had first been published in 1904, back when Terre Haute was starting to flex its muscles as a full-grown American city. The editor, Don Nixon, perhaps saw his paper as a counterweight to the metropolis that might otherwise become too impersonal, too jaded, too far above its raisin'. In 1927, the cost of the *Saturday Spectator* was 10 cents, over three times what the dailies charged. Week after week, the resulting dialogue among the deeply committed broadened and deepened. These were the residents who had chosen Terre Haute as their home for the duration.

Appropriately, from time to time the *Saturday Spectator* ran a story of the prodigal son returning home from a stint in the big city. The actual reasons for this return were seldom mentioned, but it always carried the whiff of repentance. And so, a piece entitled "No Place like Home" related the story of one David Hufflinger, who had left town 20 years earlier following the death of his father. David Hufflinger had migrated to Boston, a veritable stage villain which the readers of the *Spectator* considered sophisticated, rigid, and impersonal; the very antithesis of America's hometown: Terre Haute, Indiana. It appeared that David Hufflinger had returned to town just to confirm this.

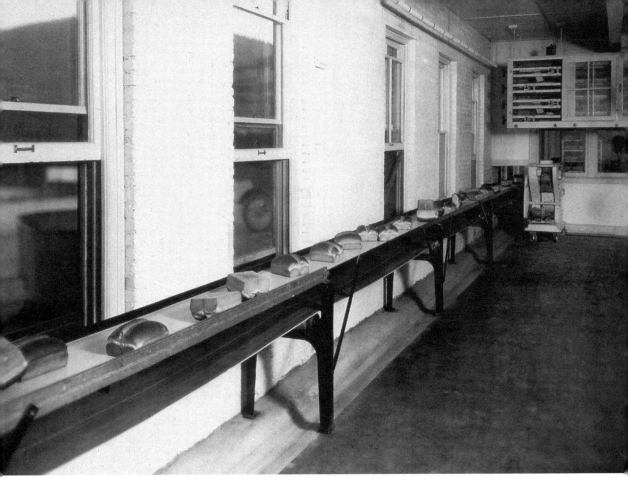

Vigo Bread Company
Assembly Line
Martin Collection, Indiana
Historical Society

Terre Haute is a place of friendly faces where people greet you with "Hello Dave, How are you?" and where they care whether you live or die which is more than is done in the cold, frigid politeness of the East. Just to walk up and down the streets is a joy to me.

Gradually over time, as those walks and those questions of concern became less common, the perceived differences between Terre Haute and Boston began to vanish as well. The increased mobility of the country dictated that urban areas offer similar services for increasingly similar needs. Any local distinctiveness was generally seen as a relic of the past. Over the course of the next half-century, the *Saturday Spectator* increasingly found itself reporting on a town that pretty much sounded like any other, which isn't really news. In 1980, the *Spectator* finally ceased publication. Appropriately, one of its last covers showed the demolition of Root's Department Store downtown.

(N) Ulysses Saucerman—r 2031 S. 7th

Michael Schaack (Catherine)—*baker*—h 628 Lafayette

A dues-paying member of the Bakers and Confectionary Workers' International Union of America. Meetings for the local were held at the Labor Temple at Fifth and Walnut on the first Saturday night and the third Saturday afternoon of every month. This schedule was put in place to accommodate a membership maintaining a six-day work week that included both day and night shifts. This was, nevertheless, a vast improvement over the 12- to 14-hour shifts that characterized working conditions for bakers before the establishment of the union in 1886.

Commercial baking was undergoing tremendous upheaval in the 1920s. Already, the union local had begun to distinguish between machine work and hand work inside the shops and companies it served. The general philosophy behind a labor union is to treat any profession represented as a skilled craft and require that it be compensated as such. In bakeries that were union shops, a jobber, the lowest-paid position, earned $8.00 a week. Gradually, a novice would move through the ranks of apprentice and benchman until finally attaining the title of foreman, ovenman, or mixer, which could pay as much as $45.00 weekly.

Mike Schaack was one of the old guard, having joined the union on July 10, 1910, back in the days when over 90 percent of the bread in America was home-baked. (*See* Jerry Fitzgerald.) An intensive effort by the Terre Haute local to establish itself in the nearby town of Clinton, Indiana, had met with mixed results. While recruiting had gone well, many grocers in Clinton had refused to carry packaged bread stamped with the union seal. Over the course of one year, the local had lost six recent members.

Another ongoing concern was maintaining solidarity within the existing membership. A few weeks prior to the annual Labor Day parade, a motion was made to exempt members from the traditional $5.00 fine imposed for not marching downtown. After a long discussion, the motion passed. Although the final vote was not recorded in the local's minutes, one might imagine that Mike Schaack stood squarely in opposition.

Eugene D. Schell (Blanche)—*machine operator*—Up-To-Date Manufacturing Company—r 629 N. 9th

When it first began operations earlier in the century, the company manufactured wire-mesh farm fencing. Fewer family farms, more processed food—so, true to its name, Up-To-Date Manufacturing moved with the times. By 1927, the company was manufacturing tin cans.

But considering the fact that the American Can Company would be constructing an enormous new factory along the Wabash River in the next six years, maybe the year 1927 was as up-to-date as they would ever need to get.

Otto Scholtz—County Poor Farm

Mrs. Bertha Schroeder—*matron*, Citizens Independent Telephone Company—h 31 S. 16th

If the job title has a disciplinary ring to it, that's because there were some strict rules that needed to be followed. Along with Indiana Bell and American Telephone and Telegraph, the Citizens Independent Telephone Company provided phone service for the estimated 15,000 telephones in Terre Haute,

The American Can Company
Martin Collection, Indiana
Historical Society

Indiana, in 1927. Although the Dresser and Walnut exchanges had been added to supplement the familiar Wabash prefix, completing a local telephone call still required operator assistance.

To deal with a volume of more than 100,000 calls a day, the company had in place a staff of 76 female telephone operators. The shifts were 8 hours long. Meals were provided and meal times regulated through the supervised employee dining room. Among Bertha's tasks was enforcing the 20-minute breaks allowed to the operators every two hours. This break was especially welcome after the peak period from 9 AM to 11 AM when about 20 percent of the day's calls came in. A furtive cigarette, a short conversation with a friend, anything to vary the numbing routine of answering a buzzing prompt with the words "Number, please." No wonder operators cultivated a distinct edge to their voice.

However fair Bertha Schroeder might have been, the numbing monotony of the shifts frequently left tempers short. Maybe the most difficult challenge for Bertha was realizing that many of the women working the board resented her very presence. Both sides might have loosened up just a little as they approached the inevitable. In the summer of 1926, the Citizens Independent Telephone Company announced that the switch to automatic equipment was a little over a year away.

Fred Schultz—County Poor Farm

The Citizens Independent Telephone Company

Joseph A. Schultz—*usher*—r 227 S. 9th

No steady place of employment listed. In 1927, the job apparently involved enough in-demand skills that someone could freelance. Theaters, prize fights, funeral homes, always some work available for a man with good night vision and a keen eye for the empty seat.

Mrs. Carolyn Sears—*waitress*, Union Station Restaurant—r 625 S. 22nd

Ruben Sears—*dishwasher*, Farmers Hotel—r 128 S. 4th

Mayme Ellis, the cook at the Union Station Restaurant, owned the bungalow at 625 S. 22nd and apparently rented a room to her waitress. Their address was a good distance from work. The women likely traveled back and forth together on the Crawford Street trolley. (*See* Darrell D. Donham.)

George Woodsmall, the owner of the Farmers Hotel, also provided rooms for his dishwasher and his waitress, Gladys Neill. Considering the very early hours of breakfast at the hotel, a daily commute any longer than a few footsteps would have been impractical.

Joseph Sevick—County Poor Farm

(N) Shepple Shade (spouse of Henry—*waiter*, Hotel Deming)—h 1514 Poplar

James P. Shea—(Hoosier Smoke House)—h 230 S. 5th

James owned this business at 20 South 7th Street with T. G. Moore. In addition to cigars, the Hoosier Smoke House also featured a soda fountain, a candy counter, and a friendly motto: Always Ready to Serve You. One added feature for the summer of '27: a baseball ticker service which employed the latest Wall Street technology to provide updates on major league games.

James would spend at least some of that summer strolling the two blocks back and forth every day from the shop. A Mewhinney's Paris Mint for the way there. A Hoosier Poet cigar for the walk home. Feeling Indiana every step of the way.

Tollie Shelton (Rose A.)—*shoeshiner*, W. D. Fuqua—h 2501 N. 15½

Well, that settles it. Woodsie for a shave and Tollie for a shine. The close proximity of the barbershop to both of Terre Haute's train stations might have made this the perfect first stop for a long-delayed homecoming. Likely, either man could fill you in on everything that had happened since you'd been gone. (*See* Howard C. Harkness.)

Albert M. Shepard—County Poor Farm

Erwin P. Sheridan (Ruth)—*locomotive engineer*—h 1209 N. 20th

Glenn Sheridan (Dorena)—*locomotive fireman*—h 1211 N. 20th

By the 1920s, the two main sources of Terre Haute's economic strength had already passed their peak period of profit and influence. Bituminous coal, which continued to be plentiful in the Wabash Valley, was being surpassed by anthracite coal, which produced less smoke. During the second decade of the twentieth century, the number of mining enterprises within the state of Indiana declined by 50 percent.

In 1927, the tipping point for railroads in the United States had just recently occurred. The total number of railroad miles operated throughout the country had fallen by 1,700 miles between 1920 and 1924. Beyond that, the only long-term future for railroads was their struggle to exist. Between 1930 and 1980, America's railroad track mileage would be cut in half.

Terre Haute, Indiana, had a long-established tradition with railroads. Labor activist Eugene Debs's first job was scraping the grease off of huge steam locomotives at age 14. Five years later, he joined his first union: the Brotherhood of Locomotive Firemen, Vigo Lodge #16. By the 1920s, a strong connection between unions and the railroad lines had been forged. There were five railroads running through Terre Haute: the Chicago and Eastern Illinois; the Chicago, Milwaukee, and St. Paul; the New York Central or the Big Four; the Evansville and Indianapolis; and the Pennsylvania Railroad.

The Pennsy, as it was commonly known, remained the largest railroad employer in Terre Haute, although in 1927, the town was still feeling the aftershock from a company decision four years earlier. Terre Haute was for years the hub of the railroad's Peoria Division. Repairs on all cars and locomotives west of Pittsburgh were done at the Vandalia railroad yards, a sprawling facility south of Spruce Street, 100 yards east of Union Station. Then in 1919, the Pennsy shops experienced a bitter strike. The job action divided workers and management as well as the workers among themselves. When the resolution was finally in place, it was hoped a healing had begun. Nevertheless, in October of 1920 the Pennsylvania Railroad announced it would cut 250 jobs from its Terre Haute facility.

Then on March 6, 1923, the Pennsylvania Railroad abolished its Peoria division altogether and with it hundreds more skilled positions. The Passenger Car Paint Shop had already been converted to a company gymnasium the year before. Company athletics had always been a source of pride among the railroad workers at Pennsy. The 1899 men's tug-of-war team from the Vandalia yards was never defeated. As recently as 1922, the Pennsy women's basketball team from Terre Haute had finished second to a team from the main terminal in Philadelphia, the company's headquarters.

The year 1927 found the brothers Sheridan still working on the railroad. Erwin had ascended to the coveted position of locomotive engineer and Glenn was attempting to follow in his big brother's footsteps. It took at least a year of excellent job performance for a fireman to advance to engineer. In the process, there was plenty of opportunity for Glenn to cop some licks off his brother. The two lived side by side on North 20th Street, just a short walk from the Vandalia yards. The fireman worked alongside the engineer in the cab of the locomotive. Beyond stoking the engine with coal, Glenn would assist in various duties: watching for and checking track signals, monitoring the locomotive's speed and performance. Occasionally, along the lonesome stretches, his brother might even allow him to yank the steam whistle.

But the years would not pass as agreeably as the miles. Glenn Sheridan would turn 28 in 1927. With each succeeding year, there seemed to be less need for trains, less need for the workers who ran them. The Pennsy had already announced they were taking off six trains running from Terre Haute east to Indianapolis and west to Effingham, Illinois. Two years passed, then four, and Glenn remained a fireman. His misfortune was to live and work during a time when the presence of the railroad was starting to decline in America. Still strong enough to draw him in, but not quite strong enough to secure his future.

The Vandalia Railroad Yards
Martin Collection, Indiana
Historical Society

It was Glenn's later misfortune to die during a week when the attention of the entire nation was focused on the assassination and funeral of its president. When Glenn's obituary finally did run in the *Tribune* on November 28, 1963, it was buried on page 30. Enough trains still running through town for a proper tribute, though: a fading whistle right around midnight.

(N) Jeremiah Shoptaw—*janitor*—r 454 N. 7th

Max Showers (Anna; The Truth Store @ 417–419 Wabash and shoes @ 507 Wabash)—h 710 S. 8th

Ralph Showers—*clerk*, The Truth Store—r 710 S. 8th

Hard to say how much truth can be found hiding up the sleeves of coats or on the tongues of shoes but ultimately that's what they were selling there. After Max's death in 1944, son Ralph continued on in the family business. By then, the name of the business had been changed to Max Showers Clothing, which no doubt became an easier standard to maintain.

(N) Minnesota Shumard (spouse of William W.)—h 1529 S. 8th

(N) Journey W. Sibley (Effie)—*hod carrier*—h 1307 N. 28th

Edward Sidebottom—*musician*, American Theater—r 1135 N. 9th

Norman Rockwell did a cover illustration for the April 29, 1950, issue of the *Saturday Evening Post* entitled "Shuffleton's Barbershop." It shows a group of elderly musicians gathered after hours. Nice to think that the boys from the American pit ensemble bonded enough to occasionally reunite in subsequent years. Somewhat unlikely to happen in real life, but hey, that's Rockwell for you. (*See* Edgar P. Herrin, Paul D. Johnson, E. Clair Montgomery, Raymond Niccum.)

William Siebenmorgen (Martha; Terre Haute Carpet Cleaning and Rug Company)—h 1603 Liberty Ave.

The business had been operating at 333 North 16th Street since 1898. Bill and Martha literally lived right around the corner and had since the company's founding.

Oddly enough, this meant that they were living on Liberty Avenue in the spring and summer of 1918 when anti-German sentiments in Terre Haute reached a fever pitch. After the declaration of war in April of 1917, many schools across the country began to purge their curricula of the German language and all German literature. The president of Indiana State Normal, W. W. Parsons, directed that any book containing German doctrine be removed from the school library and subsequently burned during daily chapel. This included works by Frederick Nietzche and Herman Hesse.

On May 3, 1918, German language classes were completely eliminated in all of the city's primary and secondary schools. Three days later, another public burning of German books and maps took place in front of Wiley High School. The glow from the enormous bonfire easily could be seen from St. Benedict's German Catholic church on South 9th Street.

Public suspicion inevitably was directed toward people with German names. Many of the overt attacks, however vicious, were never reported or documented. Most took the form of angry gestures, spoken words, or silent glares. For the various businesses in Terre Haute owned by German Americans, popular sentiment was made clear by who didn't walk through the door.

In the case of Frederick Strassner, though, a brief verbal disagreement would lead to actual imprisonment. A large map had been on display in the store window of Root's Dry Goods on Wabash Avenue that detailed the battles being fought between the Allied and German forces along the Western Front. Frederick Strassner had apparently reacted to statements made by Mrs. Melissa Nelson, whose son was serving overseas. What Mrs. Nelson had said was never at issue. Frederick Strassner's reply to her was. His statement that Kaiser Wilhelm had never done anything to hurt him personally resulted in a physical assault from Mrs. Nelson and his subsequent arrest by Terre Haute police.

Frederick Strassner was then brought to trial and after a jury deliberation of 18 minutes found guilty of unpatriotic and disloyal speech. This verdict resulted in a sentence of 180 days in prison and a $100 fine. Frederick Strassner would ultimately spend ten days behind bars before being allowed to post bond. Although the Armistice ending the war would be signed just eight weeks later, the Terre Haute *Tribune* dutifully reported to its readers on January 10, 1919, that Frederick Strassner was still being kept under surveillance.

A German-American
Postcard

As any professional carpet cleaner can tell you, certain stains become more difficult to remove if they've been allowed time to set in the fabric.

Andrene Slaughter—County Poor Farm

Charles A. Smith (Dora)—*potato chips*—915 S. 9th h do

He sliced them, salted them, and then sold them right at home. Although a direct line of descent is impossible to establish, Charles A. Smith contributed in his own small way to a great hometown tradition. During the 1960s, the Chesty Potato Chip Company of Terre Haute, Indiana, would build a national reputation selling potato chips in large re-sealable metal cans. When emptied, these containers became suitable for other uses, yet another Terre Haute tradition that was already firmly in place by 1927.

Charles J. Smith (Hattie)—*spirit runner*, Commercial Solvents Corporation—h 1740 S. 11th

At the outbreak of World War I, Great Britain was relying on a substance called cordite as a propellant for their shells and cartridges. The successful manufacture of cordite required acetone, which was produced from the distillation of wood, which involved a drying process that took at least six months.

The war immediately created a desperate shortage of acetone. During a naval engagement off the coast of Chile in the early months of the war, British shells made with defective acetone fell far short of their targets and two cruisers were sunk with all hands aboard.

Up until the start of the war, the forests of Austria and the United States had supplied Britain with sufficient wood for acetone production. Now with Austria fighting alongside Germany and the United States still neutral in the conflict, the British government turned to Chaim Weizmann for a solution.

In 1916, Chaim Weizmann was a 41-year-old research chemist living in London. He had already made significant contributions to the field when he was summoned to the British Admiralty. There, the First Lord of the Admiralty, Winston Churchill, told him that Great Britain needed 30,000 tons of acetone immediately. The chemist had been experimenting with an accelerated fermentation process that had produced acetone in relatively small amounts. Large-scale production began at once in Canada, India, and France. The first plant in the United States to produce acetone using Chaim Weizmann's process was located in Terre Haute, Indiana.

After the war, it was discovered that butyl alcohol, a formerly useless byproduct of whiskey fermentation, was useful in manufacturing a quick-drying lacquer for metal paint finishes. The newly formed company Commercial Solvents copyrighted the name Butanol and began to manufacture butyl

Local Farmers at Commercial Solvents
Archives of the Vigo County Historical Society, Terre Haute, Indiana

acetate in large quantities. By 1921, orders from commercial manufacturers far exceeded the company's capacity.

Throughout this time, Chaim Weizmann had been collecting royalties from Commercial Solvents on his original patent. During the war, the British government paid Chaim Weizmann a royalty as well. It amounted to 10 shillings for every ton of acetone produced, totaling about 10,000 pounds—a modest compensation considering the vast importance of the discovery to the British war effort.

These royalties did allow Chaim Weizmann to concentrate his efforts on a far more personal mission. Since 1901, Chaim Weizmann had been actively involved with a small group devoted to the establishment of a Jewish homeland in Palestine. In 1920, the British Foreign Secretary issued the Balfour Declaration, which committed the British government in principle to the same goal.

It would take nearly a generation to accomplish, but in 1948 the State of Israel was created and Chaim Weizmann became the nation's first president. By 1927, Commercial Solvents had shifted almost entirely to the production of Butanol and Chaim Weizmann's original patent for the fermentation of acetone was being carried on the books at a royalty rate of $1.00 annually. The spirits Charles Smith carried might have been chemical, but in many ways he had simply inherited Chaim Weizmann's original job title.

(N) Mrs. Cinderella Smith—h 655½ N. 3rd

As you'd guess, many Smiths of almost every stripe living at the Crossroads of America in 1927—including 10 Henrys, 7 Harrys, 4 Jesses, 3 Clems, two widows named Mattie, and one Smith who actually was a blacksmith: Theodore. First names that were common then wouldn't appear on too many birth certificates these days. In 1927 in Terre Haute, Indiana, it was actually possible to hear the sentence, "No, you've got the wrong Bertha Smith."

Martha Smith—*matron*, Colored Day Nursery—r 1320 13½

Just to distinguish it from that other Day Nursery at 423 North 4th Street. The service was licensed by the State Board of Charities "to provide care for working mothers during daylight hours." Instituted in no small part to enable African American women to provide childcare for wealthier white families in their role as domestics.

Not that the value of this resource assured the quality of its care. Martha had recently replaced Matron Isabelle Reed. In its annual report for 1926, the Welfare League had criticized the nursery for poor management, while choosing not to address the underlying racism that required a Colored Day Nursery in the first place. (*See* Municipal Swimming Pool.)

Fred Snider—County Poor Farm

(N) Gerrit Snip (Mary)—*manager*—h 21 N. 34th

(N) Gussie Soames (spouse of Phillip—*plumber* @ 1228 Linden)—h 1203 Lafayette

Catherine Speck—County Poor Farm

James Spencer (Mattie)—*butler*—h 621 Swan

A great name for his chosen profession, whichever half of it his employer chose to use. In 1927, James Spencer was the only manservant listed in Terre Haute. Like crumpets and cricket, this was a British institution that never quite translated stateside. Before World War II, there were an estimated 30,000 butlers working throughout Great Britain. Within half a century, they'd become as rare as they were in Terre Haute. By the mid-1980s, the number of butlers in Britain had dwindled to around 70.

STANDARD HATCHERIES—**Charles Tiffany,** *manager*—All Breeds of Day-Old Chicks Shipped Anywhere—Poultry Supplies of All Kinds—119 N. 4th—Phone: Wabash 3619

Yet another reminder beyond the Farmers Hotel and the occasional dray horse that the city of Terre Haute was surrounded by some of the richest farmland on the planet.

So let's set the stage here. Heading on foot north along 4th Street from Wabash on the west side of the street, the National Hotel on your left, then just ahead to the corner of Cherry Street and Guy Jackson's Meat Market. In the middle of that block, directly across from Hook Elementary School, you hear the sound of day-old chicks—hundreds of them—right downtown. Maybe loud enough that the chorus of cheeping would reach the Hook schoolyard. Sounds like a childhood memory that might endure because it would seem so improbable to someone's descendants.

Gladys Standifer—*domestic*—r 1228 S. Center

Margaret Standifer—*domestic*—r 1232 S. Center

Likely involved a knock on the back door to the kitchen at some point during the day. In 1927, 1228 South Center was the home of the irrepressible Emmet "Bill" Cody, proprietor of the Cody Hat Company at 715 Wabash. 1232 South Center housed the Luckett family. Coen Luckett was a physician and surgeon who shared a practice with his father, Luther, on the second floor of the McKeen block at 672 Wabash.

In the coming years, live-in domestics would become as scarce as men's straw boaters. But still, the Standifer sisters' situation on South Center Street wound up setting a precedent of sorts. During the second half of the twentieth century, many of the spacious single-family homes south of Wabash Avenue would be subdivided into apartment rentals not too far removed from the modest quarters the Standifer sisters had once occupied.

Wallace Steepleton—County Poor Farm

Edith Stenberg—*masseuse* @ 801 Citizens Trust Building—r 1416 S. Center

We can't begin to count the number of misperceptions a female therapeutic bodyworker must have dealt with in 1927, especially in a town with a flourishing red light district. Included in Edith's continual effort to rise above it all was her business address: the eighth floor of the tallest building in Terre Haute. (*See* Mrs. Harriet Gay.)

Mrs. Madge P. Stephens—*physician* @ 1438 Wabash—h 203 Van Buren

Wallace W. Stephens (Madge P.)—*undertaker*—h 203 Van Buren

Dr. Madge Stephens was, no surprise, the only woman physician practicing in Terre Haute, Indiana, in 1927. Overcoming her patients' reluctance to accept a female doctor might have paled in comparison to dealing with the apprehension they might have felt once they found out her husband's occupation.

An attempt at gallows humor might have gone something like this: "If you ever find her husband sitting in the waiting room, you'd better hope he's meeting her for lunch."

Edward Stevens—County Poor Farm

Alex Stewart—County Poor Farm

Charles H. Stewart—*laborer*, Columbian Stamping and Enameling Company—r 622 Linden

Paul R. Stewart—*furnaceman*, Columbian Stamping and Enameling Company—r 622 Linden

On Thursday, June 24, 1926, Paul and Charles Stewart were arrested by Terre Haute police for swimming without suits near the Big Four Railroad Bridge on the Wabash River. The city was averaging about 20 arrests for indecent exposure annually. The extenuating circumstance for the Stewart brothers that afternoon was their company on this little outing: Miss Lorraine Ballinger and Miss Billie Nash. At the time of their arrest, all of the accused were minors. To some degree, this worked in their favor. The next morning, probation officer William Bailey severely lectured the four and then returned them to their respective homes.

The following summer, the boys would continue their worldly education by working rigorous factory shifts and living in a small house on Linden Street with their elderly parents, their brother, and their sister. The four children of Calvin and Ida Stewart provided all of the income for the household. Martin worked in the coal mines. Sister Ruth had a job as a housekeeper.

The decision on that scorching summer afternoon was to leave every stitch of clothing in a pile on the bank and then jump headlong buck-naked into the river. Walking back home from their shift at Columbian on Friday, June 24, 1927, the brothers probably discussed the events from a year ago: their arrest, their night in jail, the fact that both Lorraine and Billie had subsequently left town, before observing that it had certainly been a long, hot day.

(N) Lulu Stickel (spouse of Harry—*secretary-treasurer* of the Vigo American Clay Company)—h 1204 S. Center

(N) Missouri Stock (spouse of Edgar)—h 509 S. 4th

Jonas A. Strouse—*wool buyer* @ 302½ Wabash—r 706 S. 5th

The Columbian Enameling and Stamping Company,
Terre Haute, Indiana.

The numbers worked out something like this. A single full-grown Merino ram yielded in excess of 25 pounds of wool. That 25 pounds of wool could eventually produce about four men's worsted suits and two winter coats. In 1927, fleece from the Wabash Valley never went very far from shearing to stitching. Jonas Strouse was simply one local connection in that short journey.

This was a seasonal market. In Indiana, most of the shearing was done in April and May. Jonas might have drawn some satisfaction from the fact that animals were not slaughtered for what he sought to purchase. Not that he would reject wool taken from a sheep pelt, but as he often explained to farmers, this pulled wool was of lesser quality. The softest and finest lamb's wool was produced between 12 and 14 months. It was so valuable in fact that a lamb before its second shearing was given a completely different name, a hogg.

Wool was a renewable resource. The life expectancy of an average sheep was 10 to 15 years. Furthermore, the quality suits, coats, and blankets produced from their wool were expected to last at least that long. With the annual shearing, another cycle of seasons began. Slowly, the wool would grow. Then all at once, it was spring again.

Dorothy Stuckwish—*pianist*, Ernestine Myers—r 722 S. 17th

Jane B. Stuckwish—*student*—r 722 S. 17th

Rudolph F. (Rose) Stuckwish—*decorator*—h 722 S. 17th

Live music for live dancers. Heavy on the left hand when it was played on piano.

The Columbian Enameling and Stamping Company

A Flagman at a Rail Crossing

Actually, during the 1920s, dancers would prove inspirational for both Stuckwish daughters. Jane had been a 14-year-old freshman at Wiley High School when she entered a contest to come up with a name for a new dance hall being built on Terre Haute's east side at the corner of 29th and Wabash. The new octagon structure would feature a huge bandstand, an outdoor pavilion appropriately named Moonlight Gardens, and a sprawling solid oak dance floor with a rotating mirrored ball suspended from the center of the ceiling. (*See* Fern Garden.)

Jane decided that, given the grand aspirations of her hometown, there was every reason to believe this new dance palace would be the equal of those in Chicago, Seattle, Los Angeles, or Cleveland. It seemed logical then to appropriate the name they all shared. The Trianon opened on December 20, 1923, and at least for the next 20 years, Jane held some bragging rights around town. Count Basie, Duke Ellington, Paul Whiteman, Jimmy Dorsey, and Cab Calloway all brought their orchestras there, relying on the same basic strategy that Dorothy employed for dancers at the upstairs studio: making sure they could feel the beat right through the floor.

In 1943, when big band music started to fade in popularity, the Terre Haute Trianon became an ice skating rink, a school for watchmaking, then a factory.

Finally, in 1967, the building was demolished, which allowed Jane's hometown bragging rights to pay some late dividends when all those memories were called in.

Edward J. Sulkowski (Irlene C.)—*signalman*—h 2209 2nd

Maurice M. Sullivan—*track walker*—h 1111 N. 8th

In August of 1926, the Terre Haute City Council began discussion on the installation of automatic signals for railroad crossings, a move proposed by the railroads to replace the crossing watchman and his flag. The city engineer, Robert Tilley, had argued against the change, maintaining that signalmen like Edward Sulkowski were the better guardians of public safety.

Standing squarely on the side of automation was William Norcross, president of the Board of Public Works. Mr. Norcross argued that flagmen were capable of sudden confusion or excitement, human responses that the mechanized equipment would completely eliminate. He and his proponents already had precedent on their side, since the city had recently agreed to start replacing traffic officers at downtown intersections with stop-and-go signals.

Fortunately for Edward Sulkowski, in a railroad town like Terre Haute, this inevitable transition would take months, if not years. So, for a while longer, he still held his job.

While the railroads were eager to dispense with the human element at track crossings, they would continue to rely on it for the safety of the tracks themselves. And so throughout 1927, Maurice Sullivan was charged with the responsibility of carefully inspecting the rails in Terre Haute; a conscious process that might have produced a relative state of bliss as long as Maurice remained aware that he was walking down the middle of a railroad track.

Odie Sutherland—County Poor Farm

(N) Marcella Swim—*waitress*—h 1721 Chestnut

T

Elmer E. Talbott (Hallie D.)—*clerk*, Filbeck Hotel—h 506½ N. 7th

The Filbeck Hotel at the northeast corner of 5th and Cherry Streets was located about a block from the unmarked boundary to Terre Haute's red light district. This would provide the answer to the most common question Elmer was asked by out-of-town salesmen next to: "Can I have an extra key to my room?"

By 1927, the Filbeck had become just seedy enough and the red light district just famous enough that any desk clerk's claim of ignorance was to be regarded with justified suspicion. (*See* Butler Sisters.)

Noah J. Tanner (Rachel)—*hat cleaner* @ 16 Home Ave.—20 Home r do

Noah's business speaks directly to the enormous popularity of men's dress hats and the acknowledged need for their ongoing maintenance. Sweating clear through the hatband of a Leghorn and having the dye bleed into the straw was a common enough occurrence during the summer months. Besides, why put a shine on your shoes, a fresh flower in your lapel, and then neglect your chapeau? (*See* Cody Hat Company.)

One more timely quip from Major Hoople's lodgers in Gene Ahern's daily comic strip *Our Boarding House*—this one taken from late April of 1927. The boarders are giving the Major grief over his worn-out summer hat:

> He changed the band and gave it service stripes. Out of respect for age,
> he doesn't have to remove it for the national anthem.

Benjamin Taylor (Lillian)—*poultry dresser*—h 401½ N. 4th

The photograph was taken at the intersection of Chestnut and North 4th Street in 1933. The grocery store that had been owned in 1927 by Saleem Nasser had apparently been sold by then to the Oakley Economy Stores. Just across the street stood Paul Kunkler's drugstore. That business apparently remained essentially as it was six years earlier. Located on the second floor of this two-story building was the apartment that had housed Benjamin and Lillian Taylor in 1927: the poultry dresser and his bride of ten years.

If there is a fascination to be found in Terre Haute, Indiana, in 1927, it lies behind these second-story windows on a secondary street in a secondary town. This is an urban streetscape that is particular to this place and time: two- and three-story brick buildings combining retail and residence on a shady side street a few blocks from the downtown of a city of approximately 65,000. The 1920s was probably the last decade in which these conditions flourished in a city of this size. Today, this streetscape would only exist in metropolitan areas of at least half a million. The residential neighborhood surrounding it would likely be gentrified. The locally owned drugstore would no longer exist, nor would the job of poultry dresser. Maybe instead there would be a wine bar or an upscale restaurant on the first floor, with the manager of a museum gift shop renting the walk-up flat.

Zacharist Taylor—County Poor Farm

TERRE HAUTE ABATTOIR AND STOCK YARD CO.—Office: 19 N. 4th—
Yards: West side of Wabash River, 2 blocks north of Wabash Ave. Bridge—
Phone: Wabash 245—**William Retz,** *president*—**George A. Seeburger,**
secretary

The Corner of 4th and
Chestnut
Martin Collection, Indiana
Historical Society

TERRE HAUTE TALLOW AND GREASE FACTORY (Harrison Smith)—
11–13 Harding

All throughout the 1920s, perhaps the greatest daily challenge facing residents
of Terre Haute was sensory. Although cold temperatures or prevailing winds
could lessen the effects, the city constantly seemed gripped by an unidentified
noxious odor. The diverse number of products being manufactured and processed at various locations in the city contributed to the problem and despite
the presence of Henley Brothers Florists and Davis Gardens, the fragrances
never overcame the odor.

Olfactory emissions from a few factories in particular were singled out as
especially offensive: the chemical byproducts from Commercial Solvents, the
processed pulp from the Wabash Fibre Box Company, and the stench of slaughtered animals from the abattoir and rendering operations along the banks of
the Wabash. Since numerous factories channeled their industrial waste directly
into the Wabash River, it meant the waterway often smelled every bit as foul
as the city itself.

Another liability of being a factory town, especially one that burned bituminous coal, was poor air quality. A reporter for the *Saturday Spectator,* Hilda
Newkom, recorded her impressions of Terre Haute from the observation deck
of the Citizens Trust on a hot day in July:

> The smoke lay in layers of all colors from a mid-
> night blue and deep grey to a pale yellow fringed
> with pure black. It was impossible to distinguish

anything in the triangle between Wabash Avenue and North Sixth Street.

A pleasant way to describe the unspeakable, like the word *abattoir.* When mankind engages nature in all her forms, the results can frequently brutalize the senses. But once man's methods begin to compromise the quality of the air and water, they brutalize nature—of which man is a part. At that point, it becomes more than a momentary inconvenience for the senses.

William Thacker—*stationary engineer*, Rose Orphan Home—r do

Among his various other duties, which included supervising the plumbing, heating, and electrical systems at the Rose Home, was throwing the master switch at 5:30 AM and 9:00 PM. This controlled the harsh overhead lights in Cottages 1, 2, and 3. It was required that this task be done precisely on time, 365 days a year. But that's not really what made it the kind of responsibility that would keep a person up nights.

Harris Thomas—*trap drummer*—r 618 Harding

These days, you'd call him a percussionist. The title indicated that he incorporated more into his presentation than two sticks and a stretched drum head—a distinction from, say, whacking on a bass drum with a brass band's name on it.

In Harris's bag of tricks: various cymbals, triangle, bells, maybe even a washboard or wood block. For a lively jazz combo consisting of piano, cornet, banjo, and a small drum kit, such versatility was considered essential. The Hoosier Hotshots from Arcadia, Indiana, a novelty jazz band from the 1930s and '40s kept this particular sound alive and exported it around the world.

Henry Thomas (Thelma)—*game warden*—h 1145 8th Ave.

Game is defined as any wild animal killed by hunters for food, fur, or sport. We don't know what particular rural properties Henry Thomas supervised, but we do know why he supervised them. Poaching game was a widespread problem in the 1920s as hunters commonly exceeded bag limits and hunted particular animals outside of open season.

An editorial cartoon drawn by Ding Darling for the Des Moines *Register* would illustrate the enormous cultural shift that took place over two centuries in once-wild regions like the Wabash Valley. In the first panel, a Native American is shown bringing a single game bird back to his village. A large flock of geese fly overhead. In the second panel, two hunters are toting shotguns and dozens of game birds as they emerge from a duck blind. They are about to deposit their quarry in a building marked "Cold Storage." The caption:

> Why the Indians always had plenty
> And the White Man never has enough

This cartoon might have given Henry a cold laugh if he had ever come across it in the evening *Tribune.* The title printed underneath was "Why Game Wardens Go Crazy."

Mrs. Julia A. Thomas—*phys cultopathy* @ 205 Oddfellows Bldg.—h 638 Walnut

Physcultopathy was a strategy for daily living developed by self-proclaimed health crusader Bernarr McFadden. The basic tenets of this philosophy emerged in the early years of the twentieth century. Bernarr McFadden's Physical Culture Creed, which proclaimed the core beliefs of the movement, pretty much constitutes accepted wisdom these days. But like Eugene Debs's advocacy of government pensions and child labor laws, physcultopathy was initially considered to contain radical ideas that were summarily rejected by vested interests of the time.

In retrospect, the Physical Culture Creed appears to be a nature-based perspective offered to a society rushing to embrace technology and mechanization in most every facet of human activity. Bernarr McFadden was born in the middle of the nineteenth century and had come of age in a generation when the telephone would impact how people spoke to each other, canned foods would influence how people ate every day, and the automobile and the airplane would forever change how people covered distances. In a sense, he anticipated the response Americans would have when presented with innovations promising to conserve personal time and physical effort: they would become increasingly dependent on their use.

In a rural culture that both embraced and relied upon nature, exposure to fresh air and sunlight were simply a response to the requirements of everyday life. But as the American population increasingly urbanized, it became common for individuals to spend long stretches of time indoors, away from natural ventilation. As climate controls like air conditioning and central heating were introduced, Bernarr McFadden recognized that people would become more sedentary and increasingly out of touch with their own body's natural responses. He speculated that a complete separation from the cycle of the seasons, the lessons of nature, and a sensory experience of life itself might soon follow.

By 1927, Bernarr McFadden had written more than 40 books. Initially, his instructions on health were directed toward simple body maintenance: avoid the bad (white bread, tobacco, women's corsets) and include the good (long walks, occasional fasting, sleeping on a firm mattress). But by the time Julia A. Thomas had graduated from the McFadden College of Physcultopathy in Chicago and set up her practice in Terre Haute, Bernarr McFadden had begun to focus on particular diseases and criticize the solutions increasingly being proposed by medical science. In 1925, he wrote a treatise on diabetes, following it the next year with tracts on asthma, rheumatism, and the common cold. Bernarr McFadden rejected the use of synthesized prescription drugs as well as vaccinations. At the same time, he spoke in favor of licensing drugless health practitioners like midwives and chiropractors. This brought physcultopathy into direct conflict with the established medical community as well as state and local laws that were increasingly being enacted to restrict and regulate healthcare.

Odd Fellows Temple,
Terre Haute, Ind.

The Oddfellows Temple

Julia's response to all this was to navigate the letter of the law by employing a skillful use of words. She paid for a separate business listing under "Physicians" in the 1927 Polk Directory which included the correct office address but a revised name: Julia A. Thompson. Meanwhile, for the main directory Julia split the name of her discipline thereby separating out the common abbreviation for physician. In an earlier *Saturday Spectator* feature, she had referred to her practice by employing an alternate spelling (d-o-c-t-e-r). Apparently, these were precautions worth taking. In 1927, one of her former classmates at McFadden College, Herbert M. Shelton, would be arrested, jailed, and fined three times for practicing medicine without a license.

The constant threat of prosecution left Julia Thomas undeterred. She publicly claimed a specialty in treating "disturbances of the entire digestive tract," which she suggested were due to deficiencies in the functioning of the pancreas and kidneys resulting from the presence of toxins and low levels of nutrients in the blood.

Like many other spiritual practices, physcultopathy recognized the therapeutic properties of water. The fourth law in the Physical Culture Creed had recommended frequent baths using cold water as a tonic and hot water for cleanliness. Bernarr McFadden himself was said to have founded the first Polar Bear Club, whose members immersed themselves in the icy cold waters of Lake Michigan.

For her part, Julia Thomas advertised the benefits of vapor baths to assist with rheumatism and neuritis. To encourage the skeptical, she included a free coupon. She certainly would have found like-minded support among the other tenants of the Oddfellows Building. In Room 202, Ivan Yates offered sulphur baths, steam sweats, and hot packs to customers. A little further down the hall were the offices of the International Bible Students Association. To establish some common ground there, Ivan and Julia could have cited John 4:13: "But the water that I shall give him shall be in a well of water springing up into everlasting life."

A kind of everlasting life was Bernarr McFadden's objective all along. He confidently proclaimed that he would live to be 150. Well into his 70s, he continued to have 20/20 vision and a full head of hair. As for Julia, she would leave this mortal coil behind on March 14, 1955, just six months before Bernarr McFadden would die from an untreated urinary infection. Julia wound up a little shy of her mentor's 87 years on earth, but there was some satisfaction to be had in death after all. Her obituary in the *Tribune* the next day did include the title of "Doctor" next to her name.

Hubert E. Thompson (Hazel I.)—*foreman*, Turner Brothers Company— r 2441 Liberty

The Turner Brothers Glass Company may have been one of the clearest examples of how the local and the sustainable functioned for businesses in Terre Haute in 1927. Actually, there is evidence to suggest that this approach may have allowed Turner Brothers to continue in operation throughout the 1920s and provide workers like Hubert Thompson with a job.

Like all of Terre Haute's bottle manufacturers, Turner Brothers struggled under the constraints of Prohibition. (*See* North Baltimore Bottle Glass Company.) But since the company had always manufactured the wooden cases and cardboard boxes used to ship its bottles, the choice was made to expand that part of the business. By 1927, the company was turning out 2,000,000 wooden cases and 5,000,000 boxes annually.

The company had not completely given up on making glass bottles; they just wouldn't be going as far. Turner Brothers had entered into an agreement with the Loudon Packing Company south of town to provide them with 14-oz. glass bottles for their tomato catsup. Though the two companies never instituted a system for bottle deposit, it may have only been because catsup leaves the bottle a tad slower than beer or milk.

Early on, familiarity with the natural world had taught Turner Brothers to look to their immediate environs for needed resources. The high grade sand essential to the process of glass manufacturing had always been available in abundance throughout the Wabash Valley.

James W. Thompson (Helen A.)—*proprietor*, Plaza Hotel and *president*, Wabash Sand and Gravel Company—r Plaza Hotel

He actually maintained a third business that went unmentioned in the 1927 Polk Directory, because it was located out of town. J. W. Thompson was the proprietor of the Trinity Springs Resort some 70 miles south of Terre Haute in the tiny Martin County community of the same name.

The lure of Trinity Springs, Indiana, lay underground in the sulfur mineral waters that were widely considered to aid in the treatment of various bodily ailments, including poor digestion and rheumatism. To supplement this natural focus on physical renewal, the resort also offered dancing, swimming, tennis, walking paths, and burro rides.

The resort's activities emanated from a large three-story hotel with cloth awnings. Below the hotel was a large mineral wading pool with springs to fill clay jugs and glass bottles. The hotel dining room at the resort seated 100 and the daily menu included chicken, eggs, milk, and vegetables raised on the nearby Thompson family farm.

Trinity Springs itself numbered about 120 residents in 1927. The community featured two general stores and a second smaller hotel managed by one J. C. Lundy to handle overflow crowds during the summer season. Three miles to the north sat the tiny community of Indian Springs, population 250. Its services in 1927 included a train depot, a post office, an Episcopal church, and a resident physician. The town also featured two hotels offering an opportunity to take the waters or just sit on a porch rocker and stare at the trees.

In 1927, Trinity Springs and Indian Springs, Indiana, were largely self-sufficient communities, even if most of the actions taken to sustain everyday life were performed within residents' households. The fact that rural settlements of this size would no longer maintain basic services for their small but significant clusters of populations in the coming years speaks directly to a diminished awareness of place and interpersonal community in America, which accompanied a growing disregard for the availability and value of local resources.

The formal season at Trinity Springs Resort began with the hotel's opening, about a week before the summer solstice. It was expected that few of the guests would actually drive to Martin County. In 1927, a long automobile trip on rural roads could be an added source of noise and anxiety—which was, after all, what most of the guests were headed there to avoid. To accommodate those wishing to begin their vacation the moment they left Terre Haute, the Chicago, Milwaukee, and St. Paul Railroad ran three trains daily at 5:45 AM, 11:00 AM, and 5:00 PM directly to Indian Springs. A carriage from the Trinity Springs Resort would be waiting at the tiny wooden depot there to pick up passengers from every arrival.

Whether the healing for those visitors actually came from the mineral springs, the fresh air, or the gentle trees, the connection with nature was what done it. This was still a time when the measure of a restful vacation was not just how far you'd gone but how deep you managed to get.

Claude Thornhill—*musician*—r 2337 N. 13th

J. Chester Thornhill (Maude)—*car repairs*—h 2337 N. 13th

Claude Thornhill was still in his teens and living with his parents in 1927, but he was already regarded as one of Terre Haute's most gifted musicians. Claude had been playing piano professionally since age 11 and within a few years became popular as a featured soloist in Leo Baxter's and Jack O'Grady's local jazz combos. Leo Baxter played regularly at the Liberty Theater downtown, and Claude quickly discovered that even with all his talent he wouldn't be the main attraction on stage. A decade before Tommy Dorsey hired Frank Sinatra, Leo Baxter's Liberty Theater Orchestra featured heartthrob vocalist Eddie Page. High school girls would gather in the front rows on the weekends to listen and sigh. Just across the street at the Orpheum, Claude had a steady gig with Bud Cromwell and his Kings of Rhythm, playing numbers that allowed dance instructor Herbert Church to strut his stuff.

Perhaps Claude's most enduring hometown moment came at Garfield High School's Christmas Vesper Service on Sunday, December 20, 1925. The program's finale that night featured a quartet directed by Claude on the piano. Together, they led the large assembled crowd of townspeople, classmates, neighbors, and friends in the Christmas carol "Joy to the World." One can imagine listening outside the auditorium on that crisp winter evening, staring up at the softly lit windows of the building: Christmas in Terre Haute, Indiana, 1925—the gentle perfection of it all would have likely stolen your breath away.

After leaving Terre Haute in 1931, Claude Thornhill would head straight to New York City where he soon gained a reputation as an arranger. Within a decade, he was leading one of the most dynamic big bands on tour. In May 1941, *Metronome Magazine* would declare the Claude Thornhill Orchestra to be the best big band ever.

By the 1950s, Claude Thornhill had basically returned to his roots, performing club dates with a small combo. Finally weary of paying others, Claude accepted a job as musical director for singer Tony Bennett in 1957. He had certainly come a long way since Eddie Page and the Garfield Christmas pageant, but he would not have much further to go. Claude Thornhill would die unexpectedly at his home in New Jersey at age 56. Like many child prodigies, Claude Thornhill's potential had been so vast that his death left many people wondering if he'd ever actually fulfilled it.

TICK-TOCK TUCKER (Perry Tucker)—*Jeweler and Watchmaker*—814 Wabash—Phone: Wabash 4056

At the sign of the clock in the middle of the block.

In 1927, a personal timepiece was as essential to the smooth functioning of daily life as a sturdy pair of shoes or a pocketful of spare change. Every timepiece involved a morning ritual: a few moments winding the stem to ensure the next 12 hours of timekeeping.

It's apparent to us now that for all the effort and attention paid to time 80 years ago, individuals back then were far less obsessed with it. Perhaps they had retained that playful sensibility toward passing time that a child has. Precision was entrusted to train crews and downtown shopkeepers. But even so, it's unlikely that all of the clocks and watches at 814 Wabash would have agreed on the correct time. This is why many clock shops followed the tradition of setting the hands of each timepiece to 7:22, the precise time when Abraham Lincoln died.

Perry Tucker apparently cultivated an interest in all means of marking time. At his shop, he carried birthstones for every month: topaz for November, ruby for July. It was said that each stone contained unique properties for healing and guidance that would serve the person who chose to wear it on a cufflink, necklace, or ring.

Perry Tucker also became aware of the powerful energies often generated by people themselves. From time to time, he found himself adjusting the mechanism of a watch that had been mysteriously altered by the strong magnetic field of the person wearing it. One local schoolteacher, for instance, came in every few months to have her watch demagnetized so it could once again keep accurate time. Legend had it that Johnny Evers, the peripatetic second baseman of the Chicago Cubs, was unable to wear a wristwatch because of the energetic force field he emanated.

There were certainly practical explanations as to why a wristwatch might suddenly malfunction. Static electricity entering a trolley from its overhead wire could speed up a mainspring by five minutes over the course of a day. All from casually grabbing a handrail. As electric headlamps began to be employed on locomotives, Perry received calls from anxious conductors and engineers. Trainmen were only allowed to have 30 seconds of variation a month in their personal timepieces.

Gradually, the problem of static electric charges was solved with the introduction of composite mainsprings to replace magnetic steel. But this only deepened the mystery of Johnny Evers, the schoolteacher, and the various other characters who entered Tick-Tock's shop complaining of time gone awry. A farmer had returned numerous times with his watch before he determined that the magnetic source was actually the horse he plowed behind every day. Old horse—brand new watch. Not much doubt in his mind which one had to go.

(N) Dymple D. Time (spouse of Arthur—*operator*)—h 2210 2nd Ave.

(N) Louisa Tootle (widow, William)—h 2202 Spruce

Charles H. Traquair—*custodian*, Masonic Temple—r 635½ Chestnut

If it's really true that the janitor knows the treasured secrets of the places he cleans, then Charles would have had some amazing stories to share. That is, unless the Lodge had the foresight to make him a member first and swallow all those secrets.

Frank Triche—*proofreader*, Terre Haute *Post*—r 109 N. 35th

Professional integrity for a daily newspaper's proofreader in 1927 demanded extraordinary precision and a persistent attention to detail. Punctuation, grammar, and spelling—the knowledge of each internalized and brought to bear on a vast wordscape characterized by inflexible deadlines. The work constantly pulled one's attention to the immediate and the short term. Frank Triche was unlikely to look very far ahead, a view reinforced by the fact that he was living alone in a rented room.

All in all, it probably turned out to be a good thing. In 1931, the *Post*'s main competition, the Terre Haute *Tribune,* purchased the afternoon daily and immediately discontinued its publication. Soon after, the *Tribune* swept up the

The Masonic Temple

Post's paper trail. Today, outside of a few yellowed original copies, no samples of the Terre Haute *Post,* or Frank's hard work, exist. A conscious intention includes the willingness to accept an unexpected outcome, realizing that even a good effort won't guarantee that anything will last.

James M. Trimble (Fay A.—Trimble Sign Shop)—h 253 S. 22nd

TRIMBLE SIGN SHOP (James M. Trimble)—253 S. 22nd— Phone: Dresser 875

He was known around town as Jimmie. But despite his successful business, the first thing folks in Terre Haute were apt to mention was his other job involving sleight of hand. Jimmie Trimble was an accomplished professional magician. He was born in 1892, about a decade too late for an extended vaudeville career. Nevertheless, he would have been front row–aisle seat at the Hippodrome in April 1926 when famous illusionist Harry Blackstone brought his stage act there. At midnight on December 11, 1927, Jimmie himself would perform on the Hippodrome stage. He would be billed as the "One Man Circus."

From a performance standpoint, the development of new media technology in the 1920s squeezed magicians from both sides. The emergence of radio was about as helpful to magic as it was to interpretive dance, and as for movies, the ability of film editors to manipulate images made every magic trick look suspect while potentially turning any film actor into a magician.

Throughout the centuries, the truest test for any magician remains the ability to convince people, which coincidentally is also the truest test for any

Jimmie Trimble
Community Archives, Vigo
County Public Library

hand-painted sign. Nearly 40 years after Jimmie's passing, the Trimble Sign Company continues in business in Terre Haute, Indiana.

Jessie H. Troutman (Maebelle)—*deputy sheriff*, Vigo County—r County Jail

In Vigo County, the well-appointed home of the deputy sheriff and his family was connected directly to the county jail itself; separated, as everything else in the building was, by securely locked doors. Which somehow doesn't make it sound very comfortable, even with a nice view of the river.

Augusta A. True—*teacher*, Davis Park School—h 123 S. 12th

Clarence T. True (Elizabeth M.)—*teacher*, Gerstmeyer Technical High School—h 1800 N. 4th

Etha J. True—*janitress*, Davis Park School—h 330 8th Ave.

Frances A. True—*teacher*, Warren School—h 1 Walden

Pearl A. True—*teacher*, Davis Park School—r 330 8th Ave.

Very true, but still hard to believe.

(N) Magdelena Trueblood (spouse of Freeman—*foreman*)—h 1101 S. 18th

Trueblood was a common surname around Terre Haute in 1927, with 28 adults carrying it through birth or marriage. Although Magdelena fell squarely in the latter group, it would be difficult to match the accidental beauty of her name even if you were a parent with time enough to consider the choice.

TULLER HOTEL—**Mrs. Margaret Witty,** *manager*—European, Fireproof, and Modern Throughout—670½ Ohio—Phone: Walnut 3021

The Tuller was a small upstairs hotel with about a dozen rooms, located just east of C. G. Pugh's bicycle shop. Despite its modest size, the Tuller had developed an excellent reputation by 1927. While this reputation was no doubt hard-earned, it defied an easy description. You could say the Tuller Hotel had a certain homespun elegance, much like a wealthy uncle who relaxes with a belch and a toothpick after a gourmet meal. The Tuller was a very strange hybrid for a hotel, but somehow it always seemed to attract a loyal clientele.

Strong reputations generally originate with strong personalities, and the Tuller was no exception. The hotel had been established by one Albert Steen, who apparently located the personality before the property. It seems a woman named Harriet Tuller had been running a very popular boardinghouse in town, primarily on the strength of her outstanding meals. The hotel's naming rights may have been part of the incentive package Albert offered. At any rate, Harriet had saved enough money after a few years managing the Tuller to move to Los Angeles and lease a hotel there herself.

Harriet's departure would lead to the arrival of the Witty family. The patriarch, William L. Witty, was a gregarious man who lived the sporting life. In the 1920s that still included shooting game as a pursuit worthy of the genteel and cultured. Mr. Witty had particular affection for hunting dogs. Over the years, he had trained a long line of pointers to assist him in the field.

One legendary autumn, Mr. Witty traveled to Clay County to do a little hunting with his pointer Dann. Dann had come from good stock; the grandson of the legendary Plain Sam and Madame Butterfly. It had been a dry summer that year, so good results were anticipated. A few days later, Wm. L. Witty and Dann returned to the Tuller Hotel with a dozen rabbits and 40 quail. The game was added to the Tuller Dining Room menu the following week—a lengthy tale of Dann's tracking skills added at no extra charge.

Harriet's legacy demanded excellent food at the Tuller Hotel. Even though the Tuller operated on the European plan with meals paid for separately from the room, the consensus among guests was that a finer meal within walking distance simply could not be found. In 1927, the Tuller Dining Room's particular specialties included a homemade chicken soup, a splendid Sunday dinner at 75 cents a plate, and the coffee—which was described as something to rave about. The constant refills would also provide an incentive for long languid conversations after dessert had been served. This practice may be another reason why the Tuller took to describing itself as European.

Like any hotel operating in Terre Haute in 1927, the Tuller hosted a small handful of guests who were steady lodgers. Suite 9, for instance, was occupied by Rosemond Clarke, singing coach. After dinner, this often made for impromptu songs to supplement the good stories.

There were also a host of out-of-town regulars who chose to stay at the Tuller, many of them vaudevillians who played the Hippodrome just up the street. The Croxton Hotel at 714 Ohio actually had a longer association with theatrical performers. The great vaudeville singer Blossom Seeley married her co-star Benny Fields in the lobby of the Croxton in 1921. But the Tuller had its share of stage troupers signing the register. A life spent in the theater, after all, generally meant reciting the same lines to entertain others over and over again. For some performers, it was a treat to stay at the Tuller and just be a listener for a change.

William T. Turman (Margaret)—*professor*, Indiana State Normal School— h 1629 S. 5th

He had grown up on his parents' farm in Sullivan County, the kind of idyllic, late-nineteenth-century rural setting that inspired poet James Whitcomb Riley and novelist Gene Stratton Porter. Big climbing trees, creeks for bare feet, singing birds, and gentle animals always and everywhere.

After that thrilling childhood, William Turman attended Merom Christian Academy, spending a good amount of time perched high on the bluffs that stretched above the Wabash River. It must have seemed natural to sit on that low stone wall and watch the sun as it eased into the western horizon. William Turman was already scheming up ways to keep it alive inside. Visual art seemed as sure a path as any.

Soon, he was off to the big city: Philadelphia and then Chicago. It allowed him to study his craft and also reminded him from time to time exactly what he'd left behind. William Turman returned to Indiana in 1894, succeeding George Thompson as chair of the Department of Penmanship and Drawing at Indiana State Normal. He married Margaret Fisher the following year and they purchased a house at 1629 South 5th Street.

Thirty-two years later, the job, the marriage, and the address would still remain intact, an amazing accomplishment for any free spirit. Ultimately, the stability may have provided William Turman with a secure grounding, much like a strongly rooted oak the sparrow returns to after flights far and near.

Much of William Turman's adult life would be spent in cities, but what he painted came from his childhood: landscapes and rural scenes. He became known for his impressionistic canvases of the Wabash Valley and Brown

County, Indiana. Early in the twentieth century, a whole generation of visual artists led by T. C. Steele was discovering the natural wonders of Brown County. Meanwhile, Wm. T. Turman would remain in Terre Haute, even though part of him kept returning to those long sunsets in Merom gazing westward.

Finally, having outlived two wives and about to enter his tenth decade marveling at the world around him, Wm. T. Turman decided to leave Indiana and join his daughter and son-in-law in the little town of Taft, California. Taft was located on the eastern edge of the Carizzo Plains, a vast American savanna of peppergrass and larkspur. Beyond that stood the Los Padres National Forest and then the Pacific Ocean. This would provide the old man yet another unbroken horizon to dream on. Just in time, you might say.

(N) Mrs. Cleopatra Turner—h 221 N. 1st

Lawrence E. Turner—*pharmacist*, Buntin Drug Company—r 1449 S. 3rd

Buntin's was a locally owned pharmacy that began the decade of the twenties with two corner locations in downtown Terre Haute. Proprietor Herman Salchert then decided to sell his location at 8th and Wabash in order to concentrate on his flagship store, which stood at the intersection of 6th and Wabash.

The Buntin Drug Store at 6th and Wabash
Martin Collection, Indiana Historical Society

It seemed like a logical decision. A study of foot traffic at downtown inter-sections done in 1921 concluded that Buntin's drugstore was the busiest corner in Terre Haute. Much like the clock outside the Marshall Field Department Store in Chicago, Buntin's became a pedestrian landmark where people would arrange to meet without ever venturing inside. Certainly, the Crossroads of America a block to the east was better known beyond Terre Haute. But the fame of 7th and Wabash had been established by the juncture of two famous highways, which simply made it a preferred gathering place for automobiles rather than pedestrians.

In 1927, the thermometer that stood outside Buntin's served as the accepted standard for the city's daily air temperature. The Terre Haute *Tribune* duly reported readings taken at 6:00 in the morning and 2:00 in the afternoon on its front page. That same year, the iconic status of corner drugstores every-where would be represented in yet another urban landscape by American artist Edward Hopper. To the casual observer, the painting *Drug Store* might be located in the same downtown that also inspired *Nighthawks at the Diner,* a downtown very much like Terre Haute, Indiana (*see* Hoosier Café).

After 1927, the story of Buntin's would reflect all the changes taking place with drugstores, downtowns, and American life in general. Buntin's would be sold to Gillis's, a locally owned chain of drugstores already operating seven stores in Terre Haute. One of its locations was on the northeast corner of the Crossroads of America. So for a brief time, their new drugstore at the corner of 6th and Wabash was symbolically balanced between potential outcomes for America's future: the locally owned business versus the chain store, pedestrian versus vehicular traffic, and the likelihood that two people would be walking somewhere to meet in person rather than chatting on a cell phone.

Alice Twadell—County Poor Farm

Jacob Umble—County Poor Farm

(N) **Felix A. Unger** (Charlotte; Unger Auto Electric Co.)—r 1130 S. 10th

UNION DEPOT—east side of 9th between Sycamore and Spruce

One of the most impressive structures ever built in Terre Haute. It was completed in the summer of 1893, when railroads were still considered the future of land transportation. The Union Depot was a massive three-story building constructed of quarried red stone and pressed brick. An arched entryway led to a spacious first floor lobby with an inlaid terra cotta floor and polished mahogany benches. Ringing the lobby on the second floor were railroad offices, their milky glass doors fronted by a wide oak balustrade. Railroad dispatchers operated from the third floor.

High above all this, a breathtaking sight. As the building's designer Samuel Hannaford conceived it, if someone happened to look up from one of those lobby benches, they'd find themselves gazing at an elegant chandelier which was affixed to a stained glass skylight. During the day, sunlight cast a rainbow on the floor below. At night, incandescent lights illuminated the kaleidoscope of color. Only a whistle blast from an arriving train was likely to disturb the dreams of the expectant traveler contemplating the vision of beauty high above.

Rising even higher was a 200-foot-tall cylindrical brick tower, a kind of secular minaret. Humorist Will Rogers, arriving in town for a performance at the Grand Opera House, even referred to it. "Terre Haute," he said, "has the only depot I've ever seen with a silo on top."

The opulent railroad stations built in the late nineteenth century often suffered the fate of the great movie palaces constructed a generation later. (*See* Indiana Theater.) They were all intended to be awe-inspiring in their size and splendor. But as the economic conditions supporting them grew less certain, they were summarily neglected until demolition ultimately emerged as the only viable option.

By 1927, the conical roof that crowned the Union Depot tower had been removed. Damaged by lightning strikes and severe storms, it was deemed not to be worth repairing. This philosophy had gradually been implemented throughout the building, a response that could only invite tragedy. On the night of September 19, 1945, three boys climbed up on the roof of Union Station. In a way, they hoped to benefit from those years of neglect. Pigeons had taken to nesting in the eaves. At least, this was the rumor the boys had heard. It seemed like a good opportunity to collect a few live specimens to raise for themselves. They reached the fourth floor through the main staircase, climbed a 16-foot ladder, and stepped onto the roof in the dying light.

The roof had a severe pitch, so the boys were anxious to find level footing. Suddenly one of them fell. It turned out that 10-year-old Ralph Muncie had not fallen *off* the roof but rather *through* it. His body was lying in the lobby four stories below. He had fallen more than 60 feet.

Although the word on the street had informed Ralph and his friends about the pigeon nests, no one had mentioned the stained-glass skylight. Actually, this was understandable since over the years the accumulated soot from the

Union Station
Community Archives, Vigo
County Public Library

coal-fired locomotives had completely obscured the window and its many colors. Its dazzling display of beauty had become dispensable; no one had bothered to clean it. Incredible to think that someone had been aware of its radiance, had calculated the expense involved in maintaining it, and concluded that it was no longer worth the effort—an effort, by the way, that could not possibly have exceeded that of three young boys climbing up on the roof to look for pigeons.

Within 15 years, the entire structure would be gone. A crowd would gather on a hot June day in 1960 to watch the tower fall. Many who attended had grown up on the farm. They understood this cold necessity from their memories of the family's plow horse: it had grown old, it was tired, it had not been gently treated during its life, and now finally it had to be put down, having outlived its perceived usefulness to man.

UNITED STATES SLICING MACHINE COMPANY—F. E. Bartholomew, *sales agent*—Meat and Bread Slicers—14 N. 8th—Phone: Wabash 1276

Many an innovation would someday earn the title "the greatest thing since sliced bread," but in 1927 the world-at-large had yet to reach that pivotal moment in time. And it actually would be one moment: when the lock on the front door to the Chillicothe Bakery in Chillicothe, Missouri, clicked open on the morning of Saturday, July 7, 1928.

A man from Des Moines, Iowa, named Otto Rohwedder had developed a machine for uniformly slicing loaves of freshly baked bread. Otto had actually perfected the mechanical process some years before: his remaining challenge was how to retain freshness, since sliced bread grew stale much faster than an uncut loaf. The solution: wrap the sliced loaf immediately in cellophane as it emerged from the machine. That problem solved, Otto sold his prototype to Frank Bench of the Chillicothe Baking Company, which offered the new product to the public for the first time on that morning.

Hard to tell exactly what kind of bread slicing machine Frank Bartholomew was marketing in Terre Haute, Indiana, the year before. But by 1928, he had certainly heard the news out of Chillicothe, just as Alexander Cartwright heard about Abner Doubleday inventing baseball, or Roald Amundsen heard about Commander Perry reaching the North Pole, or some Vikings with good memories heard about Columbus.

Likely, Frank glanced up from his newspaper one day and said something to his wife, Eva. Some variation of "exactly what I've been telling them all along."

(N) Alm Utz (spouse of Earl J.—*chief clerk*, Chicago and Eastern Illinois Railway Freight Depot)—h 2323 S. 8th

A Terre Haute High School
Pep Rally
Martin Collection, Indiana
Historical Society

Ohmer D. Vance (Bertha)—Felt and Chenille Emblems, Banners, and Pennants, Monograms and Letters—1218½ Wabash, Rooms 3–4, Phone: Wabash 5810—r 2181 Crawford, Phone: Wabash 3288

Much business to be done on Thanksgiving Day when Garfield and Wiley High Schools traditionally faced each other for their annual football game at Memorial Stadium. The trophy awarded to the winner was, appropriately, a solid bronze turkey.

Students from both schools purchased their school's pennants and waved them in the stands during the game. After the final gun, the felt souvenir usually wound up hanging on a bedroom wall. It would become an essential reminder for the adolescent waking up to face another day in Terre Haute, Indiana, displayed alongside a calendar from a local business, a framed adage about ambition, or a varsity letter sweater hanging on a hook.

If Ohmer D. Vance had been particularly ambitious himself, he probably could have furnished all four.

(N) Argentina Vannorie (spouse of Luigi—*shoe repair*, Brock Shoe Repair Company)—h 1918 Locust

While some parents used a bible for reference, others apparently used an atlas.

Margaret L. Varner—*organist*, American Theater—h 206 N. 6th, Apt. 3

She performed on a massive $10,000 Chicago pipe organ that had been installed when the American Theater first opened in 1914. The following decade would form the crest of theater employment for musicians in Terre Haute. The Grand Opera House continued to maintain its own orchestra. The American, the Liberty, and the Hippodrome all supported small pit ensembles as well as an in-house organist. In 1927, all of these organists would be women. One of them, Miss Margaret Verier, traveled on the interurban every night from the Hippodrome back to her home in Paris, Illinois. If only these musicians had known that the introduction of talkies would be taking them all out together over the next year, they might have gathered for a farewell luncheon at Root's Tea Room.

Interesting to note that there was another professional musician living in the four-unit apartment building that Margaret Varner called home. Ralph Budd and his wife, Margaret, occupied Apartment #2.

Thompson L. Vaughn (Laura)—*broommaker*—h 1121 S. 21st

Probably a challenging existence, considering that in 1927 the Hegarty Broom Company was hiring other broommakers like Jacob Williamson to mass produce them at 1904 South 7th Street.

You've got to wonder if Thompson and Laura ever argued whether this man who made them had an aversion to actually using them.

(N) Euphrasia Vester (spouse of Earl W.—*laborer*)—h 1512 S. 1st

VICKROY'S ART SHOP—Pearl R. Vickroy, *manager*—Pictures, Frames, and Mouldings, Art Novelties and Supplies, Fraternal Charts and Books—911 Wabash Ave.—Phone: Wabash 2426

In the late nineteenth and early twentieth centuries, James M. Vickroy gained a national reputation by documenting community. He began as a sales agent for the M. C. Lilly Company of Columbus, Ohio, selling ceremonial swords to secret fraternal organizations. Soon he discovered an excellent opportunity and his personal calling. James Vickroy, it turned out, happened to be a talented graphic artist. He realized that he could design custom lithographs, ledger books, and certificates and then market them specifically to exclusive membership societies, giving each a sense of presence and permanence.

By 1904, more than 5,000 fraternal lodges across the United States had come to depend on James Vickroy's *Condensed Historical and Financial Ledger.* The products he designed allowed local chapters to record, perhaps even justify, their continued existence. Each individual's name was formally entered in James Vickroy's elegant hardbound books whenever they attended lodge meetings, paid their dues, or voted on new members. Perhaps most importantly, the contents of these books were only meant for the eyes of a select few within each secret society. Ornate award certificates designed by J. Vickroy—Terre Haute, Indiana, might be presented to a member in good standing or a retiring lodge president. With the popularity and quality of his products, James Vickroy was able to secure exclusive rights to produce certificates for 28 separate fraternal orders as well as the United Mine Workers of America and the Brotherhood of Locomotive Engineers. For many recipients, a certificate designed by James Vickroy became the highest honor they would ever receive in their lifetime.

James Vickroy was also aware that family lineage was essential in establishing a person's sense of place in the world, especially within families where formal documentation was absent. His handsomely designed genealogy charts were updated over generations and often were kept carefully folded inside the front cover of the family bible. One particular chart, "The Afro-American History Record" gave former slaves an opportunity to secure a personal history that very often had been one auction bid away from total extinction.

When James Vickroy died in October of 1913, his daughter Pearl took over the family business, focusing more and more on the storefront at 911 Wabash. Pearl continued to live with her mother, Nora, in the family home at 334 Kent, just a short walk from the shop.

Families and communities are not held together by paper documents any more than marriages are. But human effort and commitment can only sustain the present moment. Over time, it is the material thing that holds significance to those who come after. A commemorative record acknowledges the fact of it all: when it happened, who was there, and to a great extent what they did during their limited time on earth. This lasting presence is ultimately the reason that stone is preferred over wood when marking a person's grave.

Vigo County Poor Farm—Edward Lowe, *superintendent*—29th and Maple Ave.

The Vigo County Poor Farm

Ninety-two individuals were listed as residents of the Poor Farm in 1927. Nothing much was actually growing there besides resentment.

Allison L. Vrydagh (Mayme)—*carpenter*—h 728 S. 3rd

Allison L. Vrydagh Jr. (Marie)—*draftsman*, Johnson, Miller, Miller, and Yeager—h 1417 S. 17th

Jean Vrydagh—*teacher*, Crawford School—r 1519 S. 8th

(N) Jupiter Vrydagh (Lunette)—*architect*—1515 S. 8th h do

Robert T. Vrydagh (Anna E.)—*architect* @ 612 Ohio—h 1519 S. 8th

What you might call a full-service family. We don't know what blueprints or completed buildings emerged from all of this. But if you happen to be looking for something truly timeless, even with the likelihood that it's long since been demolished, the smart money's on Jupiter.

Clarence W. Wagner—Transcontinental Bicycle Champion, World War Veteran, Student, Adventurer, Bicycle Tourist and Lecturer—Permanent Address: 331 Ohio—Phone: Wabash 1142

He was clearly a professional, at least in the same sense that musicians and actors and artists and ballplayers living in Terre Haute were around this time. In short, here were just enough incentives and opportunities within reach for Clarence to practice his craft and keep him fed and busy week to week. Competitive bicycle races, which had emerged as a popular spectator sport in the early 1890s were still popular a generation later. Many cities had indoor velodromes that sponsored six-day marathon races. A two-man team working regionally could earn thousands of dollars in appearance fees and prize money every year. Clarence was apparently very good at it. Good enough, at least, to have acquired a nickname around his hometown: Crazy Horse.

Bicycle racing is, like gymnastics and beauty pageants, a pursuit for the young. Clarence would turn 28 in 1927. By then, cycling for him was starting to evolve into a static collection of dusty trophies, brittle newspaper clippings, and dated group photos. One of them might have captured the team from Terre Haute that had traveled to Milwaukee in 1922 to compete in the annual 100-mile road race to Chicago. Clarence posing with Graham Elliot, Elias Bailey, and Clyde Stoody—companions who would be gone from Terre Haute five years later.

For the time being, Clarence Wagner stayed put. Awards to display, stories to recount, and then the ongoing privilege of being greeted as "Crazy Horse" on the streets now and again.

But he wouldn't have all that long to enjoy it. The front page of the *Tribune* on Saturday, April 4, 1936, carried the news. It seems Clarence had invested in a surface mine in West Terre Haute with his brother. Physical risk, a big potential payoff, a partner to share it with, just what Clarence had been used to all along. Only this time, it didn't work out. An explosives charge detonated and Clarence was killed. Front page news in any event, but the headline still mentioned the bicycle first.

Nicholas Wagner—*cigar manufacturer*—1309 Ash h do

The only, and by 1927 probably the last, cigar manufacturer to operate in Terre Haute, Indiana.

Even in the 1920s, cigar making was still done almost entirely by hand. The craft itself was represented by a union local, which required a three-year apprenticeship for formal certification. Cigar leaves were skillfully wrapped around loose tobacco, known as filler, then placed into a mold, and pressed for 15 minutes. The only machinery involved in the process was a cutter to uniformly snip the ends. All told, it still probably took a little longer to make a cigar than to smoke one—a ratio that would certainly be changing in the coming years.

The smell of fresh cigar tobacco is quite strong and quickly attaches itself to clothing and skin. Since women generally considered this an odor rather than a fragrance, it created an obvious disincentive to their prospects in the cigar-making profession. Nevertheless, in 1921 the Home Cigar Company of

Terre Haute announced it had apprenticed a woman to the trade. That said, you'll notice that Nicholas Wagner was living alone.

(N) Mrs. Lola Waterloo—h 1216 S. 19th

Clara Webb (widow, James)—*waitress*, Root Dry Goods Company—h 523 S. 10th

Root's, like many downtown department stores in larger cities, featured an elegant tea room devoted to ladies who lingered over lunch. For Clara, propriety extended past the sandwiches without crusts and tongs for the sugar cubes. It involved memorizing a regular customer's last name for a polite greeting while that same person would call you by your first name for more coffee. It involved nimble steps in high heels around large purses and shopping bags while carrying a tray full of orders. It involved remembering two forks when certain parties ordered dessert. It involved providing excellent service because it was always expected, even though it was frequently ignored.

Clara Wells—County Poor Farm

WEST'S DRUG STORE (Charles W., Henry J., and Dale E. West)—*Druggists* @ 1240 Lafayette Ave.—Phone: Wabash 3184

What's not mentioned here is the full-service soda fountain and luncheonette, which in 1927 made West's Drug Store a very popular hangout for students from Garfield High School, much as Donnelly's Pharmacy at 7th and Hulman was for Wiley students. Each of these locations would have provided some classic hometown imagery: two steadies sharing a Hires root beer float with separate straws, excited laughter following a Friday night basketball game against a cross-town rival, every stool at the counter occupied by crinoline dresses and tweed suits after the Junior Prom.

Like Citizens Market and the Swan Movie Theater, West's Drug Store could be relied on every year for a quarter page ad in the *Benedictus,* Garfield's yearbook. The drugstore also stocked back-to-school supplies and high school memory books, "particularly for graduates." Sure, the upperclassmen would be changing year to year and a good portion of those graduates would make West's Drug Store a memory as soon as they descended the steps with their diploma. But the Twelve Points neighborhood that surrounded the drugstore would certainly remain, which meant children buying candy bars on the walk home from Collett School because their parents had come to purchase corn plasters and their older sisters liked the grilled cheese sandwiches and the lemon phosphates.

Nineteen twenty-seven was the last full year that Charles West and his two sons would run their family business together. After their father's death in October 1928, Henry and Dale would continue as partners until Henry's death in 1951. This put the keys to the store in Dale's hands—for nearly 20 years more.

The property at the corner of Lafayette and Maple occupied a prominent position in the Twelve Points neighborhood and whatever business stood there carried with it the responsibility of sustaining community. There was a quality of interaction taking place between customers every day at West's that gave substance to the neighborhood, such that these scenes would be envisioned by soldiers overseas as they read letters from back home. In the end, maybe it's unreasonable to expect that this responsibility, this imagery, or even the neighborhood itself would have survived much longer once the West family finally closed their business. It turns out the timing of Dale's death in 1970 was just about perfect. The need for a family-owned drugstore in Twelve Points was dying right along with him.

Albert Westjohn (Essie)—*laborer*—h 2140 Dillman

Barney Westjohn (Lena)—*laborer*—h 2118 Dillman

Benjamin Westjohn (Arline)—*glassworker*, Root Glass Company—h 1823 S. 3rd

Clem Westjohn (Gladys)—*glassworker*, Root Glass Company—h 2400 Dillman

In June 1926, Albert Westjohn had also been employed at Root Glass. He was 20 years old and married to Essie just a few months when he was crushed in the gears of a plant elevator.

Whatever the lingering effects of that accident, by the following year Albert had made himself available as a laborer for hire. In the absence of any workman's compensation, unemployment insurance, or Social Security Disability payments, he probably had little choice. Root Glass, for its part, apparently concluded they were making an adequate contribution by continuing to employ his two older brothers.

Albert must have concluded at some point that life simply couldn't be trusted to treat him any better. On June 30, 1940, he swallowed a three oz. bottle of carbolic acid and suffered the very painful death he had somehow been spared 14 years earlier. The accident at Root's, the fact that it had also occurred in June, went unmentioned in the paper. That was for Essie, Barney, Clem, and Ben to discuss at the funeral, checking over their shoulders so Albert's two sons wouldn't hear.

(N) Mollie Whalley—County Poor Farm

Alice Whitecotton—*tester*, Terre Haute Pure Milk and Ice Cream Company—r 1429 S. 9th

Audrey D. Whitecotton—*machine operator*, Lamb Manufacturing Company—r 1429 S. 9th

Belva L. Whitecotton—*teacher*, Warren School—r 2423 S. 8th

James Whitecotton—*messenger*—r 1429 S. 9th

James T. Whitecotton (Hattie)—*checker*, Terre Haute Pure Milk and Ice Cream Company—h 1429 S. 9th

Lucille Whitecotton—r 2423 S. 8th

LAMB MFG. CO.

FROM FACTORY TO CONSUMER

SERVICE APPAREL

For Men and Women

1239-1241 Wabash Avenue

TERRE HAUTE, INDIANA FEB. 29, 1928

TERMS___C.O.D.___   SOLD TO___F.O. WRIGHT, c/o SOAPER HOTEL

INVOICE NO.___841___   515 PLUM ST., HENDERSON, KY.

/12	Doz. Lot 200 Cooks coats,	size 46	2	00	4	00
/12	" " 4500 " pants,	" 40-32	2	25	2	25
	Coats initialed "F.O.W."			05		10
		POSTAGE				22
					$6	57

Mildred Whitecotton—*bookkeeper*, Terre Haute Pure Milk and Ice Cream Company—r 1429 S. 9th

A Lamb Manufacturing Company Invoice

Their family history in 1927 played out like a mystical children's story with various members of the Whitecotton clan living out at least part of their surname every day at work. Alice and James T. with all that milk, James and Mildred with a profusion of paper, Belva amid clouds of chalk dust, and then Audrey ending the tale at her sewing machine constantly being reminded of both white and cotton. It turns out that Lamb Manufacturing, located at 15 South 13th Street, produced work clothing to outfit cooks and bakers.

Grace Wiles—County Poor Farm

Robert Wilkins—County Poor Farm

Bertha Wilkinson—County Poor Farm

John E. Willey (Veda)—*timber buyer*—h 2646 Putnam

John was part of a longstanding tradition dating back to the days when 80 percent of the land east of the Mississippi River was covered in virgin forest. By the twentieth century, you might say he was part of the problem.

There is approximately three times as much timber cut down from the forests of the United States every year as is grown in a year. (Harry Graves, former chief of the U.S. Forest Service, speaking in 1920)

The forests here also, or such as they used to be, must have had their influence. Temples and cathedrals, all works of art, are designed to impress men's minds leading them into varying conditions of consciousness. The forests of sugar and beech and poplar and oak about here originally, it has been said, were the most wonderful on the face of the earth. (Franklin Booth, as quoted in the book *A Hoosier Holiday* by Theodore Dreiser in 1915)

Albert Williams—County Poor Farm

David Williams—County Poor Farm

William E. Williams (Melvina)—*treasurer and manager*, Breaden Manufacturing Company and *vice-president*, Indiana State Bank—h 131 Adams— Phone: Wabash 3456

An acquaintance of William Sidney Porter, who wrote dozens of popular short stories under the name "O. Henry." Some years before, the author had taken a liking to "Wash" Williams and, by association, his hometown. To quote from a letter Wash had saved as a memento: "I'll put that town of yours on the map . . . Leave it to me, I'll make it famous yet."

A longer life might have helped some. William Sidney Porter, who included bank clerk, mandolin player, and fugitive from justice among his numerous accomplishments, would die before he reached 50. Still, as a writer, O. Henry did his level best to keep this promise to his friend. Terre Haute, Indiana, makes an appearance in "The Enchanted Profile" and "Unfinished Christmas Story."

Anthony J. Wilson (Elizabeth)—*superintendent*, Highland Lawn Cemetery

Up until the 1920s, large urban cemeteries like Highland Lawn were popular destinations for family picnics. Giant shade trees, mowed grass, with a tiny piece of property the family had already paid for. Just made sense to put that patch of ground to use while you were still standing on top of it.

Highland Lawn was a good three miles east of downtown, but both the city trolley system and the Interurban provided a direct collection. This would provide the image of a family riding back on the Number 3 trolley in the early evening with an empty picnic basket at their feet. Likely a calm and contented group, in spite of the fact that they had spent the entire day surrounded by dead people.

George Wilson—County Poor Farm

George Wingo—County Poor Farm

Leon J. Wise (Lenora)—*metallurgist*—h 14 Wabash Apartments

The science of metallurgy involves the analysis of various metals and alloys. Precious metals like gold and silver can be chemically treated by a metallurgist to verify their authenticity and remove any impurities. During the 1920s, hazardous substances like mercury and cyanide were often used in the process. There's no place of employment listed for Leon Wise, which leaves you wondering whether a corner of Apartment 14 was dedicated to his experiments.

As a man fascinated with the properties of minerals and stones, Leon no doubt held an opinion on the legendary Terre Haute Madstone. In the middle of the nineteenth century, a widow named Mary I. Taylor possessed a small porous black rock, possibly petrified stone, that she used to treat cases of rabies. Constant interaction with the natural world created the risk of human exposure to the virus which entered the bloodstream through animal saliva. The resulting infection often proved fatal.

The treatment called for immersing the stone in water and then applying it directly to the wound. Supposedly if the stone adhered to the affected area, this would confirm the presence of rabies. The stone would then absorb the toxins from the blood. After one hour, the stone would be placed in warm cow's milk, which witnesses say would then be transformed into a viscous green liquid. The process was then repeated continuously until the stone no longer stuck and the milk no longer turned.

Although Mary Taylor never advertised her rabies treatment or demanded payment for providing it, she claimed by 1888 to have treated more than 1,300 cases of rabies, without a single death. One child, bitten in Illinois by a rabid dog, had been brought by his anxious father to Terre Haute in search of Mrs. Taylor and her madstone. It is unknown whether Abraham Lincoln actually found treatment for his eldest son, but Robert Lincoln recovered sufficiently to live well into his 80s.

The subsequent journey of Mary Taylor's madstone is a little harder to trace. By 1904, the stone had reportedly fallen into the possession of one Mary E. Piper of Terre Haute. By then, the madstone had become more of a curiosity, since a successful vaccine for rabies had been developed 20 years earlier.

The madstone was said to still be in Terre Haute in 1927, though it's doubtful that Leon Wise ever actually crossed paths with it. It's even more doubtful that his subsequent chemical analysis would have uncovered the mysterious source of its healing power. After all, while Leon could tell you whether something was pure gold, he might have had more trouble explaining why the mere rumor of it had caused everything from mass migration to first degree murder. Almost anything can acquire great power merely out of a vague consensus that it's somehow special. Whole fortunes can be made, fatal illnesses can be cured, and through it all Mother Nature will often keep the secrets to herself.

Mrs. Cora K. Wood—*assistant librarian*, Emeline Fairbanks Library—h 456 N. Center

Over the course of his life, philanthropist and steel magnate Andrew Carnegie donated more than $56,000,000 to construct 1,700 public libraries in towns and cities across the United States. This money had a few strings attached. Pianos were forbidden in Carnegie-funded libraries as were books of questionable moral content.

The construction of the main public library in Terre Haute in 1903 was also the result of a philanthropic grant: $50,000 from Crawford Fairbanks in memory of his mother. By 1927, the library had more than 96,000 books on its shelves. Mrs. Cora Wood was one of a staff of 30. During a single month, more than 60,000 volumes were circulated—nearly one for every resident in the city.

The spacious stone building perhaps held the greatest fascination for children. Beyond perennial classics like *Robinson Crusoe, Rebecca of Sunnybrook Farm,* and *The Wizard of Oz,* there were thrilling multi-volume series available, often the first books children would select and read themselves. These included the Bobbsey Twins, a popular series begun in 1904 by Laura Lee Hope, Arthur M. Winfield's Rover Boys series, the five volumes of "The Girls of Central High," and a brand new adventure series which premiered in 1927: Franklin W. Dixon's *The Hardy Boys.* The generic setting for these books was quintessentially Midwestern. It became easy for any child living in Terre Haute in 1927 to read these books by flashlight in a dark bedroom and imagine the adventures were taking place just outside the window.

For adults, the 1920s was also a very fortunate time to be reading books. James Joyce, D. H. Lawrence, F. Scott Fitzgerald, Ernest Hemingway, Willa Cather, Rudyard Kipling, Virginia Wolfe, and Edith Wharton, were all producing new work during this period. Indiana authors Theodore Dreiser and Booth Tarkington had already gained national renown. Booth Tarkington's *Alice Adams* and *The Magnificent Ambersons* had captured two of the first four Pulitzer Prizes for fiction ever to be awarded.

There were also novelists familiar to the reading room at Emeline Fairbanks whose enormous popularity would diminish with time. Ellen Glasgow wrote 16 novels in 30 years. Her book from 1926, *The Romantic Comedians,* was considered one of her finest. But even the highest honors bestowed on literature during this time could not guarantee a lasting reputation. In 1927, the Pulitzer Prize for fiction was awarded to Louis Bromfield for *Early Autumn.* Ellen Glasgow would win the award herself 14 years later for *In This Our Life.* Neither book can be found on the shelves of the Vigo County Public Library today.

High above the main desk at Emeline Fairbanks was yet another reminder that the whispered advice "fame is fleeting" spoke very loud indeed. The ceiling of the library featured a huge stained glass dome. Surrounding its rim were lighted portraits of notable individuals in art, literature, innovation, and politics. Among them, some names you might expect: Shakespeare and Edison. Some names of local or regional import: poet James Whitcomb Riley and former Secretary of the Navy R. W. Thompson. And finally, a woman who by 1927 had fallen into relative obscurity.

Rosa Boneur had been one of the most popular artists of the late nineteenth century. Her expansive oil paintings featured animals in the wild. Humans sometimes made an appearance as well, but the major focus of her work was always clear. This focus might explain why Rosa Boneur's portrait was included in the rotunda in 1903, why her legacy had begun to diminish by 1927, and why

The Emeline Fairbanks Public Library Reading Room Martin Collection, Indiana Historical Society

her continued presence was so welcome in a building housing many thousands of books. After all, a society that treasures the beauty of nature will never forsake the beauty of words.

Lucille Woods—County Poor Farm

Harvey L. Work (Clara J.)—*examiner*, Indiana Free Employment Service—h 659 Swan

"Mr. Work will see you now."

Arthur I. Wright (Agnes J.)—*miner*—h 2601 N. 13th

John Wright—*musician*—r 2601 N. 13th

It was a family with both a mining and a musical heritage. Arthur's eldest son was also working as a miner in 1927, while Number 3 son Clyde had been John's mentor as a prospective musician for hire. Just two years before, Clyde had married Edith Baldwin and left both his parents' household and the city. This left the after-dinner entertainment at 2601 to 15-year-old John.

In the spring of 1927, another aspiring teenage musician from Maces Springs, Virginia, would be traveling about 20 miles to Bristol, Tennessee, with her brother-in-law A.P. and his wife, Sara. After a successful audition for Ralph Peer of the Record Corporation of America, Maybelle Carter and her family would make the far longer trip to Camden, New Jersey, to record their first commercially released songs, including "Keep on the Sunny Side."

This song probably would have emerged as a favorite of anyone spending his daylight hours as Arthur did. Father and son had clearly come to rely on each other by then; Arthur, 57 years old and continuing to support a family that included two sons under 10 years of age and John, looking to follow Clyde's footsteps away from the mines and clear out of town.

Ivan Yates—*baths*—202 Oddfellows Building—r do

There are many examples of home businesses in Terre Haute in 1927, but perhaps only those operating in the city's red light district would be considered more intimate than Ivan's. One intriguing possibility is that his neighbor Julia Thomas had converted him to the physcultopathy movement. This could have inspired Ivan to start his day with a cold bath, thus saving the hot water for his paying customers.

(N) Delphia Yaw (spouse of James)—h 2629 Arleth

Alvin M. Yeager—*student*—r 418 Gilbert

Alvin N. Yeager—*druggist*, B. F. Yeager—r 418 Gilbert

Benjamin F. Yeager—*drugs* @ 1429 S. 17th—h 418 Gilbert

"Doc" Yeager—*Drugs*—Washington Avenue Drug Store, 1429 S. 17th—Phone: Wabash 2498—h 418 Gilbert—Phone: Wabash 4409

Florence A. Yeager (widow, Alvin R.)—h 418 Gilbert

The nickname "Doc" might bring to mind a kindly old physician with bifocals on the edge of his nose and a pocket watch for pulse readings. Benjamin Yeager was neither a physician nor was he very old—22 years young in 1927—playing the edge of medical certification with those quotation marks. And, as with Julia Thomas, the Terre Haute *Tribune* was more than willing to include the title in his obituary. Apparently a neighborhood legacy easily trumped the state licensing board.

One wonders whether Alvin M. Yeager ever considered studying medicine in an effort to settle the matter once and for all.

Mrs. Etta Yettman—*dishwasher*, Henderson Hotel—r do

The Henderson Hotel at 209 South 4th, along with the Arlington, the Farmers, and the Sullivan, was one of the four small downtown hotels that had initially served farmers attending the daily produce market back when it was located at 4th and Walnut. Now, in 1927, with the main market moved north to Mulberry Street and the farmers driving trucks, the four establishments were all just a few years from closing altogether.

You might compare Etta's situation to that of a miner who lives in a company house and shops at the company store. Owner George Henry deducted lodging and meals from Etta's pay even if it wasn't spelled out in actual numbers. But unlike the dishwashers-in-residence at the Sullivan or the Farmers, Etta was the only employee who actually lived at the Henderson, which probably broadened her responsibilities after hours.

At any rate, this was subsistence living: scraping plates, scraping by. There must have been a strong temptation for Etta to spend whatever bit of pay remained on any cheap escape from the Henderson, aware that if the hotel itself ever disappeared, there'd be even more for her to escape from.

Lewis Young—County Poor Farm

(N) Besta Zick—*student*—r 2635 N. 11th

Charles Zimmerman (Julia)—*principal*, Garfield High School—h 2731 N. 11th

Early on, he lived a nomadic life as an educator. A hundred miles or so between jobs, all within Indiana: Freedlandville, Evansville, Bloomington, Clinton. The intention behind all this wandering was probably not evident to him until he finally reached his destination. Charles Zimmerman had been gradually drawing closer to Terre Haute, Indiana. In 1921, he assumed the position of principal at Garfield High School.

Like most of the teachers at Garfield, Charles Zimmerman was already familiar with the town, having graduated from State Normal nine years earlier. He seemed uniquely suited to the job of high school principal, not only in his qualifications but also in his appearance: a calm, serious face framed by wire-rim glasses and a tightly knotted necktie. By the 1927 school year, there was little doubt among the faculty and staff that his energy and dedication would keep him at Garfield for years to come. To quote the introduction from the senior class in the *Benedictus* yearbook: "Mr. Zimmerman has been principal during the four years we have spent at Garfield. We know no other nor do we desire any other."

Over the succeeding years, he would grow to fill the classic mold even more: a little thicker around the middle, a little sparser up top, wool suit and wire-rims reliably intact. Think Principal Willoughby at Riverdale High School in the Archie comics.

By 1938, Charles Zimmerman had already served longer as principal than anyone in the school's history and still harbored big plans for both himself and his school. He would soon be completing his doctorate in education at the University of Chicago. In August, the new school gymnasium would finally be ready. Then in December, the first home basketball game against Clinton High School, where Charles Zimmerman had served as principal for three years before finally coming to Garfield.

How could you blame him for looking ahead? Nevertheless, before he ever walked through the new gymnasium, before his remarks were delivered prior to its dedication, before the glass on his office door was repainted with the title of "Doctor," Charles Zimmerman would die unexpectedly at age 54, just a few weeks before graduation. It happened on Sunday, May 1, 1938; fitting perhaps for a man who had spent his life educating young people. The news would reach most of the students when school started again on Monday morning. Enough time to absorb the enormous shock, to dedicate the yearbook in his memory, to place his name on the brand new gymnasium, and then move on with life.

Louise Zimmerman—*matron*, Police Department—r 422 S. 22nd

The crime scene photos, the mug shots, the arrest warrants; all gone by now. Acts of passion, in many cases. One of the reasons births and marriages continue to be archived carefully while criminal records seldom survive the perpetrators is so society can demonstrate which acts of passion are truly worth preserving.

GARFIELD HIGH SCHOOL—CLASS OF 1938

MARTIN

Marguerite Zwang—*musician*—r 133 S. 23rd

Garfield High School Class of 1938
Martin Collection, Indiana Historical Society

The very last name in a list of the 105 individuals who listed their occupation in 1927 as musician or music teacher in Terre Haute, Indiana—with a few piano tuners thrown in for good measure (complete list at www.hometown.indiana.edu/1927).

It's a perfect name for the coda, every bit as musical as Ebbie McFate or E. Blanche Rippetoe. Created obviously by someone with an ear for song. Thanks go to Marguerite's parents, William and Maude, who at the time were also providing lodging for their 31-year-old daughter. An indication, at least, that the name wouldn't soon be lost to marriage.

George A. Zwerner (Marie)—*branch manager*, Wabash Market—h 14 Deming Bldg.

His daddy's oldest son. Unlike the rest of his brothers, he never did join Ernest in his venture at Twelve Points with Citizens Market. Instead, he and Marie settled into a tiny second-floor apartment in a commercial building downtown.

Their immediate neighbors were a dentist office and a beauty shop. The Wabash Market two blocks away listed itself as a meat market.

Apparently, George became increasingly estranged from his family over the years. Succeeding generations of Zwerners have no memory of him, in spite of the fact that he continued to live in their hometown. George and Marie had no children from their marriage, so all that's left to characterize the man's life now are a few sketchy stories—the kind that always follow a person who gradually loses touch with his immediate surroundings. But those stories can only follow just so far. The stories about George end with allusions to personal challenges, a certain private suffering. Friends and family tend to keep their distance from that type of journey. Eventually, recorded history does too.

That journey for George ultimately led where they all do, bringing him that shared connection with others his life on earth apparently could not. It happened at 1:36 AM on Sunday, May 27, 1956—the moment George Adam Zwerner of Terre Haute, Indiana, faced death as each of us will, completely and finally alone.

Index

Tom Roznowski is a Bloomington-based writer and musician. His public radio program, *Hometown*, explores the past through stories about Terre Haute in 1926. He wrote and hosted the television special (now on DVD) *Hometown: A Journey through Terre Haute,* and has recorded three CDs of original songs. He was recently named an honorary citizen of Terre Haute.